KINGDOM OF STOLEN CROWNS

SACRED ARBOR REALM

BOOK 1

STEPHANIE STORM

Kingdom of Stolen Crowns
The Sacred Arbor Series - Book 1

Copyright © 2025 Stephanie Storm
www.authorstephaniestorm.com

Cover design by: Stick and Stone Publishing

Dedicated to…
The brilliant, bold, and fiercely opinionated ladies of the Holzer Book Club—even though there's no way I'm brave enough to let you critique one of my stories. Because—sex. You've opened my eyes to a world beyond romance novels I never would have explored on my own. Thanks for the new adventures.
Love you all. XO

Chapter One

SACRED ARBOR REALM

RUNA

"THEY'RE GAINING ON US. On foot! Can't that infernal beast go any faster?" I shouted at Kronk, the muscle of our trio of bandits, as we raced along a narrow cliffside.

Shadows shrouded the winding trail. The only light was the glow radiating off a molten river that waited for one of us to make a single misstep. Heat seared my cheek, and the horse beneath me shied away from the threat. A quick glance at the chasm below had my heart quaking in my chest.

The Blood River Bandits had been in some pretty tight spots over the years. As bad as our situation was, this was nowhere close to the worst.

And I would keep telling myself that.

Seated on the bench of a bucking wagon, Kronk snapped the reins against the back of the straining *bula*. "Yah! Move your stubborn ass, you horned bastard, or I'll carve you into steaks and have you for dinner."

The massive bovine responded with a defiant *murrr*.

Given Kronk's considerable weight when he was in his athos form, I couldn't fault the bula's insolence. Athos were naturally bulky and muscular, even more so when they shifted, lending Kronk the strength of twenty men. His gritty flesh turned to stone, covering his heavily muscled frame. Kronk, unlike me, was also impervious to harm from weapons and fire.

Lucky bastard.

Guiding his trotting horse beside mine, Drazen, the third member of our macabre trio, cut me a critical glare I was all too familiar with. Fiery light from the lava pit gleamed off the onyx horns that curled over his skull, making the infernus appear especially demonic. Like Kronk, he too was impervious to the flames that spiraled across the pool. Infernus were born in fire. Lived it. Breathed it. Worshipped it. Did untold things with it in their bunks at night that I didn't care to analyze.

"I thought you said they would all be in the temple," Drazen barked, accusation in his tone.

The angry mob of Dark Cultists who chased us—with pitchforks, no less—was not my fault. How dare he criticize my plan? These mutton heads would be lost without my leadership. Anger swarmed like a nest of widow wasps inside my ribs, or perhaps it was the heat from the flarking lava, melting me from the inside. Either way, I wasn't in the mood to deal with my brother's crap.

"It's not as if I can predict when a monk will take a piss," I snapped. The intel I'd stolen directly from the head priest's mind was spot-on. With my goddess-given abilities, I'd uncovered the cultists' schedules, blind spots, and weaknesses along with the location of the temple vault. As a sorceress, what I couldn't do was to predict *how* this simple plan would go to hell. Though it didn't come as a surprise. I worked with idiots, after all.

I dragged a sweaty strand of lavender-tipped hair out of my eyes. "At least I'm not the dunderhead who blew our cover."

Kronk's massive shoulders hitched at the reminder. "It isn't my fault that my dress was too short."

Behind the sheen of sweat slicking my forehead, my pulse pounded. "I stole those robes to help us blend in. Why didn't you wear the pants?"

"One does not wear pants under a dress," Kronk answered with an imperious scoff.

I gripped my reins, itching to wrap my hands around his thick neck. Not that I had any chance of spanning its rocky girth. "For the last time, it isn't a dress," I grated. "And since when are you an expert in fashion?"

When Kronk had hiked his leg to climb into the cart, everyone, and I mean *everyone*, saw far too much of the athos. I felt sorry for the females of his race. Although other athos considered Kronk a runt, what hung between his legs was truly terrifying and also out of place among the Dark Cultists. Apparently, the monks were all eunuchs. Who knew?

Before Kronk could reply, the cart's wheel smacked a rock, nearly tossing him out of his seat. Our stolen bounty bucked against the wooden bed, and the lid of the stone sarcophagus popped free of its base.

"Careful, you buffoon," Drazen shouted. "Damage the payload and we're screwed."

Kronk snarled back, the too-short hem of his robe flapping in the breeze, baring parts of my brother that couldn't be unseen. "I cannot damage something long dead. What does Vex want with a pile of dusty bones, anyway?"

"Why does Vex want anything?" I screeched. My panic-driven voice annoying, even to my own ears. "The bastard's a sicko."

Vex, leader of a local gang of cutthroats, was a known

3

collector of oddities. He was also someone you didn't want to anger. If we didn't need this payoff so badly, we never would have taken the job. Too many thieves had cut deals with Vex only to go missing.

Drazen glanced back at the bellowing mob, their roars intensifying as they drew closer. "Can't that slovenly beast of yours move any faster?"

"Bula are not built for speed, but for strength," Kronk defended.

"Kind of like you," I scoffed, smirking when he shot me a granite glare.

Mature sorceress I was, I stuck out my tongue in retaliation.

Beside us, a pitchfork whizzed through the air, glancing off Drazen's stubborn head.

Flark! Not the horns.

All infernus were overly proud of their ebony protrusions. Polishing them every night. Flaunting them for the ladies. *Gag.* Frankly, I didn't see the appeal.

"Now they've done it," Drazen snarled, looking very much like the crazed devil that his species resembled.

Embers puffed from Drazen's nostrils, his eyes glowing red with fury. Ever the impulsive one in our trio, he urged his horse faster. Drawing alongside the wide-eyed bula, he held up his blazing hand. Flames flickered from his fingers.

"Drazen, no!" I barked.

Too late.

His heated palm slapped the bula's hindquarters with a resounding crack, branding the animal's beefy ass.

The lumbering bula reared up like a mighty stallion. Its massive hooves exploded against the road, and it bolted. At the sudden strain, the harness around its shoulders snapped. Leather straps tangled with the creature's thick legs, Kronk's control over the beast nonexistent.

4

"Drazen, you boar-faced shit monger," Kronk bellowed, hauling back on the reins with zero success.

I needed to come up with a new plan. Now! "We need to get in front of him," I yelled at Drazen.

"Can't. Road's too narrow."

"Then throw a fireball into its path."

"The beast is already spooked. You want to give it a heart attack?"

"If that's what it takes!"

Before I could bark another order, both animal and cart careened around the next turn in the road. With Kronk clinging to the seat. Too fast! They'd never make it.

The wagon lurched up on its side, balancing on two wheels, tilting toward the fiery pit below. Icy terror flooded my veins. Kronk was fireproof. Not lava proof.

"Kronk," I screamed, pulse pumping, certain I was about to see my adopted brother plunge to his death.

As the cart tipped, he dove over the opposite side. In a shockingly agile move, he hit the ground and spun, catching the wheel. Muscles strained along his thick forearms, his shoulders expanding with the effort. With his boots sliding against the rock, he heaved, dragging the wagon into the center of the road and setting it upright.

Thank Hathor. Kronk was safe.

With Drazen beside me, I hauled back on my reins, both of us leaping from our horses to check the bed of the cart.

Empty.

No!

I raced to the edge of the trail, peering into the fiery ravine just as a splash rang out. My heart took a similar plunge.

Below, the head of the sarcophagus bobbed in an ocean of molten rock before disappearing beneath its surface with a squelching *burp*.

"It's gone," I gasped, watching as all three of our deaths flashed in my mind.

"Vex is going to kill us," Drazen groaned, scraping a hand over his ruddy face.

"Slowly. Painfully." I could see it now. Our executions would surely be public since Vex loved to have witnesses to his brutality. We'd be used to set an example. I'd watched once while he'd forced one of his captives to eat his own entrails. Bile painted my tongue at the memory.

"Not if the Dark Cultists kill us first," Kronk stated in a cheerful tone, like this was good news.

"Not helpful," I snapped at King Oblivious.

Shouts of outrage exploded from the raging mob. The devoted monks were furious to see the remains of their deity destroyed.

Goddess, save us from the righteous. Instead of aiding those in need, they demanded their followers spend coins they didn't have on building temples while devoting themselves to a bunch of bones. I'd little use for leaders who turned a blind eye to the needs of the people. In fact, I had little use for leaders. Period. Especially kings.

I spun to face the raging mob. As usual, it was up to me to clean up my brothers' mess. "I've got this."

Drazen grasped my shoulder. "You sure? Your fingertips are already blackened. You used too much power dealing with the guards earlier." The price for stealing images at a distance was steep. Physical contact was a lot easier.

"I said, I've got this." I shrugged free of his heated grip, raising my glowing hands.

With my reserves near empty, I called on the power at my center, channeling down into the earth, drawing upon Carcerem's well of energy. *Obsidian.* It was the mystical force that supported all life in our kingdom. People, plants, animals, insects, all benefited from this gift granted to us by the goddess

Hathor from the sacred arbors she created. In the end, all returned to the well.

Magic sparked along my nerve endings, swelling up from deep inside. The feeling was indescribable. Pleasure thrummed in my veins, and I swallowed a moan. The temptation to take more, to sink my mystical claws in and never let go, was almost irresistible. I'd fought this battle more times than I could count.

Remember Yaga's teachings.

The reminder grounded me.

This power was mine to command, not the other way around. Tendrils of purple magic surrounded me in a mystical breeze. My stolen hood blew back off my head, strands of ebony hair tipped with violet floated above my shoulders.

I gave life to my illusion, projecting my glorious creation. Before the monks' eyes, their lost deity rose from the lava in a burst of whirling flames and flashing embers. Golden fabric swathed her glowing body, a glittering crown resting on her head. Her gorgeous features were ethereal. Her demeanor, regal.

Not too shabby, if I did say so myself. All sorceresses had a specialty. No two had the same combination of skills, though there was some overlap along bloodlines, as there was with portal magic in my family.

This was mine. Not only did I have the ability to pull images from someone's head, but I could also create them as well. I considered my gift of illusion more of an art form than some blunt tool to be bandied about. While my creations lacked substance, no one could tell the images they perceived were false until they touched one. Because I was *that* good.

The enchanting goddess reached out to her awe-struck followers. "*At last. I am free of my mortal bonds. Thanks to these fine people. Return to the temple and pay me homage.*" When the stunned monks didn't immediately obey, flames shot out of the glowing goddess's eyes, her command rumbling through the earth. "*Return, I say!*"

In a flurry of robes and discarded garden tools, the monks scrambled, bowing and muttering prayers as they backed away. Once it was safe, I released my grip on the illusion, and my beautiful creation dissolved in a wave of sparks. Something similar happened within me as I withdrew from the well. Weakness washed through my body, my legs collapsing.

Kronk scooped me up, and Drazen rushed over, grabbing my wrist. Blackened flesh encompassed my hands.

At the sight of the damage I'd done, Drazen hissed in annoyance. "I warned you."

"I'll be fine," I mumbled, my words slurring. "The shadows will recede once I've rested." It was important for all sorceresses to balance the ebb and flow of obsidian. Take too much too fast, and there were consequences.

"We should find a place to regroup," Kronk's deep voice rumbled against my cheek. His stone-like arms were solid beneath me.

"More like hide and kiss our asses goodbye," Drazen sneered. "When we don't show with the goods, it won't take long for Vex to place a bounty on our heads."

"Let us go to Yaga. She can make Runa her special tea," Kronk suggested.

We hadn't visited the *hag* who'd raised us for several spans. In some cultures, people considered the word an insult, but not in ours. Hags were among the wisest and most respected of creatures. Like others of her kind, Yaga was a wiz with potions.

I snorted. "You're not fooling me. It's Yaga's mead you're after." Though the idea of returning to our childhood home for a break did sound nice.

"Fine, then. Yaga's it is." Drazen stalked over to my horse, collecting its reins. "As long as I'm not the one who has to tell her we lost the payload."

It wasn't Yaga we needed to worry about disappointing. Profits from this heist would have meant the difference between life and death for the villagers. This loss would set us back even further. We'd need a plan and quick. Before the false king sent his soldiers to collect payment for the quarterly taxes we didn't have.

"Can you ride?" Drazen asked.

"Tie me into my saddle, and I'll do the rest."

Chapter Two

RUNA

I CONVINCED my brothers to leave the damaged cart behind to save time. Kronk rode on the bula since the horses couldn't support his massive frame. Once we'd put a few miles between us and the monks, we ditched our robes. Drazen and Kronk wore their usual reptilian pants and close-fitting vests because it was the only material capable of withstanding both fire and abrasive skin, while I changed back into my traditional sorceress garb.

Sturdy boots covered me from ankle to mid-thigh while a fitted skirt with slits over my legs clung to my hips. Like the guys, I wore a corset-style vest with buckles on the shoulders and laces down the front. Various weapons completed our wardrobes. Some visible. Many not.

Despite my exhaustion, we made good time, arriving at Yaga's before nightfall. Our return to the village where we grew up was bittersweet. White Bridge was once a prosperous community. While the coffers had never overflowed, the crops had always provided an ample amount of food. Our herds used to grow fat, producing many young.

Today, we rode past fields that were withered with sickness. Livestock with their ribs protruding struggled to survive on fallow pastures. As we plodded along the dirt road, the scorched remains of a once proud home stood as a stark reminder of the false king's fury. The skulls of the defiant owners were mounted on stakes in the decimated yard. A shiver ran through me at the sight.

None dared to remove them for fear of retribution.

Last quarter, when the village was short paying the false king's taxes, his men demanded restitution, claiming the lives of two villagers while burning everything they possessed. The soldiers warned next time it would be four lives.

At our appearance, children emerged from their homes. They skipped beside us, their dirt-smudged cheeks glowed with excitement.

They would suffer the most should we fail to provide the taxes that White Bridge and other villages like them owed.

"What did you steal this time, Drazen? Tell us, please. Was it a chest of jewels?" a little girl with stunted horns and sunken eyes asked. Her baggy dress hung on her malnourished frame.

"Was it the king's underwear?" another joked, swiping his dirty sleeve beneath his broad nose.

"Come now," Drazen said, peering down at them with false nobility. "You know we do not steal but simply redistribute the false king's wealth. Now, off with you." He blew into his fist, then cast a handful of sparkling embers into the air. The children cheered, dancing and twirling in delight.

At their banter, something pinged in my chest. I cast Drazen a look from beneath a lavender lock. "You're good with them. Ever think you might have younglings of your own?"

He furrowed his brow, his ruddy expression growing serious for a moment. "Not with *him* on the throne." As expected, the moment of sincerity only lasted a second. The corner of Drazen's mouth crooked, and he slanted me a mischievous smirk.

"Besides, what makes you think I don't already have a half-dozen bastards roaming these lands?"

"Our brother is a virile male in his prime. I am certain he will sire dozens of offspring," Kronk contributed, his massive body swaying with the bula's lumbering movements.

"What about you, dear sister?" Drazen asked. "Ever have thoughts of settling down, claiming a mate, and popping out a litter of snot-nosed brats?"

Only every span. It was what we'd been fighting for after all, every time we robbed one of *his* conveyances. And if I couldn't have it, I'd make sure those we protected did.

Even thieves had dreams—not that I planned on sharing them with my brothers, who would use the information to torment me.

My mate would be noble. A humble servant of the people. Someone honest and hardworking, sacrificing his own needs for others, as my father had. Yet, he'd be strong, too. A warrior capable of protecting his family and property. Someone skilled enough to fight by my side. But not *too* bloodthirsty. I had little tolerance for aggressive blowhards. No. He'd only fight when necessary. But he'd be no coward, either.

At night, we'd sit beneath the stars, listening to the sounds of the kingdom, taking in a cool breeze, savoring the sweet scent of lunar flowers in the air. Then, while our children were sleeping, we'd make love on a blanket, celebrating our union in the gentle light of Carcerem's twin moons.

Instead of sharing my desires with my ignorant brothers, I answered, "Why would I settle when I have the two of you? You're all the family I need."

"There is no male worthy of our sister," Kronk grumbled, his shoulders tensing.

I worried there would never be a span that he stopped thinking of me as the lost little girl he'd discovered in the woods. Perhaps, in time, if he found his own mate, he'd come around. If not, I'd simply have to pound the realization that I was a fully-grown sorceress into his stony skull.

Drazen sighed in a dramatic, yet antagonistic manner. "'Tis true. And to be worthy of you, they'd have to get past us first. And since there are none who can defeat your formidable brothers, I'm afraid you're doomed to stay a spinster for the rest of your days."

"Har, har," I faked a laugh. I was far from innocent and suspected Drazen knew it, though Kronk was likely still in denial. You didn't grow up wild and free the way I had and remain virginal. Not that it was easy avoiding my brothers' watchful eyes. But being a kickass sorceress of illusion, I had my ways.

Finally, Yaga's thatched roof came into view. Our childhood home had changed little over the years. Crooked shutters hung beside the cloudy windows. Slivers of light shown through the gaps in the gnarled walls. Animal bones, along with a handful of crystals, and bundled herbs swung from the eves. Some were placed there with the purpose of keeping out those with ill intent. Others had more practical uses.

Once we'd secured our animals for the night, we headed for the front door. Yaga awaited us in the entryway, gnarled hands planted on her protruding hips. Silver braids rested over her shoulders, beads and feathers tangled in the pale strands.

It was good to find her at home. Many times, she was off visiting other villages. Caring for the infirmed. Sharing her potions and medicines while mentoring young spell-casters. For an elderly woman, Yaga got around. At times, her ability to be everywhere at once seemed supernatural. At least, she tended to be home when we needed her.

She scanned us with shrewd eyes, her voice cracking. "What are the lot of you doing here? Has something happened?"

Hathor forbid she greet us with a simple, *Hello, dearest children. I'm so happy to see you.*

Drazen strode forward, kissing her wrinkled cheek. "Can't an infernus visit his favorite girl?"

She stepped back, allowing him to enter while swatting him at the same time. "Don't give me any of your lip, boy."

"We ran into some trouble," I confessed, also kissing her cheek. There was no point in keeping the truth from Yaga. She'd always had a talent for knowing when we were up to no good, even without using one of her scrying stones.

Kronk followed me in, ducking his head to clear the doorway, the ceiling of the ancient hut barely tall enough to accommodate his height. Inside, a musty mix of drying herbs, damp earth, and liniment washed over me. I drew in the familiar scent, the tension in my shoulders easing.

Hollow clacks rang out, the bones and crystals that hung from the ceiling bouncing together with our entry. As Kronk forced the crooked door closed, dust stirred, jars chiming along the cupboard wall. Some were filled with food—others with things I didn't even attempt to identify.

My body yearned for the comfort of the den-like room I'd shared with my brothers in our youth and the thin pallets that waited for us to unroll them. I couldn't remember a time when we all fit comfortably. Kronk, even as a youngling, took up a good amount of space. At times, when my brothers were too much to bear, I'd slept on the dirt floor beside Yaga, next to the fire-side cot she preferred.

I sank into one of the wooden chairs by the fire and exhaled a groan of exhaustion that had Yaga's head swiveling my way.

My adopted mother took me in with a single disapproving glance. "Ran your tank dry again, did you? And look at your hands." The aged woman clucked her tongue. "I'll get the tea started."

Yaga hung the kettle onto an iron hook set into the wall and swung it over the flames in the hearth. Kronk and Drazen settled into chairs around the small wooden table while she moved to the cupboard, selecting several bottles of herbs. That done, she turned to her sons.

"Three of ya are skin and bones." She pinched Kronk's stony cheek. "When did ya last have a decent meal?"

"Drazen stole us a leg of mutton two spans ago," Kronk said.

There had been little time for much else with the false king's taxes due in only ten spans. We'd been hustling nonstop to scrounge up enough money. And still we were depressingly short. The reminder twisted a knot in the middle of my chest, responsibility weighing heavily upon me.

"The three of you need to take better care of each other." Yaga picked up a wooden spoon and promptly popped Drazen right between his gleaming horns. "I raised you better than this. You hear me?"

Drazen ducked his head, muttering, "Yes, ma'am." His arrogant, cocksure demeanor was much subdued now that he sat before the woman who'd once forced him to wash behind his ears.

The infernus was the proverbial eldest in the family and usually the first to face Yaga's anger. His parents had been on the front lines during the Great Rebellion. Or at least that is what those who'd fought against the false king called the uprising. The cowards who'd refused to join us called it the Great Folly.

Drazen's parents had fallen early in the Battle of Blood Water. The name of our little gang honored those who were lost there.

As it turned out, there really was nothing great about the uprising. The false king had swatted the rebellious like flies on bula shit, the rivers running red with the blood of the dead. Things might have ended differently if they'd had the numbers. Unfortunately, too many of the villages refused to take up arms against the new king, too afraid to fight back. Flarking cowards.

My parents had fought as well to the best of their ability. Not that it had done them any good. Still, they'd done the right thing, not compromising their values and refusing to be corrupted by the king's influence. Unlike some.

An image of my sister came to mind, and my gut clenched. While she may have been the one who betrayed us all, I was the one who'd let her. And every day since, I'd attempted to make amends.

I exhaled a deep breath. This wasn't the time to wallow in the past.

Instead, I gazed at Kronk. Whereas Drazen could charm the scales off a dragon, Kronk had a somber tone. No sense of humor. Solid. While I loved to antagonize him just to see if I could get a rise out of the stony brute, I appreciated his reliability. One never needed to question what he was thinking. Kronk would give it to you straight with little to soften the edges of his delivery.

The athos was the middle child of our family. Like me, he'd lost his parents when the false king invaded his village, taking the survivors captive. When Kronk's family refused to join his army, the king had them executed, turning their stony bodies to gravel, leaving Kronk alone in an unforgiving world.

It was Kronk who'd discovered me the night invaders destroyed my family. Scared. Cold. Hungry.

Devastated.

He'd found me and taken me to Yaga.

The three of us had been inseparable since. All orphaned by the same monster. If not for Yaga, we would all be dead. The kingdom, for all its beauty, was unkind to younglings forced to survive on their own. It was a fate I wouldn't wish on my worst enemy. Well, except for the false king. He could rot for all I cared.

I swallowed, fighting the rush of emotion. I was often emotional once I'd exhausted my magic.

Again, Yaga took charge of our bedraggled crew. "Look at

ya. Miserable bunch of rapscallions. First, I'll feed ya. Then you'll tell me why you're really here."

"Yes, Yaga," we said in unison. There were few who dared to disagree with Yaga. Especially not the renowned Blood River Bandits.

It wasn't long until bowls loaded with hearty stew sat before us. I shoveled a steaming spoonful into my mouth, moaning as the rich broth hit my taste buds. I puffed my cheeks, panting to cool the blistering chunks of root vegetables and meat, too hungry to care about my scorched tongue. Between mouthfuls, I told Yaga about our failed heist.

"Why in blazes did ya accept a contract with Vex?" The aged woman's wrinkles deepened as her cheeks turned a furious pink. "Do ya not have a brain between ya?"

Yaga's disappointment was a splinter stabbing beneath my nails. As usual, it was my plan that put us in the mobster's crosshairs. Despite being the youngest, where I led, my brothers followed.

Before I could defend my decision, Drazen jumped in. "King Idris's men will be here in less than ten spans. We didn't have a choice."

"Ya did too. Anyone but Vex would have been better. Three of ya act as though you're responsible for every village in the kingdom. You've gotten too full of yourselves."

Except, I *was* responsible. If only I'd held on tighter. Been stronger. Been braver. Fought harder when Idris attacked my family. None of us would be in this situation. If my brothers really knew what happened that night, they'd hate me as much as I hated myself.

"Folks around here are nothing but a bunch of cowards," Yaga huffed. "If they would have come together when that hell-spawn murdered his father and stole the throne, things would be much different now."

We could discuss who was to blame until we withered and

turned to dust. Unfortunately, the clock was ticking. "What's important right now is what we do about Vex." It would be impossible to help the village with his goons on our tails.

Yaga's cloudy eyes grew thoughtful. She tapped her bristly chin. "Vex is a collector. To make amends, you'll need to steal something to replace the lost deity. Something rare. Personal even."

"But what?" Kronk scratched his granite temple.

"It's not like we're friendly with the guy, certainly not on a personal level." Drazen faked a shiver of revulsion. "How are we supposed to know what will appeal to him? Other than the usual?"

"Usual?" Kronk asked.

"You know, whores, booze, weapons."

"We cannot bring him whores," Kronk said, nodding sagely.

Listening to my brothers, I fought the urge to pull out clumps of my hair. Instead, I turned pleading eyes to Yaga, silently communicating, *Please help me come up with a better idea. I can't take another minute of these two.*

Yaga heaved a resigned sigh. "Ya can't afford to make another mistake. Choose wrong, and he'll have your heads. Only way to know for sure is to consult the fates."

"Not the fates," Drazen said, a protective growl in his tone. "Not after what happened the last time."

Last time Yaga consulted the fates, she'd slept for several spans afterward. At one point, we'd feared she wouldn't wake.

"Oh, pish posh." Yaga waved a gnarled hand. "You all treat me like an old woman when I'm in the prime of my youth."

I exchanged a look with Drazen, both of us smart enough to keep our mouths shut.

"Yes. You are, Yaga." Kronk pounded the table, setting our dishes askew. "And may any who disagree feel my wrath."

"Kiss ass," Drazen muttered under his breath.

I snickered.

Yaga offered us a narrowed glare. "I tell ya, it's not time but boredom that's aging me. Lot of the younger folks here are worthless. Hell, half of them don't know the difference between a cup of piss and a decent pint of ale. And the older ones, *bah.*" She swept her hand in a dismissive gesture. "Try to rile them up for some fun and they fall asleep on ya, snoring away in their rockers. Me? I'm long overdue for a little adventure."

"Aren't we all?" Drazen smiled, batting his thick lashes.

"I'm pretty sure you have enough adventures for all of us," I deadpanned. To say my brother had a reputation was an understatement. For some reason I couldn't fathom, all species of ladies loved the horns.

Yaga heaved her creaking bones out of her chair, bringing an end to the discussion. "Welp. It's settled, then. Tonight, I will consult the fates. Tomorrow, you'll have the information ya need to clean up this mess. Maybe once the business with Vex and the village taxes are behind us, we can have a little celebration."

"I'd like that," I said, even though I didn't share her optimism. With the false king on the throne, there would be no end to Carcerem's troubles.

Chapter Three

MORTAL WORLD

VICTOR

THAT'S RIGHT. *Sneer down your noses.* For today, those who believed themselves superior to me would judge me for the last time. Just yesterday, I was one of the most powerful vampires in the nation. Titled. Influential. The leader of North America's Eastern Territories. Currently, I stood before the High Court in chains, stripped of my rank. My peers gazed down at me in disgust. It was an experience I hadn't had since I was young. Back when I was a penniless wretch cast from my birthplace into this land of mortals. Apparently, I would leave this world much as I had arrived.

When I was last in this court, with its domed ceiling, soaring marble pillars, and meddlesome spectators, I was an honored member of the hidden underworld hierarchy. Today, I stood imprisoned in a containment field meant for the worst of our criminals. Criminals I, myself, had pulled off the streets. Criminals I'd hunted down and brought to justice while the spineless bastards before me sat on their asses, criticizing my every move.

"Master Ignatius, what is your ruling?" my nemesis, Magister Tiberius Steele, asked.

Smug bastard. Oh, how I'd love to carve the triumph off the conniving jackal's face.

"Guilty," the High Court justice replied from the raised dais.

Despite my portrayal of cool indifference, rage seared my insides. To think I'd served this realm and all its supernatural inhabitants for the entirety of my long life. Ungrateful pricks. All of them. The entire underworld deserved what Tiberius had in store for them.

"Master Crenshaw, what is your ruling?"

"Guilty."

Those furious embers flared brighter.

Few gathered knew Tiberius's true agenda. For a while now, he'd led a hidden life, working behind the Council's backs to eliminate the ruling party and claim control for himself.

It was too bad I hadn't thought of it first.

Sadly, Tiberius would succeed, partly due to my failings. I'd become complacent in my role as clan leader. Grown too comfortable playing diplomat, sending others to do my bidding. It was my downfall.

"Master Rumsfeld, what is your ruling?"

"Guilty."

Again, the fury flared, scorching my chest.

Oh, yes. I was guilty. Guilty of so many crimes the Council knew nothing about. Because they had preferred to ignore my little indiscretions. They didn't care *how* I accomplished a job, only that I succeeded. Hungry to further my political position, I complied. But not without compensation. Every backstabbing male in this court owed me a favor. Favors, apparently, I wouldn't be around to collect.

"Master Reynolds, what is your ruling?"

"Guilty."

My throat squeezed, a roar pushing up from my burning chest.

I was the dirty little secret they all kept in a shoebox at the back of their closets. I knew the secrets of every leader of the High Court. Secrets I, at times, exploited as was my due. In destroying me, they covered their own asses. Or so they believed.

Tiberius was about to turn this realm on its head. The pathetic fools couldn't see what was right under their noses.

Finally, the last guilty ruling was counted.

Magister Tiberius strolled to the boundary of the containment field, a satisfied glint in his eyes. "Victor Custodis, the High Court has rendered its judgment. You are hereby found guilty of your crimes against the Council."

The verdict came as no surprise. Tiberius had fabricated enough evidence to bury me. It was laughable to be sentenced over crimes I hadn't committed when there had been so many I'd covered up over the years.

"The sentence for these crimes is," he paused, lips curling into a smug smile, "banishment. You will be cast into the prison realm, never to return."

Never to return.

An ancient image of my mother flashed through my mind—so old it had blurred and splintered with age. Still, I remembered. I'd made a similar promise to her when she sent me to this mortal world as a child. Thanks to Tiberius, I was about to break that promise. For the first time in centuries, I would set foot in the realm of my birth. To a place that had battered, abused, and rejected me. To a place I loathed even more than Tiberius.

To a shit-hole kingdom in a neighboring realm. The fools believed it was only a dumping ground for our criminals. Few were still alive to remember it was, in truth, the land of our origins.

"Due to the serious nature of these crimes, this sentence will be carried out without delay."

Of course it would. Tiberius couldn't risk me leaking his secrets. I wasn't the first to fall during this witch hunt. Nor would I be the last. He was eliminating anyone who might pose a threat to his plans. I was most definitely a threat.

Tiberius glanced over his shoulder. The head of the High Court sat on the raised dais along with his brethren. "Lord Kaius, please release the prisoner."

Four guards surrounded me on all sides. Blue energy crackled at the ends of their submission rods. The scent of ozone was thick in the air. Kaius twisted the ring on his bony finger, and the containment field dropped to the floor.

Before me, the heavily secured gateway loomed, its massive metal doors carved with the image of a stout tree with five thick branches. A jagged fracture sliced through the trunk.

The keeper of the gateway hobbled forward. His long robes hung from his narrow shoulders. With gnarled fingers, he twisted multiple dials, aligning the sacred emblems. Gears whirled, bolts slid free, and the doors glided open on their heavy track, parting the splintered trunk. At its center, a glowing fissure appeared—a violent tear between worlds.

Unlike the magic-infused portal that had once brought me here, this gateway was a scar—a remnant of when our kind had battered their way into this unsuspecting realm. Though I had little understanding of what made it work. One thing I knew for sure. It only worked in one direction. I could not use it to return to the mortal plane.

From the opening, a strange energy sparked over my skin, crawling like a thousand fire ants. The Arbor Realm's gaping maw was eager to consume me.

This was it. No one would arrive to save me from this travesty of justice.

But what of loyalty? Some would ask.

My men. My soldiers. The warriors whose *loyalty* I'd paid handsomely for fled the moment the Council seized my assets. Those who sympathized with my plight dared not challenge the Council and magister on my behalf.

As for family? I had none. No mate. No younglings. Nobody to inherit my confiscated legacy. The so-called legacy I'd bled, begged, and bartered to achieve. I'd made sure of it, never claiming a Bride in all my years. Although I'd been tempted a time or two. But only for political reasons. Never *love*. Never would I fall prey to that tender emotion. Love made males soft. Weak.

Vulnerable.

And so I stood.

Alone.

Masking the rage that boiled behind my carefully crafted mask, I strode to the gateway. Clad in nothing but tailored slacks, a collarless shirt, and an embroidered jacket, I was ill-prepared for the unpredictable elements in Carcerem. My long white hair was a beacon to predators. While I carried no weapon, at least my hands were unbound.

Tiberius dared to meet my heated gaze. "Victor Custodis, do you have any final words before you enter the gateway and accept the repercussions of your crimes?"

I turned my head slowly. In a low voice intended only for my nemesis's ears, I whispered, "I know who you are and what you've done. Soon, they will, too. When that happens, they will turn on you as they have on me."

Tiberius leaned in, his breath a whisper of venom. "I know you as well. You're nothing but a filthy gutter rat. The bastard son of a whore who cheated his way to the top. It's no wonder they've abandoned you. It's past time someone returned you to the slums of Carcerem, where you belong."

No one here knew of my shameful past. That Tiberius did

enraged me. Could it be he hailed from that same disgusting land?

Fury seethed in my gut, searing a path up my chest, refusing to be contained. In a rare burst of emotion, I lunged at Tiberius, snapping my hands around the monster's throat. Before I could enjoy his pained expression, electricity jolted up my spine. The guards beside me nailed me with their energized rods. My muscles seized, my limbs no longer my own.

"Again," Tiberius snarled.

Fire licked my nerve endings, sapping my strength. My body convulsed.

"Again!"

My blood boiled. Liquid trickled from my nose and eyes as my fangs tore into my lips.

"Magister Steel, enough," barked an aged voice. "If we wanted him dead, we'd have ordered his execution."

"Fine then," Tiberius conceded. Quieter, for my ears only, he snarled, "Watch that first step. I hear it's a doozy." To my guard, he commanded, "Send him through."

The guard slammed his foot into my stomach, and I plunged into the portal.

Swirling lights flashed in my vision. Icy fingers ripped at my flesh. Pressure built in my head, spikes driving into my eardrums. I spun in a vortex. I had vague memories of the sensation of being everywhere and yet nowhere while plunging through space. Nausea twisted my innards. My brain spun inside my skull.

Just when I feared the torment would never end, it stopped.

I windmilled my arms for balance, my legs wobbling. Sunlight stabbed my eyelids, its harsh light searing my skin. If I'd been a youngling, my pale vampire flesh would have fried on the spot. Fortunately, age had its benefits. Once my vision adjusted, I took in my surroundings.

"By the gods!" Vertigo washed over me, and I reeled back. Far below loomed the forest floor. Beneath my feet was a narrow, twelve-inch ledge. The portal had deposited me on the side of a cliff. The rift between realms was now a solid wall of rock with no sign of the gateway.

Dizziness threatened to pitch me over the edge, and I locked my knees in place. My limbs, weakened from the guards' rods, barely obeyed. I swiped my hand under my nose, eyeing the crimson streak on my fingers. *Fucking Tiberius.*

He thought to be rid of me so easily? Anger ignited my being, and I glared out at the foreign landscape. Without my title, my wealth, or my connections, I might as well have been dead. Power was everything, and at the moment, I was less than worthless. I hadn't spent centuries rising through the underworld ranks to have my many achievements stolen.

I clenched my fists, gathering that fiery rage inside me. I would find a way back to the mortal realm, no matter the cost. Once I returned, I would take back everything they had stolen and slaughter those responsible—starting with the magister.

I roared my vow into the abyss. "You hear me, Tiberius? I'm coming for you! This isn't the last you've seen of Victor Custodis!"

Golden sparks exploded behind my eyeballs. Lightning crashed beside my head. I threw my arms up, protecting my face from the explosion of stones that threatened to pulverize my flesh. "What the—"

Thunder rumbled, and I pressed against the rock wall. What was this? A storm when there wasn't a cloud in sight?

What sounded like the sonic boom of a jet rolled out from the cliffside and down into the valley, raising a circular ring of dust in its wake.

Trees swayed far below, birds launching into the sky, squawking their outrage at the disturbance.

Stone cracked, and a fracture sliced between my feet. "By the fates," I gasped, straddling the growing chasm. Down it raced, carving a serrated path through solid rock. My heart hammered, lodging behind my tongue as I searched for an escape. I needed a fingerhold. A vine to grasp. Anything!

The ledge crumbled, and I plummeted. Jagged shards tore at my back. Stones battered my frame. I urged my sluggish limbs to grasp some small ridge, some outcropping to slow my descent— to no avail. Flesh scraped off my scrabbling fingertips. My shoulder collided with a boulder. Pain exploded.

Then, finally, I stopped.

Was I dead? Groaning, I eased to a sitting position, cursing at the agony such a simple task caused. Not dead, then. Nothing seemed broken as far as I could tell. I rolled my shoulders and cursed. Blazing daggers speared my tendons. At least it wasn't dislocated. Anvils hammered my temples, and I clamped my hand to my forehead, wincing when my fingers came back crimson. Shallow cuts covered most of my body. My costly clothing? Ruined.

"Curse this disease-ridden realm!"

Here but a few minutes, and I was already injured, vulnerable, and bleeding in uncharted territory. Flashbacks of my childhood seared my memory. When I'd lived here as a youngling, it was the same. I'd been filthy. Broken. Scorned.

Weak.

That would not happen again.

My thoughts trailed off when the stench of rotten eggs and decaying vermin invaded my nostrils. I waved my hand before my face, coughing. "What is that smell?"

I'd landed at the edge of the woods, directly in front of a large cave opening. Scattered around me were piles of bones. Would it have killed the fates to drop me in the lobby of a five-star hotel?

"Surely, the gods are shitting on me today."

No sooner had the words passed my lips than a low growl rumbled from the depths of the cave. No. Not a cave. A den.

Some creature had taken advantage of the various criminals the Council deposited here. And I was about to be its next meal.

Glowing eyeballs peered down at me from the darkness. Up high, near the ceiling. So, it was big. The creature's foul stench wafted from the entrance with its movements. Strong enough to bring tears to my eyes.

Weapon. I needed a weapon.

I forced my shaking muscles to obey. "Argh! Blasted Tiberius!" Bit by bit, my limbs responded, and I struggled to stand. Sparkling lights danced before my eyes, my head swimming. Bile rushed up my throat, and I willed the putrid liquid to remain in my stomach. If I survived, there was no telling how long it would be until I found sustenance.

Through the spots dancing before my eyes, I zeroed in on a lengthy femur. It would have to do. I lurched toward the pile of bones and extracted my weapon, holding it aloft with quivering arms. None too soon.

The creature emerged from its dank hole. First, its gruesome maw appeared, lined with three rows of teeth, dripping yellow slime. Followed by its head. In its misshapen skull, a cluster of eyeballs sat like a spider carrying its young. Body resembling that of a walrus, it shambled out of its den.

Relief curled my lips into a smirk. With stubs for its front legs, it wouldn't be difficult to evade this ugly brute. It seemed I'd been worried about noth—

The beast's tongue slammed into my ankle, firing from its bottomless gullet. Before I'd processed the speed of the movement, the sticky appendage recoiled, knocking me off my feet.

With my makeshift weapon, I hammered the man-eater's gooey tongue, my weakened arms moving with the reflexes of a sloth. Despite my feeble attack, the monstrosity reeled me in.

As far as deaths went, it was a bloody, embarrassing way to

die. Me, Victor Custodis—Clan Leader of the Eastern Territories, leader of armies, defender of the underworld, the most powerful vampire lord in centuries—devoured by an oversized slug.

When last I'd been in this kingdom, my mother had warned that I'd die here if I didn't leave. I was back mere minutes, and already, her warning was about to become a reality.

At least I could rest knowing there would be nobody to witness this travesty.

The behemoth's putrid breath crawled up my nostrils, and I gagged, wrenching back on my leg. When inches separated my foot from the bastard's slimy mouth, I used all my strength to lurch upright. Spying two openings in the thing's face, I shoved my weapon into what I suspected was a nostril.

With zero effect.

Hundreds of deadly teeth stood poised to grind me into sausage. My pride took the beating. It really was a terrible way to die.

Sparks exploded inside the creature's salivating mouth. Howling a mournful noise, it reared back.

The sticky tether dropped from my ankle. I scrambled back, struggling to regain my feet. The ground trembled beneath me, and I threw out my arms. What now? From behind me, a male built like a tank raced past. Each fall of his pounding legs rumbled through the earth. He drew back his arm, punching the cave-dwelling colossus with his anvil-like fist.

The creature belted out an ear-piercing squeal, then launched its tongue. The disgusting appendage rocketed directly at me. I ducked, and it shot past my cheek. Slimy drool splattered my face. Missed! After missing its mark, the fiend's tongue zipped back once more, preparing for another strike. Apparently, the thing had a taste for vampire.

I hit the dirt. Again. This time with a curvaceous body planted on top of me.

Oxygen burst from my lungs, and I peered into a pair of

striking violet eyes. I sucked a ragged breath while my savior scowled. Her exotic features were unexpected and—dare I admit —entrancing. High cheekbones, heart-shaped chin, full lips. It was as if the gods ripped my most secret desires from my psyche and made them real. The stranger's face was perfection.

My heart heaved beneath her—not unwelcome—weight.

Bum bump.

Generous curves rest atop my injured frame. And for some reason, I didn't mind the pain. The female's sweet breath fanned my face, her fragrance spicy and warm with a hint of cloves.

Delicious.

Another deep breath and my eyelids went heavy, my fangs stirring.

Again, my heart slammed against my sternum, only this time, accompanied by an echo.

Bum-bum bump. Bum bump.

Surprise glittered in the woman's eyes, and for a moment, she softened against me. Something foreign stirred beneath my breastbone at the act. Once more, my heart thumped. Once. Twice.

Realization dawned. The truth struck harder than the fall I'd taken from the cliff.

The second heartbeat was hers. Our hearts beat in sync. Something that only happened when a vampire found their fated mate. The one person meant for them above all others. An experience I hadn't had in a thousand years. So why would it happen here? Now?

There was only one explanation that made sense. It was a mistake. A strange side effect of my journey through the portal.

Too fast, the woman's scowl returned. Before I could decide if I wanted to clutch her closer or toss her away, she rolled off me and sprang to her feet.

"Stay down," she ordered, planting her booted foot atop my chest, claiming me like I was some mountain she'd conquered, daring to stab her flag into my wind-blown peak. I ground my teeth at the insult. Any thoughts of the female possibly being my mate vanished in a surge of outrage.

I would not tolerate this kind of treatment *from anyone.* Though I doubted I had the energy to change my circumstances.

The miscreant's ear-piecing squeals distracted me from my outrage.

"Got him," said the male whose bulging muscles were carved from granite. "Slimy *gallspawn* bastard retreated into his den."

"For now," another voice said, and I craned my neck to identify the source. This one had dark horns protruding from his forehead. "Better get a move on before it rallies."

The weight of the female's foot lifted, and I lurched upright. Though it pained me, I forced myself to my feet. *Reveal no weakness.* With a sweeping glance, I analyzed the three strangers standing before me.

If I was to find a portal home, I'd need a crew. Though most of Carcerem's inhabitants were filthy, illiterate deviants, this bunch seemed to work well together. It was unlikely I'd find better in this miserable place. With no way to pay them, I'd have to rely on my wit and charm to win them to my side.

I held out my hand to the horned male. "Seems I owe you my thanks."

The demon smirked, taking my hand in an overly tight hold. "That's right. Except we'll be taking more than your gratitude."

With a twist of his wrist, he jerked my weakened form off balance and shoved me at his muscular friend.

"What the—"

Arms like reinforced concrete clamped around my upper body. Fury ignited my weary form. "What's the meaning of this?" I fought to gasp while the bands grew tighter. Tighter. *Tighter!*

"Release me," I wheezed, my aching bones creaking. Why

save me only to kill me? Perhaps these locals were even dumber than I remembered.

As my vision tunneled, my grinning savior sauntered up, curvy hips rolling, manacles in her hands. "Welcome to Carcerem, Victor Custodis."

Chapter Four

VICTOR

VOICES PERMEATED the fog in my muddled brain. Various aches and pains made themselves known as well. Awareness took hold in an instant. I'd been taken captive. I swallowed a groan, feigning sleep. Moisture from the ground dampened my thin pants. Ropes circled my torso, pinning me against a tree. Manacles bound my wrists and ankles—the metal strangely icy where it rested against my bare flesh.

Just a few feet in front of me, I sensed a presence. Spiced pears wafted under my nose.

"You keep staring at him like that, and you'll make me jealous," a smoky voice said from further away. "After all, I'm the pretty one in the family."

"You're pretty all right," the female answered, close enough her sweet breath brushed my face. "Pretty annoying. And he's far from my type. Besides, I'm not staring, more like studying. Same way he did us earlier. I mean, did you *see* the way he looked at us? Flarking creep."

Were the sorceress and horned demon lovers? For some

reason, this didn't sit well, stirring something violent inside of me.

"Runa is right. He isn't worthy of her," said a deeper voice. Boots crunched the ground, drawing closer. "Look at him in his fancy clothes, not a single callous on his hands, covered in blood and filth. This puny male is lucky we captured him. He would not have survived one span here in Carcerem. We have done him a favor."

Clearly, this larger male wasn't the brains of the operation.

"It is odd that this infamous warrior couldn't even defend himself against one gallspawn. Are you sure we got the right guy?" The smoky voice spoke again.

This other male consulted the woman. Perhaps she was the leader? Interesting.

"Yaga has never failed us before," the female said. "Although I did expect him to be... *more*."

That she found me lacking lit a fire in my stomach. I flicked my eyes open, glaring at two of my captors. The largest held a stick as if he contemplated poking me.

Despite my exhaustion, I stared deep into his eyes, pushing a wave of compulsion into the command. "Given your disappointment, perhaps it's best you release me."

At my words, the stone male flinched as though startled, then frowned. "He even speaks like a weakling."

I gritted my teeth. Over the centuries, many a powerful being had shaken with fear when meeting me.

"You idiot," his horned partner scoffed. "He didn't know his manacles suppress magic and tried to compel you."

Enchanted manacles? That could be a problem as I was already injured.

The big guy reared back. "Does he think me some weak-willed mortal? Athos do not succumb to tricks of the mind. Our skulls are too thick."

Too thick, indeed.

The woman rose from her crouched position, displeasure in the angle of her brow. "So, this is the Great Victor Custodis."

"The one Yaga risked consulting the fates over," her massive companion scoffed. "The one she claimed will set us on the path to freedom."

I bit back an angry retort. While I was born in this backward kingdom, I'd spent my life in the mortal world. Given the short time I lived here in my youth, there was much I didn't know about the land and its inhabitants. I hadn't a clue whom or what I was dealing with.

"I fear you have me at a disadvantage," I said in an even tone. "It seems unfair that you know my name and I don't know yours."

"Very well," said the woman. "I am Runa, sorceress of Carcerem."

For some odd reason, my heart flipped as I took in her form, my blood warming. She wore the garb of a warrior maiden with boots that covered her shapely legs to just above her knees. Her fitted skirt was pleated over her thighs. On the chest of her laced corset was an ornate metal breastplate. While the women of the mortal realm changed their appearance with cosmetics, I suspected Runa's violet hair and lavender eyes were natural. Though she professed to be a sorceress, she'd yet to reveal the nature of her magic. I'd need to watch her closely lest I fall victim to her sorcery. Maybe she already had me under her spell. It would explain my strange reaction to her.

"Kronk. Athos." Her partner jabbed a finger into his chest with a hollow thud. Given the stony texture of his flesh when he'd almost crushed me to death, I'd suspected as much. Athos were a formidable race, possessing an ability to turn to stone. The indestructible nature of their bodies, combined with their unmatched strength, was admirable. To have even one in my army would be an incredible advantage.

Runa confirmed my suspicions. "Kronk is the brawn in our

little group. And very much likes to pound soft, frail things. Almost as much as he enjoys giving hugs."

Kronk offered a broad grin in response, and I nodded, warning received. I was all too familiar with the athos's hugs.

The muscular male with the black horns and the ability to throw fire was likely an infernus. In my world, they were known as fire demons and forced to shear their horns to walk among the humans. Here, not even the smoke rolling from the male's nostrils would raise an eyebrow.

"Drazen," the horned demon offered from where he lounged against a fallen log.

Before him was a small stack of branches. He blew into his fist, setting his hand on fire, then tossed the fireball into the kindling. Flames exploded, igniting the wood.

"How's that for an introduction?" Drazen said, a cocky sneer on his face.

I'd seen better but didn't dare voice that opinion. "So, sorcery, brawn, and fire. What, exactly, is *my* role here?"

"Your job is the easiest of all," the infernus sneered, holding up his flaming index finger then snuffing it out in his fist. "You're our prisoner."

"We're selling you to Vex," the athos volunteered.

"Kronk," Runa groaned.

"What?" The block-headed giant raised his hands. "It's not as if a puny male like him can best us. What does it matter if he knows?"

"And who is this Vex?" I asked.

"He's a vicious gang leader and a collector of the rare and unusual," Runa said, her voice oddly appealing, rolling through my ears. "Word on the street is you're a hot commodity, despite your apparent weakness. Rumor is you've sent many of the mortal world's criminals here. There are some who took it personally. Vex, for instance."

I pondered the odd name. "Doesn't sound familiar. Perhaps you have mistaken me for someone else."

"You'd better hope not," Drazen snorted, puffing smoke. "If you're of no value to Vex, you're of no value to us, and that would make my friend Kronk very angry."

"So, you're flesh peddlers. Slavers." Proving once again that this female wasn't my mate. The fates wouldn't have bound me to a creature so far beneath my station.

Kronk stiffened his spine. "Are not. You are our first."

"Common thieves then." Like every other bottom-dweller in this disgusting kingdom.

"Not common." Kronk took a menacing step that had me drawing up my legs.

Runa placed a placating hand on the athos's thick arm, saying, "In Carcerem, we're more like royalty, as far as our fellow thieves are concerned. Not that you are one to judge, Victor Custodis."

Ha. My crimes were exemplary compared to theirs.

She lowered to her knees beside me, close enough I could once again pick up her delightful—no, annoying—scent.

Freckles spilled across the bridge of her nose. The flaw was strangely endearing, despite her being a common criminal.

Her violet eyes took me in, scanning my features in a disturbingly intimate way. "I must confess to being curious about you." She canted her head, lavender tendrils tumbling over her shoulders. "Yaga claims you're a vampire, hundreds of spans old. Says you're from the mortal realm. That you were once a great leader there, although a deceitful one."

This Yaga person wasn't wrong. It was about time Runa and her crew showed me a bit of respect.

When she raised her hand, I forced myself to remain still, to allow her touch. Instead of striking me, she brushed my silver-white hair back from my forehead, leaning closer, whispering in a way that made goosebumps dance down my arms. "I bet there are all kinds of secrets stored in that pretty head of yours."

She had no idea.

"What do you think, boys?" Runa asked.

"Do it," Drazen encouraged, an evil smirk twisting his mouth. "Could be something useful in there. Something worth a few coins."

Do what? Apprehension flickered through the haze the sorceress had created.

When she placed her palms on my face, I flinched back, knocking my skull against the tree. At her touch, a warm tingling sensation sparked within my body.

"What are you up to, pet?" I said, attempting to hide my response.

"Runa can both project images into someone's mind and extract them. That means we're about to possess all your dirty little secrets," Drazen answered.

Outrage burned across my senses, fury sharpening my fangs. I would not allow this injustice. This personal invasion. An assault on my psyche.

Sure, I'd performed a similar act not so long ago on a young faerie who had fallen into my hands. Without reservation, I'd invaded her mind to test her mettle, claiming it was to assess if she was a danger. When in reality, I'd done it to see how she could be of use to me—even knowing it was a gross abuse of my power and an immoral assault on so many levels.

Apparently, karma was no friend of mine.

"No," I snarled. Too late.

Runa's glowing eyes held me captive, and I was helpless to look away. In spite of my attempt to engage every mental block in my repertoire, I felt her gliding right through my barriers. The female was extraordinarily skilled. It was too bad she ran with a band of thieves.

Her presence swirled within me. Not like a gentle breeze,

more like a tempest blasting through my defenses. It lit up all the nerve endings in my body, bringing me to life while sending me to my death at the same time.

In my ears, a gentle pulse pounded. My own? No. It didn't match the panicked hammering behind my sternum. The seductive rhythm grew louder, the tempo almost hypnotic, pulling me deeper and turning me inside out. What was this madness?

Beneath my breastbone, my own heart skipped and leaped to a quicker beat as though it ran a race, eager to meet the rhythm of the one in my head.

The sorceress's soft gasp said she'd felt it, too.

Did she attempt to enchant me only to get caught up in her own magic? It would serve her right.

Even more determined to keep her out, I clenched my jaw, reassembling the fractured walls of my barriers—and failing. Runa's power swam through my essence, the two mixing together in perfect harmony. Then, slamming into an obstacle.

"What is this?" she whispered. Whether the words were out loud or in my mind, I couldn't discern.

Again, she struck the barrier, causing pain to spark in my skull.

"Not possible," she growled, and I sensed her gathering energy for another blow. To my shame, I cringed in readiness, grunting as she struck again. Again. Hammering. Failing.

Hot liquid trickled from my nose and ears. Agony stole my breath. The sorceress's grip tightened, her hands crushing my face.

"No. More," my garbled objection slipped past drooling lips.

Determination flooded the connection between us. Curse the woman, she readied for another attack. My brains would be little more than porridge if she didn't stop.

"Runa! Enough!" a voice barked.

The grasping hands whipped off my face, and Runa's cry melded with my groan of pain.

Ears ringing, I blinked, finding my attacker cradled in her partner's granite arms.

"Are you okay?" Kronk trailed a coarse finger under her chin.

"What happened?" She peered up at him, expression dazed.

"You tell us," Drazen demanded, crowding the pair.

Yes, I would like to know as well. The daggered glare I sent her was sharp enough to fillet her porcelain flesh from her bones.

Runa sat straighter in Kronk's lap, pressing her palm to her forehead. "He's bound."

"He's what?" the horned infernus asked, saving me from asking the same.

"There's a shield of sorts, buried deep within his psyche. I've never seen anything like it. Whoever placed it there was incredibly powerful. The harder I pushed, the harder it pushed back."

"What fool would bind a vampire?" Drazen curled his lip. "They're weaklings. Fast, but inferior to us in every way."

I had no knowledge of any barrier. Whatever it was the little thief discovered, at least it had kept my secrets out of her clutches. To hide my own pain and confusion, I chuckled, my head lolling on my shoulders. "What's the matter, pet? Bit off more than you could handle?"

"That's it. I've had about enough of this arrogant bastard." Drazen snapped his fingers, fire blazing from their tips.

Kronk grasped the infernus's hand in his large fist, snuffing out the flames. "Brother, you cannot."

Runa groaned her disappointment. "Kronk is right. Even without his secrets, he's valuable. Twenty-four hours and we'll be free of him. Then our debt will be paid. Surely, we can tolerate the arrogant prick for twenty-four hours without killing him."

Chapter Five

VICTOR

"ONE MORE WORD, and I will gut you like the sniveling swine you are," Runa snarled against my back. The blade she'd pressed to my kidney dug deeper.

With her generous curves pushing against me, her inner thighs grazing my hips, and her spicy scent plundering my senses, I was beyond distracted. That, combined with the knife play, had many disturbing urges prodding my psyche. The experience was a first for me as I believed myself above such animalistic drives.

"Such charming words falling from honeyed lips. Do you intend to woo me, sweet sorceress?"

"Bleck," she gagged.

I fought a smile.

"Please know, you are everything I hate most in a mate."

"How so? You don't even know me," I couldn't resist saying, more intrigued than offended.

"Oh, I *know* you. Like so many leaders, you've used your authority to further your personal agenda instead of serving the people. Full of arrogance, you believe the world owes you their loyalty without having earned it. Perhaps you started out with good intentions only to be corrupted by a broken system, falling into a never-ending cycle of lies and deceit. Like the rest, the power you fought so hard to obtain corrupted you."

"Ouch," I said, unable to refute her accusations. Despite her blatant disgust for those in authority, I found I didn't hate sparring with the sorceress. She had a keen mind and sharp wit despite being an inhabitant of this land. My darker side urged me to challenge the opponent it sensed in her.

After a restless night spent beneath Carcerem's twin moons, my captors had set out before sunset, planning to enter Rottwood, some small backwoods village known for being a criminal stomping ground. Drazen and Kronk rode beside us, one on a horse, the other on a massive bovine, while Runa and I rode together. The sorceress sat behind me, dagger poised, should I attempt to escape.

And I would.

All I waited for was the right moment.

The effect of the submission rods had worn off shortly after sunrise. My injuries from my tumble off the cliff were healing at a rapid rate, far faster than they would have back home. Though I continued to feign weakness.

Given my superior intellect, it was only a matter of time before I escaped. Still, I waited. Why struggle when they were taking me exactly where I needed to go? Into a village where I might find shelter, provisions, and information regarding portals. As a bonus, my bandits were protective of their prize, providing me with the security I needed. Despite their inadequacies, they'd proved surprisingly resourceful.

Again, I allowed my body to list as though I was too tired to even sit on a horse.

"Steady, you fool," Runa growled. "Fall, and I'll drag you behind us."

I had no doubt the little thief would follow through on the threat. Though my legs were unbound, my hands remained shackled. She had draped me in a hooded cloak, likely to prevent anyone from recognizing me and attempting to steal—or kill— her prize. Both were real possibilities, considering how many criminals I had sent to this place.

"Tell me about this barrier you discovered while invading my mind," I demanded of my so-called captor. Since our journey together neared its end, I'd use the time left to gain all the information I could to ensure my survival in this gods-forsaken land.

Runa stiffened behind me. "What does it matter?"

It mattered a great deal. In all my years and dealings with the supernatural, no one had ever claimed there was a binding placed on me. I had no idea who could have done it without my knowledge—or for what purpose. Perhaps my mother put it in place, before she abandoned me.

An image of my mother flashed in my mind. Blood spilled from her lips. *"Leave this place and never return. Stay and you will only know pain. As I have."*

Growling low, I shoved the image aside. "Have you ever seen the like?"

"Never," the sorceress admitted.

"What can you tell me about it?"

"Nothing."

"Out of spite or ignorance?"

"*Flark* you, vampire."

Spite then.

"I sensed the strength of your magic." Among other things I cared not to think about. Like the way her essence seemed to caress my spirit before she attacked me with a mental battering ram. How, despite the pain, my heartbeat had skipped to match hers.

As my thoughts drifted down a twisted and outrageous road,

I almost laughed out loud. The idea that the fates had bound me to this female was too absurd to even contemplate.

"Do you really expect me to believe you know nothing of this shielding spell?"

"Believe what you want." She shrugged against my back, the movement making my teeth clench. "It makes no difference to me."

Frustration battered my composure. "You're not curious?"

"Not in the least."

"What if it's shielding some valuable secret? Something that could benefit both of us." But mostly me. What if it was something that would help me return to the mortal realm? Information about a portal, perhaps.

Runa snorted. "I seriously doubt there is much of anything in that brain of yours that would interest me."

"Revealing the shield's origins is likely beyond your ability, anyway." I found myself unable to resist taunting her.

"*Nothing* is beyond my ability," Runa grated, thrusting her blade deeper into my ribs, forcing me to stifle the stab of pleasure that ran through me. "Best you don't forget that."

Despite my body's confusing response to being the sorceress's *captive*, I couldn't help but enjoy her ire.

"No worries. Once I've escaped, I'll find someone more capable of uncovering the mystery."

Again, the blade twisted, pain spearing my ribs and stirring my cock. Inwardly, I cursed at the defiant appendage. Runa was a commoner and a lowly thief, to boot. Sure, she was beautiful and intelligent. That didn't mean I'd lower myself to bed someone of her ilk. Unless said seduction could provide me with something I needed in return. Once more, my blasted cock twitched at the idea. Rebellious bastard had turned on me.

"First of all, no one escapes Vex. Second, nobody in their right mind would help the likes of you."

"First, I don't plan to escape *Vex*. Second, I can be rather persuasive once you get to know me, little thief."

Runa's exasperated groan rumbled through my back, and I delighted in her irritation.

"I could still gag you, you know. I'm certain Kronk would even sacrifice one of his socks for the task."

"And miss out on my charming conversation skills?"

"It's no wonder your world was eager to be rid of you."

Before I could respond in a way that was sure to get my kidney speared—and my cock standing at attention—Drazen appeared at our side.

"Enough with the questions, vampire. We're here."

Lights twinkled ahead of us, and a small village rose out of the mist. The place was positively medieval. The buildings were constructed of mostly rustic materials with thatched roofs, rough-cut timber, and earthen walls. Down the center of the village, rows of buildings sat close together, the streets winding and narrow.

"Listen up, leech," Drazen said, menace in his fiery gaze. "Plan is, we enter the tavern, meet with Vex, and make the exchange. What you do after is between you and Vex. Until then, you keep your head down and your mouth shut. Draw attention, and I'll turn you to ash faster than Runa could spit on your sizzling corpse." He snapped his fingers, flashing flames.

"Noted," I agreed. I'd likely make my escape long before the exchange, anyway.

Rottwood was a bustling community, even at night. Though primitive, cobblestones paved the roads. Instead of flames, torches with glowing crystals cast amber light onto the buildings and roads. Beings from all different races strolled along the walkways. Some had massive horns curling over their heads, and others leathery wings hanging down their backs.

"Shit. Look over there," Drazen muttered.

Kronk swiveled to pin an eyeball on the trio of men who ambled down the street. "The false king's guards."

Their eyes had an odd, milky quality. Purple capes hung over their shoulders. Feathers fluttered atop their helmets.

"Don't be so obvious," Runa hissed.

"Friends of yours?" I taunted. Now, this was an interesting development. It came as no surprise that my bandits were wanted criminals. Perhaps I could use this to my advantage.

"Trust me. They're no friends of yours either," Runa answered, digging the tip of her blade into my side.

I heaved a heated sigh. She really needed to stop with the seduction, for both our sakes. "Have I mentioned how much I love a bit of knife play in the bedroom?"

"You're disgusting," she spat, easing up on her dagger. Pity.

While I sat, portraying that of a weakened lump, Runa and her team dismounted, tying their beasts to a post outside the tavern.

That done, Kronk heaved me out of the saddle before dropping me to the ground like yesterday's trash. I staggered as though my legs wobbled, swallowing a harsh reprimand. They'd soon learn how badly they'd underestimated me.

Bawdy music trickled from the open door along with the low rumbling of voices. Inside, the smell of greasy mutton, unwashed bodies, and sour ale burned my nostrils. Dim lanterns hung from the ceiling, casting the room into shadows. Not since I was an aspiring squire to a drunken knight had I set foot in such a place.

Kronk kept one granite hand clamped around my biceps while Runa remained close to my back, the small knife she held hidden by the folds of my hooded cloak.

The sorceress gestured to an empty table. "The leech and I will sit there while the two of you speak with Vex. First sign of trouble, I'll bail and take the idiot with me. If this deal falls through, I'm sure we can find another buyer to recover our losses."

Drazen scanned the patrons seated closest to us, his expression wary. "If this fails to make Vex happy, it will take more than another buyer and a chest of coins to save our asses."

The two men stalked across the crowded room, heading for a darkened table in the corner. Runa and I sat with our backs angled toward the wall, the room visible before us. The sorceress remained close, her infernal dagger ever at the ready. The idea she believed it a threat was somewhat endearing.

I rested my manacled hands on my lap. The buzz of their enchanted metal prickled my skin. "You sent the hot-head and Kronk to negotiate with the mob boss?"

"Vex is a sexist pig, kind of like you. It's best I sit this one out. Drazen isn't the only one with a temper."

"No kidding."

She clenched her free hand on the table. "The offer of a gag still stands."

"Bondage and knife play. Kinky girl."

"You wish," she said with an eyeroll.

Did I? Perhaps if our roles were reversed…

A vision of Runa tied beneath me, my dagger at her throat, held a certain appeal.

"Waitress," I said to the buxom female who'd stopped near us. "Bring us two tankards of your best ale."

"What are you doing?" Runa clamped her hand down on my thigh and squeezed.

To my frustration, my manhood took notice of her intimate grip. Probably due to the image she'd provoked.

"Blending in," I answered. "You did order me not to draw attention. Sitting in a bar without a drink in hand will look odd."

"I cannot wait to be free of you." She released me with an exasperated snarl. "One more stunt like that, and I'll deliver you to Vex in pieces."

I glanced at the male who had my bandits tied up in knots. He was a large bastard with a barrel chest, deep jowls, and a thick neck. "Vex isn't unfamiliar." I racked my memory. "Ah, yes. I remember now. Back in the mortal world, my men arrested him for slaughtering a pack of shifters and selling their body parts on the black market. I seem to recall that he didn't discriminate, murdering adults and children equally." I'd been all too happy to send such a despicable character back to the land of my birth, unleashing him on those who'd scorned and abused both me and my mother. Let the filthy inhabitants of Carcerem deal with him.

At Runa's indrawn breath, I smirked. "Are you sure you want to do business with this male?"

"You're lying."

"Am I?" I wasn't.

When she cast another worried glance in Vex's direction, I took the opportunity to study her partners. Kronk sat with his arms folded, stony face a mask of rage. Though Drazen had his back to us, smoke coiled above his head. Apparently, the negotiations had taken a turn for the worse. Good.

"Tell me, pet. How did a charming sorceress like you become a criminal?" I observed the group at a table next to us. The closest had a scabbard and sword belted around his hips. Not a bad option, but it would be difficult to wield with my wrists bound.

The glare Runa cast me was devoid of amusement. "If you think to distract me so you can grab that sword, it won't work."

Touché. My lips curled. "You wound me. Perhaps I'm merely making small talk. After all, it's been years since I sat in a bar next to a beautiful woman." This, at least, was the truth.

"First, I'm charming. Now, I'm beautiful," she snorted. "Do the women in your world actually fall for that bula dung?"

"You may find this surprising, but women have been known to fall at my feet with but a crook of my finger."

"You don't say." She batted her lashes. Her lavender eyes

sparked with an evil gleam that wasn't unattractive. "Perhaps you should switch tactics then and not speak."

This time, I was unable to stop the smirk that curled my lips.

Now, I was genuinely curious. "Fine, we will barter then. If you answer my question, I'll answer one of yours."

She narrowed her eyes, taking my measure while I considered the dagger she pressed to my side. This weapon I could wield easily with my hands bound.

As if she could read my thoughts, she offered a winsome smile. "Do it, and I'll cut out more than a kidney."

My smirk spread into a grin. "I love it when you talk dirty to me." Strangely, this, too, was another truth.

"You first." Sadly, she ignored my taunting. "Explain to me why the mortal world banished you."

"Easy enough. I was framed."

At this, she snorted a laugh. "You're kidding. The Great Victor Custodis was outwitted?"

I scowled, not appreciating her laughter. "Even the mightiest of leaders can have a bad day."

"Bad day," she scoffed.

"You've never made a mistake?"

Her smile fell. "I'm beginning to think this conversation is one."

Two tankards slapped down before us. The waitress held out her palm and snapped her fingers.

"Don't suppose you'll be paying." Runa glowered at me.

It was yet another reminder I was a pauper with nary a cent to my name. No power. No title. Vulnerable. *Focus, dammit.* It was past time I parted ways with my bandits. Still, I found myself responding in a teasing manner, unwilling to end our conversation. "I believe I am here as *your* guest by *your* invitation."

Under her breath, she muttered, "And he claims I'm the criminal."

As she slipped her fingers into a coin purse attached to her belt, a plan took shape. I could knock the ale into the sorceress's lap, grab the dagger while she was distracted, and take the waitress hostage, making my escape. And yet, for some reason, I hesitated. Our bargain wasn't fulfilled.

Once the waitress accepted her payment and disappeared into the crowd, I turned to my companion.

"I answered your question. So, tell me, little thief, what led you to a life of crime?"

Shadows darkened the exotic angles of her face, and she lowered her gaze to the tankard in front of her. "The false king. He takes more than the realm and its people can afford to give. I felt it was my duty to help restore the balance."

When she met my gaze, the depth of emotion in her expression shot right to my core. The predator inside of me woke. The same predator that, for centuries, had peeled back the layers of a person's psyche to reveal their deepest, darkest secrets. Secrets I would then exploit.

Runa had answered my question, but I sensed she'd given me a half-truth.

I leaned closer, drawing in her delightful scent. With her heightened emotions, her fragrance intensified. The spicy burn heated my insides. "And what, little thief, did this false king take from you?"

At her hesitation, my desire to take, to use, to destroy shifted. That familiar urge twisted, became something darker, more primal. Had this supposed king *touched* her? I clenched my fists in my lap, my fangs burning.

Shouts rang out from across the room.

"Raid!" a male seated at the table next to us bellowed.

Six milky-eyed soldiers wearing purple capes pushed through the front door. Curse the female and her tricks. While keeping her off balance, I'd gotten caught in my own trap.

I eyed the guards, considering the latest obstacle to my

escape plan. Conclusion? This was not the sort of aid I desired. Getting tangled up with the authorities would only delay my search for a portal home.

"Runa, run!" Kronk shouted as four of the robed guards headed straight for her partners.

The other two took one look at the sorceress and darted in our direction. While Vex remained seated at his table, a feral grin pulled wide across his jowls. It took but a second for the details of the situation to real themselves to me. Seemed I'd been handed the opportunity I'd sought after all.

"Sorry, pet. It appears you've been double-crossed."

Chapter Six

RUNA

A T K RONK'S WARNING, I leaped from my seat, dragging Victor up beside me. Fear for my brothers exploded in my chest. "Move!" I shouted, shoving my captive toward the far end of the tavern. To my surprise, Custodis did as he was told.

Dodging between the tavern patrons, we raced into a sweltering kitchen. Shouts rang out behind us. *"This way, they're in back."*

I glanced over my shoulder in time to see one of the king's men crash into a server. Greasy meat pies and foaming ale splattered everywhere. It might buy us some time, but not enough.

While the soldiers scrambled across the slippery mess, Custodis and I plowed through the rear door and out into the alley. The vampire was strangely cooperative. I had zero doubts he was plotting something. What, exactly, was yet to be seen.

The former leader had a keen mind. Of this, I was sure. Strangely, I respected this part of his personality. Like me, he wouldn't rest until he was free. Problem was, his freedom spelled my doom. Except, if the trade with Vex was a setup, where did that leave us?

I'd sort it out once I reunited with my brothers.

"Head to the right," I ordered. "We'll cut through the back alleys, then return to the main road. Maybe we can lose them in the crowd."

"An excellent plan," Custodis said.

My heart skipped an odd stutter at the praise.

"Do you and your fellow criminals do this often?" he asked, a mocking lilt in his voice.

While he may have been taunting me, the vampire wasn't far off the mark. "Of course not. We're professionals, not amateurs," I replied flippantly. An image of the angry monks with their pitchforks flashed in my mind.

I ignored the reminder of our last failure, snapping, "Talk later. Unless you want to spend the night in the king's prison." I shoved his shoulder, and we raced along the darkened alleyway. Puddles splashed beneath my feet. The stench of fermenting trash filled my burning lungs.

"Professionals," Custodis snorted. "This must be the worst kidnapping I've ever endured. Perhaps it's time you and your friends found a new occupation."

"You think you could do better?"

"Most certainly."

"Have you?" Despite my scorn for the arrogant prick, I found myself curious about the criminals the vampire had captured.

"Absolutely. Though most of my abductions ended in torture and death. Rarely did I sell my captives."

"And yet you judge us," I muttered.

Several blocks later, we reached the main thoroughfare. I scanned the road for purple capes, finding none. "Let's go." I leaned into the vampire's side, walking as though we were out for a stroll.

"Now what?" he asked.

"Now, we blend in, wait for the guards to give up, and then make our way to the meeting point where Kronk and Drazen will join us."

"That confident they got away, are you?"

"Yes." I refused to believe otherwise.

"Here," Custodis said, loosening the ties on his cape. "Put this on. Unlike you, I doubt the guards will recognize me."

It wasn't a bad idea. Custodis was likely an unknown, whereas my face was plastered on several wanted posters throughout Carcerem. I let him drape the cape over my shoulders, and as he pulled the hood up to conceal my hair, I took the opportunity to study his arresting features.

If I were being honest, the vampire wasn't hideous. Not by a long shot. In fact, when he wasn't sneering at me, he was rather attractive.

Long, silver-white hair framed his aristocratic face. Scratch that. On the surface, he projected an *aristocratic* air—impeccably dressed, with a certain refined aloofness—but a closer look revealed an almost elven quality. While his ears were rounded, there was a certain ethereal grace to his characteristics—though there was nothing feminine about the leech.

When his full lips pulled into a smirk, I stared, transfixed.

"See anything you like, little thief?"

My cheeks heated, and I dragged my eyes away, huffing. "You wish, vampire." When we started walking again, I asked, "Why are you cooperating?"

"I am not an unreasonable male. Even I can see the benefits of escaping the king's guard."

"No," I stated. "You're up to something."

He smirked as though he enjoyed my observation. "Too bad you can't read my mind."

Prick.

Too bad, indeed. The situation was unsettling, to say the least. Thanks to the strange shielding I discovered, the vampire beside me was a complete mystery. Except for the information Yaga had given us, which wasn't much. Just enough to help capture him.

And why was that? Why had Yaga set us on this path when it was clearly not the solution to our problems? Truly, I did not feel as though I was on the path to freedom but to destruction.

What was I missing?

"You two," a deep voice shouted. "Stop right there!"

My pulse leaped, and I glanced behind us. There stood two males in purple cloaks.

"It's them!" the tallest shouted.

"Get behind me." I elbowed my way in front of my captive and held up my glowing hands. Perhaps an imaginary wall of fire would deter them. I reached deep into the well of power within me, summoning the darkness at my core. Heat spread through my hands, my palms beginning to glow. Almost...

Fabric engulfed me. The cape I wore plunged over the top of my head, the hem knotting at my back. "Custodis! You son of a nerf herder, what are you—"

"Have fun in the king's prison, pet," the vampire said, then punted the back of my knee.

I collapsed with a screech of outrage.

"All yours, boys."

I registered his voice through the heavy fabric, along with the thump of racing footsteps.

"Leech! You'll pay for this, you bula flarker!" I battled the engulfing material. Rough hands yanked me off the ground and ripped the cape off my head, along with strands of my hair.

"Let me go!" I swung out my leg, only to have it captured. The guard who caught my foot twisted it, driving me back to the ground face down. Pain lanced my spine as the male drove his knee into my back, pinning me on my stomach. Both my arms were wrenched behind me, and I cried out.

As the bastards snapped enchanted manacles on my wrists, I

peered down the street in the direction my captive had bolted. At an impressive pace, Custodis sprinted away. Not so weakened, after all. The vampire was clearly an apex predator in his prime. *Gah!* I was so stupid! Believing him injured. Unable to even seat a horse. Deceitful bastard.

Despite my rage, my lips curled.

Well played.

At the end of the narrow street, a mounted soldier in a gold cloak rode into view. Four others swathed in purple stood on either side of their captain.

Custodis skidded to a stop before them.

For a moment, both sides took each other's measure. The four guards attacked in unison. The vampire attempted to bolt into another alley when a second team of men joined in, this one even larger than the first. Before Custodis could pivot, a shimmering net dropped out of the sky, the magic-infused webbing further weakening the vampire. In seconds, Custodis was face down on the ground with four guardsmen beating his immobilized body.

"Ha! Serves you right!" I belted out a laugh as the guards wrenched him up from the street. This had to be the most fun I'd ever had while being arrested. Sure, we'd kidnapped the deceitful vampire with the intention of selling him to Vex. But at least we hadn't lied about it. Unlike Victor, we were *honest criminals.*

Curious onlookers trickled out of the taverns, watching the show while Custodis's guards walked him over to join me, their captain following behind. The horse's clomping footsteps rang like a death knoll in the darkened alley.

From his lofty perch, the captain peered down at me, his face void of emotion. "Runa Starborn, illustrious leader of the Blood River Bandits. I've looked forward to meeting you. So has your king."

"The pleasure is all yours." Classy sorceress I was, I hacked a wad of spit in his direction.

"Charming," the captain sneered, turning his attention to the vampire. "And who is this?"

"Victor Custodis, Clan Leader of the Eastern Territories, resident of the mortal world," the pompous vampire answered, adding a half-bow for good measure. "At your service."

At the captain's arched brow, Custodis held up his manacled hands. "Apologies, good sir, but there seems to be some mistake. See, I was merely a captive and not a part of whatever mischief these bandits have been up to."

"Is this true?" The captain turned to me.

Regardless of my dreadful circumstance, dancing flutterflies did joyful somersaults in my stomach. Oh, this was just too good. "Nope. He's one of us. A new guy we hired to carry our bags and shovel our shit."

The vampire glared daggers at me. The intensity of his anger seared my flesh.

I delighted in the burn.

"Very well." The captain shrugged. "Tell it to the king."

"Curse you, Runa," Custodis snarled, his complaints drowned out by an approaching conveyance.

The royal paddy wagon rolled to a stop beside us. Emblazoned on its side was the false king's insignia. It depicted Idris's profile, golden bolts erupting from his skull—a symbol that did nothing to represent the kingdom's people or its land. It was nothing short of obscene.

"Load them up, and let's get underway. We've a long drive ahead of us," the captain ordered.

The guard wrenched open the door, and my defiant heart fell. Both Kronk and Drazen waited inside.

Chapter Seven

RUNA

"WELL, THIS IS A FINE MESS," Drazen huffed, slumping deeper onto the bench of the enclosed wagon. Custodis sat beside him, with Kronk resting next to me. While the vampire was still in his original manacles, the rest of us had our hands cuffed behind our backs. Like the leech's restraints, ours were crafted from enchanted metal that suppressed magic, making them unbreakable, even for Kronk.

"Flark Vex and his vile deception," I cursed. "We do not have time for another delay. White Bridge only has nine spans remaining before collection day."

"Yeah," Drazen agreed. "And I doubt our little visit to the dungeons will cause the collectors to cut them some slack."

I stared out the bar-covered window, fighting the molten wave of panic that threatened to destroy me. We were on our way to the false king. To *him*. I hadn't seen the false king since he'd destroyed my family and village. The horrifying stench of burning flesh and terror filled my senses. An image of my sister took shape in my mind. Her lilac eyes were wild as she turned to me, her sweaty hand in mine, the portal at our backs. My mother lay next to us, blood spreading across her chest. Her pale lips parted, revealing her final words, *"Runa, don't let go."* While she'd made the ultimate sacrifice to save us, I had failed in my duty to her. To the kingdom.

"I do not understand," Kronk said, drawing my thoughts out of the past, forcing me to face the impending doom headed our way. "Yaga consulted the fates."

"She did," I agreed, a tingle of unease testing my faith in the woman who had raised us.

"This does not feel like the path to freedom," he continued.

"No, it doesn't," Drazen added, a matching frown on his face. "Perhaps there's something we missed."

Yaga had never led us astray before.

"It's possible the fates are angry with us," Kronk grumbled.

"You get anything from the guards?" Drazen asked, his voice a low whisper so the men who drove the wagon couldn't hear.

"A little." When a rough-handed guard grabbed my arms before clapping me in manacles, I'd done a bit of mystical recon, stealing images from his mind. "For starters, the captain received an anonymous tip that we'd be at the tavern. From Vex, no doubt."

"We should have known this pathetic leech wouldn't be enough to appease his anger," Drazen snarled, sending Victor a disgusted glare.

"Apologies that my capture and attempted sale was a dismal failure," Custodis said. His words sliced like daggers, drawing blood.

"Before the ambush, Vex confessed the deity we lost was his former mate," Kronk added. "He'd intended to resurrect her."

"Which is why he sold us out," I groaned. Even among thieves, matters involving mates trumped business deals—most of the time.

Custodis snorted. "Any fool could have spotted that setup

from a mile away."

I shot him a glare. "You believe you're so superior to us, and yet, here you are, captured by the king's guards. Headed the same place we are."

"Due to the foolishness of others." His penetrating stare bore holes into me, leaving no doubt about whom he considered the fool.

"That makes two of us, seeing as *you're* the reason I'm here," I snarled through gritted teeth. "Don't for one second think I've forgotten about that little stunt you pulled with the cape."

"Most women do find me unforgettable," Custodis intoned.

The audacity of the male. A red haze filled my vision. My head pounded as though it might explode. "You are the most arrogant, insufferable, egotistical—"

"Guys! Guys!" Drazen interrupted my tirade. "Can't believe *I'm* the one saying this, but we need to concentrate. What's our plan here?"

I closed my eyes, heaving a deep breath. Once my pulse slowed, I shoved my expression into what I hoped was a collected mask. "From what I gleaned from the guard's mind, when prisoners first arrive, they're placed in a minimum-security holding cell for processing. There, we'll receive a torque that will suppress our individual gifts."

Drazen wrinkled his nose in disgust. "You mean the king has some kind of collar capable of snuffing out my fire?"

"Sounds like it. Good news is we did a job for one of the grunts who works in holding not long ago. Remember the one who had us steal back his mate's heirloom necklace when the soldiers confiscated it during the last tax collection?"

"I remember." Drazen snorted. "Thing was butt ugly. Why they'd want it so bad is beyond me."

"Yeah, well, he never paid us. So, the plan is, after we're processed, we'll convince him to deactivate our torques. That way, Kronk can break us out before they move us somewhere more secure. Once we're free, we'll head for the mountains where we can lay low while things cool off."

I dared to glance in the vampire's direction, waiting for his reaction. Ha! Take that for a team of incompetent thieves.

Rather than comment, Custodis rested with his eyes closed and his head pressed back against the wall, a soft smirk on his arrogant face. The bastard almost looked bored.

I kicked his foot, and he cracked one eye open.

"Enjoying the ride?"

"Except for the incessant chatter," he dared to taunt.

"Why aren't you more concerned?"

"Because I'm not going to prison like the rest of you."

Kronk heaved a massive sigh. "And they claim I'm thick headed."

"Do tell us, oh great master of denial," I said, "why are you not going to prison?"

"Because, unlike you peasants, I am valuable."

I was beginning to think Custodis enjoyed my reactions to his ridiculous statements. There was no other explanation for the crap that spewed from his lips. I schooled my expression, refusing to give him what he desired.

"How so?" I asked.

"I am Victor Custodis, Clan Leader of the Eastern Realm. A legend in my world. I've centuries of experience in leading armies. Oversaw the rise and fall of dozens of kingdoms. Guided many infamous rulers to victory."

Goodbye composure. Fury rushed my veins so fast I feared my brain would explode. "You intend to offer your services to the false king? To aid his cause?"

Of all the things the leech had said and done, this one hit its mark, slashing at me with claws and fangs.

"Runa," Kronk said softly as though he feared anything more may set me off.

"And you believe we are the fools," I said in a voice so icy even Drazen shivered. "You have no idea the crimes the false king has committed—the destruction he has caused both to the realm and those seated before you. But, by all means, if you desire to pledge your loyalty to him, do so. The two of you deserve each other."

For once, the vampire fell silent, seeming to ponder my words.

"If this is not my best course of action, then educate me," he demanded in that annoying way of his. "I am a reasonable male, after all."

"Reasonable. Ha!" I narrowed my gaze at him.

I was growing familiar with his ways. He wanted information, but instead of asking, he tried to manipulate me into telling him. Still, I conceded, curious about his reaction.

"Very well. The throne of Carcerem is carved into the base of one of five sacred arbors. Millennia ago, the great goddess Hathor gifted each of her favorite kingdoms one of these trees. Sadly, due to war, neglect, and greed, only a few remain. Those kingdoms that were able to protect these sacred treasures were blessed with magic in the form of obsidian. Carcerem's tree is the heart and soul of our kingdom. An organ pumping life into everything it touches. Those who sit upon these thrones are tasked with regulating that power. Only a child touched by the divine can handle such a monumental task."

"A descendant of the gods?"

"That's right. Only one who is god-touched can claim the throne. Lesser beings cannot control the immense flow of power and are incinerated by its strength."

"And the current king?"

"While Idris has the blood of the gods in his veins, he is the worst of all the kings before him. His body may be strong, but his mind is diseased. When his father died, he inherited the throne. From the moment of his coronation, those of us who were connected to the land knew he was a false king. When the sacred arbor rejected him, Idris retaliated, finding a way to steal what he desired, sucking the life from our great arbor's roots. That deficit affects all of us. Crops wither, animals sicken, rivers run dry."

"So, with this magical throne comes immense power."

I clenched my jaw. "Is this all you took from my explanation?"

"Yes. Yes." Custodis fluttered his manacled hands. "So, your crops are diseased, and your oxen lean. Nature has a way of weeding out the weak."

Surely, even Victor Custodis could not be this callous. "Those who defied the false king were made an example. Families were murdered, children orphaned, and entire villages were burned to the ground. If that wasn't bad enough, those who survived had their free will stolen. The milky eyes you see on the guards? The false king uses his gifts to exert his will on his followers, making them his adoring slaves."

Custodis's brow furrowed, and his expression turned condescending. "These matters involving monarchy are rarely personal. For a new king to come to power, there are those who must fall."

Furious tears stung my eyes. "You would not be so cocky if it were your family, your village, *your sister*."

"Runa," Drazen entreated. "The leech isn't worth it. Don't waste your breath on him."

I inched forward on my seat, peering into the vampire's heartless visage. "Perhaps this is why you yourself were kicked out of your world. Because you were the weak, insignificant thing that stood in the way of the new king."

To my delight, Custodis's disdainful expression slid from his face.

"You know nothing," he snarled.

Ah, I'd hit a nerve. "Don't I? Explain to me again how you

were banished, oh, great one."

At my taunt, Custodis lurched forward, baring fangs.

I welcomed the battle, hissing in retaliation. *Come and get me, asshole.* Finally, I'd fractured the vampire's stony composure.

Kronk thrust his booted foot into Victor's chest, slamming him back into his seat, causing the wagon to wobble. The vampire wheezed, his sternum cracking.

"Hey! Settle down back there," the driver barked.

"Enough," Drazen growled. "Both of you. Before you call the guards down on our heads."

Kronk released the leech with an antagonistic snarl while I preened, leaning into Kronk's mighty arm. *That's right, vampire.* My big brother was *big*, and he had my back. Always.

The vampire's pale eyes darted between the two of us, then narrowed with some strange emotion I didn't care to analyze.

We continued our journey in silence, alone with our dark thoughts. Too soon, the foliage became sparse. What was left of the vegetation slumped with exhaustion, withering with decay. Black craters scarred the ground like some beast with many tentacles had a grip on the land. Stark trees, void of leaves, lined the road, and a sense of foreboding crept down my spine. The state of the kingdom was so much worse near the source of the darkness.

It wasn't long until Slyborn Castle came into view, situated atop a rocky hill with its high walls, toothy battlements, and rounded towers. Over the massive structure, dark clouds loomed like a burial shroud. Dozens of purple flags bearing the king's image flapped around the structure, slashing the sky. Like the gallspawn creature, it seemed the stone walls contained a hundred eyeballs, the narrow windows peering down on us in judgment.

The captain of the guard rode ahead, signaling to a soldier in the guardhouse. Massive gates made of enchanted metal creaked on their hinges, allowing our party to enter. Inside the lower bailey, merchants in small booths hocked their wares. Through our barred windows, a mixture of scents wafted in the air, some savory, some sweet, though my stomach rebelled at the thought of food.

Our driver steered us onto a narrow side road, traveling around the crowded bailey to a smaller pair of doors set into the rocky foundation of the keep's many towers.

"Guess we're not getting the red-carpet treatment, seeing as how they're sneaking us in the back door," Drazen muttered.

"We'll be lucky if they don't feed us straight to the hell-hounds," Kronk answered.

Rather than deposit us outside, our driver took us into the building, horses, wagon, and all. Behind us, the heavy doors slammed shut, trapping us inside.

Synchronized boots struck the stone floor, marching in unison. Approximately a dozen soldiers entered the space. One by one, they peeled off, forming a circle around our carriage, swords at the ready.

"What the flark is going on?" I whispered. "This isn't their procedure for handling prisoners."

Where was the stock yard? The other inmates? The low security pen we could easily escape.

"Perhaps they have heard of our awesome prowess and many accomplishments," Kronk offered.

"Or perhaps they know when a noble leader is in their midst," Victor contributed.

I fought an eyeroll. I truly was surrounded by idiots.

At last, the captain swung our door open. "Lucky you. Our noble king has taken a personal interest in your crimes and will hear your case immediately."

Dread washed over me in a flood. Luck had little to do with this. There was definitely a darker power at work. One I feared I knew all too well.

Chapter Eight

VICTOR

ONCE MORE, I stood on a proverbial cliff, my circumstances taking a turn for the worse. While I was born here, I'd few memories of Carcerem's kings and castles. Perhaps because my mother and I lived in squalor, too busy surviving this brutal land to worry about such things.

As I expected, Slyborn Castle was a dismal canker sore, rotting upon a desolate land. Why anyone would want to rule in such a place was beyond me. The barbaric architecture was as stark and unwelcoming as the rest of the kingdom.

Though I'd managed to mask my reaction as we'd approached the castle, a strange energy made the hairs on my arms spike to attention. Once we were inside, the energy built to the point I feared it would splinter my ribcage, leaping out of my chest. Despite the desolation of the land, something here was very much alive.

After we exited our conveyance, armed guards ushered me and my former captors through endless corridors until, finally, we arrived at a monstrous throne room. Smoky marble with golden veins stretched out beneath our feet. Scores of spectators filled blackened benches placed on either side of a wide aisle. The cathedral-like space had domed ceilings. The supporting pillars were shaped like long fingers with claws. Ropes of crimson ivy twisted around the soaring columns. Whether it was dead or alive, I couldn't discern. Regardless, it gave the illusion that the very walls bled.

Still, I maintained my composed facade until my gaze landed on the throne. One glimpse and drool pooled in my mouth, my jaw dropping.

At the center of a raised dais was a massive tree made of ebony stone. Thick pulsing roots rolled out from its enormous trunk, delving deep into the floor and to parts unknown. Sturdy branches with copper leaves stretched up into a domed skylight. Carved into the bottom of the tree was a throne, blackened roots slithering from beneath its base.

Perched on the seat was a striking male, his rich brocade clothing woven with gold. Over his spiked silver hair was an elaborate crown designed to resemble branches. As I took the male's measure, yet another jolt ran down my spine, but not of fear. Never that. Rather, it seemed a strange thread connected us.

"Wait here," the guards ordered.

My entourage came to a stop.

On the floor before the dais, there was a large circle etched with ancient runes. A horned demon wearing manacles kneeled in its center.

"Please, sire. If I could have more time. My mate is with child and the crops—"

"Enough of your sniveling," the king snapped, his voice sharp with disdain. "You know the law, and yet, you broke it. The repercussions are clear." He held up his hand, golden light illuminating his fingertips.

"Please, sire. I beg you."

"And I grow weary of the noise." The king flicked his wrist, and the imprisoned demon let out a yowl, falling to his knees. He clutched his throat, gasping and gurgling.

The bloodthirsty crowd murmured their delight at the display. Golden flames ignited the man's body, his reedy screams echoing. Except this was no typical fire. In seconds, his writhing form became a tower of glowing embers that soon disintegrated into shimmering sparks.

I stood speechless. It was one of the most effortless demonstrations of power I'd ever seen. Behind the king, the enchanted tree pulsed as though alive. Black veins throbbed along its thick roots. From the canopy, a single withered leaf ignited, tumbling from a branch as it floated to the ground.

"Next," the king commanded.

Guards prodded our backs, urging us into the middle of the circle.

"Kneel," the milky-eyed guard demanded.

We hit our knees—all except for Runa.

"Kneel, I say." At her defiance, he clamped his gloved hand on the back of the sorceress's neck, forcing her to the ground.

The crack of her kneecaps striking the marble made me wince.

The king's eyes gleamed with delight. "Ah, the notorious Blood River Bandits. It's so good of you to join me today."

"He's heard of us," Drazen muttered out of the corner of his mouth.

"Of course he has," Kronk whispered, his shoulders drawing back.

Fools. At this rate, we'd all be ashes by the time this was over.

Oddly, Runa had fallen silent. Her body was tense, her chest rising and falling in shallow breaths. The sweet scent of her fragrance turned bitter, tainting the air with fear—like she gazed upon her worst nightmare.

Fear was a scent I typically found appealing. Only for some

reason, hers had a low growl pushing its way up my throat. I coughed to cover my loss of control. What did I care if she was afraid? Runa was a known criminal in the king's throne room. She had every cause to be concerned.

Myself, I was eager for this meeting. This was my chance to improve my situation, align with a powerful king, and find my way back to the mortal world to claim my revenge and everything that was stolen from me.

It was Drazen who spoke first. Figured. The arrogant infernus believed himself to be charming.

"Great King Idris, it's an honor to kneel before you. If it so pleases, Your Majesty, may I say you look quite royal this evening?"

The king's unnerving gaze locked on Runa and darkened with an antagonistic gleam. "And what does fair Runa Starborn think of her king's appearance?"

Static sparked along my spine at the tension between the two. Apparently, the sorceress and the king were acquainted.

Runa's rigid frame began to quake.

"Easy," Kronk mumbled in a low tone.

"Answer your king," the guard demanded, withdrawing his sword from its scabbard.

"I think," Runa croaked, seeming to have lost her voice. Likely, it was a first.

"Louder," the guard urged, taking a menacing step.

"I think you look—"

"Remember the villagers of White Bridge," Drazen hissed.

Energy crackled as a dark shroud settled over our shoulders.

"I think you look like a murderous piece of—"

Before she could finish, a unified gasp rang out. Hushed voices muttered their excitement. From a door at the side of the room, an ethereal woman appeared, gliding toward the throne.

Attired in a flowing gossamer gown that dragged along the chilly marble, the woman came to stand at the king's side. On her head was a smaller version of the king's crown. Pale lavender hair hung down her back. Her eyes were glazed white like the guards. I studied her arresting features, finding her exotic —and familiar.

"Raelynn," Runa grated in a furious snarl, the name scraping past her lips.

Both Drazen's and Kronk's thick skulls whipped in Runa's direction.

"Raelynn? I thought you said your sister was dead," Drazen hissed.

"It is a miracle," Kronk stated in that deadpan way of his, the words lacking emotion.

"My love," King Idris grasped the queen's fingers in his hand, kissing their blackened tips. Inky flesh shadowed her porcelain skin from fingertips to shoulder. Black veins spread across her chest, creeping up her neck.

"Look at us. I adore family reunions." The king beamed, pleased at his game.

Family. My ears twitched. So this was why the queen and Runa were so similar. My little thief had been keeping secrets. Perhaps I could use it to my advantage.

"I have no family." Runa sprang to her feet, violence in her snarling visage. "You made sure of that."

Too late, I realized Runa's initial fear had turned into blinding rage.

"Runa, no." Kronk attempted to stand, far too slow to intercept her. Drazen as well.

Since I was the only one with my hands bound in front, I sprang up and looped my arms over the raging sorceress's head.

Runa struggled against me, and I held her tight. Reasoning, if she angered the king, she'd place my own life in danger. This I wouldn't tolerate.

"Easy, pet. This isn't the time or place," I whispered.

To my relief, she calmed, settling in my grip.

Ignoring Runa's hysterics, the king set the queen's hand on the arm of his throne, and the great tree pulsed beneath her blackened touch. Idris groaned as if she had reached down and stroked his manhood instead.

"Yes. Yes, I know," he said over his shoulder to someone. Except there was nobody there. Did he speak to ghosts? "When I want your opinion, I'll ask for it," he muttered to an entity only he could see before straightening. Was the king mad? Hearing voices? This, too, I could use to my benefit.

With his queen at his side, he turned to Runa. "While Queen Raelynn has been a valuable and treasured addition to my kingdom, it saddens me to hear of the discontent her sister has been brewing. Just this quarter, three of my conveyances were robbed. Honestly, Runa, I expected a little more gratitude from you when I granted you your life, despite your parents' disobedience."

"You expect gratitude after you murdered my family and burned my village?"

The king heaved a dramatic sigh. "While sparing *you*. At your dear sister's request, of course. Still, you are unappreciative —stealing from my caravans, undermining the reasonable expectations I've placed on my kingdom."

"The villages cannot afford to pay your tax, and you know it," Runa spat. "Your reign is a disease, sucking the life out of everything it touches."

Gasps echoed from the crowd. Murmurs of outrage bounced off the walls.

King Idris lurched from his throne, anger darkening his conscience. "You stand before me, in chains no less, spitting this blasphemy? *I* am the true king. The divine being whose veins run with the blood of the gods. Your own sister knows this. Be grateful for your queen's generosity, or I'd smite you on the spot."

"Her generosity?" Runa choked out, seeming on the edge of losing her lunch. "My sister is a traitor to Carcerem and her family. The only one she's been generous to is herself, helping to place the false king on the throne just to become queen."

In response, Queen Raelynn pressed her blackened palm to her chest as though appalled at her sister's rabid behavior. Her flawless brow furrowed, and her milky eyes sparked with anger. "You dare to accuse me of betraying Carcerem? Calling me selfish after all that I have done for this kingdom? After all I have done for you? Do you forget the sacrifices I made?"

"Sacrifices. Ha! Momma and Papa were the only ones to make sacrifices. You. All you've done is take. And lie. And deceive. Idris would not sit on that throne if not for you."

The darkening rage on the king's face warned Runa was about to get us all killed. I thrust the suicidal female into the company of her fellow bandits.

"Your majesty, if I may?" I strode forward, drawing his attention.

King Idris arched a disdainful brow. "Who are you?"

"Lord Victor Custodis, Clan Leader of the Eastern Territories." I offered a precise bow. "Recently transferred here from the mortal world."

"Transferred, huh?" King Idris snorted. "You mean they banished you."

"Much to their detriment."

"The mortal world only sends the worst of their degenerates to my lands. Treating our beautiful kingdom as dumping grounds for their rubbish. Littering the landscape with their refuse." He turned pensive. "One would believe they did not like us. Luckily, I am not so easily offended."

I fought to hide the sneer tugging my lips. I hated this realm —and it was deliberate.

"If you are the great leader you claim to be, what are you doing with this lot?"

To admit I was their captive would sound weak. "I was merely in the wrong place at the wrong time and got caught up in their schemes. Truly, they are dangerous criminals. It's a good thing your men captured them when they did."

"What are you doing?" Drazen snarled.

"Let me guess." King Idris smirked, his tone mocking. "You're innocent and wish to be set free."

Those gathered snickered quietly.

"No, Your Majesty. I wish only to offer you my services."

"And what need would I have of a criminal who's entered my realm uninvited? Look at you. Dressed in rags, no title, no land, no prospects."

I'll admit I wasn't at my best. My long silver hair was tangled in knots. My previously pristine clothes were ruined after my fall and subsequent captivity. Currently, I had nothing to my name. Not even my title, really. Still, this was my opportunity to change all of that.

"Given my skill set and centuries of experience, I'm quite certain I can be of use to you instead of wasting my talents in a cell."

"You mean the same talents that got you captured by a band of amateur renegades? One of them female, at that."

Boisterous laughter echoed throughout the chamber.

Heat suffused my face, and I fought the urge to launch myself at the smug bastard much as Runa had.

Drazen stepped forward. "Your majesty. Don't listen to this dunderhead. We found him wandering the planes, out of his mind. Charitable thieves that we are, we took the delusional prick under our wing. Made him a junior member of our gang. Just last week, he believed he was Queen of the Pixies."

One of the bandits? Outrage washed over me. While born here, I did not belong in this shit-hole kingdom. Much less with this crew of sloppy thieves.

Chuckles rippled through the crowd. Even the king smiled.

Drazen turned to his audience. "You should have seen him dancing about in his skirt, pissing on flowers and claiming he was sprinkling pixie dust." To further his point, the fire demon pranced in a circle, lifting his knees up high.

"Enough!" the king demanded.

The room fell silent, their good humor subdued.

In the quiet, Queen Raelynn set her hand on her mate's shoulder. "My king. The vampire does have a point. I believe this particular group of criminals deserves more than to rot in a prison cell." She narrowed her eerie eyes at her sister. "What they need is to be taught a lesson in humility. To help them better appreciate Carcerem and its mighty king."

"Flark me," Drazen groaned, muttering under his breath. "Don't say it. Don't say it."

King Idris grew thoughtful. "Perhaps you are right." He raised his arms to the crowd, addressing his adoring followers. "What do you think, my good people? Do I teach them a lesson?"

"*To the pit. To the pit. To the pit,*" the crowd chanted.

Kronk elbowed the infernus, snarling low. "Way to go, idiot."

"I didn't do it," Drazen snapped.

"Clearly, they did not enjoy your pixie dance."

"They did too."

"Did not."

"It's not Drazen's fault but the leech's," Runa snarled, leveling a furious glare on me. "It's Custodis who screwed us over with his arrogant claims. Insisting that the king would find him useful."

"Which was a far wiser approach than insulting him," I retorted, then bit my lip when I realized what I had done— sinking to the bandits' level and joining in their ridiculous bickering. Even though I *was not* one of them.

The king's narrow smirk spread into a blinding smile. "The people have spoken. Lucky for all of you, the lunar equinox begins in but a handful of days, and we are short a few contestants."

For the first time since entering the palace, a sense of dread filled my being. Whatever this "pit" was they spoke of did not sound promising.

Ready to deliver his verdict, King Idris raised his palm, and all gathered fell silent.

"Criminals of the realm…" At his dramatic pause, the room seemed to hold its breath.

"Welcome to the Fallen Trials," he finished, and the crowd exploded in applause.

Chapter Nine

RUNA

THIS WAS ALL HIS FAULT. I glared holes into the back of Victor's arrogant head as our guards led us through a wide underground corridor, deep into the belly of the keep. Glowing torches illuminated our way along the darkened path. Rough stone scuffed beneath our feet. The air, damp and musty. Voices of the condemned echoed in the cavernous space.

Kronk and Drazen followed at my back. Six armed guards led the four of us past the general population cells and into the high-security units used for those destined for the pit.

During processing, we'd been forced to change into course tunics, animal-hide leggings, and soft-soled boots. Around each of our necks were four very active suppression torques. The guy who owed me was nowhere to be found. Not that we were left unsupervised for even a moment. The urge to claw at my throat was a nest of stinging ants marching up and down my spine. The lack of control I held over the situation, over my own body, threatened to send me screaming down the corridor, tearing at my hair.

"We are the Blood River Bandits. No one can defeat us," Kronk murmured in a failed attempt to lift my spirits.

"We've been through worse." Drazen's fake words of comfort were almost as effective as Kronk's.

"Have we?" I snapped. "Because by my estimations, this is the worst of the worst."

"At least your sister is alive," Kronk contributed in a bright tone.

My insides shriveled. I'd led my brothers to believe Raelynn was dead. The truth was too much to bear.

"Did she *look* alive to you?" Her arms were completely black up to her shoulders—the effects of her crimes against the realm threatening to consume her.

Served her right. I steeled my heart against the anguish and betrayal threatening to overwhelm me. Seeing Raelynn again after her treachery, adorned in jewels and silks, sharing the king's bed after what his rule had cost us made my head want to explode.

"She didn't look dead," Kronk grumbled, sounding hurt. He always was the sensitive one.

For a moment, my heart squeezed. If anything happened to my brothers, I wouldn't survive the loss. Somehow, I would find a way to get us out of this mess. Surrender wasn't an option. Too many depended on us. White Bridge would not fall as the village of my birth had.

We paused beside a wall of metal bars, the surface glowing with an eerie green light. Beyond the door was a vast room.

"Athos, creature of stone, you're in Alpha cell," one of the guards said.

"Wait. You're separating us?" Placing my brothers beyond my reach, far from where I could keep an eye on them?

"Challengers are sorted based on individual containment needs."

Behind the bars, I spotted a beast with massive shoulders,

heavy muscles, and enormous tusks jutting between its thick lips. Apparently, this cell held the strongest and most powerful of Carcerem's fallen. Kronk was a formidable opponent, even without his ability to turn to stone. Problem was, despite all the muscle, he possessed a childlike naivety that was at odds with his strength. What if someone took advantage of him?

Before entering the cell, Kronk pressed his thick forehead to mine. "I will see you soon."

"Trust nobody," I whispered. "And watch your back."

Before leaving, Kronk paused before Victor. "For any injury she receives, know I will inflict the same on you tenfold."

Warning delivered, he turned and entered Alpha cell.

"This stinks like bula dung," Drazen growled as we proceeded down the corridor. "If we would have just let the gallspawn eat the leech, we wouldn't even be here."

When we reached the next set of doors, the guard grunted. "You, infernus, creature of fire, Beta cell."

"Beta?" Drazen scoffed. "Do I look like a beta to you?"

From within the large space, a curvy female demon approached. Delicate horns curled back from her forehead. She held her cat-like tail in her hand, twirling the silky length. "Hey, Snodd," she said to the guard. "You bring me something fresh to play with?"

At this, Drazen straightened, puffing smoke from his nostrils. "Go, team Beta."

While Snodd unlocked the door, Drazen kissed my cheek. "Stay safe."

"Don't get distracted," I said before he could withdraw. "Remember, just because something is pretty doesn't mean it isn't deadly."

Snorting a huff of derision, he confronted Victor. "Know that if any harm comes to her, once Kronk has ripped off your arms, I will burn the rest of you to ash."

Why did it feel as though my brothers were entrusting my

safety to the leech? Idiots. Yet another reason why I didn't trust their judgment outside of my supervision.

Again, Victor refused to comment, heaving a sigh, his expression bored. I watched my brother enter the cell, my chest tight. The three of us hadn't been separated like this since before our time with Yaga.

We proceeded along the corridor. To my dismay, only one unit remained.

No. No way was I going to share a prison cell with the bastard who'd gotten us into this mess in the first place.

"You two. Gamma cell." Snodd confirmed my suspicions.

I eyed the bars, noting they didn't glow like the others we'd passed. "No enchantment?"

"No point with your kind." Standing toe to toe with Victor, he sneered, cupping himself between his legs. "What you going to do, vamp? Suck me to death?"

The guards behind him snickered.

"And you." Snodd crowded me, backing me into the metal door. "Without your sorcery, you're practically human."

Sure, I understood the vampire wasn't a threat, but me?

The stench of Snodd's sour breath dusted my face, and I turned my head, nearly gagging.

"Pretty, though. Perhaps we could come to some kind of arrangement." He grazed his knuckle along my cheek, and bile painted my tongue.

"Get your hands off of me." I stepped back, prepared to punt the bastard's testicles up into his throat. His buddies would prob-ably beat me to a bloody pulp. Still, it would be worth it.

Before I could commit to my attack, Victor moved closer, a strange energy charging the air. "Perhaps you haven't heard. This one is related to the queen. Can't imagine King Idris will appre-ciate the sorceress being defiled before the games."

"You're lying," the slimeball said without looking away from me.

"No, he ain't," one of the other milky-eyed guards muttered behind him. "Heard as much myself."

Seeming reluctant to admit defeat, the miscreant wound his blunted finger around one of my lavender curls. "Explains the purple hair, I suppose."

At his harsh tug, I winced, gritting my teeth.

Finally, he released me, backing away and unlocking the door. "Into the cell with you then. Any trouble from either of you, and I'll deal with you personally."

I sensed the last part he meant for me. I stifled a shiver of revulsion, entering the space.

Behind us, the heavy door slammed, and the lock hammered into place.

The minute the guard's footsteps faded, I shoved my hands into Victor's chest, knocking him back a step. "Stay out of my business, vampire. You've done enough damage for one span."

Lips pressed into a thin line of irritation, Custodis took several steps back from me. "As you wish."

I scanned our surroundings, Victor doing the same.

Along opposite walls were a multitude of open rooms. Two small cots in each. At the back was a large pit filled with sand where a pair of grunting women grappled. In the center of the communal space were several long tables. Seated on the matching benches were a handful of prisoners. Among them were a mix of males and females, all various races. At our appearance, their heads swiveled, calculating eyes taking our measure.

"Greetings, contestants," said a gentle voice.

I shifted to face a woman, who, unlike my cell mates, wore a simple, homespun shift. Two thick braids, the color of wheat, hung over her shoulders. Also, unlike the others, her smile was welcoming. In her hands was a tray with bread, cheese, and meat. My stomach growled at the sight.

"My name is Milani. I will be your servant for the duration

of the games. I'm here to answer any questions you may have. Of which, I'm sure you have many."

I suspected Milani was a *brownie*, a race of beings who thrived in the service of others. Essentially, they needed to be needed. Without that need, they often withered and died.

"Prisoners get servants?" Unable to resist, I stole a piece of bread and stuffed it into my mouth.

"Yes, all contestants receive a servant to assist them." She led us to the closest table, setting down her tray. "Meals are served here twice a span. I brought you a snack since you missed the last one. King Idris wants his competitors in top form. I've also prepared your sleeping quarters. You're both in the third room on the right."

"Together?" I coughed, breadcrumbs sweeping into my lungs.

"Yes, cell blocks are communal. The others are full."

"Of course they are," I grumbled, catching Victor's raised brow and scowling in return.

"Each morning and night, a bell will ring, signaling when it's time to rise or sleep. The guards reprimand those who do not comply."

No doubt, Snodd would be all too eager to put me in my place. "What else?"

"Engaging in violence outside of the trials is forbidden." She glanced over her shoulder at the others, whispering, "However, you should exercise caution, as there are those who sometimes break the rules."

Great. Threats surrounded me on all sides.

I met the vampire's unreadable expression, having little confidence in whose side he would fight on. Likely his own. *Bula-hole.*

"What can you tell me about the trials?" I'd heard rumors but never witnessed one.

"First, you will attend a demonstration to display your skills.

That done, each challenger receives a score so that wagers may be placed."

I feared asking but… "What sort of wagers?"

Milani's gleaming eyes widened. "All kinds. From whom may win, to which of the fallen will be the first to lose an appendage. First to drown. First to catch fire. First to—"

"I get the picture." Bubbles rolled in my empty gut. "And what of the trials?"

Victor drew closer, as eager as I was to hear the answer.

"There are three events. One event per span. Each one more difficult."

"And what do we get if we win?"

"Only those Carcerem deems rehabilitated will win. Those winners, having proven they are worthy of the kingdom's forgiveness, are granted their freedom."

I scoffed. From what I'd heard, every game, there was a survivor or two *set free*. Not one of them was ever seen again.

"What do you know about these three challenges?" Victor finally chimed in.

"Nothing." The servant's expression fell, her gaze darting between us. "The exact nature of each challenge is a closely guarded secret, known only to the king. I'm sorry I cannot tell you more."

"That's okay, Milani. We appreciate your help."

At my praise, her visage brightened. "Please, rest and eat." Milani gestured to the tray she'd placed at the end of the table.

Victor leveled the brownie with a covetous stare. "And what if I require more than food to sustain me?"

"I am here to fulfill all of your needs." Milani dipped a quick bow, flicked her braid behind her shoulder, and presented the slim column of her throat.

"You've got to be kidding," I groaned. Just like that. The woman offered her vein? I understood that a brownie's greatest desire was to serve, but this was ridiculous.

"Far be it from me to pass up a free meal," Victor said far too readily, drawing the petite woman closer and cupping the back of her head.

Watching the two of them, the possessive hold the vampire had on his prey and the hunger in his gaze, my blood heated with some foreign emotion I didn't care to analyze.

"Surely, you can't mean to..." Flustered, I waved a hand. "Here? Now?" I'd spent little time around vampires. I certainly hadn't watched one feed before.

Victor sent me a devious smirk, dipping his mouth to the woman's neck. "Unless you'd like to volunteer instead?"

I stiffened. "Has the sun frozen over?"

"No?" Victor arched a brow.

"No." I folded my arms.

Locking his eyes with mine, Victor slid his tongue along Milani's neck, eliciting a shiver from the other woman. My body responded in kind, goosebumps rising on my flesh.

"Your loss," Victor murmured. Then, with a flash of fangs, he pressed his lips to the servant's neck.

"Oh," Milani gasped, turning languid in his grasp.

Still, those antagonistic steely-gray eyes remained locked on me. Crude bastard. Sure, he could strut around crowing about titles and wealth, believing he was better than others. When it came down to it, he was just as much an animal as the rest of us.

I curled my fingers into my palms, fighting the urge to drag the other woman from his grasp. To save her. Of course. Merely to save her.

To my chagrin, her lids went heavy, and Victor unleashed a low growl, clutching his prey. I squeezed my thighs together, sweat gathering between my breasts. The sight of the vampire feeding from another woman was disgusting. That's right. Disgusting.

I should look away, *would* look away, planned to look away until Milani moaned. Vampires were rumored to secrete venom, the purpose of which was to make the feeding pleasurable. Apparently, the torque had failed to suppress this part of Custodis's arsenal.

That's it. Enough is enough.

Before I could grab the servant's arm, the leech removed his lips from her neck, and while gazing at me, slowly licked the pinpricks he'd left on her throat.

"Thank you, Milani." He held the dazed female at arm's length, steadying her while she wobbled.

"My pleasure," the servant said, trailing her fingertips over the bite wound.

I clenched my fists. The sight of the vampire's mark on the girl's neck filled me with rage. Instead of railing at him as I desired, I plopped down on the nearest bench, stuffing my mouth with a chunk of cheese.

"You're excused, Milani," Custodis said.

The servant bobbed a half-bow before scurrying away.

When the vampire settled across the table from me, my head snapped up. "What are you doing?"

"Sitting."

"Why?" I scowled—something I found myself doing a lot around the leech. If I survived this, I'd have a permanent furrow in my brow.

"Because I'm locked in a cell with a bunch of thieves and murderers with little to amuse me."

"And you expect me to entertain you?"

"You've proven very entertaining thus far," he said in that smug way of his that I'd come to loath.

I grabbed a bit of meat, chewing it as though I'd like to rip off a piece of his flesh.

"Also, your lovers have threatened to dismember me should any harm come to you. Personally, I don't want to face their combined anger across a battlefield when we enter the trials."

I choked on my meal. "Lovers?"

His gaze hardened with something undefinable. "So fickle you've forgotten them already?"

My spine stiffened. "Kronk and Drazen aren't my lovers, you deviant. We were raised together. They're my brothers."

"Interesting family."

"A family that wouldn't have been sentenced to the pit if not for you."

"For me?"

"Yes, you." I smacked the table, making the tray jump. "If you had kept your arrogant mouth shut instead of giving the king ideas, we would be in a minimum-security cell, wearing deactivated torques, and halfway out the door by now."

"Right, because the three of you were faring so well."

"Certainly nothing *good* has happened to us since you crossed our paths. In fact, I'm starting to believe the fates sent you to punish us for some reason. The deal with Vex was a complete failure. On top of that, you threw me to the soldiers to save your own ass. Then you landed us in the trials. I want little more than to be rid of you."

Fury darkening his brow, Victor turned to glance at the table next to us. I followed his gaze, noting three rough-looking males staring at me in a manner that made my skin crawl.

"Fine then, little sorceress. Good luck watching your own back."

With that, the vampire lurched from his bench, storming away. Seeing him leave twisted something inside of me.

I turned back to my meal, appetite waning. Bah. Who needed him? Not me. I was better on my own anyway.

Chapter Ten

VICTOR

"I WATCHED you feed from the servant earlier. It was quite titillating. You seem like a male who knows how to make a girl feel good," purred the woman with lank auburn curls and a luminescent sprinkling of dots beneath her eyes.

She walked her fingers up my chest, and I battled with the urge to break every one of them.

Night had fallen, the bell indicating all should be abed had rang long ago. The petite woman was a fool to agree to meet with me in a darkened corner, far from prying eyes. Lucky for her, I drank my fill earlier, so I would be prepared for this very thing.

Somehow, I'd managed to avoid the sorceress for the rest of the evening, despite the close quarters. Infuriating female. How dare she accuse me of being the source of all her problems? I was the one who was kidnapped. And by a bunch of bungling thieves at that. Runa and her *brothers* could rot in this place for all I cared.

It was past time I focused on my own goals—escaping this prison and finding a portal.

While *not* watching Runa as several of Gamma cell's predators eyed the wench, I was determined to make the most of my incarceration. There were plenty of beings here who could provide me with the information and resources I required to go home. Since the torque disabled my ability to use compulsion, I'd need to get creative.

"Talk to me, sweet, and I'll take you on a trip you won't soon forget," I demanded of the senseless female before me.

At this rate, I'd be the leech they accused me of being. In Gamma cell, drugs and alcohol were in short supply, making vampire venom a commodity.

The thought occurred to me… I was whoring myself.

I'd done far worse than this in my youth. The short time I'd lived in Carcerem with my mother hadn't been kind nor easy. The impoverished slums were especially hard on young vampires. The mortal realm wasn't much better. Except there, I was top of the food chain and stood a better chance of surviving on my own. At least this task I found more pleasurable than most.

"You mentioned you were one of the king's seers for a time," I said.

"Oh, I was. One of his best, much to my detriment." Her expression grew haunted. "Seers who tell the truth don't last long in his court."

"Tell me, what was it that heralded your banishment to the pit?" Perhaps it was something I could use.

She rolled out her bottom lip. "I tried to warn King Idris that his end is nigh. That the prophecy is true. The rightful king will soon reclaim his throne."

Nothing useful, then. What the hell did anyone care about prophecies? At any given moment, there were usually hundreds of mystical forecasts circulating. A seer's ability to see the future was even worse than a meteorologist's ability to predict the weather.

"Idris's so-called fate doesn't concern me. What do you know about portal magic?"

The seer eyed my mouth, then stroked her finger along the column of her throat. "Quite a bit. If you're willing to pay."

I exhaled an aggrieved sigh. Might as well get it over with. I enjoyed feeding from the servant, savoring Runa's reaction. Those violet eyes locked with mine while I drank from another woman, the sorceress's spicy scent deepening. I'd noted the way she'd squeezed her thighs together while pretending she was unaffected.

This, I would not enjoy.

I crooked my finger, and the woman's eyes lit up. She moved closer with the intent of wrapping her arms around my shoulders, and I shoved her hands away. "No touching," I commanded.

"But—"

Quickly, I sank my fangs into her flesh. Her stench was nothing like the sorceress's delicious fragrance. One sip, and I released the seer's throat.

The woman moaned, running her hands down her body. "Oh, that's nice," she gasped then stiffened, her muscles turning rigid. "Flark. Not now. This will totally ruin my buzz."

I studied her strange reaction. "What's happening?"

The seer's eyes turned fully white, and her head fell back. She gazed up at nothing.

From her gaping mouth, a strange voice emerged.

"When twin moons collide, the fallen king will rise.

Upon that span, a hero of gold shall bring a shift of power.

The mountains will quake, and the land will roar with vengeance.

Siblings will battle as the mighty tree weeps.

Only one will survive.

The Chosen One."

Suddenly, her head snapped up, and she grabbed the front of my tunic. Face pale, she stared at me with glowing eyes, gasping, "The Chosen One."

Seers and their bloody visions. Again, she babbled about Idris and the threat he faced from some fallen king. According to the woman, this was the sort of thing that had landed her in prison. I could understand why. No king appreciated threats to their rule. If there were any truth to her prediction, perhaps I would have investigated further, using it as leverage against Idris. That was, if I had planned to stick around, which I didn't.

Now I'd given her what she wanted. It was time she did the same before the guards caught us.

"Wake up. Now." I grasped the woman's shoulders and gave her a shake.

The seer blinked, her foggy gaze slowly clearing. After a moment, she frowned, looking at her hands on my chest. "Oh, when did that happen? Did I miss something?"

Stepping back, I knocked her hands from my tunic. "You were about to tell me how to open a portal."

"I was?" She smoothed her hair back from her face, her expression dreamy. "Boy, that venom of yours really packs a punch."

I curled my fingers into my palms. "The *portal*," I snapped.

"Keep your pants on," she slurred, wobbling like a drunkard, then smiled. "Or don't."

"You have three seconds until I tear your throat out. One."

"Fine. Fine. Sheesh. Not like we're going anywhere," she snorted. "First, opening a portal takes some big-time power, the kind of power you can only acquire through an eternal sacrifice. That sacrifice must be offered freely."

"You're talking about blood magic?"

"Yes. And only a sorceress with portal magic can perform the spell."

So, I'd have to murder an innocent. That part was easy enough. "Where do I find this sorceress?"

"Well, right next to the king, silly."

"Explain," I insisted.

The twit had the audacity to roll her eyes. "That's right. You're not from these parts. See, when King Idris first claimed the throne, our sacred arbor denied his dominion, refusing to grant him access to her power. For the sake of the realm, this could not stand. Problem was, King Idris was the only one in the kingdom with divine blood. That's why I did a reading for him and discovered the only way to remedy the situation was through a sorceress from a unique bloodline."

I narrowed my eyes, dread tightening my gut. "You're the reason he made Raelynn his queen?"

The seer planted a hand on her bony hip. "Don't look at me like I'm some common criminal. It was for the good of the whole kingdom that our king had access to its power. The Star-born females were the only line of sorceresses still living with portal magic. Once they were mated, the queen was able to open a gateway between the king and the sacred arbor."

Ah. Perhaps this was why Runa claimed her sister had betrayed the kingdom. Though why the little thief would feel responsible was beyond me and not my concern.

"Are you saying the king's sorceress can open portals?"

"Well, yes, same as her mother before her. Stupid cow, she died years ago, trying to hide her daughters from the new king. Had she merely cooperated, they all could have lived a life of luxury. But no. She was from one of a handful of villages that rebelled once King Idris came to power. Because of her defiance, the king slaughtered her husband and razed her village. If you think about it, it's rather sad, really."

"Sad. Yes," I agreed, not that I had much sympathy for peasants and commoners.

"You mentioned the Starborn women. Do you mean to say the portal magic is connected to their bloodline?"

"In theory." She hitched a shoulder. "Both the mother and eldest daughter had it. From what I understand, the youngest daughter hadn't come into her powers yet when the king and Raelynn were married."

That child being Runa.

By the gods. Runa was the key to everything.

Runa.

The back of my neck prickled, anxious teeth nipping at my flesh. Something was wrong.

I needed to hurry back.

Now!

Chapter Eleven

RUNA

THOUGH THE EVENING bell had rung hours ago, Victor's cot on the other side of our shared room remained empty. No doubt, he'd found some harlot willing to open her thighs along with a vein for him.

An image of his lips pressed to Milani's throat came to my mind unbidden. I'd spent little time in the company of vampires thanks to my over-protective brothers, who were certain every creature we met either wanted to eat me or screw me. Sometimes both.

Milani's acceptance of her fate as the leech's dinner intrigued me. Given her lusty groans, I imagined she even found it...pleasurable. Watching them, I couldn't help but be curious.

What would it feel like to have the vampire's arms wrapped around me, trapping me in his dark embrace? For him to hunger for me and no one else. I trailed my fingers along the curve of my neck, imagining that it was his mouth on my flesh. His fangs inside of me—taking.

When I realized the direction my thoughts had taken, I jerked my hand from my neck. What was I doing? This place. This prison. It was messing with my mind.

I should have been relieved to have the room to myself, free of the vampire's suffocating presence. Instead, sleep eluded me. I was vulnerable and exposed. No weapons, no magic, no brothers. Strangely, I had little fear of the vampire, confident he wouldn't attack me in my sleep.

Why that was, I wasn't certain. Just some strange gut instinct.

I desperately needed to rest. Exhaustion would get me killed in the pit. It was important that I save my strength for the battle ahead. Whatever that might entail. *Flarking trials.* While I might have blamed the vampire for our predicament, it wasn't entirely his fault.

Raelynn could have spoken up for me, demanding her mate release her only sister rather than stare at me like I was a bug beneath her silken slipper.

When we were younger, she had often bemoaned her life as a peasant. When we'd journey to the market, she'd stare off at the castle in the distance with a dreamy expression on her face. Once our chores were done, she'd often pretend she was a princess in a fairy tale, swishing through the meadow, waving to her adoring citizens.

One horrifying night, turns ago, King Idris made Raelynn's dreams come true while turning my life into the stuff of nightmares.

Memories stirred, smoke filling my nostrils. Screams of the past echoed in my ears. My vision blurred, and I spotted Father's fallen body, cut down while defending his family. We were exhausted and stressed from running. Always on the move after Idris destroyed our village and started hunting us.

My sister and I cowered behind an overturned wagon.

Our mother shivered beside us. Anguish hardened her pale

features. "Hathor, have mercy. They've found us. Your poor father," she sobbed.

"Then maybe it's time we stopped running," Raelynn snapped, tears streaking her soot-covered cheeks. "I am tired of being hungry and frightened all the time."

Mamma's palm cracked her cheek. Raelynn's shriek pierced my ears. I flinched, casting a nervous glance about us, praying she didn't bring the soldiers down upon us.

"How dare you disparage all your father and I have fought for?" Momma grated, fury and heartache in her drawn expression. "If the false king gets his hands on our magic, the whole kingdom will suffer. Not just one spoiled girl."

Raelynn silenced her sniffles behind her clenched fist, shooting a heated glare at our mother.

"Runa, child," Momma barked, her tone thick with emotion. "When the portal opens, you take your sister's hand and don't let go. You hear me?"

Portal? Now? She couldn't be serious. Her eyes narrowed to slits, and I was quick to nod my agreement.

"I mean it. No matter what. Once I'm gone, the two of you will have to take care of each other. I'm counting on you, Runa. Carcerem is counting on you. Keep your sister on the righteous path. Don't let her lose herself to her childish fantasies."

"I promise," I said naively, believing this was a promise I would keep.

I'd never seen my mother open a portal before. Had no idea what was involved. To this day, I wished I had remained ignorant.

Momma clenched the dagger she held, uttering an incantation. Purple magic whirled in her palms, and a shimmering sphere appeared. I stared in awe while Momma drew more energy from the earth. More than she'd ever taken before, making part of me ache in response. She swirled her hand, making the circle larger until it was big enough for a slender girl to crawl through.

It was so beautiful. For a moment, I forgot where I was until my mother grasped her dagger in two hands, holding it above her chest.

"Momma, no. What are you doing?" I cried out.

"A life freely given, for you, my daughters. I love you both." With one last glance at the two of us, she stabbed the blade into her heart.

As I screamed, my mother fell to the ground. Crimson swirls wafted from her body, combining with her spell, swirling together. The shimmering circle she'd created became a mirror, reflecting the image of a quiet wooded area.

Safety.

Mind reeling and my body oddly cold, I grabbed my sister's hand, obeying my mother's final wish. "Hurry, Raelynn. We must go," I said, forcing words past the fist of anguish that squeezed my throat.

"You go," my sister said through her tears, jerking her hand free.

Panicked, I grabbed it once more, holding tight to her sweaty palm. This was not the time for my defiant sibling to be difficult. "You heard Momma. We must go."

"I heard her," Raelynn choked out. "I've done nothing but listen. When is someone going to listen to me? Ask what I want?"

The whirling portal sparked and wavered. We were running out of time.

"Raelynn," I barked, annoyed with her theatrics. "Stop being a priss and come with me."

"I'm done listening to Momma," my sister said with a sneer. "And I'm definitely not listening to you. Go through the portal and continue to run and hide. I'm taking fate into my own hands. Choosing what is best for me."

"You can't do that. Momma said—"

"Momma said. Momma said," she mocked. "Tell you what. You keep doing what Momma said. See where that gets you."

Raelynn tugged back on her arm, and anticipating her resistance, I held tight, planting one foot inside the portal. Prickles of fire nipped at my toes, scratching at my ankle and tugging my leg.

"Raelynn, come on!" I barked, pulling harder. "Don't do this. We're supposed to stay together." Stupid girl never did anything she was told.

"Better hurry," Raelynn taunted as the gleaming mirror shrank around me, her fingers slipping through my grasp. I never could best her when we fought.

Fiery bites nipped at my flesh. The portal pulled me deeper, and the mirror continued to shrink. Stubborn wretch.

"Bye, Runa." She fluttered a mocking wave.

I gnashed my teeth. I sure as heck wasn't losing a limb to her foolishness. With one last glance at my sister…

I let go.

Looking back, I could have done more. A lot more. If only I'd held onto her tighter instead of giving in, demanded she enter the portal with me and dragged her by her hair, kicking and screaming if needed. Instead, I'd let her slip away, allowing her to run straight into Idris's eager arms.

With my failure, I practically set the false king on the throne myself, plumped his cushions for his royal buttocks, sat him down, and served him the kingdom on a platter.

Without Raelynn's portal magic, Idris could never have siphoned so much power from Carcerem. I told my brothers that my sister died in the attack because, in my mind, she had. Raelynn was as dead to me as I was to her.

Today, in the throne room, it was clear that she'd wanted me gone—to rid the world of the reminder that she, too, had once been a commoner. Now I was in the Fallen Trials, there was an excellent chance she'd get that wish.

I huffed a deep sigh. This line of thinking would see me blurry-eyed and exhausted come morning. At the moment, the only thing I could do about my situation was rest. Tomorrow, I'd come up with a plan. A plan that would free both myself and my brothers so we could get back to White Bridge, the only home I had left—before the collectors.

I squeezed my eyes closed, attempting to relax my knotted muscles.

A scuff echoed, making my ears twitch. I tensed. "Custodis, is that—"

Brutal hands clamped down on my limbs. One slapped against my mouth, smothering my scream. Panic exploded across my nerve endings.

The fingers on my mouth stank of grease and filth. The sting of his salty skin raised my gag reflex. It would serve them right to have me retch all over them.

Unseen attackers groped my body, tearing at my clothing. Fabric rent, frigid air kissing my bare flesh. Muted screams fell on callous ears. Outrage made my temples pound.

Gamma cell was full of bottom dwellers. The worst of the worst. The kind of criminals who couldn't win an honorable fight, so they slunk about in shadows. There would be no mercy for me from this bunch.

Claws raked my stomach, shredding my leggings. A painful grip clamped around my ankles.

How many were there? Two? Three? Spineless monsters seldom committed their crimes alone.

Sadly, this wasn't my first experience with this particular brand of assault. Except in the past, I'd had my illusions to send my attackers screaming, so shaken they'd think twice before laying their hands on another unwilling victim. Also, my brothers were usually in earshot. My last attacker never walked without a limp again. Nor was he left with the equipment necessary to commit a similar crime. Kronk made sure of it.

Every muscle in my body rebelled against the monsters' strength. To no avail. Flarking Idris and his torque. Since my youth, before coming into my powers, I hadn't felt this helpless. If they succeeded, I feared I would never be the same. The damage would be irreparable, the coward's actions a permanent scar on my psyche.

Firm hands grasped my pounding fists, shoving them over my head. Proving, once again, that I really was powerless without my sorcery. *Flark them. Flark them, their bastard-birthing mothers, and the depraved fathers who sired them.*

"Hold her tight, boys," a gruff voice commanded. "Do this right, and I might give you a turn."

To combat the terror threatening to cripple me, I imagined murdering each of them. If I survived, I'd make sure this trio experienced the most terrifying horrors ever conceived. Once we were set free in the pit, I'd conjure images guaranteed to destroy even the most twisted of minds.

The largest of them loomed over me, fumbling with the belt on his pants. My thrashing paid off, and both of my ankles broke free. Just as I raised my foot to kick him, his head wrenched sideways with a sickening *crack!* Pain and shock registered in his wide eyes, his mouth gaping before he toppled sideways.

Where my attacker once stood, Custodis appeared, a primal gleam sparking in his eyes. Icy menace crackled in the enclosed space. "You should know better than to touch things that don't belong to you," he snarled.

"What the hell?" a guy with a face like a wild boar shouted from where he'd been tossed against the wall. This must have been the reason the bula-hole released my legs.

Boar Face shot to his feet, poised to flee.

In a blur of movement too fast for my eyes to track, the vampire disabled this bastard as well. The deviant hit the ground with a terminal gurgle—windpipe crushed, arm broken, scream trapped in his throat.

Just as fast, the hands restraining my wrists disappeared. I lurched to my feet to find the final male backing deeper into the small room, hands raised.

"N-now, see here, vampire. We didn't know the female was yours."

"She isn't," Custodis stated, annoyingly calm. "I'd simply like to rest, and you are in my room."

He'd helped me because he was *sleepy*? The moment of gratitude I experienced at the vampire's timely rescue poured out of me.

"Runa. If you don't mind." He gestured to the remaining assailant. "It's been a long day, and your guest is in my way."

"Wouldn't want to interfere with your beauty rest," I spat through gritted teeth. Filled with a fresh wave of rage, I punched the last of the sniveling cowards, whipping his head around. Pain shot up my arm, and damn, if it didn't feel good. I grabbed the back of his skull and slammed my knee into his face, savoring the crunch of bone. When the screaming weakling dropped to his hands and knees, I stood over him.

"Beg me," I snarled.

"What?" he whimpered.

"Beg me to spare you." *Spare you after you made me feel weak. Powerless. Out of control.*

"Please. I'm sorry. Please. I swear I'll never—"

"Not good enough." I spun, landing a kick to his face. Blood sprayed, and he collapsed.

Soft clapping tapped behind me. "Nicely done."

Fists raised, I bared my teeth as harsh breaths pumped from my chest.

Custodis held his hands out, striking a non-threatening pose while my pulse calmed. Slowly, as if he approached a wild animal, he strode closer, one cautious step at a time. Once he stood before me, he eyed my raised fists, and a strange light glowed in his icy gaze.

"You've injured yourself."

"What?" I glanced at my bloody knuckles, confused by his strange shift in moods.

"Allow me." Gently, he claimed my injured hand and brought it to his mouth. The scent of frosted evergreen filled my senses. My eyes riveted to his lips, I watched in a daze as he pressed a kiss to my broken skin. With his heated tongue, he laved my damaged flesh, soothing the burn. Breathless, I watched him do the same to each of my knuckles until, at last, he raised his head.

When he met my eyes, I expected him to taunt me for accepting his aid—to mock my weakness or belittle me for dropping my guard and allowing three ingrates to sneak up on me. Instead, his steely gaze shimmered with something I couldn't define.

"Are you well?" he murmured.

"Well?" I struggled to comprehend his meaning as adrenaline seeped from my veins. The sudden crash turned my thoughts to goo.

"Are you well?" He glanced at the male I'd dropped.

I shook my head, my mind clearing, and withdrew my hand from his grasp.

"Yes." I stiffened my spine. "Of course. Why wouldn't I be?"

My cheeks heated. I didn't like that he'd seen me so vulnerable. After all, I was a powerful sorceress. Conjurer of nightmares. Leader of the notorious Blood River Bandits.

I lifted my chin, ignoring the tear in the shoulder of my tunic. "Where were you, anyway?"

He studied my face, seeming to see through my posturing. "Gathering intel."

"And what, pray tell, did you discover?" While I fought for

my life. Alone. Something deep within my core howled, insisting that this male in particular shouldn't have abandoned me.

His tawny brow furrowed. "I discovered I need you."

I swallowed with an audible *gulp*. Perhaps the sun really had frozen over.

Chapter Twelve

VICTOR

RAGE POUNDED IN MY VEINS, the burn a wildfire I fought to contain. I struggled with the need to fight, to smash, to hurt, to kill. When I'd returned and found Runa pinned beneath three males, a crimson haze filled my vision.

This wasn't me.

In my world, I was known for being cool and collected, completely in control at all times. It was possible something in this kingdom was affecting me—causing me to react this way.

The fire burning in my gut wasn't run-of-the-mill anger. No. This was something deeper—darker. More explosive. Like some part of me had cracked, allowing something new to escape. What? I didn't know. All I'd known for certain was those males had needed to die for touching her.

All except one.

The last was a gift.

Watching Runa end the bastard, how she took a moment to toy with the prick before taking her revenge, that dark piece of me had taken notice. Afterward, I'd been unable to resist tasting her. That simple taste might have been my undoing because even with my latest windfall of blood, I hungered.

Once I'd tossed the males out beside the garbage, making sure to snap the neck of the last, I sat on my cot. Leaning back against the wall, I propped my foot on the miserable excuse for a mattress and rested my elbow on my knee. It was a sad attempt on my part to appear at ease when everything inside twisted into knots. Still, it was important that Runa not know she might very well hold my future in her hands.

"Okay, Custodis." Runa rested on her cot with her head propped on her hand. Lavender tendrils spilled down her arm in a becoming display. "Tell me. Why do you need me?"

"The king's former seer claims your sister can open a portal to the mortal realm. Is this true?"

Runa's eyes hardened. "Raelynn is no longer my sister."

"Fine, then. Regardless of your familial ties, the queen has portal magic."

"Yes. Her magic is the reason the false king has access to Carcerem's power. Raelynn ripped a gateway between the two, forcing the connection. Taking something the realm was unwilling to give."

Like the bastards who'd attacked her. Darkness swelled at the reminder, and I took a deep breath to cool my rising anger.

"And you." I managed to say in a steady voice. "Do you share that power?"

Her dark brow furrowed. "It's an ability that's passed down through the females in my bloodline. Though I've never attempted to use it. For…" She hesitated, eyes darkening. "Many reasons. One being that it requires a significant amount of magic, forcing the caster to draw deeply from Carcerem's reserves of obsidian. Too deeply." She rubbed her fingers together.

"But it could be done."

She chewed her lip, growing more discomfited. "In theory.

Also, a sacrifice is needed. A life freely given. Idris must have done the same to claim Carcerem's power."

The seer had said as much. So, I'd have to convince some simpleton to offer up their life. It was a minor detail.

"Perhaps we could work together."

The sorceress narrowed her violet eyes. "You want me to create a portal to send you home."

"It's not as if I can beg the queen for her aid."

Runa frowned. "What you want from me... It's a big ask."

"Bigger than agreeing to kidnap a male so Vex could torture, then murder him?"

She grinned, unapologetic. "Much bigger."

"I'm sure we could come to some sort of agreement."

Her grin twisted with derision. "Look around you, vampire. You've nothing to barter."

"Not true. Agree to my terms, and I will ensure no further harm comes to you, both in Gamma cell and the pit. Also, since you are currently unable to steal secrets due to the torque, I will share any intel I gather with you and your brothers. Together, we will make our escape."

"And how do you plan on gathering this intel without your compulsion available to you? You're not the most charming vampire I've encountered."

I smiled, flashing my fangs. "I could demonstrate if you like?"

Runa's cheeks turned a delightful shade of pink. "Never mind."

"Me thinks the lady protests too much." I smirked, enjoying our verbal sparring.

"In your dreams, vampire." Runa flopped back on her cot.

"Think on it. We share a common goal. Both of us wish to escape and return home."

"I'd also like a cart full of jewels, my own castle, and a goose that lays golden eggs."

"You mock me."

"Handsome and perceptive."

She thinks me handsome? For a moment, I was thrown off target until I gave myself a mental shake. *Focus.* "We can help each other."

"You have a plan?"

Not yet. "Absolutely."

"Tell me."

"I haven't worked out the details."

"Says someone who's unaccustomed to answering to a competent woman. No deal. You either treat me like an equal partner, or we're done here."

A low growl clawed at my insides. What I was unaccustomed to was defiance. "I will tell you when the time is right."

She rolled to her opposite side, daring to give me her back. "Good night, vampire."

Infuriating female. "In case you didn't realize, your head is most definitely on the queen's chopping block. Don't think I didn't see the gleam in Raelynn's eyes. You're here because she wants you dead instead of incarcerated. Worse, she wants to watch."

Silence.

"As my partner, you will have access to information you wouldn't otherwise, aid in the games, and protection in the cells. Should I fail, that will mean one or both of us is dead, and then what does it matter? You've nothing to lose and everything to gain."

"Nothing to lose but my soul." She snorted. "Tapping into the amount of magic a portal requires could take me to a place I cannot afford to travel. The queen's blackened flesh is proof she's in over her head. If the darkness takes hold of me, as it has with Raelynn, I may never return."

An issue that held few ramifications for *me.*

"And every minute you spend here, both you and your brothers' life expectancies shorten."

She exhaled a heavy sigh, her shoulders rising and falling. "And without us, many of the villages will go hungry, falling prey to Idris's tax collectors. More than just our lives are at stake."

"Do we have a deal?" I pressed, glad she couldn't see the sweat that gathered on my brow.

"Yes, vampire," she said to the wall. "We have a deal. But one misstep from you, and I'll make sure my brothers and I are the only ones to leave this place."

I relaxed into my cot, smiling at the ceiling. "Understood."

Now I'd found my ticket home, all I needed was to facilitate our escape.

Chapter Thirteen

RUNA

HEAT from the sun beat down on my dark head, and I held up my hand, shielding my eyes. As I strode behind my fellow fallen, sand dragged at my feet. After an awkward breakfast with rumors of four contestants murdered during the night—Victor and I being responsible for only three—our guards gave the order to join the demonstration. As promised, the vampire walked at my side, my icy partner in this twisted game. Time would tell what I stood to gain or lose from our bargain.

What had to be dozens of guards led the inhabitants of Gamma cell into the pit. Around us was a circular stone amphitheater. Four stories in height, it was large enough to hold thousands of spectators. Except, at this moment, it held only a few hundred. Between soaring columns along the outer edges stood several massive statues, almost as tall as the stands. Each depicted an exalted warrior from Carcerem's history.

On either side of the king's grand pavilion, a small audience had gathered, though King Idris's seat remained empty. Silks and gems adorned well-coiffed women and some of the men as well.

It seemed some of the wealthiest in Carcerem were in attendance, a.k.a., King Idris's favorites.

As Milani explained, we'd demonstrate our skills to earn a rating. That score would help those who wished to gamble during the games to place their bids.

Three smaller rings were set in the sand before the gathering of spectators. One for each cell. Next to each ring was a rack of weapons, ready for our use. My brothers lingered at the rear of the huddled contestants.

Excitement and relief zinged through my body. I tensed to run to them, only to find my biceps gripped in a firm hand.

I glared up at Victor. "Release me. I want to check on my brothers."

"Reveal no weakness."

"What?"

"Your affection for your brothers is an obvious weakness others could exploit. Given our pact, *your* vulnerabilities are also *mine*."

My pulse pounded, and I bared my teeth at the bastard, unaccustomed to taking orders. "Wait until this torque is deactivated. Then I'll show you which of us is the weaker."

"Of this, I have no doubt. Except *they* do not need to know the full extent of your power." His icy gaze took in the surrounding competitors. "For now, it would be best to let the others misjudge you."

"So, I'm to reveal no true weakness while pretending to be weak." I rubbed my forehead. It was too early for his convoluted strategy.

"Yes," he stated simply, gazing in the direction of my brothers and scowling.

I faced them as well, only to discover Kronk twisting his fists in a snapping gesture while glaring at the vampire. Not one to be left out, Drazen thrust two fingers at his eyes, then flicked his wrist, pointing at Custodis.

Their antics made me grin, and I turned back to the demonstration.

Poised to enter the ring was a shirtless male. A single glance had my pulse quickening. Feminine murmurs from the stands said I wasn't the only one. Shimmering blue scales glimmered across the top of his muscular shoulders; sweat glistened over his washboard abs. Dark hair, angular jaw, muscular thighs encased in coarse leggings—check, check, check. Though I failed to identify his race, his body was on point.

The—not unattractive—prisoner strutted into the middle of the circle, much as Drazen would have, with a cocky rhythm to his stride, arrogance stamped on his attractive features. The torque around the male's throat flickered as it deactivated, and he turned to face a stone mannequin situated at the outer edge.

Bones crackled as the competitor twisted his neck and arched his back. He spread his arms wide, inhaling deeply. A fiery glow ignited at the center of his chest. Then, with a forceful exhale, flames erupted from his lips. A blazing stream shot forward, engulfing the mannequin in fire. In an instant, the inferno vanished, leaving only smoldering remnants behind.

I blinked at the statue. The stone glowed bright red from the heat. Had it been flesh and bone, it would be ashes. My jaw fell, and I glanced at Drazen to judge his reaction. My brother watched the demonstration with an upturned nose, unimpressed.

While Drazen's flames originated in his hands, this male's seemed to come from deep within. What the heck was he? Murmurs rumbled from the spectators. No doubt, he'd earned a high score—especially from the ladies.

As the next competitor entered the ring, my brothers strode over to us. Unaware of the "no weakness" strategy, Drazen picked me up and spun me in a circle. Once he returned me to the ground, I registered Victor's irritated growl.

"Sister! You survived the night," Kronk stated the obvious,

thumping my shoulder with his heavy hand, nearly knocking me over.

"And yet you didn't kill the leech?" Drazen arched a brow.

"Tell them," Custodis snapped, getting straight to the point. Seriously, the vampire had zero social skills. It was a wonder he'd ever risen through the mortal world's ranks.

Drazen narrowed his eyes, leaning in. "Tell them what?"

I cleared my throat, my palms growing damp. My brothers weren't going to like this. Hell, I didn't like it. "The vampire and I have come to an agreement, of sorts."

I explained quickly.

"Are you crazy? You've never even opened a portal. You have no idea what it could do to you," Drazen said, dark scowl on his face.

Even though he wasn't wrong, this was a worry for another time. We'd need to survive before I would have to hold up my end of the bargain, and the chances of that happening were slim.

"We do not need his help. He will get in the way," Kronk added, a matching scowl on his face.

The corner of Victor's mouth twisted. "I wasn't in the way last night."

Sweat trickled down my back as my chest tightened.

Drazen's brows furrowed with concern. "Runa?"

"It was nothing." I flicked a hand. "A minor altercation. I had everything under control."

Kronk grabbed my forearm, eyeing the bruises on my wrists. Rage poured off of him, and he clenched his fists, taking a menacing step toward the vampire.

"No, wait." I moved between them. Some strange impulse rising to his defense. "Not him. Custodis...*helped*." The last, I croaked past my rebelling throat.

Embers blazed in Drazen's eyes. "Tell me they are dead."

Victor sniffed as though offended. "It's been handled."

Caught in a testosterone sandwich, I started shoving,

throwing elbows. "Back off, will you? You're making me sound like some helpless damsel." They should know better.

Once I could see daylight again, I folded my arms over my chest, casting them all a petulant glare.

"Back to the matter at hand," Victor stated. "I provide Runa with protection, both in the cells and the game, along with the intel we need. During the trials, we work as a team and plan our escape together."

Drazen sputtered. "Now, hold up—"

"Done." Kronk stuck out his meaty paw, accepting the deal, and Victor reciprocated.

Smoke puffing from his nostrils, Drazen muscled up to his too-eager brother. "Wait a minute. Don't you think—"

Horns blew. An announcer shouted Kronk and Drazen's names, calling them to their respective rings.

Before they could leave, Victor stood in their path, ordering, "Hold back."

"I don't take orders from you," Drazen snapped, stalking across the sand.

Though separated by their individual rings, Drazen and Kronk worked together for their demo. With the torque deactivated, Kronk shifted and tossed a boulder into the air while Drazen set it aflame. As it returned to earth, Kronk punched the flaming missile and launched it clear out of the amphitheater. Screams echoed from outside.

Demonstration complete, they made their way to my side.

"Nicely done," I beamed, proud despite the circumstances.

Victor scrubbed a hand over his weary face, then turned to glare at me. "Your brothers are idiots. When you enter that ring, you must think of everyone who watches you as your enemy."

"Easy," I snapped, glaring back at him pointedly.

"Remember what we discussed, *partner*," he added, the reminder slamming my molars together. "Until the games begin, it would be better to be underestimated."

Horns blew, and the announcer shouted my name.

"Fine," I huffed. "You want me to play the part of delicate flower? You got it."

Fates, this was going to be embarrassing.

As I entered the ring, the torque heated against my neck as it powered down, and my sorcery came rushing to the forefront. I gasped, welcoming it home like a long-lost friend. This performance would be a challenge. How did someone act fragile?

I called on the well of power at my center, drawing a single thread. My palms warmed, and I whirled my arms dramatically as though preparing to conjure the most horrifying of images, a sight certain to strike fear in every heart. I was the Queen of Nightmares, leader of the infamous Blood River Bandits. All who stood before me would feel my wrath.

Finally, I thrust out my hands, giving life to my creation. What appeared was...

A miniature pony.

The first pranced around me. Then I added another, followed by a third, fourth, and fifth. I gritted my teeth, pretending to strain with each addition. Until, at last, I'd created twelve prancing ponies. Once the beasts had made several laps, I clapped my hands, and the animals exploded, becoming flutter-flies that twittered into the sky.

Snickers followed my display. Adding to my performance, I pressed a hand to my forehead and stumbled as though weakened.

"Runa?" Kronk's worried voice reached me as I hit the sand.

One of the guards grabbed my wrist, putting me in direct contact with his skin. Sucker. Little did he realize I had more than one ability at my disposal. He dragged my limp carcass out of the ring while the other competitors chortled, dropping me at my brother's feet. The torque around my throat heated, and my beautiful magic fell silent once more.

"Runa!" Kronk swept me up in his arms. "I do not understand. Her fingers haven't turned black. Is it the sun?"

I cracked an eye open. "Boo!"

He flinched, dropping me into the sand once more. Air knocked from my lungs, my rounded ass breaking my fall.

"Rocks for brains," I cursed and lumbered to my feet, dusting off my hands.

"I'm uncertain whether *I* want to be your partner after that pitiful display," Drazen intoned, muscular arms folded over his coarse tunic.

Sadly, it was only the leech who seemed to understand the genius behind my performance.

"What did you get from the guard?" Victor asked.

At the reminder of what I'd extracted when the male seized my wrist, I shivered. That was one trip I refused to take again. "Something about the trial tomorrow involving Carcerem's challenging landscape." That, and he found the prancing ponies a turn-on. *Gag.*

The vampire's smirk of approval sent a shiver coursing through me. Instead of analyzing my reaction, I decided to simply enjoy the ride. It likely wouldn't happen again.

The announcer projected his voice, calling out, "Victor Custodis."

Before entering the ring, the vampire selected a delicate sword. Something designed more for a petite woman than a warrior. At the edge of the circle, he stabbed his weapon into the sand. Then, he removed his course tunic, stripping down to his leggings while the audience's animated discussion quieted. With their curious attention on him, Custodis strolled to the middle of the enclosure, indifference in his expression. Once there, he pressed his palms together, growing quiet. The rise and fall of his chest shallowed, his breaths slowing.

Unable to resist, I eyed his physique, expecting flaccid muscles on a milk-toast frame. Instead, muscle I didn't expect to find in an aristocrat bulged beneath his pale skin. Long white hair spilled down his back, falling over his wide shoulders. Sunlight played off his lean torso and defined arms. The vampire's ridged abs glistened with sweat, his sculpted form warming under the unforgiving sun. I squirmed, wanting to fan my cheeks—due to the heat, of course.

Slowly, gracefully, he swept an arm out to his side, leaning into the motion, causing firm muscles to flex in his thighs. The controlled, precise action had me holding my breath. Then, he echoed the movement on the other side. By the time he'd repeated his warm-up four more times, I was breathless and near to passing out.

Speed increasing by slow increments, he brought his palms closer. Circling his arms as though he tamed the wind, forcing his unseen prey to submit to his will. Bending and twisting, he moved his body, conjuring some imaginary spirit. The two sparred, Victor defending, then attacking.

Again, his movements quickened when suddenly he flipped, seizing the sword.

My breath caught at the flawless motion, my eyes riveted to his performance.

I'd never seen the like. The competitors before him had offered examples of brute force and violence. I was *accustomed* to brute force and violence. Lived in it. Wielded it. Enjoyed it. In contrast, Victor's demonstration was all about finesse and artistry. His movements were that of a skilled dancer.

Blood pounded in my veins, and my mouth went dry. Would he be this disciplined with—*everything*?

Weapon in hand, he twirled the slim length as though it were an extension of his lithe body. The metal sang, whistling through the air. My heart sang as well, taking flight.

His dance took on a new, more vigorous cadence. This time, he sliced his invisible partner into precise ribbons. With the deadly sword, he taunted his prey, threatening to end them at any moment. And yet each cut appeared magical, much as I imagined I'd find the vampire's touch.

Thrusting, plunging, undulating.

Beneath the relentless glare of Carcerem's sun, it seemed his skin glowed, shimmering with a golden light.

Sweat trickled between my breasts.

His speed increased. Oxygen grew short. My head swam.

Until…

At last, he leaped. Spun. Slammed his blade into the sand. Ending his prey.

Ending *me*.

I exhaled the breath I held, goosebumps breaking over my flesh. I stared, transfixed, while the vampire remained frozen like some glorious statue of virility.

His performance, unlike my debacle, was… orgasmic.

Applause erupted, waking me from my trance. Boos rang out as well. The women cheered while the men and other competitors scoffed. Some of their insults hit my ears.

"What a pretty boy. What's he going to do? Bore us to death."

"Look at me. I'm a dancing princess with a dainty little sword."

Clearly, they all had sword envy.

There was nothing boring about Custodis's performance. Nothing at all.

Chapter Fourteen

VICTOR

"You performed well, Master Custodis."

I strode behind the servant on bare feet. A silent Runa padded at my side. She'd had little to say since we'd left the pit. Nor had she met my eyes.

"Yes, I did." It was a good performance. One full of grace and refinement. No doubt the other competitors were eager to pick my bones clean after that display.

I cast a sideways glance at the sorceress. Did Runa find my presentation appealing? I'd felt her eyes on me. Her heated gaze prodded me to greater heights. I'd strived for mediocre but couldn't bring myself to perform so dismally in front of the woman who'd once held me captive.

"Here we are," Milani said. "Gamma cell's bathing chamber."

Before us was a pool worthy of the ancient Greeks. In the center, there was a large, sunken expanse of steaming water. From the tiled walls, gurgling streams emerged in gentle water-falls for those who preferred a cascade. Bubbling nooks waited to soothe aching muscles. In those secluded hideaways, I noted several writhing couples.

Runa's head swiveled in the same direction, and her indrawn breath whistled in my ears.

I resisted the urge to study her expression. What would I find there? Shock? Arousal? I wondered strictly from an intellectual standpoint, of course. After all, now we were partners, I needed to understand the nature of who I worked with.

Milani turned to us. "Tomorrow, you will face your first trial." The baleful gleam in her rounded eyes hinted she didn't expect to see us again. "Tonight, you shall rest and rejuvenate. In the morning, I will assist you with your costumes."

"Costumes?" Runa asked, breaking her uncomfortable silence.

"Why, yes." Though it seemed impossible, the servant's eyes grew larger. "During the Fallen Trials, contestants are presented before the king, his most honored lords, and leaders from other kingdoms. It's important that you represent Carcerem in a favorable light."

"Favorable light? Ha!" Runa scoffed. "Then maybe he shouldn't have selected his competitors from the realm's dungeons."

"But who else among us would have the most reason to survive, representing Carcerem's undying spirit?" Milani asked, her expression bordering on fanatic. Another one of Idris's fans, no doubt.

I met Runa's eyes. With that look, we held a wordless conversation. Both of us agreeing—the servant's ignorance was astounding.

At the realization that we'd begun to speak without speaking, an act reserved for those who were far more intimate, spiders crawled through my insides. While I'd admit I found the sorceress attractive, she was merely a means to an end. The tool that would enable my return home.

"Fine garments, lavish bathhouses—these kinds of luxuries are wasted on criminals," I informed them.

Runa snorted an inelegant sound, then turned a gaze of longing to the heated pool before us. "Shut up, vampire. Though tomorrow we may perish, tonight we *live*."

I imagined the little thief had never experienced such luxury. I scoffed, turning to express as much, only to find Milani helping the sorceress disrobe.

Cultured gentleman that I was, I failed to notice how the servant drew the coarse tunic over the sorceress's head, revealing her lean torso and creamy expanse of flesh. The way her generous breasts swelled over the top of the plain fabric band containing them. I also paid no mind when her leggings soon followed, sliding down her shapely thighs. Thighs that were toned from her time on a horse and yet still supple. Nor did I care about the simple undergarments she wore, the coarse fabric cut high enough to bare her generous cheeks.

Sweat trickled down my temple, my blood heating. Did they have to keep it so warm in here?

"Master Custodis?" I blinked as if awakening from a trance to find Milani standing before me. The reality of my actions struck me. What was I doing? Ogling the chit was beneath me. What was I, an animal? I looked up, noting others appreciating the same sight.

Filthy ingrates. Perhaps I'd pluck their eyes from their skulls. Deep in my chest, a low rumble emerged. I tensed at the odd show of emotion. Was that a...growl? Surely not. It was this place. It was doing something to me. While I struggled to unravel my reaction, Runa waded into the water.

"Shall I assist you?" Milani asked.

"Quickly," I ordered, not wanting to let Runa out of my sight. Who knew what kind of mischief the sorceress might find without my supervision?

In moments, Milani had me out of my sandy clothing. Unlike

Runa, I stripped down to bare skin. Why not? My physique was flawless. Despite all the battles I'd fought over the years, not a single scar marred my flesh.

Liquid warmth encased my toes. I stepped deeper into the pool, taking a moment to note Runa's direction.

Our eyes collided. The sorceress's gaze slid over me in a heated caress. Across my chest, down my defined abs, then lower to my stiffening shaft, which seemed to have developed a mind of its own.

Traitorous bastard. My body reacted as if she'd reached out and stroked me.

Smirk pulling at her full lips, Runa raised her eyes to mine and quirked a challenging brow.

A challenge my cock was all too eager to answer. What the hell was with this place? Was there something in the water? My control was better than this. I hurried deeper until the water covered my hips.

Runa led the way to a small alcove and submerged herself in the steaming bath. Bubbles shot from the walls, and I sat beside her. Jets pummeled my back, relaxing my muscles. Elbows propped on the ledge behind her, Runa let out a moan.

Twitch. Twitch.

Curse my rebellious shaft.

"By the fates, that's delightful," she purred. "I believe I have sand in places I didn't know existed."

I clenched my jaw, refusing to notice the way her position thrust out her breasts.

When I failed to respond, she angled me a glance. "Why so tense, vampire? Worried you'll be sullied by the bathwater of honest criminals?"

"Honest," I snorted.

She narrowed her catlike eyes. "Not everything is as it appears on the surface, you know. Aristocrats are always so quick to judge."

"Or perhaps things are exactly as they seem. Lie, steal, cheat, plunge a knife into someone's heart, you're a criminal."

"And you've never lied, stolen, cheated, or killed?"

I fought a smile. "Never."

Runa barked a laugh, the sound erupting like bubbles in the finest of champagne. She tilted her delicate chin, peering down her nose at me. "You know, you're not the only one with a silver tongue. While speaking with some of our competitors, I learned that Reuben stole food to feed his family. Dexter accidentally dropped a lantern and was convicted of arson. And Adolph attempted to free his ailing mother from debtor's prison and was captured. There are many here who are more than criminals."

"I suppose you'll say you are one of them. That you are wrongly accused. A generous outlaw stealing for the good of others."

"Oh, no." She grinned. "I'm guilty as sin. The worst this place has ever seen."

My lips curled. "Yes, you are."

Again, her laughter had my insides twisting. I tensed my stomach, quelling the reaction. This female, this thief, shouldn't have this kind of effect on me or any effect at all, for that matter.

In rebuttal, I uttered a disappointed sigh. "Your opinion of the others is rather naive. Reuben killed the shopkeeper and two of his customers in his endeavor. Dexter razed a building containing his ex-wife and her new lover. Adolph gutted a guard who had three children while rescuing his drug-addicted mother."

Runa sank deeper into the water. "It's all in your perspective, I suppose."

Given her casual response, she hadn't believed a word of my lies. Interesting. There were few capable of seeing through my manipulations.

Feet scuffed behind us, and I tensed.

"May I help you with your bath, Master Custodis?" Milani asked.

Of course, the simple-minded servant would want to touch me. I glanced in Runa's direction, finding the narrow glare she directed at the other woman amusing. Could it be my partner didn't appreciate the servant's attention? Perhaps she was annoyed at witnessing proof that I was, in fact, irresistible to the opposite sex?

"Yes, by all means," I said with a flutter of my hand.

Two slim legs hit the water flanking me. Milani sat on the ledge, placing my frame in the cradle of her thighs.

"I selected a special fragrance for you. One I'm certain you will enjoy."

"Very well," I agreed absently.

Sudsy hands caressed my upper back, Milani's fingertips kneading my flesh.

I had to admit it felt divine. "Harder," I groaned, and the brownie complied.

Heat seared the side of my face. The source—Runa's daggered glare.

Finished with my shoulders, the servant guided my head back to rest in her lap, then proceeded to bathe my chest. While I found her ministrations relaxing, her honey and wheat fragrance singed my nostrils. She smelled nothing like the sorceress's spicy fragrance of pears and cinnamon.

With my upper body spotless, Milani trailed a hand up the inside of her thigh. "If you'd like, Master Custodis, it would be my honor to nourish you before your first challenge."

She offered her femoral? It had been a while since I'd fed in such an intimate fashion. The effects were known to be rather orgasmic. However, the thought of Runa watching me while I fed from the woman held a certain appeal. Before I could utter a word, Runa shot upright in the water.

"That will be enough, Milani."

"But—"

"You are excused," she snapped.

"Yes, Mistress Runa," the servant whined, withdrawing from the water and slapping away on sodden feet.

Rather than resume her relaxing soak, the sorceress exited the pool and settled behind me as Milani had. One shapely calf on either side of me.

I tensed, expecting to feel her slim fingers wrap around my neck.

Twitch. Twitch.

Bloody hell.

"What are you doing?" I asked, my voice a husky, grating sound.

"Tending to you, oh, fierce and mighty warrior." She slapped a sudsy cloth on my back, making me flinch. "Does this not please you?"

Twitch. Not at all. "I do find it pleasing when those beneath me know their place," I dared to taunt. Soapy fabric smacked my face, and I whipped the offending cloth away. Fire stung my eyeballs, and I tilted my head back at Runa.

"Do you have an issue with the servant tending to me?" I asked, genuinely curious as to her response.

Runa sputtered. "No, well, yes, but no." She stiffened. "Of course, I have a problem with people being treated like slaves."

"And yet, you allowed her to assist you too."

"That's different."

"Is it?"

"Men are such idiots, desiring women who will wait on them hand and foot."

"You think this is what I desire?" I had no interest in brainless simpletons. In the past, I'd courted educated females with impeccable bloodlines and solid social standings. If our liaison would further my own agenda, all the better. Females who were nothing like the little thief.

"Don't you? Shall I wash your hair next, oh, mighty lord?" Runa simpered, resuming her role.

"Absolutely not." I'd no desire to have it yanked from the roots.

"Don't you trust me?" she purred.

"Have you given me a reason?"

"You don't trust me, and yet you let that female sit at your back."

"The servant wasn't a threat." Runa, however…

Angry fingers threaded through my damp hair and pulled. Lips brushing my ear, Runa snarled, "And now that *I* am sitting behind you, what does that make me? Friend or foe?"

It was an excellent question. One I shouldn't answer.

Instead, I angled my chin, offering the sorceress my throat. "You tell me. Do your worst, little thief. If you dare."

Strangely, it was both an insult and a compliment. I'd little concern the minx would kill me. After all, we had an accord. Runa was many things. Foolish wasn't one of them. I had something she needed.

Twitch. Fates, save me. Not you!

For a moment, the sorceress seemed to consider my offer, and something deep inside quivered, eagerly awaiting her response.

With an angry splash of her legs, Runa slapped her hands down on my head and shoved.

Water sloshed over me in a deluge, shooting up my nostrils and burning my sinuses. I surfaced with a roar to find my attacker storming away. I studied the furious swish of the sorceress's generous hips, not hating the view.

Despite my anger at being dunked, a smile cracked my lips. I couldn't remember a time when I'd had this much fun while my life hung in the balance.

Chapter Fifteen

RUNA

AFTER A SLEEPLESS NIGHT, the morning of the trials greeted me with little sympathy for my exhaustion and far too much fanfare. After being paraded around the amphitheater in the back of magically driven chariots, the "fallen" currently stood within the sandy pit.

The stands surrounding us were filled to capacity, forming a cage of flesh and bone. My eardrums trembled from the onslaught of the cheering crowd. The roar was almost too loud to bear.

None had ever described me as shy or reserved, and yet I struggled with the need to curl inside of myself. Far too many eyes peered down at me, measuring my value, determining my worth.

Over a lavender gossamer shift and ass-baring briefs, I wore a corset trimmed in glittering crystals. My long hair had been twisted into spiraling curls, and a beaded circlet rested across my forehead. On my feet were a pair of sandals with straps that crisscrossed the length of my calves. Instead of the skilled sorceress that I was, I'd been made to resemble a delicate sheep anxious to be slaughtered.

Flarking Raelynn. She must have had a hand in this—so eager to humble and humiliate me. Well, she'd soon discover I wasn't easy to subjugate.

"That's right, ladies. Cheer for your favorite." Beside me, Drazen flexed his spectacular muscles, turning a circle. Golden bands with flames etched into the metal circled his bulging biceps. While his chest was bare, black leggings clung to his muscular thighs, leaving little to the imagination. Finely detailed flames were stitched along the outer legs. Even I had to admit his costume suited him. Unlike mine.

"You are embarrassing," Kronk grumbled, dressed in brown leggings made to resemble fractured rock. Over his broad upper body, he wore a leather harness with iron studs and a rustic chest plate designed to cup his bulging pectorals.

"And you are jealous," Drazen taunted.

"It is ill-advised to encourage their attention. To be a favorite is to be a target," Victor stated.

I scanned his costume with a critical eye, noting the intricate braids that drew his long silver hair back from his aristocratic face. Braids Milani had spent an excessive amount of time plaiting this morning. The rich brocade tunic, woven with metallic threads, gave him a rather king-like appearance.

"Will you be able to run in those?" Drazen scowled at my feet.

I squared my shoulders, ignoring the breeze that blew up the back of my skirt, flashing my ass. "Who says I'll be running? Once this torque is deactivated, the others will run from me."

Trumpets blared, and though it didn't seem possible, the crowd grew louder.

One of the females I recognized from Gamma cell twitched nervously in front of me, muttering, "We're all going to die. All going to die."

Thanks to the orbs that floated over each of our heads, her mental breakdown was projected onto the rotating carousel of magical images that hovered high above us. The orbs would project our every move during the games.

King Idris entered his royal pavilion, the queen trailing behind him. His doublet, a luxurious garment woven with gleaming metallic threads, sparkled as if sprinkled with starlight. Raelynn sparkled as well, the tiny crystals on her costly gown catching the light and scattering rainbows.

The king strode to a raised platform near the railing, raising his arms. "Great people of Carcerem, I welcome you to the Fallen Trials."

The crowd roared. Much more of this, and my eardrums would bleed.

"We're going to die! We're going to die!" The terrified woman grasped her head, rocking back and forth. Poor girl was losing her shit. No way she'd make it to the end of the competition.

The false king lowered his arms, gesturing for the crowd to quiet, which, of course, they did immediately. *Brainless idiots.*

"The competitors gathered before you are criminals of the kingdom." Idris's magically amplified voice echoed through the stands. "All are guilty of heinous crimes that threaten the peace and prosperity of our lands."

This time, the spectators responded with hate and violence. "*Boos!*" thundered in our ears. Cups of mead were thrown into the aisles.

"We're going to die! Going to die!"

"Hey. Settle down. It's going to be fine," I lied. The screamer was most definitely going to die. I reached out to pat the distressed female's shoulder. Big mistake.

The second my hand made contact, she belted out a screech and bolted through the other competitors scattered before us. No one cared to stop her.

"Going to die!" she shrieked, sprinting to the edge of the ring.

"Wait!" I shouted. "You can't—"

Sparks exploded as the woman hit the invisible containment field. Flames engulfed her body. Inhuman screams erupted from her throat. In seconds, she'd turned to ash, her remains floating away on a breeze.

Once more, the crowd was back to cheering. Bloodthirsty deviants. And they claimed we were the criminals.

"Ah, yes." King Idris chuckled. "I was getting to that part. Residents of Carcerem need have no fear, for the suppression field will contain all threats to the kingdom's safety during the trials."

A shiver ran through me. The screamer wasn't wrong. Flark, we were screwed. Firm fingers squeezed my own. I glanced down. When did I grab the vampire's hand?

Double flark. I shook off his grip and lifted my chin.

Drazen glanced between the two of us, a dark frown on his ruddy face.

"*Blah, judgment for your crimes. Blah. Blah,*" Idris droned on, his voice an irritating buzz in my brain.

I tuned out most of his blathering to focus on the woman who lingered behind his throne. Not that I cared about the traitor, but I noticed Raelynn wasn't allowed to sit beside her royal mate. Instead, she stood next to him like one of his servants. Bet that burned her greedy ass.

As though she felt my scrutiny, she turned her attention to me. While meeting my eyes, a twisted smirk distorted her face. No doubt, she was eager to see me fall during the coming challenge. That we shared even a drop of blood between us was a mystery.

Never one to bow beneath my sister's taunting, I flicked my fingers under my chin and blew her a kiss, the gesture meant to mimic a kiss of death. The classier version of sliding one's finger across their throat.

To my delight, her smirk faded, replaced by an ugly snarl. When we were younger, Momma used to warn us our faces would freeze like that. I only wish it were true.

I dialed into the false king's long-winded speech.

"There are three challenges. One per span. Each represents different aspects of our dear kingdom. The first span will demonstrate her land, the second her heart, and the last her many inhabitants. In these trials, Carcerem shall determine which of the criminals are deserving of redemption. Those who are deserving must persevere against the kingdom, themselves, and each other. Last one standing will have earned their freedom."

At this, the competitors cheered louder than the crowd. I imagined it would be the last time any felt the desire to do so.

"Well, that was vague as hell," Drazen grumbled. "Land, heart, inhabitants?"

"Stay together," Victor ordered. His icy gaze scanned those around us. "Do not lead until we see what unfolds. Let the others spring the traps."

I stiffened at the order. Our temporary partnership didn't make him our leader. Not by a long shot.

"Agreed," Kronk said far too readily.

My palm itched with the urge to slap him upside his thick head.

In the royal pavilion, King Idris raised his arms. Raelynn's blacked hand rested on his shoulder. Golden energy glowed in his palms, growing brighter. Brighter.

"Let the Fallen Trials begin!" the king roared in an otherworldly voice, the deep tenor rumbling through the amphitheater.

Blinding light exploded from his hands, engulfing everything it touched. The force that blasted over my skin nearly knocked me on my ass. Stony arms wrapped around my frame as Kronk shielded me with his body.

Sand pitched and rolled beneath our feet.

"What's happening?" I shouted as if anyone else had a clue.

Our entire world seemed to come apart, then reassemble in unexpected ways. The stands dissolved, the audience vaporizing.

Deep in my center, where my magic dwelled, a dark ache seized me. Ice scraped along my nerve endings, my life force burning me from the inside out. Except this pain. It wasn't mine.

No.

It was Carcerem's.

Our noble king defiled her. He stole her power for himself. My *sister* used her magic to aid him—for their entertainment. What they had done was vile. One of the worst crimes an individual could commit. Nausea rolled through my gut, and I fought with the urge to vomit.

As my stomach churned, the scene shifted. The amphitheater vanished, replaced by miles of endless shoreline. Before us, a restless ocean churned. Its waves crashed with frothy intensity. At its heart lay a small island, marked by a lone red flag. Suspended above the sandy mound, an enchanted timer glowed, counting down from twenty clicks.

The king had used the realm's magic to create a compelling illusion. Unlike mine, this one had substance. Over the pounding waves, I registered the sounds of the crowd. While they still watched us in this magical environment, we could no longer see them.

"Now what?" Kronk asked.

Scattered along the beach were the other competitors. Like us, they glanced around in confusion.

"What? No instructions?" Drazen asked.

Victor stared out across the water. "Given the flag and timer. I'm assuming we're meant to get to the flag in twenty clicks. Those who don't make it in the time allotted won't live to see the next challenge."

"Fabulous," I huffed, reaching for my reserve of power,

finding it eager and ready. "I think the torques are deactivated." To test my theory, I held out my hand, conjuring a raven. The illusion came easily, then darted off, flying for the horizon.

"Mine as well." Drazen snapped his fingers, creating a single flame, then snuffed it out.

"Good. We're going to need it," Custodis said, his keen eyes taking in everything around us.

Several wooden boats rested along the shore. Those competitors who were closest to them turned on each other, fighting to claim one.

"Boats are out." I strode to the edge of the water. "I suppose we could swim."

"No. Wait." Victor grabbed my arm. "Look." He nodded.

Eager to beat the others, a number of competitors charged into the water. With quick strokes, they swam away from shore.

"Over there," Drazen pointed.

Directly in front of a small group, water twirled, gathering speed. Screams rang out. Several of the swimmers were caught up in the whirlpool. As the first group vanished beneath the surface, violent waves began to crash. Growing bigger, more powerful, they rolled and tumbled, headed straight for the few who had managed to claim boats. Waves pounded the flimsy timber. Wood splintered, and the boats came apart. As the passengers struggled to hold onto the broken pieces, massive waves claimed them, dragging them under.

In the distance, cheers erupted, the king's audience enjoying the show. *Filthy bastards.*

"Athos can manipulate stone," Custodis stated. "Can Kronk raise them from beneath the water?"

"If Kronk creates stepping stones, we could cross on foot," I finished the vampire's thought. "Do it." I smacked Kronk's iron arm, then shook out my stinging hand.

"Very well." Kronk took a knee, plunging his fist deep into the sand. Then, with a brow furrowed look of deep concentration, he summoned his magic. The ground trembled beneath our feet. Out in the water, bubbles exploded in a violent stream. Along the surface, dark mounds erupted, slimy stones the size of adult bula emerging from the depths.

Adrenaline sped through my veins. This might actually work.

"Kronk, you're a genius." I ignored Victor's contribution.

"*Ten clicks*," said a mechanical voice.

"Hurry," Victor ordered, and we took off at a sprint.

One at a time, we leaped from stone to stone. Frigid water sprayed our bodies, wetting our clothes and hair.

I blinked my blurry eyes. We were getting closer. Hope welled inside of me.

"Brace yourselves!" Drazen shouted over the roaring water.

A massive wave exploded against the stones, threatening to knock us off our perches.

"Runa!" Before I could brace for the next impact, a larger wave crashed into the pillar I stood on. It slammed into my chest, knocking me off my feet. I tumbled, knees and elbows cracking on the rock. With the deluge threatening to suck me under, I dug my nails into the slippery stone surface, finding little to stop my fall. Flark. I was going in.

Stony fingers clamped down on my wrist. With one hand, Kronk dragged me up, setting me on my feet.

"Behind us," Kronk shouted over my head.

I spun to look. Others had taken advantage of our path, leaping across the stones, gaining on us.

"Drazen, your flames," Victor shouted from the rear.

"Duck," Drazen yelled, launching a fireball.

The flaming orb sailed over Victor's head, barely missing him. It crashed into a guy with green scales. The creature squealed, falling into the water, where the waves quickly swallowed him.

"*Five clicks*," said the disembodied voice.

"Move," Victor shouted.

This time, I didn't balk at the order. I leaned back and hurled my frozen body at the next foothold.

Only a few steps to go. We were so close.

I reared back, prepared to make another jump. Bolts of lightning whizzed past my nose.

"Hey!" I threw out my arms, wobbling on my perch.

"Argh!" Kronk bellowed behind me.

He'd been hit. Panic washed over me until I remembered his skin was made of stone.

Still, no one messed with my brother. I spun in a circle. Where were those bastards? To my surprise, one of the boats had survived. While two of the occupants paddled, the third flung magical lightning bolts at those closest to the island.

I braced my legs, drawing power from my core. My hands warmed, and my illusion took shape. In the water beside me, an enormous sea monster broke through the churning waves. Razorblade fins, daggers for teeth, bulbus eyes—my baby was glorious.

"Go get 'em, boy." I hurled my illusion at the boat, and my sea creature took off. Water rolled off its charging back.

"There! Over there!" voices yelled. "What is that thing?"

Halfway to the boat, my beautiful beast reared its ugly head and roared.

Screams rang out. Mr. Lightning Bolt blasted energy into the illusion. The other two began paddling, their movements erratic, their boat spinning in panicked circles. Apparently, paddling wasn't in their skill set.

"*One click,*" that infernal voice warned.

"Move your sweet ass, Runa," Drazen bellowed.

My feet struck the next stone with a tooth-rattling jolt. The next one as well. Then the next. My leg muscles burned. The sound of the others following behind me propelled me to move faster. Seconds remained.

I hit the sand and tumbled, rolling out of the way. My teammates followed, piling onto the beach.

Horns blared. Time was up.

Heart racing, I sat up. "Kronk, Drazen?" *Custodis?*

"All here," the vampire answered, even though I hadn't included him in my concerns.

"Nice sea monster," Drazen praised.

I snorted a laugh. "It was. Wasn't it?"

We glanced around the island. Cheering echoed from far away. Those infernal orbs hovered over our heads. Flark. I'd almost forgotten our audience. I was so focused on surviving. Plenty of the other competitors had survived as well. Pity.

I flopped back on the sand, catching my breath. "That wasn't so bad."

"Right," Drazen growled, flicking droplets off his muscled arms. "Great fun if you're a fan of water."

He never had enjoyed being submerged, which made bath time as a youngling particularly entertaining.

Horns blew, and I tensed. What now?

Chapter Sixteen

VICTOR

IDRIS'S magic burst over my skin, the sensation like a thousand spiders skittered over my flesh. I savored the tantalizing sensation, some hollow part of me eager to soak it in. Oh, what I could do with that kind of power.

Beneath us, the ground rumbled and surged.

"Here we go again," Drazen snarled.

I looked to Runa, and she met my eyes, her expression stark.

Who knew what this next challenge would bring?

Once more, the landscape changed. Water drained from the ocean as if it plunged down a drain—along with anyone who'd failed to reach the beach. Gurgling screams rang out, ending with a *slurp*.

Around us, trees erupted from the ground. Sandy beaches turned to forest. Earth cracked and trembled. Kronk reached for Runa, holding her tight to his side. She might claim him as her brother, but they certainly weren't blood. At the sight of his thick arms circling her frame, a low growl rumbled in my chest.

Laughter rang in the distance, the king taking far too much

pleasure in his creation. The crowd exploded in applause, praising their monarch for his latest design.

Keeping Runa and her brothers in my peripheral, I scanned our new surroundings. Thick woods surrounded us. Overhead, a mystical image shimmered into view. Pictured was a ravine with another one of those infernal red flags on its opposite side. The picture faded, becoming a map. Beside it was another timepiece. This round, we had thirty clicks.

I was really beginning to understand the bandits' hatred for their false king. How dare the bastard run us around like lab rats for his amusement?

"Let me guess," Drazen drawled. "We have to find our way to the flag, through who knows what, and over the bottomless ravine all in thirty clicks."

"Apparently." I dusted sand from my damp clothes.

Thick woods obscured the other competitors from my view, though I picked up the low rumble of their voices, along with the crack of snapping branches. "The others are moving forward. We need to as well. Only better. Faster."

"I will lead," Kronk commanded, barreling through the underbrush. Twigs snapped against his brawny frame. He plowed through Idris's illusion like a mighty bulldozer.

The block-headed athos did have his talents. The rest of us followed in his wake, stepping over fallen trees. Once more, I brought up the rear. Runa stomped through the brush in front of me, the sway of her hips hypnotic. I shook my head, in need of a distraction.

"Do you recognize this place?"

"What?" Runa cast a glance over her shoulder.

"The false king claimed that Carcerem would determine our fates. By chance, is he recreating varying aspects of the kingdom?"

Runa slowed, walking to my side. "It's possible." She

quieted, deep in thought. "The ravine he showed us could be the Devil's Throat."

"Which is what, precisely?"

"Deadly," Drazen contributed.

"While I've never visited," Runa said, "it's said to be a bottomless chasm. Those who tumble into its depths are rumored to fall for eternity."

"And to reach the flag, we need to cross this insurmountable obstacle," I surmised.

Before us, Kronk came to an abrupt stop, forcing Drazen to collide with his unforgiving back.

"What is it?" I demanded.

"We've reached the field."

I glanced around Kronk's massive girth. Blood-red flowers carpeted the area ahead, their blooms bobbing waist-high.

"It's too easy," Runa murmured.

Drazen pointed to the far edge of the clearing where some of the other competitors had gathered. They uttered curses, turning in a circle and swinging claws at the foliage.

"They are being attacked," Kronk said.

Fending off their unidentified attacker, they bolted into the meadow.

Runa shifted on her feet, growing restless. "They're getting ahead of us."

"Let them." I clasped her forearm.

Halfway across the field, the others began to slow. Screams rang out. They slashed and clawed at the surrounding blossoms. Blood gurgled from their lips, and they tumbled to the ground, obscured by the flowers. Cries and bellows of pain rent the air. Over the sounds of agony, our invisible audience cheered. Then, suddenly, all fell silent.

"What the hell was that?" Drazen gasped, puffing a ring of smoke.

I took a knee, eyeing one of the buds. Tiny rows of serrated teeth lined its gleaming petals. "The flowers are carnivorous."

Runa's scream whipped my head around. Face first, she struck the ground. Some unseen force dragged her backward, deeper into the woods.

"Runa!" Drazen hit his knees, grabbing her hands, doing his best to haul her back.

Around her ankles were several vines covered in serrated thorns. The harder Drazen pulled, the harder they pulled in return.

"Get them off! They're tearing me in half!"

Runa's scream twisted my insides, stirring something primal inside of me. Kronk and I dove for the vines at the same time, grabbing them below Runa's feet and pulling.

"Tear them!" I shouted.

Kronk nodded, clutching the tendrils in his massive hands. Muscles straining, he ripped through the vegetation, breaking one at a time until Runa was free. She tumbled into Drazen's arms, panting.

Before I could check her for wounds, she thrust out her arm, eyes wide. "Behind you!"

Dozens of vines slithered out of the woods, headed right for us. This must have been what sent the others fleeing into the field. A field we dared not enter. Both Drazen and Runa scrambled to their feet, glancing at the slithering plants, then the blood-red blossoms.

"We have to go forward if we're to make it to the flag. Try your flames," she said to Drazen, gesturing to the flowers.

He nodded, blasting the blooms in front of us with a stream of fire. High-pitched screeching pierced our ears, the blossoms burning to a crisp. Just as quickly as they died, the outer edges of the cleared space filled in, growing until the path was once again covered.

The infernus was useless here.

I eyed Kronk beside me. Without warning, I drove my shoulder into his side and shoved with all my considerable strength.

Off balance, Kronk stumbled into the bloodthirsty field.

"Kronk!" Runa yelled, her mouth a gaping expression of horror.

Kronk held out his arms, frozen in place, afraid to move. He glanced down, then back at us. "I'm okay. They cannot penetrate my flesh."

Runa exhaled a sigh, then turned to me. "Did you know?"

I shrugged. "I suspected."

Fury darkened her violet gaze. "You—"

"We must hurry." Kronk returned, scooped Drazen onto one shoulder and Runa onto the other, then headed off into the field.

Leaving me behind? *Nice try.*

I tensed to jump. Pressure circled my ankle, jerked my leg, and I hit the ground. Dirt and rocks scraped beneath me. The vines dragged me into the forest.

"Bloody bastards." I rolled and sat up, grabbing my ankle. Once I had a grip on the vine, I bared my fangs, sinking them into the bitter vegetation and tearing through its green flesh as if I were a youngling with his first meal.

Once free, I darted to my feet and sprinted for the field. Kronk and the others were several feet ahead now. I had no time to waste. At the edge, I leaped.

Landing on Kronk's muscular back was like running head-first into a stone wall. Still, I clung to his shoulders, bracing my legs against his sides. The athos stumbled beneath the impact, uttering a curse but thankfully keeping his feet.

Distant cheering resounded over our heads. The audience was excited by our continued progress. Four glowing orbs followed in our wake.

Beside me, Drazen lifted his head. "Nice of you to join us."

"Missed me, did you?" I arched a brow, struggling to maintain my grip.

"It was nothing you didn't deserve for almost feeding my brother to a bunch of demented flowers," Runa snarled from her position over Kronk's opposite shoulder.

Before I could argue my case, Kronk had reached the other side. He shrugged, dropping his siblings to the ground. Before I could manage a dignified dismount, two powerful hands grabbed me, and I sailed over Kronk's head. My back slammed the dirt, oxygen punching from my lungs. I gasped, staring up into the athos's inverted face.

Kronk leaned over me. The promise of my demise was a glimmer in his eyes as he pounded his fist into his palm. I croaked in response. Seeming appeased, he nodded and stormed away.

Chapter Seventeen

RUNA

I STOMPED through the woods behind Kronk. Despite our supposed alliance, the vampire wasn't one of us and never would be. Again, he'd put a member of our group at risk. Same as he had in the alleyway and the throne room. Other than Idris, I'd never met a more self-serving bastard. Custodis was just another corrupt leader, faking concern to fulfill his own agenda. It was a fact I needed to keep in the forefront of my mind, no matter what slipped past the devil's manipulative tongue.

Kronk slowed in front of me. "I think we found the ravine."

Together, our group moved forward, one cautious step at a time. Our next obstacle stretched out before us. Mist rose from the vast chasm, the sounds of the forest echoing off its steep walls. The opposite bank might as well have been an entire continent away, the length impossible to cross.

I dared to glance into the immense pit, toeing a rock and kicking it into the ravine. The stone pinged once off the rim, then into the hole. Not another sound emerged. It never hit bottom. I shivered, inching back from the edge.

Voices hit us from either side of our group.

"We're not alone," Drazen said.

We scanned the cliffside. Others had made it here, too. In small, ragged groups, they gathered along the edge.

I glanced to my left. "There's a bridge."

Though calling it a "bridge" was a stretch. Frayed ropes held together rotted boards, several of which were missing. The rope passage swayed in the breeze, seeming on the verge of collapse.

Others noticed it as well. Shouts rang out. Two of the groups rushed to the entrance at the same time.

"This should be interesting," Drazen muttered.

After a brief tussle, one of the competitors made it to the crossing first. With little hesitation, he raced onto the rotting surface. The ropes pitched and groaned beneath his weight. I held my breath, waiting to see if he would fall.

Would we need to use the bridge as well? No way that rotted thing would hold Kronk's weight. And I sure as hell wasn't leaving him behind. An image of my sister's sweaty hand in mine rolled through my memories, and I winced, pushing the thought aside.

Behind the first man, a second followed. Then another. And another.

"I can't watch." I smacked my hands over my eyes, peering between my fingers.

Sure enough, the rope snapped, and half of the wooden planks gave way. Screams rang out as several of the competitors plunged into the bottomless void. Some managed to hang on, clinging to the rope, slowly making their way across, hand over hand.

"The bridge is a death trap designed to thin the herd," I said.

"Agreed. We'll need to build our own, as we did in the water challenge," Custodis answered, his icy gaze locked on one of the trees.

He turned to Kronk. "Think you can knock one of those over?"

Kronk nodded, lines of determination furrowing his thick brow. "Let's find out."

Standing behind the tree Victor indicated, Kronk rolled his shoulders and cracked his neck. Palms planted against the mossy bark, he stabbed the toes of his boots into the ground, stomping footholds. That done, he leaned his considerable weight into the trunk and shoved.

Thick muscle rippled across my brother's broad shoulders. Veins stood out on his giant biceps. His stony complexion turned pink, then red, then almost purple. I chewed on my thumbnail, uncertain who would break first, the tree or my brother. Finally, the wood splintered and cracked. Branches swayed over our heads.

Demanding arms circled me, pulling me back. "Out of the way in case it rebounds."

The vampire's frosty cypress scent filled my nostrils. Some defective reflex kept me from breaking free of his grip, allowing his touch instead.

I watched in awe as the tree tilted toward the chasm. Kronk unleashed a mighty roar, and the wood splintered, the noise like lightning had struck the ground. The treetop hit the opposite bank and bounced.

We all held our breath. If it twisted too far, it would plunge into the darkness, taking our hope for survival along with it.

Instead, it settled on the other side.

Kronk dusted his hands, grinning. "I did good, huh?" Then his gaze lowered to my stomach, and his grin turned to a dark glare.

I glanced down, finding the vampire's arm around me, and jerked free. "Better than good. Let's go before the others join us."

It wasn't like we could keep our plan secret, what with the explosion of cracking wood and screaming birds.

Drazen caught my hand, holding me back. He narrowed his eyes on Custodis, offering a mocking bow. "Leeches first."

"Very well," Custodis said, climbing up on the broken stump. Arms out, he balanced, taking a few practice bounces. When the tree held, he took measured steps, inching further until he cleared the ledge, standing over the chasm, free of any handhold, net, nor safety rigging to keep him from plunging to his death.

"Perhaps we should go one at a time," I suggested.

"No time for that." Drazen glanced over his shoulder.

Shouts rang out. The others were coming.

With no further encouragement, I climbed up, following the vampire.

"Move your ass, blood sucker," Drazen shouted.

We scrambled across the makeshift bridge, with Kronk bringing up the rear.

Heart pounding a frantic rhythm, I dodged branches, careful of each footstep. The fallen trunk wobbled, shimmying beneath our combined weight. Wood cracked, and I screamed, dropping to my hands and knees.

Frozen, I stared at the bark under my palms. Don't look. Don't look. Don't…

My gaze shifted. Below me was a vast chasm of nothingness. Vertigo washed over me in a flood. My head swam, and I swallowed back bile. The panicked woman's cries from earlier echoed in my ears. *We're going to die! We're going to die!*

"Runa!" a smoky voice called my name. "Runa, you have to go!" he repeated.

No. No. No. I was fine right where I was. What was the hurry?

Heat warmed my backside. Orange light erupted. "Damn it, Runa. Snap out of it. I can't hold the bastards off forever."

Smoke burned my nostrils. I blinked and peered out across

the fallen tree. Surely, Victor had reached the other side by now. Hell, he was probably already at the flag, feet kicked up, watching my brothers and me on one of those ridiculous floating screens. Like the dead woman, my mental breakdown would be broadcast for the world to ridicule.

Laugh it up, Custodis. Enjoying the show?

Beneath my nose, a hand appeared. I blinked, forcing my eyes from the relative safety of the trunk. The vampire's silver-gray stare held me captive.

He really did have nice eyes. Something in his hypnotic gaze pulled me in. Warmth spread through my veins, my head growing foggy.

"Take my hand," an angelic voice said.

I'd do anything for that voice. I swallowed, licking my dry lips.

"Take my hand. Your brothers are counting on you."

What? My brothers?

I placed my palm into my savior's grasp, and he helped me to my feet. "Eyes on me. One foot in front of the other."

Someone screamed, the shriek fading as if they had fallen into a deep well. Cursing and the whoosh of fireballs roared behind me. Still, I did as the voice commanded, following in his path.

"Flark! It's on fire!"

"Drazen, you fool!" a deeper voice shouted.

"I'd like to see you hold off a dozen men while balancing on a log," the first yelled over the rumble of hungry flames.

Pounding footsteps thundered along our improvised bridge. "Move! It's going up quick."

As we neared the end, my legs wobbled and lurched beneath me. "Jump, Runa," the angelic voice said.

We dove off the tree, hitting the ground, thank the goddess. Two bodies hit the dirt beside me.

Though I had leaped to the ground, something soft had

broken my fall. The fog cleared, and I raised my head. Custodis rested below me with his eyes closed. Reality returned by slow degrees. He'd helped me?

I wiped a smudge from his cheek, smoothing back his silver-white hair. His chest inflated on an inhale, and he opened his eyes, scanning my face. But not with the harsh judgment I expected. No, this was something softer. Something that looked an awful lot like genuine concern.

"What did you do?"

He frowned. "Only what needed to be done."

Instead of angelic, I now found his voice annoying. Realization dawned. Flarking vampires and their stupid powers. "You compelled me." He took my choice away—my free will, my control.

"Yes," he said simply.

"That's not possible. Sorceresses are impervious to compulsion."

"And yet you were susceptible to mine."

No way. Except that would explain why I had trusted him. It was the only reason I'd taken the vampire's hand. Warmth permeated my damp clothing where I pressed against him. Victor's heated palm rested on my bare thigh. Instead of releasing me and jumping away as if he feared I would sully him, he stroked my flesh. My bones turned molten. It had been a long time since anyone had touched me this way.

I eyed his firm lips. What would it be like to kiss this male? Would he be icy and cold or wild and primal? I suspected the latter. Many who appeared controlled and contained were hiding something darker underneath. A tremor ran through me at the thought, and his pupils dilated, his breath quickening beneath me.

"Ahhem," a voice cleared.

I peered up to find my brothers standing next to us. Smudged with soot, they stood with their arms folded, matching expressions of disgust on their faces.

I flinched, jerking free of the vampire's embrace and snapping to my feet.

The vampire stood up as well, glancing at the burning tree. "It's about to—"

Wood cracked. Embers exploded into the air. The flaming bridge tumbled from its banks into the ravine. Those who'd braved the fire, attempting to cross, tumbled into the void, screaming and cursing.

Drazen propped his hands on his hips. "Well, we crossed the ravine. Now what?"

I mimicked his stance. "Must you keep asking that? Every time someone says, *now what*, bad things happen."

Dark laughter rumbled from above.

Chapter Eighteen

RUNA

HORNS BLEW, and the roar of the cheering audience rose over the noise of the forest. Golden energy swept over me, threatening to push me over the ledge. Shit. Not again. The landscape wavered, shifting and changing.

I stumbled, falling against Custodis, and the ground dropped out from beneath us.

Together, the vampire and I plunged into a dark tunnel.

"Curse you, Idris," Drazen's voice echoed from a distance before fading away.

"What's happening?" I shouted.

"Hang on to me," Victor barked, clamping an arm around my waist.

I clung to his shoulders. No way did I want to fall into some dank hole in the ground *alone*. Even if Custodis was my only option, he was better than nothing.

Smooth stone slipped beneath our bodies, and my stomach slammed into my heart. We could end up anywhere—a lava pit, in a nest of golden-tailed scorpions, or the layer of a gallspawn.

Suddenly, the tunnel ejected us, sending us tumbling into a tangled heap of arms and legs.

Our ragged breaths broke the silence as the glowing orbs overhead illuminated the space. Solid stone enclosed us on all sides. We had landed in some kind of cavern.

Victor pushed himself to his feet. "Are you hurt?"

I rubbed my throbbing shoulder, rising as well. "Just a few bruises. Where are we?" I turned a circle, calling out, "Kronk? Drazen?"

Water dripped in the silence.

"I believe they fell into a separate tunnel." The vampire dusted his hands.

I surveyed our new surroundings, relieved to find no animal scat, bones, or man-eating plants. Behind us was an elevated shaft we had no hope of climbing out of. In front of us was a single opening.

"Time's wasting. I will lead," Custodis said with zero discussion, heading deeper into the passage.

I followed, snorting, "By all means. Lead away." If the vampire wanted to be the first to face the unknown, who was I to disagree? A wise leader didn't let ego get in the way, knowing when to let others rise to a challenge. Me? I was allowing the vampire to rise. Hell, maybe he'd even learn something from the experience.

I inhaled, and my nose twitched. Instead of muck and mold, the air was sweet.

"Do you smell that?"

"This isn't some crude joke about flatulence you share with your brothers, is it?"

"Are you serious?" I snapped, tone biting with disdain. Although, it was totally something my brothers would do. Only *once* had I fallen for the pull-my-finger gag. *Once.*

The walls of the cavern closed in on me, and my chest squeezed. I wasn't afraid of small spaces, but following someone

I didn't trust deeper into a dank hole had each breath I took feeling tighter than the next.

What I needed was a distraction.

I frowned at the back of the vampire's silver head. "What about you? Do you have any family?"

Custodis walked in silence. Just when I'd given up on his answer, he said, "I did. Once. Long ago."

"Siblings?" Sweat trickled between my breasts, and I fanned my heated cheeks. It was strangely warm for being underground.

"Perhaps. I can't be sure. My mother wasn't mated. I never knew my father."

"Is she still in the mortal realm?" Maybe that was part of his reason for wanting to return.

He snorted a self-deprecating sound. "It may surprise you, but I was actually born here."

I grabbed his arm, pulling him to a stop. "Hold on. You mean to tell me you're a native of Carcerem?" Yaga didn't mention that.

He pulled his arm free and continued along the path. "I was sent to the mortal world as a youngling."

"So, after all your bluster and disgust for this realm, you're actually a native."

"I am not one of you," he grated.

"If you say so." Arguing with a delusional aristocrat set on denying his own roots was pointless. Besides, what did it matter if he was born here? It changed nothing. Certainly not my feelings for the arrogant lord.

I drew a deep breath, sweet perfume filling my lungs.

Something wasn't right. Dank tunnels shouldn't smell *good*. Warmth flooded my veins, and I shivered, my nipples pebbling against the fabric of my dress. I inhaled another breath of the sweet fragrance. There was something vaguely familiar about it.

Custodis muttered a low growl, stumbling a step before catching himself.

My head spun, and I pressed my palm to my sweat-slicked forehead. "I feel funny," I murmured, my voice a husky rasp. "We need to get out of here. Do you see anything?"

"We're nearing another opening."

Finally, we cleared the tunnel, stepping into a vast, open area. "Oh, wow," I gasped. "It's beautiful."

Glowing crystals illuminated the space. On one side was a turquoise pool, the water shimmering in the soft light. Scattered around the walls were clusters of purple flowers with fuchsia centers. They clung to the rock in small clumps, their seductive fragrance filling the air.

"Why would Idris include this in his challenge when his goal is to punish and torture us?" There had to be a catch.

"These flowers..." Custodis strode closer to one, eyeing its dramatic blooms. "I've seen them before—in a book."

"Please tell me they're not carnivorous." Sure, I'd lived in Carcerem my entire life. That didn't make me a specialist on every twig and leaf.

"No. But their effect can be almost as deadly. We must leave this place. Now." He drew a breath then groaned, bracing a hand on the wall. Energy pulsed, vibrating through the ground.

What was that? Was he hurt? Strange, but that didn't sound like a groan of pain. I studied his tension-riddled frame, staring at his tortured expression, then his straining shoulders and lean torso.

Finally, I let my gaze drift lower to the impressive bulge in his pants.

Gulp. Nope. Not a groan of pain, more like...

Lust.

Victor Custodis was aroused.

At the discovery, my blood heated, warmth pooling between my thighs.

He wasn't the only one.

"Fates. The flowers. They're an aphrodisiac." Simply saying it out loud had a soft moan parting my lips.

At the sound, Victor snapped his head in my direction. His eyes shimmered with a golden light. "Their pollen unleashes inhibitions. Hold your breath," he snarled through gritted teeth.

"Too late," I gasped, a haze clouding my brain with every inhalation.

I needed...to leave.

Thoughts grew fuzzy, my blood heating.

"I need..." I trailed off, my tone rasping. Warmth spread through my center, and I squeezed my thighs together, moaning. "I need to be touched." I glided my hand down my throat to my chest, trailing my fingers over sensitive flesh.

"Damn you. Stop that."

"Stop what?" It wasn't as if I was the one in control here. My fingers had a mind of their own. That wandering hand dipped beneath my corset, shoving the cups of my bodice down, leaving my breasts in little but the transparent shift. Through the thin fabric, I teased my pert nipples, sending jolts of pleasure shooting through my belly.

Victor's glowing eyes watched my every move, burning me with the heat of a thousand suns.

I liked his eyes on me.

Watching.

Wanting.

Down, my traveling hand wandered, touching me much as I imagined my lover would, following the curve of my waist, blazing a tantalizing trail over my hip.

Just as I reached the hem of my short skirt, I met the vampire's hungry stare and smirked.

"Runa," he choked, claws raking down the stone wall.

"Runa what?" I asked in a breathy whisper, guiding my fingers up the inside of my thigh.

"Don't." Rocks broke beneath his desperate grip.

The vampire was seriously pent up. When was the last time he'd let loose and blew off a little steam? Did he ever?

I didn't live a life of restraint. I took what I wanted, when I wanted it, particularly if it felt good. Life was too short, especially with the false king on the throne.

"Don't what?" I dipped my fingers inside my undergarment, stroking my swollen sex. Fates save me, I'd never been so wet.

Wind gusted. Victor moved in a blur, and my spine hit the wall. An iron grip held my hands above my head. I blinked, drawing into focus the vampire's snarling visage.

Despite the rough stone scraping my flesh, I groaned, eyes rolling into my skull. The warmth of his body branded mine, and I arched my back, seeking more of him.

"Runa," he gasped, his expression a mask of both pain and pleasure.

I tipped my face to his, our noses touching. "Release me and we can both feel good."

"Can't," he said in a broken voice.

Despite the coolness of the cavern, sweat dampened his brow, trickling down his temple. Eager for a taste of him, I pressed my lips to his jaw, then drew my tongue along that single bead of moisture.

The vampire shuddered against me. "What are you doing?"

"Tasting you. Would you like to taste me?" I tilted my head to the side, baring my throat. I'd heard a vampire's venom could be quite orgasmic, which was exactly what I needed right now.

"Damn you," he panted, pupils dilated, eyes locked on the vein that fluttered in time with my racing pulse. "This is wrong. There's something we must do. Something..."

He furrowed his brow, squeezing his eyes closed.

I breathed deeply and exhaled a heated sigh. In this moment, there was nothing more important than the two of us.

Thanks to his distraction, I managed to wiggle one of my arms free. I grasped his wrist and steered his hand to my chest, pushing it to my breast and enclosing his fingers around my flesh.

Transfixed, he gave me control, offering no objection when I drew his hand down my side, under my skirt. Drawing one leg over his hip, I steered his heated palm beneath my undergarment. With no further direction, he stroked my sex.

"Is this what you want, pet?" he purred in my ear.

"Yes," I moaned. "I need you to ease me. Make me burn."

He gripped my hair, snarling against my lips. "You don't know what you're doing."

"You sure about that?" With my other wrist free, I caressed his inner thigh, cupping his impressive erection through his pants. I remembered the vision I'd had of him in the bathing chamber. It was one I'd called to mind many times. Oh, to have that thick length inside of me now.

His entire frame shuddered in my grip.

Still, he shook his head. "No. No. There's an important task. Something urgent."

I drew a deep breath of the tantalizing perfume that surrounded us, and my sex spasmed. He was wrong. The only thing that mattered was this feeling.

With little warning, he jerked free of my grasp, stumbling back. Fangs bared, he glared at me, his glowing eyes consuming me. Energy pulsed between us. The ground trembled, not that I cared. The walls could fall in, trapping us together forever. *Yes.*

The predatory gleam in his gaze prickled the hair along my nape. Something deep inside pushed to the surface. This creature. He was dangerous, not to be trusted.

No. I rejected the idea. This vampire was my salvation—the only one who could save me from the fire burning in my veins.

I reached out to him, and he flinched. His reaction snapped my hand back, seizing my heart in my chest.

"Run," he grated.

I frowned, studying his menacing profile. "Run?"

"Yes," he snarled. "Before it's too late."

He was rejecting me? Hurt twisted my guts, and I curled my arms around my waist. "But—"

"Now!"

His command rattled my bones, the dark fury in his tone stirring some deep-seated sense of survival.

Without another word, I spun and bolted, my head a tangle of contradictions. My instinct for self-preservation made me shove one foot in front of the other while the warmer, deliciously tingly parts of me screamed, *Return to him. You're going the wrong way!*

Footsteps hammered the stone behind me. He was so close.

Go!

No, stay!

No, go!

Bright light filtered through the darkened cavern. The clamor of several thousand voices rang in my ears. Fresh air billowed through the tunnel on a gentle breeze, the scent sunny and clean. My head pounded, my thoughts clearing. It was the end of the challenge. I was almost there.

My langued muscles firmed with determination, and my racing stride lengthened. Flark, what had I been thinking? Go! Definitely go!

Behind me, a primal growl rumbled, and my pulse leaped. Claws scraped my shoulder. The vampire was gaining on me. Whether he hungered for blood or...*gulp*...more, I couldn't determine. Regardless, this time, he wouldn't find me docile prey.

Sunlight flashed in my eyes. This was it. I'd reached the end. The vampire's fiery breath dusted my neck as I dove through the tunnel's exit. Sand padded my fall, and a large body landed beside me. Victor's weighty frame pinned me to the ground. He straddled my hips, his hand circling my throat. I blinked, peering up at him.

Victor blinked down at me as well, panting. Goddess, but he was a sight. For a moment, I forgot where we were, simply taking in all that was Victor Custodis. Silver-white hair surrounded his head, wild and untamed. His usually icy gaze was a hot, searing gold. Twin fangs gleamed behind his full lips. Gone was the emotionless demeanor he chose to portray. In its place was something else. Something powerful. Savage.

Though we'd left the flowers in our wake, a heated shiver ran through me. I didn't hate this hidden side of my icy partner.

Custodis blinked, and by slow degrees, the golden light in his eyes faded. "Runa?" he groaned, and his grip on my neck eased. Shock registered in his expression, and he rolled, then pulled me up off the sand in a rush.

At the sudden movement, my head reeled, and I wobbled, pressing a hand to his chest.

He grasped my upper arms, peering into my face. "Are you okay?"

Why does he keep asking me that? It wasn't as if he actually cared. Or did he? I nodded my answer, not trusting my voice.

Slowly, I became aware of the arena around us, other competitors strewn about the pit, the hovering orbs. *Flark! The orbs!*

The roar of cheering voices stabbed my ears. Custodis's name fell from worshipful lips. Many celebrated his performance and prowess in the game. While my name was often followed by jeers of harlot, whore, tease.

Fire blazed in my cheeks, memories surfacing. By the goddess, the flowers had reduced us to our most primal state, and the audience had watched every moment.

Nausea twisted my stomach, and I slapped a hand to my mouth. The weight of countless ridiculing stares pressed down on me. Sharp breaths wheezed between my fingers.

Custodis gripped my chin, the contours of his face hardening. "Reclaim your control. It is they who should be ashamed."

He was right. What sort of sickos signed up to watch a bunch of criminals experience this kind of hell? They were the ones who should have been embarrassed. I met Victor's silver gaze and nodded my agreement.

"Do you see my brothers?"

The side of his mouth curled into a mockery of a smile. "Over there."

I glanced in the direction he indicated, only to find both of them rising from the sand where they'd been dumped from their tunnel. Drazen's eye was swollen shut, and he held his ribs. Kronk's harness and part of his hair were seared.

Dread tied a knot in my twisting gut. I'd always feared the span my brothers turned on each other with no one to intervene. At least they'd survived. The two cast sullen glares at each other. I hastened to their sides.

Drazen scanned me with his good eye. "Are you injured? The leech didn't hurt you, did he?"

"Nope," I croaked, cheeks flaming anew. Apparently, our primal halves had emerged in different ways. Lucky for Kronk and Drazen.

"How are you?" I asked.

Kronk shrugged one massive shoulder. "I went easy on him."

"Did not. It's I who went easy on you," Drazen snarled.

Kronk took a menacing step in his direction, pointing a blunt finger at his missing eyebrow. "Did not."

"If I hadn't, you'd be dead."

"And your bones would be splinters."

"Guys! Enough!" I dared to step between them, slapping a hand on each of their chests. "What happened in the tunnel, stays in the tunnel. None of us are responsible for what happened under the influence of those flowers." I raised my head, meeting Victor's mocking smirk, and lifted my chin, daring him to comment.

Kronk reached over me, placing his hand on Drazen's shoulder. "Runa is right. We were not ourselves. I forgive you, Brother."

"Forgive me?" Drazen barked, then froze, tipping his nose toward me and sniffing.

He snapped his eyes to mine and sniffed again. "Why do you smell like the leech?"

"What?" I offered a wobbling smile. "Don't be ridiculous."

Kronk jammed his nose in my hair and sniffed as well. "Our brother is right. You stink of—"

"That's enough." I threw elbows, squirming free of their intrusive sniffing. The bula-holes needed to keep their nostrils to themselves.

Horns blared, interrupting my family squabble. I huffed a sigh, for once thankful for the king's intrusion.

"Let us congratulate the winners of our first round," Idris boomed. "And thank our dear kingdom for rendering judgment upon those who were unworthy of her forgiveness. Take note, for those gathered before you will move on to compete in the second round of our trials. Tonight, our champions feast. Tomorrow, they return to the pit."

Around us, the crowd broke into applause. The thundering of their hands, deafening. Soldiers marched into the arena, herding the prisoners into our appropriate cells. My brothers stormed past us, casting glares at Victor as the guards led them away.

As we passed the royal pavilion, I caught the queen's smirk. No doubt she'd loved watching me humiliate myself, performing like a whore before the masses. One span, very soon, I would wipe that smile off her face.

Chapter Nineteen

RUNA

POUNDING music thumped over the din of low, muttered voices. Long tables loaded with food filled the space. The scent of greasy meat and stale ale permeated the air. My brothers and I had secured a place at a table in the back of the room. Drazen sat beside me while Kronk sat across the table, shoveling food into his maw.

After a trip to the bathing pool, we'd been ordered to assemble for dinner. Tonight, all three of the prison cells dined together. Only half of the almost one hundred competitors had made it through the first set of trials. Tomorrow, that number would likely drop by half again.

I glanced to where Victor stood across the room. Arm braced on the wall, he peered down at a flushed female who simpered back at him. The expression on the vampire's face was soft, half-lidded. Seductive. I should know. I'd seen that same look mere hours ago.

My blood heated at the memory. The way he watched my every move as I'd pleasured myself in front of him. How he pinned me against the wall, his body hard where mine was soft. The hungry spark in his glowing eyes when he demanded that I run. Funny, but I hadn't minded the chase.

"What's happening between you and the leech?" Drazen startled me from my thoughts.

I jerked my head around and met his dark scowl, my cheeks warming. "I have no idea what you're talking about."

"Don't you? You watch him," he drawled. "He watches you…"

"You're imagining things." I stole another glance at Custodis, only to find his steely gaze locked on me. For a second, it seemed his eyes flashed gold before turning gray again. The same had happened in the caverns when he'd watched me. There'd also been a surge of energy I couldn't explain. Was it a side effect of the trials?

"I don't like it." Kronk pounded his beefy fist on the table, reclaiming my attention. "He's grown possessive of you."

At his statement, my insides quivered. I brushed the sensation aside. "Has not," I scoffed. "If he watches me, it's because he doesn't want to lose his one shot at returning home. I'm nothing to him but a means to get what he truly wants."

"And what is he to you?" Drazen asked, ever the one to ask the most unsettling questions.

I stared at my brother, my mouth opening and closing while I searched for an answer.

"Hello, beautiful," a deep voice said from my right. "I must be in a museum because you truly are a work of art."

My eyes rolled before I even turned to face the loser who'd dared to sit next to me. I'd seen him before, during the performance demonstration. He was the one who could belch fire. The guy was pretty, I'd give him that, but I knew his type. Dark hair, sparkling blue eyes, chiseled body. Overly confident that his good looks would be enough to make up for his shallow personality.

Drazen leaned around me, giving the male a pointed glare. "And you are?"

"Thorne Blackwing, at your service."

I shifted back in my seat, gathering my legs beneath me. "Goodbye, Thorne Blackwing."

"No, wait." The charmer's smile fled.

I eyed the hand he'd dared to lay on my arm, and he winced, withdrawing.

"What do you want?" I asked.

He cast a glance around the room, an air of desperation in his mannerisms. "I want in."

"In what?" Drazen said. "And if you say my sister, know they will be the last words to ever leave your lips."

I wrinkled my nose. "Gross, Drazen."

"I want into your alliance," the attractive interloper answered. "I think we could work well together."

There was no point denying the existence of our partnership. The entire kingdom had seen us competing as a team. Many of the other contestants had paired up as well.

This time, I managed to gain my feet, standing beside him. "Not a chance."

"No, wait." Once more, his desperate grip held me in place. "Please."

Icy evergreen swept through my senses, the air stirring. "Touch her again, and you will lose a limb." The vampire's warning ended on a spine-shivering growl that did lovely things to my insides.

And now it was a party. Kill me now.

Clueless of the danger he was in, Thorne thrust his hand out to the vampire. "Victor Custodis, I'm—"

"Thorne Blackwing. Yes, I know."

The blue-eyed charmer beamed. "You've heard of me."

Custodis peered down his nose at the man. "I've made it my business to know everyone here."

Thorne's sparkle returned. "Then you understand I can be an asset to your alliance."

Kronk paused between mouthfuls, food slipping down his chin. "We do not need your flames, Thorne Blackwing. You are not an asset."

Drazen snorted. "Kronk is right. We already have the fiery end of things covered."

"Perhaps." Thorne smirked. "But do you have this?"

He tugged on a leather cord he had around his neck, extracting a gleaming skeleton key. "This little baby will open any door in the place, even if it's warded," he whispered.

Victor canted his head. "Now, where did you get that?"

Thorne leaned closer, winking. "I have an *in* with the queen's handmaiden. She gave me a token of her affection so I could attend to her needs with none the wiser. Mind you, the key is spelled to only function for me, so no funny business."

Victor's expression turned calculating.

I cut the attractive interloper a hard glare. "Only funny business going on is yours." I'd never met a male with so much sex appeal who could be trusted. It was bad enough I was forced to work with the vampire. No way did I want to add the flirt with fire breath to the mix.

While Thorne stowed his key down the front of his tunic again, Drazen scanned him with a speculative eye. "If you have a magical key, then why are you still here? Unless you're lying, and it's nothing more than the key to the nearest latrine."

Thorne firmed his jaw. "Maybe I want to be here."

"What a liar," I scoffed. "Nobody in their right mind would place themselves in the trials deliberately."

Perhaps realizing this required some honesty, he admitted, "The king has something that belongs to me. I entered the trials to get it back."

While I sensed no deception, his hidden agenda could interfere with our own instead of aiding our escape. "And what do you get out of this deal?"

"Word is your vampire is peddling venom in exchange for intel. I've got a key but no way out. All known exits are heavily guarded. What I need is the location of a hidden door that is rumored to exist. This door is said to lead to an underground passage that will lead us under the wall. Find that door, and I'll provide the key, along with transportation out of here."

I planted my hands on my hips. "Sounds to me like you snuck into the trials to recover some stolen trinket with no way out. Talk about poor planning."

"One"—he held up his index finger—"I came here with at least half of a solid escape plan, minus a few details. Two, did I mention my stolen item was incredibly valuable?"

Kronk stopped eating, leaning closer. "How valuable?"

Something in the guy's manner didn't sit right with me. While his words sounded truthful, there was an odd tension in his shoulders that said he wasn't giving us the whole story. No way I was trusting some random treasure hunter when my brother's lives were on the line.

I shook my head, preparing to shut him down. "Listen, I—"

"Deal," Victor stated.

My teeth snapped together. "Deal?"

"Yes. Deal."

No. Hell no. The fallen vampire leader was not in charge. I slapped my palms down on the table. "And since when did you become king?"

At my question, gold sparks glimmered in his eyes, and the low rumblings of some sort of strange energy hummed over my skin.

Before I could comment on the odd sensation, a servant ambled behind us with a sweets-loaded tray in his hand.

Unlike most of the brownies who served Idris, this one was male and quite a bit larger than the others.

I eyed his offering. "What is this for?" The rest of the food was served on large platters and placed on the tables.

"A special treat. Compliments of Queen Raelynn."

"Yeah, no thanks." I recoiled as though he'd handed me sea slugs.

"Pass that over here," Drazen said, and the servant extended the tray.

"Drazen, are you cra—"

Pastries, along with the platter, exploded against Drazen's chest.

My brother belted out a roar, teetering on his chair legs, coated in creamy confections.

Chunks of cake and icing splattered the floor, and I slipped on a sugary glob. "What the hell?" This was no accident but an attack.

The servant whipped around, daring to give the raging infernus his back. In the man's hand was a dagger. My heart pitched. In a flash, the blade descended. His target—Custodis.

Faster than my eyes could track, Thorne sprang to his feet and captured the assassin's arm. At the same time, the vampire grabbed the servant's hand and twisted. Bones snapped and popped, the attacker screaming his rage. Next thing I knew, the male staggered backward and collapsed. The bloody dagger protruded from his chest.

It all happened so fast. I could do little but splutter.

With the threat contained, Custodis took a knee at the male's side. "Tell me who sent you."

The guy stared at the ceiling, unseeing. Blood gurgled from his lips.

"The Chosen One must not ascend," he coughed, and the light faded from his eyes.

"What was that all about?" Drazen snarled, flicking cream from his ruined clothing.

The vampire plucked the dagger from the man's sternum.

Squelching sounds had my dinner rising, eager to escape my stomach.

Carved into the hilt were strange runes.

"Anyone know what the markings mean?" He glanced around our group.

Thorne dragged his gaze from the dagger, his expression hardening. "Never seen them before."

I narrowed my eyes at him. "You sure about that?" He was far from convincing. If the new guy wanted "in," hiding secrets wouldn't put him in my good graces.

Horns blew. Guards shouted, "Everyone back to your rooms."

I SAT on the lumpy cot, glaring up at Victor. "What do you mean, you're heading out?"

"I can't lie around when there is work to be done. Hidden doors to be located."

I huffed an irritated sigh. In other words, veins to be tapped. "We need to discuss what just happened. Someone tried to murder you."

He shrugged. "I've made a lot of enemies over the years. Many of those enemies ended up here in Carcerem."

I studied his form in the soft light. The clothing Milani had brought him stretched tight across his shoulders. The seams on his thighs strained the threads that held them together. Either she'd miscalculated his size, or he'd packed on a couple of pounds since our incarceration. And not in the same way Yaga's sweet buns did to me.

Something was happening to the vampire, and he refused to talk about it. "There's something going on with you. The vampires I've met, strong emotion turns their eyes silver, not gold. Several times now, I've seen yours turn gold."

"A trick of the lighting," he snapped with impatience.

I firmed my chin. "It isn't my imagination. In the cavern, there was this pulse of energy. I felt it again in the dining hall."

He held up his hand, saying in that imperious tone I'd come to loath, "I don't have time for feminine concerns. Remain in this room. Do not leave." With his command issued, he headed out the door.

Thoroughly dismissed, I stared at the place where he had stood, mouth gaping. He did not just bark orders at me. No one spoke to me that way, not even my brothers.

I punched my fist into the lumpy mattress, hissing, "Better sleep with one eye open, Custodis."

Whispered voices hummed outside my doorway, and I peeked out. Two women, towels thrown over their arms, strolled in the direction of the bathing room. Were they meeting my vampire?

My hands curled into fists. Pinpricks of pain spiked my palms, and I uncurled them, wincing at the small cuts my nails made. *What am I doing?* He wasn't *my* vampire. He wasn't *my* anything. I couldn't care less what he did with his fangs.

Perhaps I would head to the bathing chamber for a soak and gather my own intel.

Not that I gave a heated fart for Victor's orders, but did I dare? I definitely didn't want to get caught alone in this place. Especially after the attempted assault I barely escaped last night.

"Psst," a voice hissed.

I tensed, peering into the gloom beyond my door.

Crystal-blue eyes peered back at me. "Over here."

"Thorne?" I tiptoed into the dining area, whispering, "What are you doing outside of Beta cell?"

He offered me a blinding smile that I was certain had wrecked many hearts. "We didn't have much time to talk earlier. I thought we could get to know each other."

I pursed my lips. He was in possession of a key that could

prove useful in our escape. That didn't mean I trusted him. Not even a little. Since Victor agreed to let him join us—without consulting me—it couldn't hurt to try to get a better read on the guy. Reclaim control of the situation. Perhaps I'd work my wiles on him, soften him up, and get him to let down his guard. Even without my powers, I was still a sorceress with skills.

"Fine," I said, careful not to sound too eager. "I was headed to the bathing chamber. You're welcome to join me."

His smile widened, a delightful dimple blooming in his cheek. "Lead the way."

After a couple breathless moments of darting through the shadows, we both stripped down to our undergarments and sank into a steaming corner of the chamber's pool.

I swallowed a groan, letting the warmth of the water melt my tension.

"You're insane to risk coming here like this," I murmured.

He leaned back, resting his elbows on the ledge. "Maybe, but at least you know the key works now."

Said key rested between his nicely defined pectorals. I allowed my curious gaze to wander over his body, not bothering to hide my interest. He was attractive, in that rakish, bad-boy way. Which usually worked for me, but for some reason, tonight, it did little to stir my blood.

"What are you anyway?" Dark blue scales dusted the tops of his very bare, very broad shoulders. The rest of his skin was sun-kissed tan. I couldn't get a read on him. Not that I was familiar with every species in existence.

He shrugged. "Shifter."

"What kind? I didn't see you shift during the trials."

Dimples speared his cheeks. "My animal is shy."

I snorted a laugh. Nothing about this male was shy. Remembering my mission, I trailed my finger along his forearm. "That attack today at the banquet. Your reflexes were incredible."

"I couldn't allow any harm to come to my new partner." His

166

deep voice lowered to a purring rumble, indicating he wasn't talking about Drazen or Victor.

"You were worried about me?" I pointed to my chest.

He followed the gesture, his sparkling eyes lingering on the bit of cleavage that swelled above the water. "Why, yes. You are the queen's sister, after all."

"Not many people are aware of that." With his gaze fixed on my finger, I caressed the fullness of my breast. "Have you been asking the others about me?"

"What can I say?" He shrugged. "The queen's handmaid likes to gossip."

"And you like to listen." I'd have to watch myself with this one.

"It's not a crime."

"No. But can I trust you're not sharing things with her in return?"

"How can I trust you won't tell someone about my key?"

"Self-preservation."

"Exactly. I hear the queen isn't fond of you. No offense, but I'd prefer she not know we are acquainted."

I gathered my wet hair off my shoulders, holding it against the base of my neck, offering a coy smile. "So, I'm to be your dirty little secret."

To this, he cocked an eyebrow, eyes warming as he took in the picture I'd presented. "How dirty are we talking?"

I shifted my position, coming to rest before him, propping my palms on his knees while also pressing my breasts together. "That will depend on whether I decide if you are trustworthy."

"And how would a male go about earning this trust?" He lifted a swirling lock of my lavender hair from the water, letting it slide over his fingers.

"For starters, you could answer a question for me."

"Go on."

"That sigil on the dagger. The way you reacted... I think you've seen it before."

He pursed his lips as though fighting a smile. "Think so, huh?"

I inched closer, settling my frame between his knees, whispering, "I do."

"I may have seen it around." Thorne relaxed deeper against the pulsing jets, a male content to watch the show—curious to see how far I was prepared to take this.

"What is it?"

"It's the mark of a religious sect that believes the prophecy is true. They just disagree on the interpretation."

"You mean the prophecy about the lost king returning to Carcerem to set us free?"

"Yes. Except they don't think the lost king is our savior. They believe he is the beginning of the end. One destined to destroy, not save."

I tilted my head. "Isn't Idris already destroying us?"

"Sure, but his style is more death by a thousand cuts. According to this sect, if the lost king defeats Idris and claims the throne, what's left of Carcerem will be destroyed."

"If that's their concern, then why did they attack Victor? He's a simple vampire, not some lost demigod returned to smite us all."

His sparkling blue eyes darkened, his expression shuttering. "Case of mistaken identity, perhaps?"

"Perhaps." Or maybe the shifter knew more than he was willing to say despite my gentle seduction.

"How long have you known him?"

I hitched a shoulder. "Not long."

"Come now. You have to give me more than that. Do you think I don't know when a beautiful woman is playing me to get information?"

Touché.

I smiled. "Don't act like you're not enjoying the game."

"How did you meet Victor?"

"My partners and I captured the vampire after his realm banished him."

"He's from the mortal world?"

I failed to see the harm in answering. "More or less. He was born in Carcerem and sent to the mortal realm in his youth."

"Why?"

"I haven't a clue. Maybe because even as a child, he was annoying as hell."

"Runa?"

Speak of the devil.

Victor hastened to the side of the pool. Behind him, a blonde with a dazed cast to her eyes stumbled past us, heading toward her room.

Custodis snarled, glowering at us. "What is the meaning of this?"

I stiffened at his tone. "Just a little meeting of the minds."

The vampire's deep growl sent a shiver down my spine. That damn golden gaze of his was back. The one he denied existed.

He sliced the shifter a daggered glare. "You don't belong here."

Energy jolted through the water in a crackling wave, and I flinched at the sudden shock of power that rippled over me. Thorne flinched as well, and his muscular thighs flexed beneath my palms.

Rather than respond to Victor's aggressive tone, he gazed up at Custodis, his expression scrutinizing.

Yeah. Good luck, buddy. I'd spent days with the vampire and had yet to figure him out.

Before I could formulate a rebuttal about bossy males who needed to know their place, firm hands grasped my forearms, yanking me out of the water and free of the shifter's lap.

"Hey! What are you—"

"Time for bed," Custodis snarled. Then, his icy gaze traveled down my body and my now transparent undergarments. Air gusted over my damp flesh, and suddenly, a towel whipped around my frame.

Holy bula-crap, the vampire was fast.

"You, return to your cell," he barked at my bathing partner while I wobbled, tucking the length of material under my arms.

The orders, as well as the manhandling, set my teeth on edge. "I will go to bed when I—"

In yet another whoosh of dizzying speed, Custodis swept me into his arms and had us back in our room in seconds.

The minute my feet hit the ground, I came up swinging.

My fist rocketed through the air, and I spun in a circle, losing my grip on my towel. Regaining my balance, I turned to confront the vampire, fists raised. "Touch me again, and you'll pull back a bloody stump."

Instead of protecting himself from my wrath, he directed a long searing look at my exposed skin and snarled, whipping his tunic over his head.

"Put this on. Now," he snapped, tossing the garment at my face.

"Bula-hole!" I stomped my foot, jerking the offending fabric off my head. Seriously, what the hell? The vampire was as bad as my brothers. Maybe worse.

When he continued to glare at me, I pursed my lips, stabbing him with my eyeballs. "You going to watch?"

He snapped a smart turn, giving me his back while I removed my wet undergarments and tugged his tunic over my head.

Taking advantage of his turned back, I smacked my palms against his bare flesh, hard enough to leave handprints. "What the hell was that all about?"

Rather than answer, he used that damned vampire speed again, snapping an arm around my waist and dragging me with him when he laid on his cot.

Resting against his naked chest, I struggled in his hold. "Release me."

Instead, his grip tightened. "You've already proven that I can't trust you not to sneak off."

I sputtered a hacking cough. "Trust me? I'm not the one slinking around with harlots, sucking soiled blood. And for your information, I didn't sneak off. I was working Thorne for intel. Much as you were working your latest conquest."

"What did you tell him?"

"Me? Tell him?"

"He's a skilled manipulator. The male has obviously targeted us for a reason. The assassin with the tray was likely a set up to allow him into our ranks."

"What? You're crazy."

"Nobody is faster than I am. Especially not some unidentified shifter, and yet he grabbed the assassin's knife before me. He expected the strike."

"Then why the hell did you agree to work with him?"

He squeezed me tighter. "Keep your enemies close."

I grunted, my lungs straining. "Ha. Ha," I wheezed, pinching his chest until his grip eased. "Point made. Now, let me go."

"You're sleeping with me tonight."

Goosebumps pebbled my chilly flesh, and I settled deeper in his embrace, absorbing his warmth. "Give me one good reason why." Besides the fact that my frigid bed no longer appealed to me.

"I promised your brothers I'd protect you."

Yeah, right. I doubted he held a sliver of respect for my family, nor did he strike me as someone who kept his promises.

Fatigue had my head dropping to his chest. "Seems to me it's you who needs protecting."

"Sleep, little thief," he commanded.

I was too tired to resist, drifting off in the arms of a vampire.

Chapter Twenty

VICTOR

THE BLINDING rays produced by Carcerem's sun threatened to blister my eyeballs. My ramshackle team stood beneath her judgmental gaze. The acrid breeze did little to cool our sizzling flesh, sweat trickling down our faces. Had I been in the mortal realm, I'd likely be a pile of ash right now. While I was no youngling, even my resistance to the sun's effects would have been tested by the intense rays. Thank the gods, my sensitivity to the sun didn't seem to be a problem since I'd arrived.

Restless energy hummed under my skin, and I fought the urge to tug at my restrictive torque. Fatigue pulled at my limbs. I'd slept little last night, though Runa had no such qualms, the curvy sorceress resting peacefully in my arms.

I hadn't slept beside a female in...well, ever.

With Runa at my side, every noise seemed amplified. Every fluttering shadow was a demon to be slayed. I was the only thing standing between her and the monsters. The key to my future was a fragile creature, despite her incredible gifts. It was unsettling, knowing my fate resided in her slim hands. Hands that had held tight to me late into the night. As if she feared I'd vanish while she slept. Her unconscious behavior made me wonder who she'd lost. Who had slipped through her fingers?

Could it have been a mate or lover?

At the thought, my fangs burned beneath my gums. A furious snarl formed in the back of my throat. I swallowed against the sensation, gliding my tongue over my teeth.

I'd need to control these urges lest they make me sloppy in the battle today. Once I was free of this uncivilized realm, I'd no doubt they'd disappear. Whatever was happening between me and the sorceress was temporary, at best. I had a life to reclaim and vengeance to enact. Females were a distraction I didn't need nor desire.

I gripped the sword I held. None of my informants had a clue what this day might bring. All I knew was every prisoner was armed.

Despite the well-balanced blade I'd claimed, I felt unprepared for what awaited. It was a disturbing sensation, to say the least. Back in the mortal world, I'd been two steps ahead of everyone I encountered. Well, except for one.

Horns blared as King Idris strode to the front of his royal pavilion. His queen trailed behind him. Costly metals adorned his garments. Carcerem's crown of golden branches circled his spiky silver hair. The queen wore a daintier version with her lavender mane set into braided coils around her head. Tiny jewels decorated her gown, reflecting the sunlight. Together, they presented an envious display of wealth.

"Good citizens of Carcerem," Idris boomed, using magic to project his voice, "welcome to span two of the Fallen Trials."

Applause and cheering erupted.

"Yesterday, our repentant criminals faced the judgment of our great kingdom's lands. Today, they will encounter her people in their various forms. After all, it is the inhabitants of Carcerem who are her heart and soul. That heart is multi-faceted, both with darkness and light. This challenge will consist of three parts. First, our competitors will face the realm's darker side."

Idris lifted his hands as his queen placed a steadying palm on his shoulder. A blinding surge of golden light burst from his form, flooding the space. Energy lashed against my skin like a thousand fiery tongues—painful, yet not unbearable. I planted my feet, standing firm against the onslaught while others collapsed to their knees.

Runa's soft groan of discomfort rang in my ears. Though she clutched her hand to her chest, wavering, she managed to stay on her feet.

From deep inside of me, some dark voice purred in approval. *Fierce female.*

Before us, pillars of sand emerged from the ground, one for each contestant. Those pillars trembled and shook. The writhing masses began to solidify, forming arms, legs, and heads.

"What the flark is this nonsense?" Drazen shouted.

Long hair hung over the shoulders of the sandy figure before me. His proportions took on the shape of a formidable male with an aristocratic edge. Chin held high, he appraised me down his upturned nose. In one hand, he clutched a sword. An exact copy of the one I held in my own.

I raised my free hand, swiping a trickle of sweat from my brow. The king's creation mirrored the motion.

"Seven hells. They're us," Drazen gasped, hopping on one foot, staring as his sandy replica mimicked the movement.

"We're to fight ourselves?" Runa turned to me, her jaw gaping in disbelief.

Horns blew. The flamboyant king thrust his glowing hands into the air. The torque around my neck heated, the restraint deactivating.

"People of Carcerem. Let the trials begin."

With those words, the sandy figures charged, angry snarls roaring from their inhuman lips. I raised my blade just in time to block the strike from my doppelgänger. The power of his hit rang up my arm. His strength was impressive—as it should be since he was supposed to be me.

"This is madness," Runa shouted, blocking a well-aimed kick from her twin.

A weapon made of sand, yet no less deadly, zinged past my cheek. I ducked and spun, barely missing the tip of my assailant's blade. He was good. I'd give him that.

Still, there was nobody in this world with my kind of skill—except me. Idris had no hope of duplicating my level of experience. Muscles flexed across my shoulders. I shot forward and thrust my sword into the creature's heart.

There, it stuck.

While the abomination smiled at me, I heaved on the sword's hilt. My supernatural strength did little to extract my blade.

The sand creature waggled his index finger at me as though I were an errant child. To my bemusement, the bastard grasped the blade of the sword and pulled my weapon from his chest. Before I could retreat, his unyielding fist connected with my jaw.

Pain erupted, and my head spun.

Runa stumbled backward as well. Panting, she turned to me. Blood trickled from her brow. "She knows my every move before I make it."

"Same," I uttered, then looked up. "Duck!"

"*Argh!*" Kronk flew over heads, his massive form hurled by his mirror-self.

Runa glanced at me and blinked, her cheeks pale. "That's a first."

I bet. The only creature strong enough to toss Kronk like a stone skipping across water was…Kronk.

I eyed the creature before me, the sandy devil doing the same. He canted his head, a dark smirk flirting upon his lips. His stony eyes flicked in Runa's direction, and his smirk became a devious grin.

With little warning, the demon before me lunged for Runa. It figured the bastard would seek to destroy the only thing I valued in this infernal kingdom. It was what I would have done. Our mirror selves knew our weaknesses and intended to exploit them. In turn, Runa's assailant turned her back on the sorceress and spun to engage her brothers.

"Runa," Drazen huffed when the abomination jumped on his back, pounding him with her fists. "Make her stop."

"Stop her yourself," the sorceress shouted, dodging a slice of my doppelgänger's sword. "I've got problems of my own."

Purple energy glowed in Runa's palms. She clapped her hands, and suddenly, six of her stood before her attacker. Unlike the creature Idris made of sand, these were picture-perfect versions of the sorceress.

I scrubbed my eyes. Which of them did I defend?

All six of her images took a fighting stance, flicking their fingers. In unison, they taunted my replica, saying, "Bring it, bula-hole. Give me your best shot."

Just as confused as I was, my double chopped and hacked through the first mirage, then the second. The moment he prepared to slice into Runa Number Three, his head tumbled free of his body. Defeated, the fake Victor returned to its origins, that of a pile of sand.

Behind the mound of debris, Thorne Darkwing stood with a broad smile on his face.

"My ladies," he offered Runa and her projected selves a courtly bow, then darted away.

With another clap of her hands, the sorceress dissolved her illusion, leaving one of her. Well, one original and one composed of sand.

Manipulative bastard. It would take more than that for Thorne to weasel his way into the sorceress's good graces. I turned to her to confirm as much, only to find her smiling at the shifter's retreating form. Before I could remind her of where her loyalties lay, Kronk's hoarse bellow rang out.

"Runa, my sister. Forgive me," Kronk cried.

Across the ground, a sandy replica of Runa's head rolled before stopping at our feet.

The flesh and blood Runa gaped at me, swallowing with an audible gulp. "That is disturbing in so many ways."

"I had no choice." Kronk staggered to her side, wrapping her in a hug and hoisting her up.

She grunted in her brother's tight grip. "Forgiven."

"Release her, Kronk. Before you break her as well," I ordered.

The athos let go of his sister, dropping her to the ground where she wobbled before straightening.

"What do you think?" Drazen joined us, gesturing to his mirror-self, whose sandy proportions were now frozen in place. The heat of the infernus's flames had turned it to glass. "Quite the work of art, if I do say so myself. Maybe Idris will let me keep him."

"Fates forbid we have to deal with two of you," Runa snapped.

Around us, several of the competitors continued to struggle against their sandy selves. I noted quite a few had fallen in the battle.

Horns blared.

The signal, while a relief, also stirred a new wave of dread. It was time for the second phase of the trial. I heaved a growling sigh, muttering to my team, "Here we go. Be prepared for anything."

The king moved to the head of his pavilion, gesturing grandly. "Good people of Carcerem. First, our competitors faced the worst of our kind. Next, they will face the best." Again, the queen placed her hand on his shoulder. Golden light blasted from his raised palms. Fiery sparks nipped at my flesh as the king's power washed over me.

"What do you suppose he means by that?" Drazen asked, legs braced, ready to defend himself.

Before anyone could answer, the earth trembled. Along the outer wall of the arena were a dozen statues of Carcerem's fallen heroes. Their chiseled forms stood three stories high. Stone cracked like lightning striking overhead. The towering giants broke free of their bases. Their powerful bodies stormed into the pit.

Heavy footsteps trembled through the ground. Beside me, Drazen stared at the massive defenders, mouth gaping. "He's got to be kidding."

"Afraid not," Runa groaned.

"How the hell are we going to defeat giants made of rock?" the infernus asked.

"We don't," I said. "All we need to do is to stay alive until the clock counts down."

"Right." She nodded. "Keep moving. Don't get squished. This should be fun."

Contestants raced around the pit, screaming as the beasts pounded their way across the sand. One of the giants raised its mighty boot, slamming it down on a horned male who wasn't as fast as the others.

Gagging sounds parted Runa's lips, and her complexion turned pale. One giant in particular fixed his stony gaze on us. His marble lips curled. The earth shook as his charging strides threatened to knock us off our feet.

Kronk narrowed his eyes at the statue. "Isn't that—"

"Morpheus, champion of the Battle of Dorbron. Flark. Here he comes." Drazen set off with Kronk at his side.

Runa and I kept pace with her brothers. Clouds of dust kicked up from our pounding heels.

I peered back at our assailant. The towering hero raised the mighty sword he held, swinging it as though he swatted flies.

"Duck!" I shouted, and the four of us hit the sand. Just in time. Stone swept over our heads. The massive blade whistled as it sliced the air.

Before the giant could right himself, Drazen popped back on his feet, hands flared, menace in his expression. Fireballs launched from his palms, exploding in the monster's face.

Morpheus flinched, recoiling. Off balance, the giant lurched backward a step.

Bones crunched. Another contestant fell beneath the creature's enormous foot. Once he righted himself, he leveled his furious glare at the infernus.

"You angered him," Kronk stated the obvious.

"You think?" Drazen turned his frustration on his brother. "You think I angered him?"

"Guys?" Runa eyed the giant.

"If you shot fireballs up my nose, I too would be angry." Kronk folded his thick arms while the giant took a pounding step.

"Guys?" Runa repeated.

I clutched her forearm, pulling her away from the approaching giant.

"Like you had a better plan," Drazen sneered.

"Guys!" Runa shouted.

"Run, you fools!" I slung the sorceress over my shoulder.

"Victor, wait! What about my brothers?" Runa pounded my kidneys.

I ignored her concern. "Can't help them if you're dead." Nor would she be able to help me.

The squabbling siblings finally glanced up and blanched.

Smiling an evil grin, our giant opponent raised his leg, eager to smash Runa's kin.

We dove to safety as Morpheus's mighty foot slammed down.

"No," Runa cried out, peering at the cloud of dust behind us.

An image emerged from the sand, coughing and waving his hand. "Flark, that was close," Drazen said.

"Do you see Kronk?" Runa shouted.

I peered through the fading cloud, seeing nothing. I grimaced. Kronk was powerful but slow. It was possible he hadn't moved in time.

"Kronk?" Drazen turned a circle, panic in his tight expression. "Kronk!" he bellowed.

Morpheus snickered, his laughter booming throughout the arena.

Moisture gathered in Runa's eyes, and she lurched to her feet. "No. No. No. Not my brother," she screamed, a dark gleam mixing with her unshed tears. She stood before the former champion, hands raised, energy sparking in her palms. Before she could unleash whatever nightmare she'd conjured, the giant wobbled.

Peering down, the creature frowned. Cracks formed in the giant's boot, spreading across his arch. Thunder cracked, stone splitting like two icebergs colliding. Craggy fractures splintered the warrior's ankle, shooting up his calf. The beast threw back his head, roaring his fury at the sky.

"Look!" Runa pointed. Beneath the giant's shattering instep, two much smaller yet sturdy legs rose from the sand.

"It's Kronk!" Drazen jumped, punching the sky.

Hands pressed beneath the monster's wobbling foot, Kronk powered through his deadlift like Atlas with the world perched on his shoulders. With every inch he gained, more fractures shattered the giant's leg, racing up his thigh to his hip. I gaped at the athos's strength. I knew they were strong, but this was incredible.

Cheering voices permeated my shock. The arena went wild with the athos's achievement. "Kronk. Kronk. Kronk," they shouted, stomping the stands.

With a mighty heave, Kronk stood upright, legs braced, Morpheus's boot trapped in his grip. Then, with a final burst of strength, he shoved. Morpheus wobbled, flailing his arms.

Rearing back, Kronk slammed his powerful fist into the giant's fractured foot, and the splinters that had stopped at the giant's hip shot up his torso.

Great. Here we go again.

The stone giant was coming apart. Right on top of us.

Once more, I scooped Runa into my arms, barking at her brothers, "Out of the way!"

Chunks of broken granite rained down on our heads. Laying on the speed, I sprinted out of the path of the falling rubble. Near the edge of the pit, I skidded to a stop and set the sorceress on her feet, glancing over my shoulder at yet another cloud of dust.

As the cloud settled, an image materialized in the middle of the arena. Hands on his hips, glaring at the pile of rocks before him, was Kronk.

Seeming satisfied with his win, he spat on the debris, then dusted his hands.

The spectators went wild, tossing cups of ale, flowers, and lacy unmentionables into the pit.

Kronk gazed back at them with a bemused expression on his chiseled face. He fluttered a three-finger wave at his adoring fans.

Horns trumpeted, and my muscles tensed. Would it kill the king to give us a moment to breathe?

All around the arena, the stone giants froze, then broke into sparkling gold fragments. The king's power dissipated.

Again, bodies littered the floor of the pit. Some little more than greasy smudges.

Idris approached his podium, clapping in an exaggerated fashion. "Well done. Well done. I'm happy to tell you that after this last challenge, only twenty-three competitors remain. Sadly, only twelve may compete in the final trial."

Beside me, Runa shivered, her expression bleak. "Milani told me we'd started with one-hundred and seven."

"So far, our contestants faced both Carcerem's criminals and her heroes. Now, it only seems fair that they face Carcerem's people. After all, it is you, distinguished citizens, who are the backbone of our mighty kingdom. Therefore, it is you who will judge the contestants most worthy of competing in the final round tomorrow."

"What the hell does he mean?" Drazen glanced at Runa.

The sorceress bit her lip. "I don't know, but it doesn't sound—"

Golden bands clasped our arms and chests. The grip was tight enough to cut off our oxygen. My head pounded as my ribs creaked in Idris's magical grip. Around the arena, every competitor squirmed, trapped by the king's golden magic.

Idris held out his cupped hand like he squeeze the life from our bodies. As his arm lifted, we lifted as well. Beneath my feet, the sand disappeared. My incapacitated frame floated above the ground, rising high above the pit.

Runa's quiet whimper whipped my head in her direction. She and her brothers dangled above the sand. Violet eyes wide with terror, she peered at the circle of competitors.

"It is time to vote, good citizens. Today, each of you will be judge, jury, and executioner." Golden light illuminated a muscular female with blood spatters on her furious face. "Gaze upon this fierce competitor and tell me. Does she live to see the final challenge? After all you have seen, is she worthy of fighting for the realm's forgiveness? Or does she die, right here, right now, a deserving recipient of Carcerem's justice?"

At this, the crowd went wild. Booing and cheers filled the stadium. Many held their thumbs up while most stabbed theirs down, chanting for the woman's death. Above us, a magical counter shimmered into view, tallying the votes.

It was barbaric. After all that we'd been through, the king

would let the citizens decide our fate? Nothing about Idris led me to believe he was a *fair* ruler who cared about the opinions of others. To him, this was merely part of the game he played. A roll of the dice to see who would make it to the next round. I had little doubt he'd rigged the outcome and placed a hefty sum on the winner of this particular challenge. Hell, I would.

"Oh, too bad," Idris said, tone laden with false sympathy. "Looks like this champion has reached the end of her journey."

In grand fashion, Idris spread his arms wide, then slammed his palms together. Golden light exploded, the fiery sparks nipping at my flesh. The woman uttered an agonized roar, and the band surrounding her detonated. Blood sprayed. The contestants nearest to her were blasted with a mixture of gore and rendered flesh.

Runa made gagging noises. I swallowed the bile burning my throat. It was a brutal way to go, even by my standards.

"Next!" Idris declared cheerfully, enjoying his demonstration of sadistic power.

I'd known and supported some bloodthirsty kings in my time. Idris threatened to outshine all of them. I didn't believe a being was born good or evil. Most were shaped by their circumstances and driven by their needs. This false king could be the exception.

The next five contestants raced by. Two of them, the crowd embraced. Thorne Blackwing was among the few who passed. Three met a gruesome end.

Sweat dampened my palms. My bandits were next.

Golden light illuminated the athos's stony expression. Despite the circumstances, he faced the threat with his chin raised. He stared out at the audience, daring them to murder him.

Fortunately, after Kronk's skillful display with the giant statue, he was a crowd favorite and passed with little issue. Drazen as well. Lucky for him, there were a number of ladies in the audience who found his posturing attractive.

"One spot left, and yet we have two competitors," Idris drawled.

My heart leaped into my throat, wrestling with the bile I struggled to keep down. The air thickened, pressing against my chest like an iron vice.

Only Runa and I remained.

Kronk and Drazen thrashed in their bindings, calling their sister's name. Their voices were raw with desperation.

"Blessed goddess, hear my prayer," Runa whispered, bowing her head. Confessing her sins? Praying it was me that Carcerem murdered? The tremor in her voice unsettled me, threading through my veins like poison.

Then that damned golden light shone down on my head, and I froze. Runa glowed as well.

"What's it going to be, dear citizens?" Idris chuckled, savoring the moment, relishing the control he wielded over our lives.

"The sorceress…" Runa's golden beam flared brighter, her expression stark in the blinding light. The bitter smell of her terror wafted in the breeze, fracturing my insides and waking something primal inside of me. It stretched and strained that feral part of me I usually denied. It clawed at my sternum, desperate to be released. *Protect her.*

"Or the leech…" The king's energy surged, a searing presence pressing down on me.

I struggled to breathe. This heavy, useless feeling at my center. It was worse than when I'd faced the Council in the mortal world. Again, I was restrained, powerless while others held my fate in their hands. Except this time, I wasn't alone, having more than myself to worry about. Instead of rage, there was a tightness in my chest, a jagged sensation in my gut. An emotion I hadn't experienced in centuries.

Fear.

I glanced at the woman next to me, and the sensation sharpened, twisting into something unbearable. The realization struck like a crack of lightning, splitting my world in two. I wasn't afraid for my own welfare. I feared for Runa's.

It was the first time I could recall truly caring about someone else's survival other than my own. An experience I loathed—a weakness I couldn't afford. And yet, I had no choice. The damage was done the moment this fierce sorceress crashed into my life. Even then, our heartbeats had aligned. And I...

I was the fool who'd ignored it.

Who'd denied fate's irresistible call.

There were some who spent their entire existence hunting for the gift I'd been handed.

Handed and rejected.

I closed my eyes and strained my ears, the piercing roar of the crowd slashing my sensitive eardrums. Icepicks stabbed my brain. And yet no amount of pain could dissuade me from pinpointing the one sound I craved. The pounding rhythm that called to me above all others. Runa's racing heartbeat reached my ears, frantic and uneven.

My own pulse pounded in kind. A sledgehammer knocked at my chest. Every beat threatened to crack me open and spill my innards upon the sand for all to see. Faster. *Faster* it hammered, sprinting to a quicker pace.

And then, as Idris's revolting screen projected what should have been a private, sacred moment between two eternal souls above our heads for all to see—I heard it.

I heard it!

The perfect synchrony of our pulses. Two beats, one rhythm.

Duo corda, amor unus, semper. Two hearts, one love, forever.

I'd lived almost a thousand years and never expected to find the one female who was meant to be mine—and mine alone.

The fates had decided, and their cruelty knew no bounds.

Runa Starborn was my mate.

A sardonic laugh rattled my chest, an edge of hysteria clawing at its surface. Of course, she was my mate. Only destiny could be this merciless, binding me to someone moments before we were separated for all of eternity. Given the path my life had taken to date, it should come to no surprise that I would find my mate while the blade of a guillotine's blade pressed against our throats.

No longer could I deny the truth. No more ignoring how my instincts screamed that the sorceress was *mine*.

"Runa," I wheezed, the name sacred on my tongue.

My mate peered at me, resignation dulling the fire that I admired so much in her lavender eyes. "I am the thief and you the clever leader."

"No," I growled. She believed she was about to die.

Tears wet her eye lashes, trailing down her cheeks. "Promise you will watch over my brothers."

"Runa, I cannot—"

"Then lie and make me believe you," she demanded, jaw tightening, voice steely even as it wavered. "So that my soul may rest."

"I swear," I said, and she exhaled, as if surrendering, until I added, "I swear, should Idris end you, I will place his severed head on a pike. *Then* your soul will rest."

A startled laugh burst from her lips, tears dripping off her chin. "Not what I requested, but I almost believed it."

As she should. I meant every word. This beautiful, courageous woman didn't deserve to die in this manner.

Above us, the magical screen flickered. The ticking numbers settled on their final count, deciding our fates.

"Very well, Carcerem. It appears we have a winner," Idris boomed.

The crowd roared, but I avoided looking at the totals.

"Victor Custodis, welcome to the final round."

186

The cheers rang hollow in my ears. Darkness splintered my psyche. Cracks formed.

It was a cruel and brilliant game the king played. Even though I'd won, I'd lost. Like Runa's brothers, I wanted to shout, curse, and thrash. None of that would help Runa in her final moments.

Instead, I met her eyes. She'd not go through this alone. I wouldn't look away, no matter how difficult it would be to watch my mate slaughtered.

"I'm with you, pet," I murmured in my most soothing voice.

"Runa!" the sorceress's brothers roared their anguish.

I resisted the urge to bellow my shouts of outrage, adding my pain to theirs. Runa needed me, and I would not falter.

Beneath the confusion, another sound emerged.

Across the circle, a scaled demon sputtered and gagged. I darted a quick glance in his direction. Blood leaked from his eyes, nose, and mouth. Blisters, like tiny, agonizing bubbles, erupted on his green skin, as if he boiled from the inside out.

Was he dying? My pulse skipped. Hope teetered on a razors edge. Every muscle, every cell strained with the possibility.

I'd never desired another's death with this level of intensity. Not even Tiberius Steele's.

"Help. Help me," the creature gurgled, then fell limp in his restraints.

Slime and excrement dripped from his decimated frame.

The demon was dead.

Gasps and cries echoed from the horrified audience.

Witnessing so much gore had never made me happier. Dare I hope it would change the outcome of the spectators' votes?

Idris glared at the demon's bloody corpse, golden sparks flashing in his eyes. Clearly, he didn't appreciate the unexpected disqualification of an approved champion. He spoke to someone over his shoulder, though there was nobody there. Muttered curses flew past his lips.

It wasn't the first time I'd noticed he conversed with shadows. Apparently, the false king was both evil and psychotic. A terrifying combination.

Once the king finished with his imaginary conversation, he turned back to the audience, a dark scowl of irritation creasing his face. "It seems one of our challengers no longer qualifies for the finals. Therefore, the sorceress may remain." He flitted a hand as if Runa's life meant nothing. "This trial is concluded. As a reward, the winners will attend a ball hosted by the queen and I this evening. Long live Carcerem."

With little fanfare, the bands restraining us dissolved. Twelve competitors plummeted to the ground. We hit the sand in undignified sprawls. Weak with relief, I collapsed, wrecked by the experience. Top was bottom, and bottom was top.

I gazed at Runa, fighting the urge to go to her. From the back of my head, a deeply ingrained voice whispered, *"Reveal no weakness."* Mates were a vulnerability. No one could know what the sorceress was to me. That knowledge would put both of us at risk. That darkest, most primal part of me refused to endanger my mate, much less myself.

I rose from the sand, locking my legs into place. Drazen, however, suffered no such qualms, racing to his sister and sweeping her into his arms. A low growl rattled my teeth at the sight of another male's arms around her.

Like a handful of survivors emerging from the wreckage of a storm, we stumbled through the pit, taking note of who'd fallen and staring at each other with dazed expressions of shock.

With Runa alive and well, I was uncertain how to proceed. Given our interactions, I suspected she didn't know we were mates. Nor did I have any knowledge about how sorceresses formed eternal bonds. I'd need time to process it all before figuring out how I'd handle the information. So much had happened in such a short period. It was overwhelming, even for me.

Chapter Twenty-One

RUNA

YARDS OF SHIMMERING fabric swathed my body from breast to ankle, the rich purple so dark it was almost black. Milani had worked tirelessly to prepare me for the survivors' ball.

Feathery sweeps of gold and bronze dusted my eyelids, making my natural lavender eye-color sparkle like gems. Glittering combs pinned my sleek curls away from my face, leaving the rest to tumble down my back—my *exposed* back. The elaborate gown was low enough to reveal the dimples above my hips.

Who was this woman staring at me from the gilded mirror?

Since the moment Idris's golden light blazed down upon my head, ordering the crowd to dictate whether I lived or died, I'd felt…different, changed by the experience, oddly hallow, and yet fulfilled by the life-and-death encounter.

As I eyed my reflection, it seemed as though I still played one of Idris's twisted games.

I raised my hand, and my doppelgänger raised hers as well.

It was me but *not me*.

Since the ill-fated span I'd captured a banished vampire,

nothing in my world had made sense. At times, it appeared that the events of the past few days were a curse. At others, it seemed they were fated.

Earlier, when Idris held my life in his hands, that sense of fate had grown stronger. In that moment, when death held me in her grasp, I prayed to the goddess, begging her to give me strength. Almost immediately, my fear had washed away, replaced by the feeling that, dead or alive, I was right where I was meant to be. That my existence was somehow tied to the vampire.

Strangely, while my brothers screamed, fearing for my life, it was Victor who'd helped ground me. In what I believed were my final moments, it was his gaze that I'd sought, his face I wanted to see.

Was it possible that fate brought us together for a reason?

What that reason was, I hadn't a clue. If only Yaga were here to help me figure it out.

I glanced at the opulent bedroom. All the finalists were given their own rooms. Likely to keep us from murdering each other in our sleep and ruining the king's fun. Like me, Yaga would have turned her nose up at the expense of the lush furs, ornate furnishings, and rich bedding. The cost of this room alone would feed White Bridge for many seasons. Seasons where, without the Blood River Bandits, many would starve.

Fury rose in my gut, and I spat on the priceless rug, grinding the toe of my sparkling sandal into the wet spot. These were the kind of riches my sister had sold her soul to obtain.

Unlike Raelynn, my only desire was to leave this place and care for my people.

I paced to the door and back, nibbling my thumb nail. The final trial was tomorrow. Traditionally, it was a fight to the death. The last one standing would win. Instead of traipsing around in finery, entertaining King Idris's court, we should be fighting our way out of this place.

If Thorne could be believed, all we needed to escape was the location of a hidden door. Custodis promised he'd uncover its location.

And yet, here we were, close enough to the end that deaths claws tickled my nape.

Tomorrow, I'd face my brothers in a life-or-death challenge where only one of us might walk away. Idris must know we would never harm each other. He'd likely have a contingency plan in place to give us no choice. Being forced to harm one of my brothers was a punishment worse than death.

Had I survived the trial this span only to watch my brothers fall?

If Custodis didn't come through, I'd need to take matters into my own hands. What that would entail, I wasn't sure. Just that under no circumstances would Idris take away my free will and force me to harm them. I'd sooner die.

Before the panic could rise to choke me, knocking sounded, locks tumbled, and a uniformed guard opened the door. "It's time," he commanded, his words slightly slurred.

He extended his hand to me. Twin punctures marked his wrist.

I arched a brow and met his blurry eyes. Catching my pointed look, he winced, snapping his hand down.

Interesting.

Six guards escorted me through several long hallways to a massive set of double doors.

Gentle music and the low murmur of voices traveled to my ears. I took a deep breath to soothe my trembling nerves. Surely, a royal ball couldn't be any more intimidating than facing an opponent on a battlefield.

Both doors swung open, and the guards made it clear I could either step into the room or have a dagger thrust into my back.

It wasn't a simple choice to make. The dagger held a certain appeal.

At my appearance, a booming voice announced my name. Heads swiveled, and dozens peered at me as though I were the prized lamb at the local fair. The gamblers measured my worth. I imagined their voices in my head. *How long will she survive in the challenge? Chances are she'll go first. What good is the gift of illusion in battle? She's sure to die. Terrible odds. No hope of winning.*

Bula-holes.

I sucked a tight breath, scanning the room, noting familiar faces. The other competitors were already here. I was the last to arrive. Last, but not least. I raised my head and stalked into the space like I was the baddest thing in a pair of strappy sandals to ever walk the realm.

I almost pulled it off until a striking male with sleek silver hair and determined gray eyes made me miss a step.

Custodis.

He cut a path through the crowd like an arrow launched from a bow. Target? Me.

Again, that sense of fate washed over me, along with a flush of self-awareness. My confident swagger faltered. I'd never been overly conscious of my appearance, dressing more for ease of movement than style. Even now, I couldn't care less what the royals thought. However, there was one opinion that mattered.

He stopped directly in front of me, motionless except for those predatory eyes of his that missed nothing. With a look, he consumed me, stole my image, locked it away, and held me prisoner with just his stare. And yet he said nothing.

He wasn't the only one speechless.

My hungry gaze took him in, committed his likeness to memory, and burned it into my psyche.

His smoky gray tunic was richly embroidered with metallic stitching. A perfect match for the unyielding glint in his eyes. The tailored fit accentuated his broad shoulders, lean physique, and powerful build. But it wasn't his clothes that demanded my attention, it was his stature. Victor Custodis had an air of lethal grace about him that no other male could imitate. Standing before him sent a chill rolling down my spine. But not one of fear, no, this was something else.

No one had made me feel like this in a very long time, if ever.

I clasped my hands, fighting the urge to fidget. "Don't just stand there. Say something."

"I have no words." His voice emerged on a rasping growl that twirled a spiral of warmth through me.

The Great Victor Custodis was speechless. This was simply too good to pass up. I offered him a coy glance from beneath my lashes, whispering, "Try."

In response, he claimed my hand, pressing a heated kiss to the inside of my wrist. Sparks shot along my nerve endings, and I shivered.

"Come." His grip tightened. "Dance with me."

Not waiting for my agreement, he dragged me into the mass of spinning bodies.

"I don't know how to waltz," I said to his back. Instead of the exuberant reel the villagers preferred, this aristocratic dance was stiff with intricate steps.

Ignoring my objection, he spun me into his arms, grasping my waist. "Follow my lead."

I snorted a sardonic huff. "Me? Follow you?"

With Custodis guiding me, we twirled across the dance floor. Look at that? I did know how to waltz.

Somehow, without breaking stride, he managed to draw me closer, pressing his mouth to my ear. Surely, now, he would compliment my appearance.

"I located the door," he whispered, sending a tingle down my arm.

Screw compliments. This was far better. "Then why don't you sound happy?"

"Because it isn't a door but a drainage tunnel, located in the pit beneath the sand. The grate sits in front of the king's pavilion. Like all the exits, it's locked and warded."

Disappointment had me tripping over my feet. Victor steadied me.

"But not guarded because it's completely exposed and impossible to reach." I exhaled a heavy sigh. "It will never work."

"I have an idea, but I'll need to speak with Thorne."

Our entire escape plan rested in the hands of a male who'd already betrayed us and a mysterious shifter with ulterior motives.

Too soon, the music ended with those around us bowing to their partners.

"All hail!" a deep voice boomed, and heads swiveled as the ballroom doors swished open in a dramatic fashion. "King Idris and Queen Raelynn."

Both the king and my sister made their grand entrance. Thorny crowns rest upon their heads, the gilded branches glimmering beneath the glowing chandeliers. Rich fabrics encrusted with costly crystals wrapped their lean frames. Priceless jewels circled Raelynn's neck, dripping from her earlobes.

So much waste. I turned my back to the spectacle.

Tomorrow, we would find a way to escape this place. We had a plan. Sort of. An impossibly difficult plan. Sure, we would likely die before we even got close to the hidden gate—but it would be a good death. A warrior's death. Monuments would be erected in our names. Okay, not monuments. More like minuscule trinkets farmers would hang from the tailgates of wagons.

Oblivious to my impending meltdown, Victor passed me a glass of something bubbly. Lady that I was, I downed it in three gulps.

Despite my spinning head, I noted the room had fallen quiet.

Fabulous. I was going deaf. I stuck a dainty finger in my ear and wiggled it.

"Runa," Victor murmured, a bite of warning in his tone.

I spun to find His Holy Royalness behind me. "Flark." I grasped my chest, cursing before I could stop myself.

Unaffected, King Idris passed my empty glass to the vampire, whose benign expression had turned to stone.

"Dance with me," Idris commanded, the same as Custodis had earlier.

Revulsion slinked up my arm where the false king touched me. The sensation was like snakes slithered along my shoulder and down my torso, where they coiled in my stomach.

This man was everything I hated most in this world.

I glanced around the room, searching for an escape, noting the locks on the doors, the windows too high to reach, and the guards in my path.

"Don't," Idris ordered. "Tonight, you are more beautiful than a thousand night-blooming flowers. I'd hate to see one hair on your fair head defiled."

I barked a laugh of hysteria at his silken words. Finally, I received the compliment I'd sought. It was a shame it was from a serpent, instead of my vampire lord.

Except, perhaps this was the break I'd been hoping for. Custodis wasn't the only one capable of uncovering secrets.

I met the vampire's steely gaze while speaking to the false king, saying with false cheer, "Why thank you, you your highness. I'd love to dance with you."

Idris guided me through a waltz with the same finesse Victor had moments ago. The weight of a hundred eyes bore down on me.

"Tell me, King Idris, do you often dance with convicted criminals?"

"Only the most attractive ones."

I summoned my most winsome smile, fluttering my lashes.

"I imagine you have something special planned for us tomorrow? You simply must tell me. I promise it will be our little secret."

Idris snorted. "Is that the best you can do? I confess I expected a little more seduction on your part before you attempted to manipulate secrets out of me. Looked forward to it, in fact."

I pursed my lips, huffing a disgruntled sigh. "Well, I do despise you. I suppose I'm just not as good at faking my attraction as my sister."

The false king grinned, flashing a neat row of perfectly white teeth. "And now you seek to enrage me. You should know I find your lack of subtlety quite amusing. What's next, begging and tears?"

Honestly, my plan was simply to keep him off balance and see what he revealed. Though I worried I didn't have the patience to pull it off. Espionage was far easier when I could rip those secrets right out an unsuspecting mind.

"Hardly," I pouted, rolling out my bottom lip. "Pain and torture were next on the agenda."

His bark of laughter raked my eardrums. "Pity. I would have enjoyed seeing you on your knees."

Now, it was my turn to miss a step. Disgusting bastard. In his dreams.

We glided past my sister, who stood among a group of fawning women, her angry glare shooting venom at me.

Idris followed the direction of my stare. "Your dear sister. She is unwell."

My head swiveled, detached from my body. If I was capable of such a feat, I imagined it would spin around on my shoulders. "And whose fault is that?" I snapped, failing to contain my temper.

His grip on my waist tightened. "You know she came with

me willingly. Sees me as her hero, in fact. As she should. After all, I saved her from a life of mediocrity."

The desire to draw blood bloomed across my senses, and my teeth sliced into my tongue. And so, I managed to say nothing while screaming inside.

In my silence, Idris continued, "I also wanted to save you that night. Except your mother's portal spirited you away from me."

Spirited me? My mother sacrificed herself to save me. Raelynn too. Only to have that gift stomped into the mud.

Immune to my turmoil, Idris asked, "You share your sister's ability to create portals, no?"

"I don't know." Though I suspected that I'd inherited the same ability from our mother. In truth, I'd never tested the depths of my darkest magic since it required a blood offering. It was a side of my gift I'd refused to experiment with, especially after losing my mother. Until Custodis offered me a deal.

Idris dipped his deceitful mouth to my ear, much as Victor had, only with a far different effect. "I could be your hero as well."

Was Raelynn unwell to the point he sought a replacement for her? Perhaps I was better at gathering information without my gift than I realized.

Despite my rolling emotions, I managed to keep my tone even. "At what price? Would you free my brothers?"

Instead of answering, he scoffed, his hot breath dusting my shoulder. "I noticed you didn't include the vampire in your concerns. Dare I pray there is hope for you and me?"

Before I could vomit on his overpriced shoes, the song ended. My sister's snarling visage swam in my vision. Wonderful. He'd managed to bring us directly to her.

"Look at the two of you together," Idris taunted. "Just like old times."

"Yes, old times." I didn't bother to hide my scowl.

Raelynn glared back at me. "Congratulations on surviving the trials."

An image flashed through my memory. One of blood gushing down Momma's dress and the portal open before us. My sister's refusal to escape with me. Her abandonment. My failure.

"To you, too," I choked out.

She canted her head. "How so? I certainly wasn't among the criminals cast into the pit."

I flicked a pointed glare at her blackened hands, the darkness spreading from forearm to shoulder. The price of her betrayal was displayed beneath her glittering ballgown. Her damaged flesh was proof she abused her power, taking more than the realm could bear to give—than her body could handle. Every time she aided Idris, she helped him to suck the life out of our world. How long would it be until it consumed her in return?

"Can you honestly look me in the eyes and claim not to have stolen that which doesn't belong to you?" I asked. "What would Momma say if she could see you now?"

Tension grew like eager weeds between us, unwelcome, binding, twisting—choking.

It was our mother who'd preached to us the importance of balance. Who taught us to regulate the ebb and flow of obsidian.

Raelynn's hands curled into claws. Outrage darkened her expression, energy crackling.

I thrust out my chin, welcoming her challenge. When we were younger, she used to easily take me in a tussle. But that was before I'd come into my powers. Before I'd grown and started training, riding, and thieving to provide for our people. All while she sat on her royal ass, watching them starve.

"Runa." Victor's voice pulled me from the trance. "You looked thirsty." He thrust another bubbling glass into my hand.

"Ah, the banished vampire leader, never far from our dear Runa's side," Idris finally spoke up as if his queen and I were not moments from throwing down. Then again, he'd probably enjoy such a spectacle.

Raelynn pursed her lips into a false impression of compassion. "Isn't that cute? The leech waits on her. I believe he's grown attached to the harlot. Who could blame him? After all, you saw the way she behaved in the tunnels."

Fire heated my cheeks.

Idris flushed as well, his golden eyes gleaming with a disturbing light. He scanned my figure, muttering in a roughened tone, "It was a titillating display."

"Disgusting, more like," Raelynn snorted.

"At least I didn't sell my soul for a crown." Before I could sink my claws into my sister's flesh, Victor pressed against my side. His firm grip circled my waist.

Raelynn puffed her chest. "Are you going to allow a common criminal to speak to me this way?"

Idris ignored her squawking, his focus remaining riveted on the vampire who'd tugged me slightly against him. Static sparked against my flesh where I leaned against Custodis, his palm hot against my stomach.

The king's eyes narrowed as if he'd felt it, too. "There's something different about you, vampire. Perhaps the challenges have done you good. Maybe you're more like the criminals than you believe."

"I suspect the air here agrees with me," Custodis answered in a tight tone. "That and the rigorous exercise."

Idris arched a dubious brow. "Your surname. Custodis. It doesn't ring any bells. Who are your parents?"

Victor stiffened against me. "I only knew my mother."

I studied the play between the two men, sirens ringing in my mind. Idris's sudden interest in the vampire didn't bode well for any of us.

"You're a bastard, then." Idris chuckled. "Oh, that's rich. You know, vampires hold little power here. That's why so many fled to the mortal realm like cockroaches running from the light."

Victor's rage was such that heat radiated from him, searing me through the thin material of my dress.

"Haven't you heard?" Victor said with tightened lips. "It's beings like cockroaches who thrive in the dark. It would be foolish to underestimate such a creature."

"I must admit, I was surprised to see you perform so well in the trials. Even the spectators have taken a liking to you. You've become quite the crowd favorite. I can't fathom why, given that you lack the gifts the others possess. And yet…there's something about you."

Idris leaned in, scrutinizing Victor with an unsettling intensity as if sheer focus could unravel his secrets. As if, by staring hard enough, he might glimpse the truth hidden beneath—the very truth we were desperate to conceal. Our plan to escape.

"It's almost as if the gods are on your side. One might say you succeeded through divine intervention."

What was Idris talking about? Did he think to accuse Victor of cheating?

"I assure you." Victor snorted. "The gods are no friends of mine."

"Where did you say you were from?"

Shouts rang out.

"Out of the way, you stupid bastard."

"Who are you calling stupid, you sack of bula dung?"

Glass shattered.

I gasped, glancing toward the brawl. "Is that—"

"Drazen and Thorne." Victor bowed to the king. "Please excuse us, your highness. There's a matter that requires our attention."

Guards rushed to protect the royal couple, preventing Idris from asking further questions.

Victor towed me along with him, leading me away from the

king. Across the room, a soldier dragged Thorne to his feet. The mysterious shifter met my panicked stare with a flirtatious wink.

My alarm turned to admiration, a smile playing at my lips. It was his timely diversion that freed us from Idris's crosshairs.

Well played.

Noting my appreciation, Victor snorted a disgruntled huff. "Anyone can pick a fight."

"Yes, but there are few who do it with such style." I raised my drink to the shifter. I prayed he'd show the same consideration while helping us to open that hidden door tomorrow.

Chapter Twenty-Two

RUNA

DESPITE MY EXHAUSTION from both the trials and the party, sleep eluded me. The uncomfortable floor I slept on didn't help.

Something large thudded against my bedroom door, and I jolted.

"You'll keep walking if you know what's good for you," I shouted, clenching the vase that rested beside me. Locks tripped, and sloppy footsteps stumbled through the doorway of my quarters. Holding my breath, I peered beneath the bed frame. From my position at the backside of the bed where I lie between the bed and the wall, I made out a pair of linen-clad legs and bare feet.

Men's feet.

I braced for battle. Flarking guards. I knew I couldn't trust them. No way I was letting anyone catch me unaware again.

After the party ended, we'd been escorted back to our rooms. Milani had helped me undress, twittering on about how exciting it was to serve not one but two finalists in the trials. While her status among the brownies might have been elevated, mine hadn't improved. I was still a prisoner in Idris's castle, subject to both the king's and my sister's whims. Honestly, I trusted the guards not to stab me in my sleep more than my sister.

Wait a minute.

If my intruder was one of the guards, he'd still be in uniform. Fates save me if this was Idris invading my room.

I clutched the vase tighter. It was a pathetic weapon but all I could find in this useless space.

"Runa?" My name was a slurred, rasping whisper.

I struggled to place the voice. Idris wouldn't whisper in his own castle.

"Runa, are you awake?"

Is that...?

Again, I eyed the pale, dare I say, elegant feet.

Feet that haven't walked through the hillsides barefoot in quite some time. If ever.

My would-be attacker wobbled a step, then shuffled toward the bed. Earlier, I had placed pillows down the center so it would look as if I was asleep and unaware. While it was an amateur move, all I needed was a moment or two to prepare.

"Bloody hell. The chit sleeps like the dead," the intruder grumbled to himself, standing over fake Runa. "What if some deviant were to sneak into her room while she slept?"

What if?

"And yet she's shown zero appreciation for my protection. What would she have done without me?"

Custodis. It was definitely Custodis.

I lurched from my hiding spot, vase held aloft. "She'd have done just fine. Better in fact."

"*Bah!*" The vampire reared back, losing his balance before he disappeared.

"Oh, fates," I gasped, scrambling across the mattress, laying on my stomach to peer over the other side.

It was there I found the mighty Victor Custodis sprawled on the floor, his brow lined with confusion.

"What is wrong with you?" I snarled down at him in a harsh whisper. "Are you trying to wake everyone in the palace?"

"You know, you're quite attractive from this angle," he slurred, peering up at me with glassy eyes. "Lovely, in fact. Then again, you're lovely in everything. Even those burlap tunics they made us wear. Did I tell you how beautiful you looked tonight? Most beautiful woman I've ever seen."

Now I get the compliment? "Are you drunk?" Could vampires get drunk?

"Most definitely." He struggled to his feet, wobbling at my bedside.

I sat back on my heels, mouth gaping. "How?" He hadn't drunk that much alcohol at the party. Seeing as how he was a vampire, I imagined it would take an entire cask to get him this inebriated.

He scratched his chest. *His delightfully bare chest.*

Goddess save me. Where were his clothes? The uptight aristocrat had come to me half-dressed in little but thin linen pants.

Damn the bastard, but drunk looked good on him. The glow of the twin moons shone through the window, casting his lean body into perfect shadow. Every contour of his chiseled torso was on display. May the fates strike me down, but I could swear he'd grown larger since we'd first met. His carved and elegant muscle was now bulkier, growing more defined. No way was he hiding all of this under his fine suit when he'd arrived. Whatever Carcerem was doing to him, I was here for it.

"I did it for you, my treasure."

I scrubbed a hand down my face, clearing the fog. Despite the tingles his words evoked, I asked, "By any chance did you hit your head when you fell?"

He performed an awkward twist and flopped into bed beside

me. I peered down at him, and he stared back. Gold flecks twinkled in his glowing eyes.

I didn't care what he claimed. This color was unnatural for a vampire. Despite the torques we wore, energy practically sparked off his skin.

"Did what for me?" I leaned closer.

"Drank them, peddling my venom."

I stiffened. "Drank whom?" Did he dare visit me after gorging himself on his whores?

"The guards." He sighed. "All of them. Yours and mine. In all my years, I've never consumed so much blood in one sitting."

By the goddess, he really was intoxicated. I flopped onto the bed beside him.

"Why?" I dared to ask.

"Because my instincts demanded that I remain at your side tonight," he growled, disgruntled at the admission.

My pulse skipped. Next question a bit breathier, I repeated, "Why?"

"Because I've never needed anyone as much as I need you."

Oxygen seized in my lungs. Nobody had ever said anything quite so moving to me. The vampire was full of surprises tonight.

While I suffocated on the emotion, he stirred, frowning at the ceiling. "After all, you're the only one who can help me regain all I've lost."

"*Puh.*" I release the breath I'd held, my exhale punching from my throat. Bastard. My heart shrank beneath the weight of his words.

"Before coming to you, I also paid Thorne a visit."

"Lucky Thorne," I huffed.

"Together, we formulated a plan. Tomorrow, when the torques deactivate, you will create an illusion to hide our activities while Kronk removes the sand covering the hidden passage and Thorne unlocks the grate with his enchanted key. He claims to have someone on the outside ready to assist us."

Hopefully, Thorne was sober for this conversation. "And what of the trials?"

"While the three of you work on our escape, Drazen and I will provide protection from whatever it is that Idris unleashes upon us."

"You intend to take on the other challengers—and who knows what Idris sends our way—with just Drazen at your side?"

He stiffened beside me. "You think I can't?

Goddess, save me from males and their egos. "I guess it doesn't matter what I think since it's the only plan we have."

Silence stretched between us. My late-night visitor fell quiet, staring at the ceiling. Apparently, he'd gone to all the trouble of sneaking into my room simply to protect his investment. Because all I was to him was a means to an end. I, too, stared at the ceiling as I pondered the bigger question. Was that all that he was to *me*?

My mind flipped back to the span we met. The span I'd tossed him to the ground to save him from the gallspawn. For a second, as I rested on top of him, there had been a moment. A spark that exploded between us. The sensation had felt important. At the time, I'd blown it off, believing it was the fates at work, putting me on the path that would protect us from Vex while providing for White Bridge. Which obviously wasn't the case.

He turned to his side, propping his head on his hand. Silver hair spilled over his shoulders, his steely eyes sparking with gold. His winter-green fragrance enveloped me, clouding my senses. I stared back at him, spellbound.

Touch feather-light, he trailed a finger along my temple and jaw, then brushed his thumb over my lips. My lungs swelled. My heart raced. Then, those teasing fingers drifted lower, over my collar bone, and along the thin strap of the silken nightshift I wore, teasing the outside of my breast, causing my nipple to pearl.

"You're so beautiful like this."

"Like what?" I gasped.

"Soft."

Soft? As in weak?

I pursed my lips, and he followed the action, mesmerized. "What do you m—"

Victor crashed his mouth into mine. At first, I was too stunned to react and then...

Then.

Sparks exploded inside of me, and I kissed him back, applying pressure of my own. At my response, a throaty moan rumbled in the back of his throat. Gone was the uptight leader I'd known. In his place was a passionate, hungry male who kissed me like he was drowning, and I was the only thing keeping him alive.

My brain floating in a haze, I hardly noticed when he moved, pinning me beneath him. His hips settled between my thighs. The warmth of his bare chest seared me through the thin material of my shift. Very little separated us. Needing to touch him, I skimmed my hands down the flexing muscles of his shoulders.

Hot and minty, his tongue teased the seam of my lips, and I opened, eager for a taste of him. The kiss deepened, and my mind emptied. The only thought left, one of *more.* In that moment, we were no longer captives of a mad king, but two people consumed with each other.

He snaked his fingers into my hair and tugged, breaking our kiss. "What sort of spell are you working, sorceress?"

Panting, I peered up at him in confusion. "Spell?"

"I feel..." He squeezed his eyes closed, and when he opened them again, two golden orbs glared back at me. "I feel raw, fractured..."

"Out of control?"

"Yes," he hissed.

"Same," I whispered.

While I was no scholar, I knew the threat of certain death was known to evoke strong emotions in people. Desperation being one of those emotions. Tonight, I ached to share a sense of connection with someone—to know I wouldn't be alone as I faced the gallows. The desperate need to feel *good*.

I dragged my foot up his calf. "Question is, what do you plan to do about it?"

His golden eyes brightened, scanning my body. "What would you like me to do?"

"Touch me." I arched my back.

He dragged a hand across my shoulder, sliding down the strap of my gown, baring me to his hungry gaze.

"Where shall I touch you?" he asked, blowing a hot breath over my eager nipple.

"My breast," I groaned, squirming in his grip.

His glowing eyes darkened with something undefinable. "Beg me," he demanded with a flash of fangs.

Anticipation scratched beneath my heated skin. Irritating bastard. I should have known he'd be commanding in bed.

"Please, Victor. Please touch my breasts." My plea emerged on a rasping exhale.

As if he couldn't wait, he didn't waste time with a reply. Instead, he plumped my flesh, his mouth descending to my stiffened peak.

"Yes," I purred as the heat of his tongue laved my aching nipple—swirled, stroked, leaving me panting.

Warmth flooded my core, and I rocked my hips, delighted by the hardened shaft that pressed between my thighs.

He groaned, grabbing my hip. "Be still, pet. Or you may incite more than you bargained for."

The vampire's command had the opposite effect. An image of our naked, writhing bodies flooded me with heat.

Tonight, something had come over me. Perhaps it was the pull of Carcerem's twin moons drawing together. Sane Runa should have punched him the second he kissed me and thrown him out of my room. Crazy Runa was throwing caution to the wind, as well as her common sense. Why not? Tomorrow, we'd face impossible odds against a ruthless opponent. Tomorrow could very well be our last. But tonight...

Tonight, we'd live.

Chapter Twenty-Three

VICTOR

"I DON'T WANT to stop. I want all of you, just this once," the enchantress beneath me admitted. While I hadn't figured out what finding my fated mate meant to me, I didn't see any harm in exploring our mutual attraction.

The vision of Runa with her nipples pearled, arms over her head, eyes glistening with need, stirred something primal.

My head swam, my brain floating in a red haze. I'd never felt this befuddled. Was it her or the copious amount of blood I'd consumed?

No, something deep inside of me urged. It wasn't the blood.

It was something better.

Darker.

Stronger.

It was the sorceress who was intoxicating.

Energy ignited in my veins, energizing my tired body. At my center, a primal instinct prowled beneath my skin. It pushed at the barrier of my psyche, trying to break free. Anticipation pounded.

I drew a deep breath. Runa's scent filled my senses, the rich flavor of her desire caressing my tongue. My captive peered back at me, her lavender eyes sparking with need and a touch of apprehension.

Good, she should be wary. For some reason, centuries of self-control had flown out the window tonight.

I squeezed my eyes closed and shook my head. Clarity escaped me.

There was a reason I should put distance between us.

What it was, I couldn't recall.

Nor did I care.

From the moment I'd laid eyes on the daring female, I'd found her fascinating. Sparring with her, matching wits, fighting at her side, I realized I'd not enjoyed the company of another this much in decades. Though half the time, I considered her infuriating.

Tonight, I'd noted the interest on Idris's face. Worried he'd take advantage, I'd come here, driven by an urge to protect her from any who dared to knock on her door. With her beneath me, that urge had become a hunger. A hunger that drove me to consume.

"One night," I answered. Yes, I was a noble leader on a quest of immense importance. But I was still a man. Surely, I could allow myself this singular indulgence.

"Just one." She held up a finger. "Then after, we pretend this never happened."

I smirked. "If you think you can give me up after one night."

"Silly vampire," she scoffed. "I'll have forgotten your name by morning."

"Perhaps, but the whole castle will remember the way you screamed it," I countered, my blood-drunk brain clearing by the minute, my focus turning to something I desired more.

"Show me," she said, dragging her slim hands over her

tempting breasts before her lusty expression turned serious. "Tonight, I don't want to think. Just feel."

"Arms above your head," I commanded.

She narrowed her eyes at me, a flash of defiance in her lusty gaze.

"Now," I growled, and slowly, she complied.

"Good, now don't move them."

"Or what?" She nibbled her plump lip.

"I'll punish you."

Her indrawn breath indicated she didn't hate the idea.

The women I'd laid with in the past were elegant, simpering creatures. Quite often, they wanted something from me, and I from them. Their every gesture was controlled, contrived.

My little thief was none of these things. She was like a wildling I'd captured and now attempted to tame. Which of us would be the first to submit was yet to be seen.

I claimed her mouth, kissing her until we were both breathless, then trailed a path to her jaw. Tasting, teasing, I followed the graceful column of her neck and down once more to her exposed breast. There, I tormented the stiffened peak until she writhed in my grasp.

I glided my hand down her arm, taking the strap of her gown with me, and raking the material down to her waist.

"Lift," I ordered, dragging her garment down her hips. I tossed the fabric onto the floor, withdrawing so I could admire my handiwork.

The sorceress was a sensual goddess. Full breasts with dusky nipples, a narrow waist, and rounded hips. Her legs were toned from days spent riding. Thin scars marked parts of her body. Injuries, no doubt she'd received while pursuing a life of crime. Again, I was reminded this wasn't a polished socialite who lay before me.

"Custodis." She squirmed beneath my predatory gaze, reaching for me.

"Arms," I snapped, and she uttered a groan of frustration. Cock straining the front of my thin pants, I lay beside her. Starting at her shoulder, I painted her flesh with my fingertips, stopping when I grazed a scar in her ribs.

"Where did you get this?"

"Broken window."

One she'd likely smashed and used for her escape. "And this?" I grazed another.

She frowned, growling, "When you claimed I'd scream your name, I didn't think you meant in frustration."

I fought a grin. "You cannot blame a connoisseur for pausing to admire a masterpiece."

At my honeyed words, she rolled her eyes. "In case you haven't noticed, I'm a sure thing. No need for wooing."

"Very well." It's all the warning I gave before grabbing her and rolling her on top of me.

She straddled my hips, disheveled hair tumbling over her full breasts, a bemused expression on her face.

"Think you can do better?" I challenged.

"Most certainly." She bit her lip, her eyes darkening with a determination that had my manhood twitching.

She ran her scorching palms down my chest, and I held back a groan. I'd not allowed anyone to touch me in such a way in eons, refusing to give up control. With Runa, though, I couldn't resist giving her free rein of my body, curious to see what she would do. Since we'd become allies, there had been an unspoken tension between us, both of us battling to determine who would lead our ragtag team.

At my restrained response, an evil light glimmered in her violet eyes, and she tried again. Only this time, it was her nails that raked my flesh, the burn a perfect mix of pain and pleasure. My pectorals jumped beneath her ministrations. She smirked, hooking her fingers into the waist of my thin pants.

There, she stilled, canting her head at me in question, and I nodded. At my agreement, she dragged the pants down my hips and tossed them away. Biting her plump lip again, she stared at my eager cock.

"Why, Lord Custodis, I believe you've been holding out on me."

"I have been told that I'm a spectacular specimen of the vampire race."

"And humble to boot," she scoffed.

I snagged her wrist and placed her heated palm over my aching shaft. "You disagree?" I asked on an exhale.

When I released her hand, Runa stroked my length from base to tip.

"It will do."

I couldn't keep the groan from escaping my throat. The sorceress had magical hands.

She angled her body over me, her full breasts grazing my chest while her talented palm continued to stroke, and I was nearly undone.

Exhaling a growl, I cupped her head and smashed my mouth into her lips. My little thief opened, allowing me entrance, and our tongues battled, fighting for dominance. Pain pierced my bottom lip. The metallic flavor of my own blood danced along my palate, igniting a fire in my veins. The little minx had bitten me.

Despite the tangled locks I clenched in my fingers, Runa shoved free, breaking the kiss. "Now, now, vampire. You said it was my turn."

Before I could growl an objection, she slid down my torso, tasting, licking, nipping. When she gripped my hips, peering up, my breath lodged beneath my ribs.

"Eyes on me," she commanded before her pink tongue darted out, laving my manhood like a carnival treat.

My lids grew heavy, and I struggled to keep my eyes from rolling back in my head. "You fight dirty, pet," I groaned as her mouth closed around me. I didn't dare to look away for fear she'd stop.

Gods, but the sight of her plump lips sliding on my cock threatened to drive me mad. "Runa," I grated.

"Hmm?" she hummed, and the vibration combined with her talented mouth nearly caused me to lose control.

"Runa," I tried again. Damn her, but she added a twist of her tongue that had me seeing stars.

"Runa!" I fisted her hair, and she finally released me, gliding up my body to straddle my hips.

She ground her slick folds against my throbbing shaft in retaliation and leaned in close, saying against my lips, "That's right, vampire. Scream my name."

"Little vixen."

She uttered a yelp as I rolled her beneath me.

"You'll pay for that."

She grinned. "I regret nothing."

I'd soon have her singing a new tune. "Is that so?" I caressed her from breast to thigh, then tugged her leg over my hip. My fingers skated through her slick folds, and she exhaled a soft moan.

"Did you enjoy toying with me?"

I circled her clitoris, and she threw her head back. "Hated it," she lied, causing me to thrust my fingers into her silken channel.

"Your body tells a different story." Feeling how wet she'd become while pleasuring me sent a current of heat through my straining cock. As she started to thrust against my hand, I pulled away.

"Vampire," she growled in annoyance.

"Victor," I demanded. "Tonight, you will use my given name. Say it again."

"Fine," she snapped. "Victor!"

"That's one." I crawled down her body and placed my shoulders between her thighs.

Seeing my intent, she ran her fingers through my hair. "Oh, yes. Please."

Rather than give her what she wanted, I nuzzled the inside of her leg, tonguing a pulsing vein I found there.

"Victor," she groaned, twisting her hips.

"Two," I muttered, then devoured her sweet sex like a blasphemous man with his salvation.

"Oh!" she cried out. "Flarking hell." Her hands fisted the sheets beside her hips, her lithe body tensing in my hungry hold. "By the goddess, that's brilliant," she cried.

I growled low, keeping her prisoner and refusing to release her until she gave me what I was after.

"I'm close." Her hips rock, her head thrashing on the pillow. Finally, she exploded against my tongue, her sex pulsing. "Victor!" she shouted, her back arching off the mattress.

Satisfaction rolled over me. "Three." I smirked, admiring her sex-drunk expression. My sorceress peered back at me with glazed eyes. Realization dawned in her expression, and she huffed a laugh.

"Told you you'd scream my name."

"Not fair," she whined.

"Not to worry, pet. We're just getting started."

RUNA

I should have known sex with Victor would be like nothing I'd ever experienced. No male had ever taken the time to savor me if that is what this could be called.

Most of my experiences—when I succeeded in ditching my meddlesome brothers—were hot, heavy, and over before they'd started.

Being with the vampire was nothing like that. Even now, he challenged me.

Goddess, save me, but he had that gleam in his eyes again.

I reached for his beautiful shaft once more. His hard length glided through my hand. The groan he exhaled drew my lips into a smile. Power flooded my veins. The idea that I'd managed to stir the vampire's primal side sent a delightful tingle through me. It was I, Runa Starborn, thief, rebel, convict, who'd managed to get under the Great Victor Custodis's skin.

He grabbed my hand and kissed the inside of my wrist. The hot caress of his tongue shot tingles up my arm.

"Playtime is over, pet. Be a good girl and do as you're told."

"Afraid I'll unman you with a simple touch?"

"Little thief, there is nothing simple about you," he grated. "Arms over your head."

"Yes, oh, bossy one." I rested my hands over my head, arching my spine. After all, my breasts were rather spectacular, if I did say so myself.

Victor grunted in answer, his eyes devouring me. "Now, spread your legs."

Trembling with anticipation, I did as he commanded. "Like this?"

His hum of appreciation raised goosebumps along my flesh. "You truly are a beauty."

The way he looked at me, I felt beautiful, desired. Spread before him like a sacrifice, I trembled. What would he do next?

"Touch yourself. Like you did before in the cavern."

"What? Now?" My cheeks heated.

"Now," he purred. "Unless you're not up to the task."

I growled low at the challenge in his tone. Was the male trying to drive me mad?

I'd soon show him which of us was stronger.

"As you wish." I trailed my hands down my chest, pausing a moment to tease and twist my nipples. Pleasure coursed through me at the contact, and I groaned. To my delight, Victor watched my every move, his golden gaze riveted to my every action.

"You know," I taunted, "I always say, if you want something done right…" I danced my fingers along my stomach, then over my jutting hip bones.

"Do it, Runa. Touch yourself for me," Victor said in a broken voice. Every muscle in his body was carved of stone. He seemed frozen in anticipation, his posture that of a predator ready to strike. A chill danced down my spine.

I wanted him to break. To give up his rigid control. For me.

"Like this?" I grazed my fingers over my mound, gasping as my over-sensitive flesh swelled.

"Yes," he groaned. "Now, stroke your clitoris." Resting on his side near my hip, he took his shaft into his hand, circling his fingers over his swollen head.

Distracted by the sight, I did as he ordered without thought. Anticipation tied me up in knots. Victor knew exactly what I wanted, and yet he refused to give it to me. The devil.

Eyes locked on my circling fingers, he bared his fangs, hissing, "Faster, pet."

His stroking fist moved faster as well. I panted, uttering a groan, and my hips began to rock.

"Tell me. Are you close?"

"So close," I panted.

"Don't you dare come," he snapped.

"Ugh! No more games." My sex pulsed, my will eager to break before his. "End this."

"Beg," he growled.

"Curse you," I shouted, tossing my head, my body on the brink. "Please," I snapped.

"Please what?"

"Please, Victor, may I come?"

"No."

"What?" Tears burned my eyes. I couldn't take anymore.

In a blur of movement, he pinned me to the mattress, his delightful weight sinking into me. Thank the fates.

"You'll come on my shaft or not at all." His hand circled my neck below the torque.

I peered into his glowing eyes.

"Understood?" His scorching cock prodded my aching sex, and in that moment, I feared I'd have given him anything he demanded if he'd only ease me.

"Crystal clear." I rocked my hips, trying to take what he denied.

"So greedy," he groaned against my lips, and then finally…

Finally.

He thrust.

Lost to sensation, I threw back my head, crying out, "Yes!"

"Sweet sorceress, I warned you I'd make you scream. Fates save me, but you feel too good."

He thrust again, and his grip on my throat threatened to cut off my breath. "Tell me who owns you."

My brain floated in a lust-filled haze. Goddess, but I needed release!

"You," I rasp, and he thrust again.

"Louder," he ordered, hitting a spot deep inside of me that had my walls clenching.

"You. You own me."

As my reward, he struck a pounding rhythm. My breasts bounced, my mind spinning.

"Who?"

"Victor," I groaned.

"Scream it." His hips slammed into mine, our flesh slapping.

Stars spark in my vision. "Victor!" I exclaimed, my nails raking his flesh.

"Good girl. Now, come with me."

Lightning crackled through my nerve endings, and I

exploded. Sparks detonated. My entire body tensed, bowing off the mattress.

My vampire was out of control, thrusting wildly. I hooked my ankles around his back, savoring every stroke. My soul soared somewhere beyond my physical self. If this was the after-life, I didn't want to live. Starlight sparkled behind my eyes, and a brilliant flash burned through my eyelids. By the goddess, Victor had made me climax so hard he'd blinded me.

"You are mine."

Victor's roar rang in my ears, and I smiled, panting through the ripples of pleasure pounding my flesh. His hand on my throat turned scorching, his touch one of pleasure and pain. I loved every second of it.

Regrettably, I returned to my body.

Once I'd landed, I snorted a laugh, blinking my blurry eyes. "That was…"

I gave up. As he'd said to me at the ball, there were no words.

Despite my lack of vocabulary, Victor rolled on his side and pulled me close, tucking my face beneath his chin.

"I know," he stated, arrogance in his tone.

I could feel him smiling against my hair and prayed he didn't say something demeaning to ruin the moment.

Instead, he held me in a protective embrace. "Sleep, pet. I will keep the monsters at bay."

And I did, drifting to sleep.

Chapter Twenty-Four

RUNA

"I'M GOING TO KILL HIM," I muttered, glaring at the back of Victor's silver head. Oblivious to the daggers I stared at him, the vampire rode ahead of me in the bucket of a golden chariot. Once again, Idris paraded us about the pit, each contestant riding in their own magical, driverless chariot.

After my night with the vampire, I'd woken to an empty bed, which wasn't all that surprising. What shocked me were the burn marks on my sheets. Spread around me was a starburst of thin black lines. On closer inspection, I realized they were burns. As if one of us had literally detonated at some point. I had a vague memory of seeing sparks but never imagined it was *real*.

Victor had some explaining to do, especially since the bigger issue wasn't the sheets.

Horns blared, and confetti and streamers rained down on us. The chariots formed a tight circle, and we disembarked.

I stomped across the sand, coming to stand directly in front of him. Fists propped on my hips, I gestured to my throat and the shimmering handprint that marked my skin. There was no way he hadn't seen it, leaving me to deal with the consequences alone.

"Are we not going to talk about this?"

Custodis stared over my head. The only indication he'd heard me was the clenching of his jaw.

"This isn't the time."

"Not the time?" I screeched. "We're about to die. There may be no other time. You branded me."

"Not the time, Runa," he repeated in that disdainful voice I'd come to hate.

I slapped my hands on his chest. "Did you notice the burns on my sheets?" When he ignored me, I slapped him again. "You owe me an explanation. What the hell is going on? Did you know this would happen?" I pointed to my neck.

This time, he at least had the decency to glance in my direction. As the weight of his eyes slid over his mark on my flesh, something primal flashed in his gaze. Just as quickly, it disappeared behind that frigid mask he liked to wear.

"I did not," he intoned, his words so icy I wondered if I'd imagined that flash of emotion. "And lower your voice. There are no less than five thousand eyes and ears on us."

"Oh, *now* you want me to be quiet," I said through gritted teeth. Last night, he'd demanded I shout his name to the rafters. Today, I was the dirty little secret he didn't want revealed. Was bedding a criminal below the illustrious lord? Did I embarrass him? Despite the fact I knew I was a skilled thief and powerful sorceress, my heart still took a hit. Filthy bastard! I was the one with the reputation to uphold.

"What's wrong?" Drazen trotted over to my side. "Thorne told us the plan, and we need to be ready when the challenge starts." He frowned and glanced at me, then at Victor, before whipping his eyes back to me once more.

"What the..." He glanced back at Victor and snarled. "You did this?"

For some reason, he took Victor's blank stare as confirmation. "I'll flarking kill you!"

Drazen charged as the trumpets blasted. Sand shifted. The three of us whipped into the air. I dropped to my knees as my stomach sailed into my toes.

Beneath each of us was a semi-transparent, glowing disk. Each floating platform was the length of five paces. I held my arms out and carefully rose to my feet. Scattered throughout the pit, the other competitors floated on similar disks, like we were pieces on a game board.

Idris approached the front of his royal pavilion, a crown of branches gleaming on his silver-blond head. "Welcome, loyal citizens of the kingdom, to the final span of the Fallen Trials. First, our challengers faced Carcerem's land. Then her people. Today," he paused dramatically, "they will face her beasts."

A sudden, unsettling rumble made me whip my head around, my heart pounding in my chest. Yesterday, where there were massive statues, today, there were gigantic gates. Gears squeaked, the bars of the metal doors shuddered, and slowly, they lifted.

My issues with the vampire forgotten, I trembled at the sight of those massive cages opening. "Flark, but I have a bad feeling about this," I muttered under my breath.

"Good people, I present to you my beautiful menagerie," Idris boomed. "A rare and unusual collection that I've spent years assembling."

He rattled off the exotic names of his creatures as his "pets" emerged. One snarling monster at a time, Idris's beasts made their grand entrance. Some charged out of their cages only to be brought up short by the chains on their necks. I'd little faith the restraints would remain in place for long.

Most of Idris's pets I'd never heard of before due to their rarity. Regardless, each was more terrifying than the last. Every one of his enormous beasties had a combination of fangs, claws, spikes, and who knew what else. Goddess forbid the false king keep a collection of cuddly *cottonpelts*.

The swords each of us had strapped to our backs would be little protection against Idris's monstrosities.

"And last but not least, I present to you the prize of my collection."

Golden energy flashed in his palms. Beneath the royal pavilion, a massive gate materialized, this one larger than the rest. From the darkness, a pair of reptilian eyes took shape, framed by a coarse muzzle and a maw of bone-crushing teeth.

Ice scraped through my veins. No. It couldn't be. They were rumored to be extinct.

VICTOR

From beneath Idris's pavilion, a massive dragon prowled into view. Its inky emerald scales were so dark that they devoured the light, casting an eerie shimmer across its hulking form. Thick, corded muscles rippled beneath its hide, each movement exuding raw power. Its long neck curved with a predator's grace, leading to a set of massive jaws—engines of pure destruction, capable of tearing through stone and flesh alike. Towering over the battlefield, the beast was three times the size of any monster in Idris's collection.

It was both breathtaking and terrifying—a creature of legend, too rare, too magnificent to be shackled by the will of a madman.

I glanced at Runa to check her reaction. The wide-eyed expression of terror on her exotic face stirred something savage within me.

From the back of my skull, a presence snarled, *"Protect your mate."*

I woke this morning, having slept for what felt like minutes, with this *voice* inside of my mind. The voice, while it sounded like my own, was different, stronger—powerful.

It urged me to do incomprehensible things.

For starters, it had urged me to feed from Runa—to cover her with my seed and plant my youngling deep in her womb as if I'd already claimed her as my Bride.

Which I most certainly had not, despite sharing the most pleasurable encounter of my life with her.

When claiming a Bride, a traditional incantation was uttered, and blood was exchanged. Afterward, eternal fang marks branded a Bride's throat. The male, too, if he so desired.

Runa did not bear my fang marks. Thank the gods. Claiming a Bride, even if she was my fated mate, was the last thing I needed at the moment.

Still, it had taken every ounce of control I possessed to crawl out of our shared bed. It was then I noticed the scorched sheets and my shimmering handprint on her throat. A mark that had left me feeling, dare I say—possessive. While it was far from fang marks, I'd *enjoyed* the sight of my brand on her throat.

In that moment, I'd never felt so primal, like one of the lycans in my world that I'd often mocked for their lack of control.

Even now, the urge to grab Runa and slaughter any who opposed me hammered against my skull. My lack of focus only further proved how mates and relationships led to weakness. Right now, I couldn't afford to be vulnerable. Not when Idris held my life in his hands.

I steeled my resolve. Despite the appearance of the dragon, which currently sat on top of the grate we needed, our plan remained feasible. It *had* to be. Especially after all I'd done to prepare for our escape. Much to my detriment last night.

I tuned into Idris's blathering. The more I was around the male, the more I loathed him. Over the years, I'd supported many kings. This one did not deserve to sit on the throne of this kingdom. I sensed it in every part of my body. As Runa and the others claimed, he was the false king.

I shoved my tongue against the roof of my mouth, his voice making me want to claw my ears from my skull.

"*Kill him. Take what is yours,*" the voice hissed.

I shoved the murderous urge down. Idris's death was not on my agenda. I'd nothing to gain from freeing Carcerem. What did I care about those that had once scorned both me and my mother?

Unbidden, an image of my youth flashed through my mind. I crouched in a puddle where I'd fallen, hand pressed to my blackening eye. Neighborhood children threw rocks at me, chanting some horrid song about fatherless bastards. Their parents looked on, doing nothing while their children abused the son of the neighborhood whore.

Idris's voice pierced the image, and I shook my head to clear it. "This final challenge is a fight to the death. The last contestant standing will have earned Carcerem's forgiveness for their crimes."

Runa's sister placed her hand on the king's shoulder. Golden light flickered in the false king's palms, and the chains on his beasts dropped into the sand. All except for his prized dragon, the one creature who had wings.

I flexed my legs, ready for the moment our torques would deactivate. Beneath us, a dozen creatures licked their chops, eager to devour their next meal. With my alliance of five, that left seven contestants who would love nothing more than to end me. Intimidating odds—for someone with half my skill.

We'd stick to the plan. Runa could easily cast an illusion to distract the dragon while concealing our actions. Drazen and I would protect our allies while they used their gifts to open the grate.

With any luck, we'd be gone before Idris even realized we were missing.

Once more, Idris stepped to the edge of his pavilion. "Oh, and one other thing. Today, the competitors' torques will remain active. This final lesson is one of humility. A great number of these criminals believe themselves to be predators. Today, they will learn what it feels like to be prey." He smirked, glancing in my direction. "Let the trial begin."

Bloody bastard. Dread turned my heart to stone, plunging it into my stomach. This was a disaster. With the torques on, Kronk couldn't shift the sand, and Runa couldn't create a diversion. There was no possible way we could dig through several feet of sand to the grate without being slaughtered.

I dared to meet Runa's stark expression. Even if we managed to defeat the other competitors before Idris's beasts ripped us apart, only one of us would leave this place.

Mind racing, I reconsidered my strategy. One, there was no escaping. Two, my alliance was now worthless. With our plan gone to hell, Runa's brothers would kill me in a heartbeat. Three, the only way I'd survive was to outlive the competition. That included Runa.

This last part gave me pause.

Because I needed her.

For the portal. Yes. Except the portal was no good to me if I was dead.

"She is mine," the voice growled.

Silence!

My legs wobbled, the disk shifting beneath me. Caught in the grip of Idris's magic, the competitors sailed around the arena like stones skipping across water. Kronk drifted toward me. Ruddy expression tinted green, he clamped a hand over his mouth. Apparently, sailing through the arena didn't agree with the athos. I could use that weakness to my advantage if I struck quickly.

It was him or me. Conclusion?

Runa's brother had to die.

I braced to jump when my disk wobbled and tilted. My ass

struck the platform, and a sword whizzed over my head. Some bloody bastard had snuck up on me from behind. This was unacceptable.

I sprang to my feet and faced my attacker. Heavily muscled, the horned demon snarled, baring three rows of razor-sharp teeth.

"Do you kiss your mother with that mouth?" I taunted. The gibe was a classic I'd learned from watching my well-paid soldiers train. *Former* soldiers who'd quickly abandoned me when my assets were frozen.

"Kiss yours," the demon snarled and lunged.

I ducked beneath the arms he tried to sling around me and sliced my sword along his ribs.

The demon roared and nearly plunged off the side of the platform. The edge forced me to stop as well. As I recovered my balance, I discovered a new issue. The disk I stood upon sank beneath our combined weight.

Below us, in the sand, several of Idris's creatures had gathered. They smacked their lips, salivating and peering up at me. Any second, we'd be low enough for them to jump onto the platform.

The demon seemed to notice as well. He lunged, and I braced for impact instead of dodging. This time, I managed to tuck my shoulder, slam it into his gut, and hurl him over my head into the pit.

His high-pitched scream rang in my ears. Snarls and snapping followed, then gurgling.

At the violence, the crowd erupted. Their bloodthirsty cheers threatened to turn me deaf.

Before I could recover, the disk tilted, and I hit my knees. Behind me, two clawed feet gripped the rim of my platform. The horned creature struggled to get a grip, dangling several feet above the sand. It must have jumped. With its heavier weight on one end, the platform tilted dramatically. I struggled to find a handhold, finding nothing as I skidded on one hip.

Eager for its meal, the creature licked its bulbous lips and opened its massive jaws. Rows of serrated teeth waited eagerly to saw me into bite-sized morsels.

Not today, miscreant. I planted a foot on its upper and lower lips. Bracing myself above its gaping maw, I slashed my sword through one of its feet, severing the appendage. Screeching hit my ears. As the creature fell, I sprang back, propelling my body back to the center of the glowing platform.

With the monster gone, my disk floated higher, rising above the danger in the sand. I breathed a sigh. Though my relief was temporary.

Across the arena on a wobbling platform, I spotted Runa. The sorceress battled with a contestant with scaly skin and pointed ears. Their swords clanged. She seemed to be holding her own until a second attacker drifted closer.

"You idiot. No," I snarled. Already, Runa and her adversary had sunk halfway down. The added weight would put all of them on the ground.

Uncaring of the danger, the second competitor jumped. Runa's disk tilted, and the three of them plunged to certain death.

"Runa!" Kronk's bellow spun my head around in time to watch the athos jump off his platform. His massive form exploded against the sand, raising a cloud of dust.

"Kronk, you fool." Now, two members of my former alliance were in the pit.

I glanced from them to the swinging platforms nearby. No one on the ground could possibly survive. Letting them die would improve my odds. All I needed to do was to maintain my lofty position and wait for the others to fall as well.

Below, Runa's scream sank steely fingers into my chest. I clenched my jaw hard enough to crack my molars. *Don't look. You can't help her. Only one may survive.*

Another scream, and those fingers cracked my ribs apart and ripped out my heart.

I peered over the side.

Below me, Runa stumbled before righting herself. Four bloody claw marks scored her shoulder. Crouched before her was a creature that was part saber-tooth panther, part velociraptor. The sorceress backed away from her prowling attacker. I held my breath, surprised the beast had yet to pounce when a blast of heat and flame demanded my attention. Flark. That was why. While trying to escape the panther, Runa was now dangerously close to the dragon.

"Runa. Hang on. I'm coming!" This time, it was Drazen's bellow. He hit the sand before racing in her direction from the far side of the pit. He'd never make it in time. Where was Kronk? I searched and discovered he'd been intercepted by a crustacean-type creature with large pincers for hands.

Their sister would be dead before they reached her.

Once again, my disk shifted beneath me and sailed across the arena, stopping directly over the sorceress. What madness was this? It couldn't be a coincidence. I glanced over at the king. Idris smirked back and fluttered a two-finger wave. Bloody bastard.

It was a test. He was playing with me, curious to see how I would react. To see if I would come to her aid. No doubt, he'd wagered a vast number of coins on the outcome.

Chapter Twenty-Five

RUNA

MY ARMS SHOOK from fear and exhaustion. Pain seared my injured shoulder. The *duskcat* I faced was feline—ish. Its pointed ears pressed back against his blocky head. Black fur stood up in a threatening spike down its spine. Canines the size of my forearm protruded from its snarling lips. Green poison dripped from its razor-sharp whiskers. At the tip of its club-like tail was an assortment of spikes.

As I retreated, it advanced. My feet stumbled over something, and I nearly went down. The beast snapped, and I swung my sword, managing to slice its muzzle. It reared back, pawing its nose. Out of the corner of my eye, I spotted the thing that tripped me. One of my opponent's severed legs.

Bile painted the base of my tongue. Monster Kitty had caught the bastard the moment we'd fallen. Snatched him right out of the air. While I'd run for my life, the creature juggled the male, playing with its prey before ripping him apart.

A similar fate awaited me.

Curse Thorne and his stupid plan. We'd foolishly hung all

our hopes on a mysterious shifter and Victor's intel. Intel he'd gathered from criminals, assassins, and venom addicts. Now, it was too late to pivot. Our alliance was void. I had little doubt the selfish vampire lord would murder us all to gain his freedom—despite the incredible night we spent together. From span-one, he'd made it clear all he cared about was himself. Satisfaction flooded me that my death would strand him in Carcerem for eternity. Not that there was any guarantee he would survive.

I prayed one of my brothers would be the winner. Both were skilled fighters even without their gifts. If even one of them survived, perhaps my death would have meant something.

Arching his spine, Monster Kitty whipped out a massive paw, attempting to slice me in half. I twisted, flipped backward, and struck out with my sword. Two of the duskcat's claws landed in the sand, and the creature yowled, recoiling.

Ha! Score one for the chew toy. When Monster Kitty hesitated to attack, hope flickered inside of me. I bared my teeth, snarling, "That's right, furball. There's a lot more where that came from."

My feline nemesis glanced over my head with wide, dilated eyes. Hissing a screech of fury, the creature darted away.

One little injury and the bastard ran for his life.

"Go ahead, you hairball-hacking prick. Run away!" I shouted.

Hot, acrid wind blasted the back of my head, blowing purple tendrils over my shoulders.

Icy terror froze me in place.

Gulp. My harsh swallow echoed over the arena's magical sound amplifier. Shallow breaths rattled my chest, and I forced my feet to shuffle a circle in the sand.

Behind me, I faced a pair of large nostrils. Those nostrils rested above a terrifying maw filled with bone-crushing teeth. The teeth were set into a reptilian muzzle capable of swallowing me in one bite. Above the nostrils were a set of serpentine eyes, clouded white with the king's influence.

Idris's deep chuckle reached my ears just before the dragon reared back. At the base of its throat, a fiery light glowed. The reach of its flames would extend far beyond Drazen's. I'd never outrun the blast. There was no escape.

Fine then. If I was about to die, I wasn't going out as a coward.

I raised my chin and thumped the hilt of my sword against my breast, shouting, "Long live the rebellion. Down with the false king!"

The dragon opened its mouth. Flames flicked from the depths of his throat. The creature's hot breath heated my flesh.

I closed my eyes.

Goodbye, my brothers.

Hard muscle slammed into my body. Oxygen exploded from my lungs. The world spun, and I flew several feet before hitting the ground.

I blinked sand from my vision. Sucked a desperate breath. Flames rained down on my savior in a deluge. Blasting him where I'd been seconds ago.

"Victor," I gasped.

The vampire stood beneath the full force of the dragon's flames. Body braced. Hands fisted.

Horror washed through me.

"No," I cried. Despite the unbearable heat, I didn't dare look away, raising my hand to shield my vision.

Instead of collapsing, he held steady beneath the dragon's fiery assault. His muscular form was an immovable boulder in a raging river. His clothing incinerated in an instant, turning to ash, exposing his body. Rather than blister, Custodis's skin fractured like broken ice across a frozen pond.

I gaped at the sight. What was happening?

Blinding light shone through the cracks in his exposed flesh, and his golden eyes glowed with a fiery brilliance. Curling strands of silver hair whirled around his head. The effect made him appear like some avenging god. Splaying his hands, Custodis arched his back, tipped his face to the sky, and roared at the sun.

Energy exploded.

The wave slammed into me, and the force threatened to shatter my bones. Every object, every creature, every person in the immediate vicinity hit the ground. My frantic pulse pounded in my ringing head. There was no possible way he'd survived that blast. How could this happen?

I coughed debris from my throat and peered through a cloud of dust. Standing at the center of the blast circle was Custodis.

Gone was the tightly wound vampire lord. In his place stood a fierce golden warrior. He was like some imposing mystical entity, finally released from an eternity in prison. Formidable. Commanding.

Ready for war.

Energy electrified the atmosphere. Every inch of his flawless body glowed with an eternal light.

A divine light.

Silence reigned. Nothing stirred. Even the air seemed afraid to move.

Then, slowly, one by one, voices rang out.

"It's him."

"Our king has risen."

"The chosen one."

"The prophecy is true."

Those low murmurs started to chatter like a buzz of insects.

I gawked at my vampire. No, I refused to believe it. The male I'd captured, fought beside, argued with, *slept with,* couldn't be divine. This was Idris's work. A fictional spectacle meant to entertain the masses.

Seeming unaffected by the chaos surrounding him, Victor

peered back at the roaring spectators. His expression was an emotionless void. Lord Custodis had checked out. Who remained was a mystery.

"Victor?" My voice emerged a rasping croak.

His glowing gaze slid to my sprawled form, and he scanned my body with little recognition.

"Victor," I tried again. "It's Runa. Are you okay?"

Gah! What a stupid question. He was definitely not okay.

His eyes darted to something behind me, then narrowed. I turned as well.

Slicing through the mayhem, one lone figure dashed across the pit, dodging dazed, unmoving obstacles.

"Now, you spell-casting bastards! Do it now!" Thorne shouted at the stands, sprinting past both myself, then Custodis, only to leap onto the dragon's back.

Reality sliced through the confusion in my foggy brain. We were still in a pit filled with deadly monsters. And Thorne had clearly lost his mind.

I lurched to my feet. "Thorne? What... How... Why?"

Whipping the enchanted key from his tunic, the shifter slammed it into the lock on the dragon's collar. The beast's chain dropped into the sand with a metallic *chink*.

And now the beast was free.

I was alive. Victor exploded. And Thorne straddled a dragon.

My brain threatened to fracture. Shock emerged from my throat on a screech. "Thorne, you idiot! What are you doing?"

"Hurry! Do it now!" Thorne bellowed again, dropping to the ground.

Do what now?

Voices screamed from the stands. I pressed a hand to my throbbing forehead, glancing around the arena. What had to be a dozen figures dressed in dark robes sprinted into the walkways. Spread throughout the space, they raised their hands, their deep voices chanting. Purple light glowed in their palms.

Were they the ones Thorne kept shouting at?

By the fates, this was all too much.

As Thorne sprinted past me again, I snagged his arm in a death grip.

"Dammit, tell me what's happening!" I snarled.

"Told you I had a connection waiting for us on the outside." He offered me one of his dazzling smiles. "Look."

Around us, the shield Idris had put in place to protect the audience and contain his prisoners began to spark and fizzle. Raelynn's scream erupted from the royal pavilion. My sister clawed at her skull, convulsing. Idris caught her before she could fall, barking orders to his men.

"They're breaking the containment spell," I gasped.

Thorne smirked. "That's not all, sweetheart."

The torque around my neck heated, then dropped to the ground, as well as every other torque in the place.

Yet another explosion rocked my world, and I wobbled, peering at the sky. The purple haze had vanished. They'd done it. They'd broken the shield.

"Runa." Thorne captured my attention, commanding, "Time to do your part."

"What?" I stared back, still reeling.

"Get Kronk. Stick to the plan!"

"Kronk?"

"Here," my brother grunted, appearing beside me. He planted his hands on his thighs, panting as though he'd run a great distance.

"Torques are off, shields down," Drazen shouted, racing to join us, puffing smoke. "Let's get the hell out of here."

"Right." I rubbed my blurry eyes.

"Hurry. We don't have much time." Thorne sprinted back to the dragon, where he proceeded to flap his arms. "Fly, you big ugly bastard. You're free. Fly!"

Thorne was rescuing the dragon. The one who, moments ago,

tried to roast me. In what world did this make sense? None. I was definitely concussed. Possibly brain damaged.

Without warning, the mystical creature turned a circle, and we stumbled back. Gaze clear of Idris's influence, the beast sliced us a dark glare, then turned to face the pavilion. The shield was gone, the royals vulnerable. People screamed. Those seated closest to their king scattered.

Idris peered up into the face of the beast he'd dared to imprison and paled. Flames blasted the royal pavilion, the dragon unloading a stream of fire directly at the king.

And just like that, the dragon became my favorite monster of all time.

Flames surrounded the golden bubble Idris succeeded in forming around him and Raelynn while his guard burned to a crisp. Once the beast had run out of breath, all that remained of the royal pavilion was a charred circle of smoking ash. Idris and his golden bubble somehow managed to survive the blast.

Pity.

After snorting a puff of smoke from its nostrils, the dragon extended its massive wings and leaped into the sky, sending a plume of sand whipping around us. I was really beginning to hate sand.

Drazen grabbed my face. "Diversion, Runa."

Right. Drawing power up from my core, I waved my glowing palms, creating a swarm of widow wasps, then doubled, then quadrupled its size. Again. And again. I swirled my arms in sweeping circles, twisting my creation into a swirling cyclone. It spun around us, then I pushed my stinging tornado outward into the pit, then further into the stands. Both the remaining spectators and Idris's creatures ran screaming from the deadly cloud.

With my part finished, Kronk drove his fist into the ground. The place where the dragon once sat shifted. Large mounds of sand slid to the outside of the pit. Just as Victor promised, a large grate came into view. Thorne raced over, easily disabling the enchanted lock with his key, and Kronk heaved open the heavy gate.

"Let's go." Drazen held out his hand to me.

I shook my head. "What about Victor?"

I glanced over to where I'd last seen the big glowing…whatever he was.

Victor stood before the king. Fists clenched. Murder in his shimmering eyes. Idris glared back at him from the charred remains of his pavilion. A ball of energy swirled in his palm.

Thorne raced to Victor's side. "My king. We must go. This isn't the time."

Victor's head swiveled in an eerie fashion. His golden gaze took me in before locking on the handprint he'd left on my throat. I swallowed a lump of apprehension.

Wrestling with my fear, I held out my hand to him. "Come with us. With…*me*. Please."

Without another word, he turned on his heel and strode in my direction. Still glowing. Still naked. Before I could utter a yelp of objection, he swooped me up in his arms and leaped through the grate into the darkness.

Chapter Twenty-Six

VICTOR

I DRAGGED open eyelids made of lead, drawing in my surroundings. Nothing about the room nor bed I slept in was familiar. One thing was certain—I was no longer a prisoner of Slyborn Castle.

While even the nicer parts of Slyborn had a coarse, primitive quality to them, this place had an air of refinement without being blatant in its display of riches. Silks and velvets in shades of emerald and bronze softened the room while ornate rugs rested on the marble floors. The furniture was crafted by an artist's hand, the lines almost delicate while seeming indestructible. Soft light illuminated the space, magical fixtures casting a warm glow.

Beside me, Runa slept curled up in a high-backed chair. Soft breaths fluttered a lavender lock that had fallen across her cheek. Other than the circles beneath her eyes, she looked well, wearing a plum-colored dress with a richly embroidered bodice, cap sleeves, and a loose skirt. Her bare legs were folded under her. A pair of boots rested beside the chair. Far from prison garb, the richness of her garments indicated she'd been afforded some care and consideration.

While none of these observations were alarming, they didn't explain how I'd gotten here.

I raised my arm, finding it, too, was made of lead. Fates, but I was exhausted. I eyed my pale skin, and a faint image of a golden light came to mind. Was it a dream?

"Victor?" Runa stirred, rubbing sleep from her eyes. "You're awake."

"Am I?" I felt...off. Though I appeared whole, I sensed something was different. My body was heavy while my soul was almost...lighter?

"Where are we?" My voice cracked.

She bit her lip, sitting up straighter in the chair. "What do you remember?"

I frowned, struggling to recall. "The dragon."

She winced. "And?"

"Fire. Pain. Then..." I trailed off, again glancing at my hands. Had I imagined the explosion of power that followed? Why wasn't I dead?

"You saved me," Runa said, her voice a reverent benediction. "Sacrificed yourself to save my life."

I dared to meet her eyes. Emotions flickered across her conscience, tripping something soft in my chest.

Memories stirred.

It was the same look I'd seen in my mother's eyes. Right before she'd plunged a dagger into her own heart and thrust me into the mortal realm. A look I'd witness before she'd abandoned me.

That tender look was an expression of weakness.

Something that would drive a male to act on emotions instead of logic.

No.

This I could not allow. Fated mate or not, attachments of the heart made a male vulnerable. My ambitions, my goals, came first. Always. Power was everything. The *only* thing.

My mind raced. "You're mistaken. That doesn't sound like me." The walls closed in, the air growing thin.

It was one thing for a female to become obsessed with me. Even fall in love on occasion. This was to be expected. It was quite another for those feelings to be reciprocated. Ever. Which they hadn't. Not once in all my years had I ever returned a female's infatuation. Despite the shimmering mark that remained on Runa's throat, I wasn't some besotted fool. Until I'd determined what I would do about finding my fated mate, it was vital for the sorceress to have a clear understanding of our relationship. I needed her to create a portal. Nothing more.

At my rebuttal, Runa stiffened, hurt darkening her violet eyes. "I was moments from death. You shoved me out of the way."

I shook my head, firming my jaw. "I remember peering down at you from my platform." While debating whether I should let her die, that damn inner voice had reared its head, telling me Runa was mine and nothing would separate us, not even death.

"And then?" Runa pressed.

I swallowed past my tightening throat. "I fell."

"You...*fell*." She stiffened, pursing her lips. "And landed directly between me and the dragon...by accident?" Her voice rose.

I arched a brow, daring her to challenge my explanation.

"You know what?" She flopped back in the chair, folding her arms. "Never mind. We have more pressing issues to deal with than what might have been the only selfless act you've ever performed in your life."

Silence stretched between us until she finally said, "What do you remember about our escape?"

"Nothing." My memory was a wasteland.

"I feared as much. You...weren't yourself." She untucked her legs, sitting upright in the chair and adjusting her skirt. "As it turned out, Thorne was telling the truth. He'd allowed himself to be tossed into the pit. His benefactor hired him to save you. According to their deal, she'd help save the dragon if he got you out as well. After you *fell*, a bunch of his guys broke the containment spell. We escaped into the grate, where more of his friends intercepted us. The tunnel exited near a swiftly flowing river where they'd hidden a handful of small boats. After a span's journey, they brought us here."

"As captives or guests?"

"Guests." She paused. "I think. Kronk, Drazen, and Thorne are resting in their own rooms. They healed our injuries, fed and clothed us. Still, I'm not completely clear on why they've come to our aid. Nor do I trust them."

She was smart not to let her guard down. Lucky for her, I'd woken and would sort it all out.

"Where is 'here' exactly?"

"I believe that answer is best explained by letting you see it yourself. Think you can stand?"

I snorted. "I'm not an invalid."

My heavy legs dropped to the floor like they were made of stone. I covered my wince, forcing my cumbersome frame out of the bed.

Runa's gasp reminded me of my lack of clothing.

I smirked. "Nothing you haven't seen nor enjoyed, pet."

"Me and half the realm," she grumbled.

Somehow, I managed to shuffle to the balcony.

"Welcome to Copia." She pushed the doors open wide.

Breath lodged behind my aching ribs.

What lay before me was something out of a fairy tale. Far below, rolling hills of green painted with swathes of lavender and pink covered the landscape. Nestled between the hills were dozens of multitiered homes with glistening roofs. In the distance, a frothing river journeyed across the countryside. At the head of it, a waterfall gurgled. Mist danced along its banks, giving everything a mystical quality.

I peered down at Runa.

Warm sunlight cast her exotic features in an ethereal light. As she gazed out upon the land, her expression was soft, serene. A gentle smile played at the edges of her full lips.

To my surprise, I found my arm wrapped around her waist, pulling her close while we shared the view together.

She waited for my reaction. Before I registered the act, my fingers caressed her cheek. "Breathtaking," I admitted, peering into her fathomless violet eyes.

Her face reddened, her expression shuttering, and she withdrew from my touch. "Come. Let's get you dressed. There's someone here who wants to meet you."

Her withdrawal left me chilled. "Who might that be?"

"Queen Elowen."

After a humiliating struggle, where Runa helped me dress due to my weakened state, I wore new clothing crafted of exquisite fabric. Heavy gold embroidery embellished the jacket's lapels and cuffs. The cut of the garment was made for a king.

Soon after, we exited the room and were escorted by a pair of guards dressed in dark robes, stopping before a set of ornate doors. The heavy oak doors swung inward with a groan, revealing a vast throne room. My second since my arrival in this foreign world.

For once, I failed to contain my reaction. My jaw dropped.

At the top of a raised dais was yet another tree, much like the one in Idris's castle.

Unlike Carcerem's sacred arbor, with its single trunk, this tree was a complex structure of hundreds of thinner branches, interwoven to form a wide, sturdy base. Above that, thousands of smaller limbs formed a lush canopy full of metallic emerald leaves. Carved into the foot of the tree's base was a wide seat of tiny woven branches braided to form an intricate throne.

On that throne sat a resplendent queen. Her robes and gown were a rich forest green. Her thick silver hair was braided into elegant loops. On her head was a crown of golden branches inset with gleaming emeralds. While far from aged, there was a sense of wisdom about her not found in those of their youth.

"Ah, Victor Custodis and his charming sorceress. Come forward," Queen Elowen commanded.

Runa sputtered a cough when the queen called her mine, and my lips curled.

Our guards led us to the foot of the dais where the queen peered down her nose at us. Her shrewd eyes scanned every inch of my person. "You appear much improved."

"Yes, Your Majesty." I offered a courtly bow. "You have my deepest gratitude for coming to the aid of both myself and my allies."

"Yes, well." She sniffed. "I believed it was past time someone took you in hand since you were failing so miserably on your own."

I stiffened at her tone. "Please forgive my ignorance, but I do not understand." Was I tasked with some job other than surviving in this ridiculous land?

"Of course you don't. That mortal world you lived in has twisted you into something even I hardly recognize." The queen fluttered a dismissive hand. "The moment you arrived, I felt a disturbance. I'd hoped, at last, the balance would be restored. Needless to say, I was disappointed to discover you were a competitor in that barbaric game."

"As was I, Your Majesty."

"Your performance was embarrassing, to say the least. That one of the divine should scurry about like a powerless rodent in Idris's maze was a dark stain upon us all. It wasn't until the dragon broke your enchantment that I began to understand the reason for your dismal showing."

Again, she spoke in riddles. "I was unaware of any enchantment."

"Apparently, your true nature was concealed sometime during your childhood. Since your arrival here, that enchantment has been weakening. It was the dragon's fire that finally broke it, allowing your true self to emerge. Your divine self."

The explosion of power, my glowing flesh. It wasn't a dream.

However, her insistence that I was divine was surely a fantasy and too farfetched to be believed. "If I am truly divine, then how did this come to pass?"

The queen scoffed. "No sovereign should sink so low as to explain procreation to a simpleton."

I gritted my teeth. "My mother was not divine. She was merely a vampire and a peasant at that. She begged and scraped for everything we possessed. Sacrificed her own needs to provide for me. Despite her valiant efforts, we lived in squalor."

"And what do you know of your father?"

"Only that I was the product of an affair that brought her much suffering and heartache. Once I was abed, he'd visit her in secret. I never even knew his name." Nor did I care to.

"Then I'm sorry to be the one to tell you. Your father was none other than King Helix, Idris's father. You are King Helix's bastard son. Helix himself was also a bastard, his sire being one of the gods. Being a demigod, he passed that divine spark to his offspring."

"That's...not possible." My frozen brain moved as though wading through snow.

"Isn't it? King Helix was a virile male in a loveless marriage."

Runa wavered at my side. "I'm going to need a minute." She braced her hands on her knees and hung her head, hyperventilating.

"Are you saying I'm the son of the demigod, King Helix?

And, at some point, had an enchantment placed on me to suppress my divine power?"

"Precisely." Queen Elowen nodded.

I'd already known I was a bastard. The realization that I was a *royal* bastard meant little to me. I certainly hadn't benefited from my god-given heritage. Neither had my mother.

"If you ask me, it's incomprehensible that someone suppressed your powers all these years. I couldn't imagine a more desperate act. Whoever did this must have been faced with no other choice. I mean, the long-term effects of such a spell are dreadful. Then again, I would expect nothing less from the inhabitants of Carcerem."

After her shocking news, I dreaded what else she had to share. "What effects?" I forced myself to ask.

"Well, look at you. Can you even summon a spark of magic?"

"I...do not know."

She held up her hand, her fingertips glowing gold. "Hold up your hand and order the power to come forth. It's an innate ability. One that should require little effort."

I held up my hand, feeling something stir inside of me. I snapped my fingers, and sparks shot from my fingertips, then sputtered and fizzled.

The queen snorted a disgusted huff.

"It's exactly as I suspected. Your well of energy is empty. The connection between you and the realm's pool of obsidian is long broken. It could take decades to replenish your divine gifts. Such a disappointment. You're of no good to me until you're strong enough to restore the balance."

"Which balance would that be?" I asked.

Runa straightened beside me, massaging her temples, grumbling, "Helix's son, and he isn't even aware there's a balance." Her face remained pale, and she refused to meet my eyes.

"Fates save me, you really are ignorant." The queen's voice

snapped with impatience. "Since your half-brother Idris claimed the throne, the realm's equilibrium has been off, and not just in Carcerem, but in all five of the surviving Arbor Kingdoms. My seers assured me that in time, all would be well. That the true king would return one span. I had such hope when I sensed your arrival."

Given my lifelong absence, I was subject to an excessive amount of blame. I gritted my teeth. "I fail to see how my arrival was to accomplish such a lofty goal."

She smacked the armrest of her majestic throne. "Are you daft? Because you're the lost king of Carcerem. The one who will fulfill the prophecy."

Beside me, Runa sucked a noisy breath and braced her palms on her knees once more. I worried she might pass out, tempted to crumble beside her. Thoughts raced through my mind, colliding.

The queen arched a regal brow. "You didn't know?"

"No, Your Majesty." Flark me. It was bad enough I was a royal bastard with broken magic. Now I was prophesied to save a realm?

She shook her head, for the first time showing an ounce of apathy. "I imagine this news is quite the shock, then. You were taken from your home at a young age. It's a shame your mother didn't prepare you. Nonetheless, you're here now, and there is much work to be done. That is, should you choose to stay. I was disappointed to learn you plan to return to your disgusting mortal world."

"If Carcerem's throne is rightfully mine, then how is it I ended up in the mortal world? How did all of this come to pass?" After her revelations, I had a million questions and few answers.

"The story is a long one." She sighed. "Frankly, I've little interest in the tale of your youth, only the outcome. Since my time can be better spent elsewhere, I've summoned my most trusted seer to explain everything to you. Guard." Queen Elowen gestured to one of her men at the back of the room. "You may send her in."

Bells jingled behind us.

Runa turned before I did and gasped. "Yaga!"

The sorceress spun and dashed down the aisle, embracing a haggard old woman with long gray braids.

The aged female released Runa long enough to narrow her cloudy eyes on me. "Young man, we've much to discuss."

"So, it would seem," I muttered.

Chapter Twenty-Seven

VICTOR

AFTER OUR MEETING with the queen, we retired to one of the royal sitting rooms. Yaga sat in a chair near a crackling fireplace, pipe in hand, peering at me through the smoke. Runa sat at her feet as if she was loath to put an inch of distance between them.

While Runa had spoken with Yaga, she'd yet to say a word to me or meet my eyes. I found it unsettling. For some strange reason, I desired to know what she thought about my divine heritage.

Yaga stroked Runa's dark head with gnarled fingers, the act motherly. From what I'd discerned, this was the woman who'd raised Runa and her brothers.

It explained much.

Watching the two of them stirred a distant memory. One of a woman with flowing silver curls. I sat on the floor at her knee, fire crackling at my back while she trailed gentle fingers through my short locks. It was a moment of contentment and safety. The last I could remember.

I'd waited patiently while Runa reconnected with her mother.

That patience now neared an end. "Queen Elowen mentioned you knew the story of my past."

"I do."

After a stretch of silence where I suspected the woman had fallen asleep, I said, "Can you tell me this story?"

The hag grinned, revealing gaping teeth, and I stifled a shiver.

"Thought you'd never ask."

Swallowing angry words, I curled my fingers into my clenched fists. *Must not slaughter the hag.*

She took a deep puff on her pipe and exhaled, beginning her tale. "Long ago, there was a noble king," she stated sagely. "A *divine* king with the power of the gods. King Helix ruled over a prosperous land. And though the king loved the people as they loved him, he grew lonely and decided to take a queen. Soon after, she bore him a son named Idris."

Runa snorted her distaste for this part of the narrative.

"For a time, the king was happy. Except, the queen, she was a frigid, calculating soul. Before long, it became clear she'd mated with the king, not out of love but greed.

"Again, the king grew lonely. Until a beautiful female vampire crossed his path. More and more, the king visited the woman, and soon, he became obsessed with her. That obsession produced a son."

"I'm to assume I am that son?" I scoffed. If she wanted me to gasp and wail in surprise, she was to be disappointed. After all I'd been through, there was little that could shock me.

Yaga's cloudy eyes locked on me, tracking my reaction. At my continued silence, she huffed a sigh.

"The vampiress was an intelligent woman. She knew if anyone were to discover the affair, she and her child would become targets of the king's enemies. So, she met with a powerful hag from a neighboring village and begged for a spell.

One fashioned to hide her child's identity. Sensing this child had an important future, the hag did as the vampiress asked."

Runa leaned back from her adopted mother, frowning. "It was you who put the shield on his powers."

Yaga grimaced. "For all the good that it did. Not long after that, the queen learned of the king's infatuation, and she flew into a rage. Fearful the king's bastard would jeopardize her own son's claim to the throne, she sent assassins to kill the vampiress and her child.

"Fearing for her son, the king's mistress fled in the middle of the night. She sought the aid of a young sorceress rumored to have a unique gift and begged the woman to help. The sorceress offered to open a portal to another land. However, she warned the price of such a spell would cost the young mother everything."

At this, Runa stiffened. "One of my ancestors did this?"

"Yes, child." Yaga stroked her hair. "Your great-grandmother."

Meaning, between Yaga and Runa's grandmother, our lives had been intertwined since the beginning. A connection that wasn't lost on me.

"So it was, with a heavy heart, the king's mistress sent her child into a foreign land."

An image of my mother flooded my brain. One of her crying, kissing my cheeks, and then thrusting a blade into her chest.

Portal magic required a blood sacrifice. My mother sacrificed herself to protect me.

I wasn't abandoned. Rejected. This news should have offered me some comfort. It didn't, as I was no longer a child who cared about such things. The story Yaga told felt long separated from me. As if it had happened to someone else.

"The king mourned the loss of his lover and son. When he discovered what his queen had done, he cursed his remaining child, ensuring the realm would reject Idris when it came his time to rule.

"Furious, the queen plotted, and when her son was old enough to claim the throne, murdered the divine king. When the kingdom's sacred arbor rejected the cursed son, his mother urged him to capture a sorceress who could force a bond. Problem was, a sacrifice was needed. Knowing her actions were the cause of his curse, the queen surrendered her life so that her son could access Carcerem's power."

Shadows from the flickering flames haunted Runa's expression. "So, not only did my sister open a connection between the two, she was ultimately responsible for the queen's death."

Yaga nodded. "Sadly, the eldest son was more like his mother than his father. He abused the power granted to him, using the tree to drain Carcerem until the kingdom was a withered shell of its former glory. For a while, it seemed all was lost until a prophecy came to light. One that claimed Carcerem's one true king lived and would someday return. Which brings us to now." Her discerning gaze took me in.

In her eyes, I felt...

Judged.

Lacking.

My defenses rose in response. "It's a lovely story."

The hag narrowed her cloudy eyes. "You don't believe me."

Runa's glare now matched the hag's. That I'd dared to question Yaga.

"I've learned to put little faith in prophecies over the centuries. Most never come true. Others were invented by drunken soothsayers, selling snake oil and fortunes trying to make a buck."

"Careful, vampire," Runa growled.

"It's okay, dear," Yaga stated in a way that made it clear it was anything but okay. "Those without faith often have trouble believing things they haven't seen with their own eyes."

"You forget," I snapped, "I have experienced the effects of this so-called prophecy firsthand, along with everything it might have set into motion. First, upon having all I've worked for stolen from me before I was banished to a barbaric land. Next, by falling off a cliff into the jaws of a gallspawn. Then, by being sold to a gangster who promptly shipped me off to Idris, who treated me like a game piece."

Yaga opened her mouth as if to speak, and I cut her off. "Did I mention I was recently burned alive by a dragon?"

"And you are better for it," Yaga declared with a thrust of her bony chin. "All of it."

"Better?" I snapped my fingers, emitting sparks that fizzled and died. "Behold my god-like power. One look, and I'm certain Idris will quake in his royal boots. Tell me again how I am the lost king sent to save a decrepit kingdom filled with criminals and commoners."

Runa scoffed. "Don't waste your breath, Yaga. The vampire believes in nothing of real value. He puts his faith in the almighty coin. That which cannot be bought has little value to him."

"I have faith," I spat. "Faith in myself."

Runa snapped to her feet, standing before me. "And that is why you ended up on that ledge, exiled and alone."

I rose from my seat as well, not one to be looked down upon. "I'll tell you what I believe. I believe my mother was right to send me into the mortal world, saving me from a miserable life in this rabid, uncivilized land."

"Perhaps it is you who doesn't deserve the kingdom." Runa took an aggressive step forward. "By your own words, all you care about is yourself."

"Because I am the only one who's never let me down. I owe this realm nothing. And now we are free of the pit, I owe *you* nothing as well." I stabbed a finger into Runa's chest. "I held up my end of our deal. It's past time you held up yours. You promised me a portal."

Instead of shrinking in the face of my anger, Runa thrust her nose an inch before mine. "Still, you hound me about your flarking portal. Even though you've just found out you are the only one who can save Carcerem's people, your only concern is returning to the mortal world."

"Finally, you understand."

"Is that the reason you 'fell' saving my life? Because you'd prefer to die than be stranded here?"

"Exactly," I snarled.

Runa's palm exploded against my cheek. Though I could have stopped her, I welcomed her fury. It fueled my own. Fury felt better than the pain and confusion I experienced during Yaga's story.

"You disgust me," Runa snarled, then bolted from the room.

Silence reigned, my fury-driven breaths the only sound.

At length, Yaga heaved a heavy sigh. "Well, that was disappointing."

"Yes," I growled. "I'm getting that a lot lately."

Again, silence fell between us while Yaga tapped her whiskered chin, glaring into the crackling fire.

"Perhaps I was wrong then. Both when you were a youngling, and again, when I sent my greatest treasure to you." She shifted her bony frame, squaring her slumped shoulders as if she'd come to some difficult decision. "Very well. Victor Custodis, if power is all you want, then power is all you shall have. If you still insist on returning to the mortal world, then you should not go back empty-handed."

"What do you mean?" I cast her a leery glance.

"I mean, you've made your point. For all you've suffered, I believe you are overdue a reward. The choice is yours. You can return to your realm broken and exiled or return as a god."

"I'm listening."

She narrowed gleaming eyes that seemed to see nothing and yet everything at the same time. "I must warn you. The journey will be difficult. And to start, you must do something you've never done before."

"That is?"

"Apologize."

Chapter Twenty-Eight

RUNA

The rush of water sliding against a rocky beach echoed in the distance. Flutterflies danced upon a briny breeze, alighting on delicate pink and purple blossoms. At the center of the queen's royal garden, a multi-tiered fountain gurgled with turquoise water. Manicured hedges lined the path to an enchanting gazebo with curved arches. Ivy wrapped around the stone pillars, creating a flowing canopy that trailed over the domed roof.

On any other span, I'd have found it captivating. I plopped down on an iron bench tucked beneath the gazebo, glaring at the tranquil view. Maybe Victor was right. Maybe the prophecy was nothing but the ramblings of seers gone mad.

But what if he was wrong?

Since my parents' deaths, all I'd desired was to redeem myself for the wrong I'd committed. To make up for the fact that I'd failed to fulfill my mother's dying wish—preventing Raelynn from putting Idris on the throne. So, I stole enough to pay their taxes, keeping their homes from burning. Stole to keep their children fed. Yet it was never enough.

While Idris drained the obsidian from the land, bleeding the kingdom dry, I'd lie awake at night, dying inside and praying for a solution.

Except if Victor Custodis was sent here to be the kingdom's savior, the fates must surely be blind.

I closed my eyes, picturing Custodis on Carcerem's throne, and, strangely, it wasn't too difficult. He certainly had the bearing of a king, wearing his arrogance like a crown. While bossy and demanding, I couldn't discount his leadership skills during the Fallen Trials. There were many times that I'd floundered, not knowing what to do next, but Victor always seemed to have a plan. He'd made snap decisions that saved our asses time and again. Sure, the vampire had been heartless when it suited him, but he'd also acted with confidence.

Then there was the dragon. Victor could deny it all he wanted, but I knew that he'd leaped to my rescue, believing he would die. Proving he was willing to sacrifice his life for others when the mood struck. Were these not the actions of a noble ruler?

Perhaps Victor didn't believe in the prophecy because he hadn't grown up here and didn't love the land or its people.

Nor me, whispered a tiny voice deep in my conscience.

I tensed at the thought. What did it matter what the vampire felt about me in the grand scheme of things? I certainly hadn't developed any tender emotions toward him. My heart twisted like a hardened rock scraping beneath my breast. Nope. No feelings at all. That he could so easily walk away from me after the time we spent together had no bearing on the situation.

Hell, my own sister had abandoned me for power and wealth. It shouldn't come as a surprise that someone like Victor would do the same.

So why the heck did my chest ache?

Footsteps scuffed the ground. I whipped around. Custodis

approached me with slow, careful steps, as one might a cornered animal.

"What are you doing here?" I snapped.

"Searching for you."

My heart flipped at his answer, and I ignored the sensation. "Why?"

"To apologize."

I snorted. "Yaga sent you. Didn't she?"

He came to stand before me, leaning against a stone pillar. Sunlight turned his silver hair to spun gold. His broad shoulders filled out his tailored jacket, and his biceps strained his sleeves. Despite his lack of magical reserves, there was a delicious air of power about him. He looked nothing like the fallen lord I'd pulled from the gallspawn's jaws. Carcerem had done this to him, breaking him out of his stuffy shell. He was thriving here, and yet he rejected her and what she could offer.

"Runa, I'm sorry."

Yaga definitely had sent him. "No, you aren't."

The corner of his mouth quirked. "No. I'm not."

"Then why are you here?"

"I've…nobody else to talk to."

I sensed this was also the case in his mortal realm. That he'd chosen to confide in me might have straightened my shoulders, just a bit.

"Do *you* believe in the prophecy?" he asked, his shrewd gaze studying my reaction.

"Honestly, I…" My knee-jerk response was to declare that I absolutely believed, especially if Yaga said it was true. When in reality, I had doubts. "I don't know. Even if I did, what does it matter when you do not?"

"I do not," he confirmed.

"Then what *do* you believe?" This time, instead of throwing the question at him as a challenge, I genuinely wanted to hear his answer.

He heaved a heavy sigh. "I believe fate is what we make of it. It is our own choices that determine our future."

"I don't...disagree," I dared to admit, causing his brows to shoot into his hairline.

"However," I held up my palm before he read too much into my admission, "for a moment, let's take the prophecy out of the equation. You are still a divine being, descended from a demigod, who is intimately connected to Carcerem. The only one capable of sitting on the throne. How can you look at the suffering Idris has caused the land and its people and *choose* to turn your back on them?"

He narrowed his eyes. "You mean, why wouldn't I desire to rule over a desolate kingdom that cannot sustain itself? A place of filthy criminals and peasants who'd love nothing more than to stab me in the back? Where I'm not top of the food chain, and everything in this place wants to eat me? Why wouldn't I sacrifice my entire life to save them when they'd sooner spit on me in return?"

I winced, having little to contest his argument except to add, "You could be king?"

"King of a dung heap." He scoffed.

The insult stirred my temper. "You say that because you've only seen the worst of our kingdom."

"There's more?" He arched a brow.

"Of course, there's more," I bit out. "You've experienced Carcerem as the main course of a gallspawn's meal, then as a captive, then as a prisoner in a twisted game." Now that I put it all together, it was no wonder he was eager to leave. He'd yet to experience the beauty of our kingdom. The heart and resiliency of its people.

Yaga would have realized the same. She certainly didn't send him to me to apologize. The conniving old woman was up to something. I simply needed to figure out what part she wanted me to play.

"Why did you really follow me out here?"

He didn't even have the decency to act contrite for his duplicity. "Yaga says there is a way to restore my power. One that won't take decades."

My chest tightened. "Ah, it all makes sense now." He hadn't come to confide in me. He wanted something.

"She claims there's a temple created by Hathor. A place of rejuvenation and rebirth I could visit. Only one being knows of its location. A divine creature the goddess created for the sole purpose of guarding her secrets. Yaga believes you could help me find them."

I knew better than to think he desired this for the good of Carcerem. "So you will be at full strength when you return home."

"Yes. That is my intention. Better to return a god than an exiled criminal."

Yaga, in her wisdom, wouldn't have shared this information without some purpose. I doubted that the reason was to help him seek his revenge in the mortal world.

If there was even a tiny possibility that he was the kingdom's savior, I had to give him a chance to redeem himself. Same as the fates had given me. My heart skipped at the realization. Victor Custodis would be my penance for failing my kingdom so long ago. *This* was the reason Yaga sent me to capture him that fateful day. Why she'd placed me on the path to freedom. Carcerem's freedom.

Since I was the one who'd found Carcerem's lost king, I would be the one to bring him back into the fold. Victor was a celestial being who'd lost his faith. Who'd had his connection to Hathor's sacred obsidian severed. Surely, once I helped him to reconnect, he'd understand why he needed to stay—to set Carcerem's people free.

And the taxes White Bridge owed in a matter of spans? They'd be safe if the lost king decided to stay. To fight.

I schooled my features, trying to hide the flush of hope rising in my heated cheeks. "You know, technically, I agreed to create a portal for you. I never said when. I mean, it could be years before the stars and the moons align properly." Yeah, I'd totally made that part up.

He stiffened. "My kingdom, my world, was in peril when I left. Each minute I'm detained here takes me further from my goal."

"Not to worry," I said, flipping my lavender locks over my shoulder, enjoying my moment of power. "I will open your portal in due time, as well as help you reach this temple. However, in exchange for this amendment to our original arrangement, I'm going to need something in return. First, you will grant me three boons. Requests you may not deny."

"You're blackmailing me?" His lips curled, interest gleaming in his eyes.

"Absolutely." I tilted my chin. "I am a criminal, after all."

Strangely, he didn't seem angered by my admission, more like...*delighted.*

He prowled closer, and I resisted the impulse to sink on my bench like cornered prey. Dammit, I was the one in control here.

"Agreed," he purred in a heated tone that sent a tantalizing tingle down my spine. "As long as the stakes are not life-threatening or these requests do anything to lengthen my stay."

That was far too easy. Perhaps I should ask for more? "Very well," I stated primly. "Second, there is the small matter of your portal requiring a sacrifice. A life given freely."

"Yes."

"That offering will be Vex. Once your power is returned, you should be able to control him as Idris controls his slaves. You will convince him to sacrifice himself."

"Done." He planted his hands on either side of the backrest, caging me.

His minty cypress fragrance washed over me, heating my

blood. I bit my lip. *Focus, Runa.* "Also, on this journey, you will subject yourself to all the wondrous things this world has to offer while keeping an open mind." There was a chance once he'd seen Carcerem's sweeter side, he'd rediscover his connection to the land and its people.

"While not complaining or belittling its people, nor your guide," I added.

"Now, you're pushing it, little thief."

Yes, I was. *Eh.* Two out of three wasn't bad.

He grasped my chin. "I didn't realize you were such a skilled negotiator."

I tipped my face to his, our mouths a single breath away from connecting. "I'm skilled at a number of things. It's a shame you won't be around long enough to experience all of them."

With that, I shoved my palms into his chest and sprang to my feet, darting free of his embrace.

"It's going to be a long, cold journey, vampire," I purred on my way out of the gazebo, adding an extra swish to my hips. "Hope you're up for it."

His low, frustrated growl had a bubble of laughter rising in my belly.

"So do I, little thief. So do I."

Chapter Twenty-Nine

RUNA

"No. ABSOLUTELY NOT!" I shouted at deaf ears. Literally. "Kronk, dammit. Put her down. Yaga, you are not going."

Kronk hefted Yaga's aged bones up onto the cart's bench.

She landed with a thud. "Careful, boy, or you'll damage my posterior. I've been told it's my best feature."

While we prepared for the journey to Amberdale, a location Yaga had seen in a vision, a small crowd had gathered around us to watch the show. It was no wonder with the scene the hag was making.

For both Custodis and myself, two swaybacked horses waited. Not the queen's finest steeds, by any means. No, those would draw too much attention. Behind our mangey nags was a coarse, wooden cart pulled by a slack-jawed bula. Drool dripped from the beast's chin. And yet, that wasn't the worst part.

In the back of the cart was a load of prime, grade-A, kiln-dried bula dung. We'd be traveling as merchants on our way to the market. Bula dung was used as fuel in many of the more destitute villages. Our disguise, though loathsome, was genius.

While the product had worth, there would be few bandits eager to rob us of our wares.

"Drazen." I turned to the only brother who may see reason. "Tell her. It's too dangerous."

"Already tried." Drazen sighed, a puff of smoke rolling from his nostrils.

"And?"

His brow furrowed. "And she threatened to cast a spell guaranteed to grow fungus on my manhood."

I screwed up my face at the nauseating image he'd created.

Again, I attempted to argue with the hag I loved with every piece of my shriveled heart. "Yaga. Please. I have a terrible feeling about this. Custodis and I can make this journey without you."

"Yes." Yaga settled her thick skirts around her bony ankles. "However, even if you somehow manage to find the guardian of the Empyrean, they will not speak to strangers, only trusted friends."

"I could make them talk," Custodis finally contributed while double-checking every buckle and strap on his mare. I suspect he did so in an attempt to avoid a confrontation he couldn't win.

Yaga sputtered a laugh. "*That* I would like to see."

"Yaga, it's not safe," I tried again, not ready to give up. "Idris has teams of soldiers hunting us. On top of that, the trek to Amberdale is a difficult one. The roads are full of thieves and murderers." The well-known marketplace sat within Carcerem, along Copia's border. People from both kingdoms traveled there to trade and do business with pockets full of coins and loaded carts. And the thieves knew it.

"Then I guess it's fortunate that I'll be riding with the best of them," Yaga said with a wink.

My chest swelled, and I ignored the flare of warmth her words evoked. "I won't be wooed by your compliments, Yaga. The road to Amberdale is no place for..."

The glint in Yaga's eyes warned I should not complete this sentence. "Girlie, do I look like a fragile bag of bones to you?"

Drazen and Kronk coughed and sputtered. One gazed at the sky, the other at his very interesting shoe.

Yaga cast them a glare she'd used often in our youth. That single look knocked the smiles off both their faces.

She acknowledged their compliance with a nod. Then shifted her attention back to me. "Your concern is wasted on this old woman. I can handle myself. Been doing it since before you were born. I'm going with you. That's final."

Drazen interrupted before our argument could escalate. "Thorne asked me to send his regards and wish you a safe journey. He wanted to be here to send you off himself, but his dragon was being difficult and demanded his attention."

"Far be it from me to distract him from his care of his dragon." I shivered. "Though I would have liked to tell him goodbye and thank him for his aid in the pit. But no matter, I'm sure we'll meet again."

While Thorne had explained the deal he'd made with Queen Elowen, his connection to the dragon remained a mystery.

"I hear the beast is enjoying Copia's plump sheep," Drazen offered. "I'm sure it will recover in no time."

Before I could comment, firm arms clamped around my torso from behind. My lungs squeezed, and my ribs threatened to snap. "Kronk," I croaked.

"I will miss you," my brother muttered, putting me back on my feet.

Spots danced before my eyes. Before I'd recovered, Drazen swept me up as well, searing me with his is excessive body heat then releasing me.

In lieu of hugs, both offered Custodis a dark scowl.

"Keep both of them safe," Kronk started, then hesitated. "Or bad things will happen. To you." He punched his palm, the warning nowhere near as terrifying as he'd intended. Discovering our former captive was the lost king of Carcerem and a divine entity had taken the steam out of my brother's threats.

Custodis nodded, and I was relieved when he didn't smirk... much. "I promise to treat Yaga and your sister with the utmost respect."

I resisted an eyeroll. Yeah, right. Like that would happen.

Since the Blood River Bandits were easy to recognize when we were together, my brothers would linger at Copia for a bit. Not that this was a hardship to stay in an enchanted castle with fat larders and bottomless casks of honeyed ale.

I locked eyes with Custodis. "Guess it's time to activate the enchantments." Around both our necks were silver chains with smoky crystals attached—gifts from the queen for our journey. My illusions would prove too tiring to maintain for the whole trip. Burning through that quantity of power would have my flesh blackened from fingertip to shoulder before we were done.

I grasped the crystal, uttering the magical phrase. Sparks skittered over my body. Victor and I studied each other as the glamour took effect.

Victor's striking silver mane turned a greasy brown, and his gray eyes faded to something more akin to swamp water. On the bridge of his nose, a crooked bump formed. His noble chin rounded, his jaw turning jowly.

I picked up a hank of my own violet hair, finding the lavender ends now a dirty blonde from roots to tips. I touched my face, discovering that my nose was misshapen and my high cheekbones sagged.

"Wow." Drazen grunted. "If I hadn't seen it with my own eyes, I'd think you were a stranger."

"Good," I stated with a firm nod. If my own brothers didn't recognize me, then it was unlikely anyone else would.

"Well, what are ya waiting for?" Yaga bellowed. "I ain't getting any younger. Onward, into the great unknown!" She cracked the reins over the back of her bula, and the bovine lurched forward with an irritated *merrr*. Yaga's cart, loaded with bula dung, rocked on its axle, expelling a noxious odor.

"Right." I grimaced and swung my leg over my worn saddle. Not wanting to ruin Yaga's adventure, I didn't comment on the fact that the "great unknown" wasn't an unknown at all, but a well-traveled path to a popular village.

"Wagon ho!" Yaga cackled, throwing her fist in the air as if she led a fierce army.

"On…ward," I mumbled, urging my mount forward with a kick of my heels.

In response, my mighty steed peered over her bony shoulder at me.

I made a kissing noise to my aged beast. "Go on now. Carrots if you're a good girl."

My nag answered with a whinny at the promise of treats and thrust one gnarled hoof before the other.

Victor also mounted his nag, trailing at the rear as if loath to be seen with our ragtag band.

I had no such qualms, holding my head high. I guided the lost king toward a secret temple that would ignite his magic. At my side was a notorious soothsayer of unfathomable power. Together, the three of us were Carcerem's last hope—whether Victor knew it or not.

Fates save us.

Many miles later, my enthusiasm for our quest ran thin.

"This lumbering beast is chafing my nether regions," the vampire griped, his voice like claws raking my spine. "This is no way to treat a king," he repeated for what might have been the hundredth time. For a guy who didn't plan on sticking around, he was really enjoying his royal status.

Yaga trailed behind us so the odors rising from her cart wouldn't make our eyes water. "What's that?" she bellowed over her rattling wheels.

"Nothing, Yaga," I shouted.

"What?"

"Nothing."

"Yes. I agree. Let's stop for a moment." She hauled back on the reins, bringing the cart to a stop.

Custodis cast me a dark glare. "Again? At this rate, it will take a week to reach the village."

"You are welcome to convey your concerns to her yourself."

At my suggestion, the vampire blanched. The last time he complained to Yaga that she was taking too long, she'd popped off her boots and proceeded to take her time, trimming her gnarly toenails with a small knife.

While I helped Yaga to the ground, Custodis secured our horses. Once he returned, Yaga slapped an empty waterskin into his chest, which he caught with a grunt.

"Here, boy. Go refill that for me."

"Yes, ma'am," he grumbled, heading into the woods to find the stream we followed. Apparently, not even the mightiest of kings dared to say no to Yaga.

I watched him stomp away with a sigh of appreciation. The vampire had a nice backside even the queen's glamour couldn't conceal.

Yaga's gaze seared the side of my face, and I turned to discover her taking my measure.

"What?" My cheeks warmed.

"He has a fine ass, that one."

"Yaga," I groaned.

"Have you tapped that yet?"

"Yaga!" I squawked. So what if I had? Once. Because I was certain we were dying. That didn't mean I had any intention of repeating the act, no matter how good it was. My blood warmed at the memory.

"What?" Yaga shrugged her hunched shoulders. "He's a virile, divine being. You're a talented sorceress in your prime. What's the problem?"

I spluttered, a long list racing through my mind. "The problem is, he cares nothing for anyone but himself." Except in bed. Then, he'd been quite generous. I squeezed my thighs together, ignoring the spark the memory ignited.

"Doesn't seem that way to me. The lad can't keep his eyes off you."

"You're mad." I glanced in the direction the vampire headed, then back. "Really?"

"Seems to me he's caught your eye as well."

I frowned. "He has not. The male is insufferable. He's selfish and arrogant, and he…smells." Like the forest mountain tops. And the way he kissed, there was no doubt he was a divine being.

Yaga's shrewd eyes bore into me. "Perhaps *you* could be the reason he stays."

At this, I commenced with the spluttering and coughing. "Me? Believe me when I say that a male like Victor Custodis does not want a thief at his side. Besides, I'm already doing as you wanted, being his tour guide on his path to enlightenment."

Yaga planted her hands on her hips. "Know what I think? I think despite how desperately Carcerem needs him, you're holding back because you are afraid of what will happen if the prophecy is right and he remains."

I fought the urge to brush away her observation, instead forcing myself to answer truthfully. "You've seen what the power of the realm has done to Raelynn. That kind of power in the wrong hands can become something dangerous, something deadly. You do not know him as I do. He's ambitious. What if the fates are wrong and he…"

"What if he turns on you as your sister did?"

There was one thing in this world that I knew with absolute certainty—*power corrupts even the purest of hearts.*

I shook my head. "Perhaps he *was* destined to be a great and noble ruler. Once. A long time ago. But the world he lived in, it sullied him. What if he agrees to stay and claims the throne, only to become—*Idris*."

Yaga puffed out her chest, growing indignant. "The fates do not make mistakes. *I* do not make mistakes. I sent you to him for a reason. Your paths are intertwined. If you ignore what you feel for each other, it could have dire consequences for both of you."

I was beginning to think Yaga came on this journey not to help with the temple guardian but to play matchmaker. If that was the case, she wasted her time. Whether he decided to stay or go, he'd never be *mine*.

Muttered curses alerted us to Custodis's return. He lurched free of the brambles. Twigs stuck out of his hair while mud clung to his pants.

"Gods, but I hate this place." He sliced me with a look that threatened terrible things should I ask questions.

Stomping past me, he thrust the waterskin into Yaga's hands. "Your water, my lady."

"Took you long enough," Yaga huffed, returning to her cart.

With her back turned, the vampire raised his hands as if to wrap them around her throat.

"Custodis," I snapped, and he swiveled his head in my direction. "We need to get moving if we're to make Amberdale by nightfall."

"Then perhaps some of us should learn to hold their bladders."

"Some of us heard that," Yaga growled.

I cast a glance to the heavens, offering the gods a prayer to keep me from murdering both of them.

To my relief, the rest of our journey went smoothly. With Yaga only needing one additional stop, we arrived in Amberdale at sunset.

As we rode down the main thoroughfare, sounds of music and laughter reached our ears. Succulent flavors of smoked meat and baked goods wafted on the breeze, making my mouth water.

People in colorful skirts and capes paraded down the sidewalks, splendid crowns of woven ivy decorated with feathers, twigs, and berries adorned their heads. Across the path, a brightly painted banner read, *Amberdale Harvest Festival.*

"Well, imagine that!" Yaga cackled. "What a coincidence. It just happens we're in time to help celebrate the harvest."

I shot her a pointed look from beneath a dingy lock of hair. "Funny coincidence. That we happen to be here on the same span as their festival."

I had a terrible suspicion Yaga wasn't taking our mission seriously. That suspicion was confirmed once we'd secured our rooms for the night and stabled our animals.

Standing outside our lodge, Yaga turned to me, a childlike gleam in her cloudy eyes. "I think we should split up. We'll cover more ground that way."

"And how are we to recognize the temple guardian without you?" I asked.

"Oh, you'll manage." She fluttered a gnarled hand. "Besides, the guardian can take on many different forms. You'll need to use your senses to find them, not your eyes. Heck, even Hot Britches there could feel them if he bothered to listen."

Custodis swiveled his head my direction, cocking a brow. "Hot Britches?"

"It's nothing." I dodged his curious gaze. "Fine, then. We'll spread out and meet back here at…"

I turned to Yaga only to catch the back of her hustling form. Her direction—the nearest booth pedaling tankards of fermented moon berries. "I swear that old woman is going to be the death of me."

"What is it, exactly, I'm supposed to *feel*?" Custodis asked.

I shrugged. "I don't know. Sometimes, for me, Hathor's energy is like a tugging sensation in the center of my chest."

He cocked an eyebrow at me, and I exhaled an irritated sigh. It wasn't an easy thing to describe.

"Perhaps we should stick together." There was no point in sending him out to scout alone when he didn't know what he was searching for.

My stomach chose that moment to let out a yowl.

"Food first, then," Custodis said.

"Agreed."

We selected a pub that wasn't overly crowded and settled into a table in a secluded area. I glanced away from scanning the crowd to find Victor staring at me. "What?" I touched my face, a jolt of worry washing over me. "Is my glamour slipping?"

"Just reflecting on our first date," he quipped.

I lowered my hand, snorting. "Oh. Date. Ha, ha. You mean the one where you sacrificed me to the king's soldiers to save yourself?"

"I seem to recall it was the one where you clapped me in chains in order to sell me to a gangster."

"Good times." I smirked, sipping from a tankard of ale we'd ordered earlier. My half-eaten meat pie rested before me.

Between the cozy atmosphere, my full belly, and—make that my *second* tankard—I was in a rare mood. A mellow mood. The first I could recall in a long while. Sure, Idris's men were hunting us, and we were on a mission to find a rare, shapeshifting temple guardian. But right now, that seemed a far-off threat.

Also, it was literally my mission to make sure Custodis had a good time.

Seated in the corner, a musician strummed his lute, singing a gentle ballad. In the middle of the room, a circular pit crackled with playful flames. The comforting scent of roasted meat and flakey baked goods settled over me like a warm blanket.

"So, do you?" The vampire was more relaxed than I'd ever seen him as well, sitting with his legs stretched out, his elbows slung over the armrests of his chair.

"Do I what?" Though my stomach bulged, I couldn't resist taking another bite of buttery crust.

"Date?"

Flakey pastry sucked down my windpipe, and I coughed, quickly gulping a swig of ale. When I could breathe again, I said, "In the traditional sense? No. I've little time for such things."

"What with all the thievery?"

"Exactly." I nodded, ignoring the taunt in his tone. "And then there are my brothers."

"Ah, yes. I've met them."

"And you?" I dared to ask, already dreading the answer.

"Everywhere I went, females threw themselves at me. It was exhausting."

I blinked, staring at Custodis's blank expression. His bottom lip quivered, and his face spread into a broad smile. Even with the glamour disguising his features, the effect was breathtaking.

"Liar." I kicked his foot, a strange warmth settling in my chest.

He cleared his throat. "There were social functions I would attend for political gain. Because of my station, I was not free to indulge in the company of just anyone. Those who stood at my side were selected carefully for who and what they represented."

"Sounds romantic." Not that I knew anything about romance, what with the few moments I managed to steal without my brothers around. "So you were never allowed to simply be yourself?"

"There were standards to uphold. Appearances to be kept."

"Same." I sighed.

At the vampire's raised brow, I felt the need to explain. "I'm pretty sure my brothers still believe I'm a lily-white innocent."

To Custodis's credit, he didn't even crack a smile. Point to the vampire.

His lack of response dared me to whisper, "That and there was the issue of my identity. The one plastered on wanted posters around the kingdom. Idris had placed a hefty sum on our heads. I had to be careful."

He nodded his understanding, wisely keeping any disparaging comments to himself.

Another point to the vampire.

I'd almost dare to say we were getting along. For once.

I tilted my mug to my lips, polishing off the last of my ale as a thought occurred to me. "Know what? My brothers are miles away. And my identity is secure." I tapped the crystal on my chest.

"True," Custodis said slowly, his eyes strangely warm as they traveled over my glamoured face.

My heart pounded with the temptation of freedom. "I mean, look at us. Nobody knows who we are. For all they know, we are two dung dealers."

Victor wrinkled his nose, then his eyes brightened with a kindred light. "You have a point. Tonight, we are peasants. Commoners." For once, he didn't say this with an edge of disgust.

"The most common of commoners," I agreed, my voice rising with excitement.

His smoky gaze took on a calculating gleam. "The temple guardian likely isn't going anywhere with the festival in full swing."

"Nope." I smacked the table. "Plenty of time. There's no reason we cannot keep our senses open while having a bit of fun." I mean, I had plotted to show Victor the better parts of Carcerem, after all.

"No reason at all." He grinned.

"What do you say to being nobody with me? Just for a night."

Custodis raised his tankard, and I lifted mine in kind.

"To being nobody," he declared.

"To being nobody." Our rims clinked, and a pact was made.

Chapter Thirty

VICTOR

"DEFINITELY NOT. I REFUSE." I glared at the offensive object Runa thrust under my nose.

Moments ago, the sorceress confirmed that Yaga was tucked safely into bed. Her snores echoed into the hall of the inn now her quest for adventure was satisfied.

The night was ours to explore.

We'd claimed a coarse table beneath a brightly striped canopy. The dirt-packed dance floor beside us teamed with twirling villagers. Huddled tightly on a short platform, a ragtag group of musicians played a rhythmic song with an enthusiastic beat.

"Have I led you astray yet?"

I scowled. "The puppet show was fairly disturbing." It wasn't often that you discovered an exact replica of yourself made from sticks and scraps charging across a miniature stage.

Runa laughed. "I thought you were quite dashing when you defeated the mighty dragon."

"I'm pretty sure my silver hair was stolen from a horse's

ass." The fairytale was a comedic reenactment of my adventures in the pits. Apparently, news of the lost king's return blazed like a wildfire across the land.

"Why anyone would want to entertain children with that story is beyond me."

Runa grew serious. "You've given them hope."

"It's a shame that hope is based on fiction." The villagers assumed I was there to save them. They assumed *a lot.*

At my declaration, Runa grew somber, her joy sliding away like globs of caramel on tart fruit.

The loss of her smile kicked me in the stomach. I turned her attention back to the dessert she held. "Tell me more about this treat you insist I try."

She waggled the goo-covered sweet under my nose, her smile returning. "I promise you have not truly lived until you've tried a candied fire zapple."

In answer, I pressed my lips together.

Runa used my silence to work more of her wiles on me, rolling out her bottom lip, blinking thick lashes. It was a childish tactic that was beneath her and delightfully entertaining.

I'd not seen this playful side of her before. She was a much different person without her brothers and the threat of Idris's trials hanging over her head.

I had to admit, I didn't hate it. "Nice try. The answer is still no."

So far, I'd experienced—or rather Morgue Sweatzer, a name Runa had given me—had experienced everything the festival had to offer, from drinking games to something called "arm wrestling," a game of strength in which I'd excelled. To a challenge with feathered darts where Runa had won a miniature dragon figurine, which she'd promptly gifted to me, tucking it into my pocket.

I had to draw the line somewhere.

At my continued obstinance, Runa narrowed her sparkling

eyes. Even with the glamour, I sensed this look meant trouble for me.

"Remember those boons you promised me in exchange for my help?"

I groaned. "I knew that would come back to bite me."

She held up a finger. "I'm calling in the first one."

"Fine," I growled. It wasn't enough that we'd sampled every fermented brew in the village, carved hideous faces into gourds, nor lost several coins while gambling on a maze full of racing rodents.

"May I remind you I prefer to consume a liquid diet."

"I'm aware. As is half of Carcerem."

Was that...a note of anger I detected? Something akin to jealousy, perhaps? The thought titillated.

I opened my mouth, and she tucked the sugared fruit between my lips. Before she could withdraw, I trapped her fingertip, grazing it with an extended fang, hard enough to break the skin.

The sorceress inhaled a breathy gasp yet didn't pull away.

Despite the sticky treat, Runa's unique flavor washed over my tongue. My eyelids grew heavy, a low growl rumbling in my throat.

Runa's luminous eyes turned languid, her breath coming in short pants.

Of all the veins I'd tapped since my arrival, hers wasn't one of them.

Runa was *forbidden fruit*.

And may the gods help me, I prayed this taste of her wouldn't be my last tonight. I grasped her wrist and released her finger, taking care to draw my tongue along the quivering digit.

"How—" Her voice cracked. "How was it?"

"Delicious," I purred, desire heating my veins.

"Would you," she gulped, with her eyes still riveted to my mouth, "like more?"

"From you?" I kissed the inside of her wrist, her fingers trapped in my hand. "Always."

"Holy bula dung," grated a coarse voice. "Would you get a load of you two?"

I broke free of the enchantment the sorceress had me under and turned my attention to a woman seated at the end of our table.

At least, I believed the creature to be female. Thick tusks jutted from her bottom lip. Her flesh had a greenish cast to it, and her nostrils sat within a broad nose. Beside her was a male with similar features.

"Excuse me?" I asked in my most disdainful voice, irritated at the interruption.

Pain erupted in my shin, and I cut a glance at Runa, who waggled her brows at me. Oh. Right. I was Morgue, the peasant. King of the Dung Merchants.

I cleared my throat, relaxed my posture, and drawled, "What's this now?"

"Little old to be newlyweds, ain't ya?" the woman asked.

"Newlyweds?" I scoffed, only to receive another kick under the table.

I cast Runa an evil smile in retaliation. "Nah. Me and my old lady been mated for five turns."

"Best two turns of my life," Runa crooned, again batting her lashes.

"Well, nonetheless, good to see a couple keeping the spark alive. Me and my Eldorth are still randy as two nymphs. Though it can be difficult to find a moment with a pair of pups running about." She hiked her thumb at a group of children who tussled in the dirt. Two had tiny tusks. One of the younglings stood separate from the others, staring over at our table. Little fellow had a strange gleam in his eyes and a head full of explosive orange hair.

I frowned. Odd little chap.

"Morgue and I have half a dozen little ones of our own," Runa said. "Right, Morgue?"

"That's right, Fungaria. That's why we locked 'em in the cellar for the night. Everyone deserves an evening off."

At the female's horrified gasp, I realized my mistake. What did I know about younglings?

This improvisation earned me another kick. "Dance with me," my blushing bride demanded.

"I couldn't possibly, my love. See, I have this throbbing pain in my shin."

"You'll live," Runa bit out, pulling me upright.

We joined the outer circle of the writhing group. I eyed the couples next to us with their spry, stomping feet.

It wasn't a waltz, certainly not a foxtrot. "I do not know this dance," I declared, managing one step back toward our table and obtuse friends before Runa snagged my wrist.

"Boon number two." She held up her fingers.

And to think I'd found her attempt to blackmail me earlier charming. She'd been speaking my language, after all. I'd lost count of all the people I'd manipulated over the years. Though I'd expected her to demand something far more dastardly than sweets and dancing. Preferred it, in fact.

"Must I?" I growled.

"You must."

"Very well." I sighed, and off we went.

As it turned out, the dance was exhilarating, reminiscent of an Irish jig. The entire group moved as one, coming together with our arms raised and then stomping back to form a larger circle. Being agile and quick on my feet, I picked up the steps with ease.

Runa's elbow hooked with mine, and we twirled in a circle. The dance floor whirled. Laughter sparked in her eyes. A joyful blush darkened her cheeks. Despite the glamour, she demanded my full attention. I didn't need to see her true face to know she was more beautiful than any other female. In this world and mine. It was possible the fates weren't *completely* mad when they selected her for me.

Dancing with Runa, I felt freer than I had in decades. Unburdened. In that moment, I was no one and yet everyone.

Emotions engulfed me—more than I'd experienced in years. It was odd, taking pleasure from such simple things or pleasure in much of anything, for that matter.

Too soon, the song drew to an end, and we bowed to our partners. My body and mind reeling, I slumped onto a hay bale near the dance floor.

The band started a rowdier tune, and Runa tapped out a smart rhythm before me, tugging my hand. "One more," she begged.

"You go on," I demanded.

A posse of dancing females swept by, recruiting Runa into their ranks. She spun away from me, a broad smile upon her lips.

As I observed from the sidelines, contentment rising in my center, a small figure settled beside me on the hay bale. Uninterested in the interloper, I watched Runa twirl. She really was a sight to behold.

Grubby fingers pulled at my sleeve. *Tug. Tug.* I dragged my attention away from the sorceress to focus on the young boy who sat at my side.

"Your face looks funny," he declared in a squeaky voice.

In response, I arched a brow and returned to the dancers. The center of my chest drew tight, and I rubbed the ache. What was this?

Tug. Tug.

This time, I didn't bother glancing down.

"Why does your face look that way?"

The tightness in my chest grew stronger, and my focus sharpened. Something felt off. Could it be the feeling Runa described? I sat straighter, scanning the crowd.

Tug. Tug.

"Her face is strange, too. Why is her face strange?"

"What?" I said absently. Again, that sensation pulsated. Was the guardian near? I scanned those closest to me. None of them appeared divine. Rather, the opposite, in fact. Most stumbled about, fairly inebriated.

Tug. Tug.

At last, I scowled down at the child beside me. It was the little outcast. Bright orange hair stood up at odd angles along his head.

"Return to your mother, boy. I've no time for this."

His heavy sigh brushed my forearm. "As you wish."

With the child's disappearance, the tightening in my chest eased, and I frowned, scanning those gathered, finding nothing out of sorts, except for one thing.

Runa's spritely twirls around the dance floor had ceased. Looming over her was a gruff-looking male with bulging biceps and thick shoulders. His body swayed with the beat while the sorceress had gone stiff as she twisted the wrist he clasped in his grip.

Without registering that I'd moved, I found myself before Runa's unwanted suitor.

"Release her." The last word emerged in a snarl.

The beast who held her captive scowled down at me. I glared back, tilting my head to peer up at the drunken oaf.

"The lady is with me." He dared to poke my chest. "If she was yours, you'd be at her side."

From the corner of my eye, I caught Runa's fingertips flicker with purple sparks. Bad idea. If she used her magic, our cover would be blown.

Appearing to de-escalate the situation, I held up my hands, backing away, playing the role of coward. "My mistake, friend."

The purple energy in Runa's fingertips fizzled, and she planted her hands on her hips, outrage in the glare she shot at me. "Are you kidding me? Damn right, your mistake. What kind of husband refuses to defend his wife?"

Heart jumping, I backed to a table loaded with empty tankards. Anticipation tingled up my spine. "The kind who is always subject to scrutiny and hampered by politics."

Her brow furrowed. "Seriously, you've never been in a bar fight?"

"Never. Fortunately, Morgue isn't held to those same lofty standards. And you did promise to introduce me to all this world has to offer."

I'd fought in many wars and commanded armies across dozens of battlefields. What I hadn't done was brawl like a common thug.

Runa cringed. "I didn't realize we were marking things off your adventure list. Does it still count if we're not in a bar?"

"Absolutely." I swung the empty tankard. The mug exploded against the dullard's thick skull.

I grinned back at Runa, who watched me with a shocked expression. Perhaps I'd taken this excursion into the commoner's realm too far?

Too late, I registered the heavy fist that collided with my jaw.

My head spun, and I found the pain invigorating. That was until Runa jumped onto the back of my attacker, biting his ear.

A high-pitched whine deafened me. My vision tunneled.

Runa peered at me, the fiend's earlobe clenched between her teeth. Another's blood stained her sweet mouth.

Red painted the landscape. This male would die. The moment Runa released her prey, I slammed my fist into his face. Blood exploded from his nose, and he toppled. Luckily, Runa jumped free before he collapsed like a felled tree—directly on top of a fully occupied table. The villagers seated there leaped to their feet.

Runa pointed an accusing finger at a random male who happened to be near me, and the furious mob charged the innocent bystander. Aggression stampeded through the inebriated crowd. Battle cries rang out, and those gathered turned on each other.

The sorceress faced me with wide eyes. An all-out brawl was more than I'd bargained for and significantly more attention than we needed.

"Let's get out of here before the authorities show up," I shouted over the raised voices and cursing.

"The lodge is too far. This way." Runa raced ahead of me.

We sprinted down the alley and into the stable where we'd boarded our animals. Together, we ran up a rickety flight of stairs and into the hayloft.

Once there, Runa cracked open a small loft door that overlooked the street and breathed a sigh. "I don't think anyone followed us."

She glanced at me, eyes sparkling, color in her cheeks. "That was—"

"Exhilarating," I finished.

Her laughter chipped at my stony heart.

"You've truly never been in a bar fight?" She shut the door, sealing us inside.

Adrenaline from the brawl and our escape rode me. Blood running hot, I stalked closer, Runa taking a step in retreat. "There's also one other thing I've never done."

"What's that?" she asked, her tone breathy.

I closed the distance between us, trailing my fingers down her arm in a teasing caress. "Tumbled a milkmaid in a hayloft."

At this, she tipped her head back, laughter erupting from her full lips.

"So I'm to be a milkmaid now, instead of the wife of a dung merchant?"

"If I'm to experience all of this realm's greatest wonders." I cupped her cheek, noting the flush of pink that colored her skin at my compliment. "Remove your glamour, little thief."

She nibbled her bottom lip, then nodded, grasping the medallion and uttering the incantation. I removed mine as well. We gazed at each other, eyes tracking, savoring, reconnecting with our true identities.

"The span isn't over," Runa whispered. "We're still commoners, right?"

"We are whoever you would like to be."

A frown creased her brow, and her expression turned earnest. "Then for this one night, I'd like to be yours."

At her words, my stony heart cracked. I wanted this, regardless of the fact that tomorrow, when we woke, everything would return to normal. Runa would stand with Carcerem, and I with the mortal world. But here and now, the two of us existed outside of reality.

Runa was fierce, loyal, and intelligent. Even vicious at times. She made me *feel* things I'd never experienced with another.

Throughout my life, I'd collected many treasures from various lands—spent millions of dollars filling out my collection. The shelves in my study at home were teeming with these rare and unique oddities. Runa was the greatest treasure of all.

What is mine, I keep, my subconscious whispered.

"Show me what lies beneath your disguise, little thief. Reveal yourself to me."

Chapter Thirty-One

RUNA

SINCE THE DAY an arrogant vampire lord tumbled into my hands, nothing about my world had made sense. He was Carcerem's savior and my downfall. Whether he claimed the throne or abdicated, he could never be mine. But for one night, I could put that reality aside, pretending we were two souls finding comfort in each other. Pretending we were peasants with simple goals and desires. Pretending what we were about to do together meant nothing.

I shoved every thought from my mind but one. I would exist in this moment. Claim it as mine. The memory would be mine to keep and one he would never forget.

"Choose, vampire, which of my identities shall I reveal to you?" I wasn't about to drop all my barriers, making myself vulnerable. "Your tired and neglected wife of five decades?" I unfastened the buttons on my frumpy dress, shrugged out of the sleeves, shoved the course material down my legs, and kicked the garment onto a bed of straw.

Standing before him in my moth-eaten shift, I groped my

breasts, saying in a false voice, "Take me quick, Morgue, before the younglings break out of the cellar."

Victor coughed a laugh. "It concerns me how easily that role comes to you."

"Careful, husband, or I may fall victim to a horrible headache." I cast him a glare before turning my back to him. "Perhaps you'd prefer the shy milkmaid?" I offered a coy smile over my shoulder while I slid the strap of my chemise down my arm.

Slowly, with teasing movements, I followed with the second strap. Then, bending at my waist, I guided the fabric over my hips and down to the ground where it hit with a masculine sounding exhale.

Breasts bare, in little but a pair of skimpy undergarments, I spun, prowling a path directly to him. "Or maybe I'm the leader of a band of thieves, an evil sorceress with a penchant for seduction." A devious grin tugging at my mouth, I placed a hand in the center of his chest and shoved.

Custodis fell upon a mound of hay with nary a word of objection.

With the vampire under my spell, I set a foot on either side of his hips and lowered to straddle him. "Tell me. What's it going to be?"

He grinned, enjoying my game. "That depends?"

I canted my head in question.

"Who do *you* want your partner to be?" His eyes flashed with mischief.

Suddenly, I found myself rolled and pinned.

"Am I the neglected husband who must take his pleasure quickly before my wife falls asleep or the younglings escape the dungeon?" He ground his impressive erection against my core, grinding in rhythm that made me breathless before grabbing my breast in a rushed manner that had a rare giggle threatening to emerge.

"Or am I the coarse farmhand, eager to experience anything the milkmaid will allow me to get away with?" He plumped my abused breast, then feasted on my puckered nipple. His skillful tongue circled, laving, tempting me in a way no simple laborer could pull off.

Desire pooled at my center, heat flooding my veins. I grasped his silken hair, arching my spine. "Farmhand," I gasped. "Definitely the farmhand."

"Or perhaps I'm the dashing descendant of a god?" He nuzzled a path along my ribs, his lips brushing my skin, and I held my breath.

"A divine being thrust into a strange world?" Across my stomach, he burned a trail of heated kisses and gentle nips.

"Determined to ravish any sorceress who dares to make me her captive?" His tempting mouth brushed my center, his warm breath penetrated my undergarment. Over the hated fabric that separated us, he nuzzled the sweetest of places.

"Divine," I croaked. "I was wrong. You are definitely divine."

At my admission, my vampire dragged the offensive barrier aside and slid his tongue the length of my slick channel.

"Ah!" I tossed my head. Every nerve ending between my legs lit up at the attention.

"If I were truly a god, would you pray to me?" He teased with a long stroke that had me writhing.

"Pray?" I gasped, confusion swirling through the lusty haze in my mind.

His talented tongue paused in its ministration, firm hands tightening on my thighs, and I wanted to cry at the loss.

"Pray to me, little thief," he commanded.

I discovered I'd do just about anything in that moment. "Please, my lost king, my divine vampire." The second I caved, he set back in, laving, stroking, tormenting. Words left my mouth. What? I hadn't a clue. He was my imaginary husband, my fantasy lover, my heavenly conqueror.

"Close. I'm so close. So—" Stars exploded behind my eyes. Sparks erupted along my nerve endings. Victor's hungry groan rang in my ears as he wrenched every pulse, every ripple of bliss from me.

Fabric rent, clothing shuffled, and Victor's heated flesh pressed against mine, skin on skin. I curled my legs around his naked hips, caressing his shoulders.

VICTOR

Runa's orgasm was the sweetest of victories. In that moment, I truly felt like a divine being. Over the centuries, sex had been a necessity, a political advancement, or the consummation of a pact. It had never been *this*.

With Runa, my pulse raced, my heart skipped, and my soul sang. Together, we were witty, playful, and passionate.

Real.

This was what I'd been missing with my perfunctory coupling. Despite the game we'd played, Runa was my devoted wife, my dream lover, my seductive sorceress. Everything I'd desired, yet didn't know I needed.

In my moment of distraction, I ended up pinned beneath my curvaceous conquer.

Runa peered down at me. A predatory glint blazed in her eyes. Slim fingers curled around my throbbing cock and a low growl rumbled in my throat.

"Tell me, what am I to do with this divine king that I've captured?"

At the first tempting stroke of her skilled hand, my eyes rolled back.

"Shall I pull him from the jaws of a hungry beast and lock him up in shackles?"

Before I could formulate an answer, Runa's mouth covered my nipple, her teeth grazing my tender flesh while her talented palm did wondrous things to my aching shaft.

Her molten tongue set off on a delightful journey down my ribs, over my abdomen, and across my hipbone.

Speechless, I took in the sight of her full breasts brushing my thighs, the hungry gleam in her violet gaze, and her plump lips, inches from my manhood, noting the caress of her hot breath feathering my flesh.

"Shall I keep him prisoner to my wicked desires?" Runa's tongue made a slow journey from the base of my shaft to the aching tip. Then her wicked mouth closed over me, and I forgot the question. In an embarrassingly short amount of time, she had me on the brink.

It took everything in me to make her stop. "Enough, pet. Before you unman me."

I seized her shoulders, guiding her back up my body where she straddled my hips. A playful smile danced upon her swollen lips.

"Tell me, vampire, have you ever been ravished in a hayloft?"

Despite the state of my aching cock, I couldn't recall being this entertained during sex. "Can't say that I have."

"Good. Then let me be the first." Runa guided my erection where she desired me, lowering her welcoming heat along my shaft and taking me into her body.

"Flark," I growled her favorite curse, grasping her hips and thrusting.

"Oh, that's nice," she purred, planting her hands on my pectorals and rocking her hips.

In moments, she found a seed-stealing rhythm that had me seeing stars. If I continued to let her have her way, I'd never last.

"Nice?" I snarled. "I'll show you nice."

I grasped her waist and rolled, pinning her under me.

"Curse you, vampire," she groaned. "I was enjoying that."

"You've had your fun, pet. Now, be a good girl and allow me to have mine."

Her violet eyes narrowed in warning. "Be a good—Oh!"

I drove my cock into her slick entrance, silencing her protests. With every rock of my hips, pressure built at the base of my spine. Desperate hands clawed at my shoulders. The sorceress's thighs squeezed my flanks, urging me on. Harder. Deeper.

"Oh, that's it. Faster," she ordered.

I claimed her mouth, kissing her until we were both gasping for air. "No more commands," I growled against her lips.

The handprint I'd left on her throat had darkened, glowing with a celestial light. Upon seeing my mark, possessive urges rose inside of me like a gathering storm.

My divine half might have claimed this female, but tonight, it was the vampire's turn.

Fangs extended from my gums. "Earlier, you granted me a mere taste. Tonight, I want all of you."

Runa's gleaming eyes dilated in response. Anticipation blazed across her cheeks. "No vampire has ever taken my blood."

At her admission, a primal presence stirred in my psyche. This pleased me. "You and I, we've experienced many firsts this evening."

"Why stop now?" she murmured, tilting her head, exposing her neck.

Hunger stabbed my gut. Before she could rescind her offer, I lowered my head and sank my fangs into her throat. One sip and I was lost.

All vampires connected with their prey's essence when they fed. It was the reason blood needed to come straight from the source. Runa's was the most delightful of nectars. Her essence washed over me. In that connection, I sensed a magic that was uniquely hers, mixed with tendrils of courage and devotion. The responsibility she bore for those weaker than her, even kindness, but also a sense of ruthlessness, and a spirit that would never surrender, never quit.

Beneath her unique signature, there was something else. Something bigger than the two of us. It welcomed me like a lost friend. Its touch felt like home, safe and nurturing. Its power was immense. Instinctively, I sensed this was Carcerem. As a sorceress, Runa was connected to the kingdom and drew her strength from it. This same connection was a siren's song calling to me.

Runa's throaty moan forced my attention back to her lush body. My aching cock. I released her throat, and she uttered a whimper of protest.

"By the fates, it's all so clear now," she gasped.

I wondered at her meaning, but the demands of my body blinded me to all but the feeling of her slick heat surrounding me.

Runa's legs clamped around my hips, and she tossed her head, crying out as her orgasm exploded through her. The tight, pulsing grip of her channel sent me over the edge as well, and I buried my cock deep into her depths, shouting my release. Jets of pleasure erupted from me, filling and marking the female beneath me. Spasms rocked our writhing bodies, and my muscles were powerful and yet weak all at the same time.

It seemed my very soul left my body, floating somewhere above me. My vision turned gold. Once I'd returned to myself, the sensation of gentle, stroking fingers slid over my shoulders and back.

"Still with me?" Runa chuckled.

"I... Yes." I couldn't remember a moment when I'd lost myself so completely with a woman. The experience left me shaken.

I rolled to my back, taking Runa with me and tucking her

into my side. She angled her leg over my thigh and nestled her face under my chin.

"That was incredible," she whispered.

"That was..." Beyond incredible. I had no words.

"I think I get it now."

I struggled to focus. "What's that?"

"The venom."

"Ahh." Despite my wandering thoughts, a smile tugged my lips. I toyed with a strand of her lavender hair.

"I mean. It had to be the effect of your venom, right? Because that was...like nothing I'd ever experienced before."

"Yes, the venom," I agreed, though I'd never seen a female react in such a way. It certainly didn't explain my own reaction.

Strangely, while feeding from her, I'd sensed no desire to utter the incantation that would claim her as my Bride. Perhaps because she was already mine?

Regardless, I had a nagging suspicion that what happened between us was more than sex. It was a spiritual interaction between mates. The idea chilled me. Primal urges rose at the thought. Urges that demanded the sorceress was mine forevermore.

Yes, said a voice from deep within my psyche.

Despite Runa's efforts, I had not changed my mind about staying here. Carcerem's people were little more than savages. Delightful savages who made the finest fermented brews, danced feet-stomping jigs, and took pleasure in the simple parts of life. None of that was for me. Was it? It wasn't. Of course, it wasn't.

Chapter Thirty-Two

RUNA

MY EYES FLICKED OPEN, and my breath caught. What woke me? The jolt of alarm soon faded when I realized I lay on a pile of itchy straw, my naked limbs intertwined with Victor's. I took in his soft features as he slept. He was almost too pretty to be male. Every line of his patrician face was perfectly balanced. His nose, cheeks, brows, chin, each angle was strong and proud. It was as if the gods themselves had sculpted him.

I suppose they had.

His body was similarly made. Sublime in every way. From his lean muscles, defined abs, angular hipbones to his… *cough*… I forced my eyes away from his manhood. That part of him was also divine. Lucky me. My lips curled, and I rubbed the base of my throat. The place where he'd marked me with his handprint warmed.

Despite the cloud hanging over us, I couldn't remember having so much fun. Yesterday at the festival, I'd seen a side of the vampire I didn't think existed. From the wonder in his eyes, I suspected he hadn't known of its existence either. I enjoyed being the one to reveal that aspect of him. I wished we could have more days like yesterday together.

My chest tightened, and I exhaled a heavy sigh. There was no point in wishing for impossible dreams. We both had a part to play. His was far loftier than mine.

Thunder cracked, and the stable walls rumbled. Dust rained down from the ceiling, screams ringing out.

I shot to my feet, coughing. "What was that?" I stumbled to the loft door and peered out. It was still dark outside.

Victor stood at my back, alert despite the harsh wake-up call. In the street below, villagers fled to the east, some arming themselves as they went. I glanced in the opposite direction, and needles prickled my skin. Soldiers in purple capes flooded the road from the west. Some on horseback, many on foot.

"It's Idris's men." Alarm shot through every nerve in my body.

"Get dressed." Victor shoved my clothing at me before stabbing his legs into his pants.

"They've found us." I whipped my shift, then my dress over my head. "How the hell did they find us so fast?"

"I don't know, but we need to leave."

"I'll get Yaga." I stomped into my shoes. "You ready our horses."

Victor's firm hand clamped around my upper arm, and I peered into his steely eyes. Face set in stone, he said, "We have to leave her, Runa."

"What?" Maybe I'd misheard. "I am not leaving Yaga."

"She will slow us down," he stated in an emotionless tone.

"So what?" I wrenched my arm from his grip. "If Idris somehow found out we traveled here, he may know Yaga was with us. If he captures her, he'll harm her to get to us."

"Yaga knew the risk." Gone was the male from yesterday. The imaginary male who didn't exist.

"You son of a bitch," I spat, my heart withering. "You made

me forget. I got so wrapped up in being nobody with you, I almost forgot who you really are."

"Runa..."

"Good luck with the temple," I snapped, a piece of me dying inside. "Look me up when you're ready for that portal. I will gladly send you where you belong."

With that, I turned my back on the lost king and raced down the rickety steps.

Lost king, I fumed. Lost king, indeed. Kronk was more of a king than Custodis.

"Runa. Dammit. Wait!" I ignored the vampire's snarls.

I needed a weapon. Carefully, I scanned the stalls. With few options, I grabbed a long-handled shovel and slipped out the door.

The roads outside the stable were utter chaos. Across the alley, a woman screamed, running from a soldier on a horse baring down on her. With one swift slice of his sword, the woman's scream was silenced.

She was unarmed and little threat. The soldiers were slaughtering everyone who crossed their path. Images burned in my mind. Images of a similar night. My father's lifeless eyes stared up at me. Bodies lined the streets. My mother called to me and my sister. Her voice was a horrified whisper, *Runa, Raelynn, this way. Hurry.*

"Runa." The sound of my name snapped me out of my memory and into my current nightmare.

Victor stood behind me, pitchfork in hand.

"What are you doing here?"

"Protecting my...investment," he growled.

I ground my molars. "Right. Just stay out of my way."

On the road in front of us, a foot soldier headed toward the stables. His dark head swiveled as he searched for fresh prey.

Victor shuffled closer. "What's your plan?"

I stepped from the shadows. "Hey, bula-hole!"

The soldier spun in my direction as I swung my weapon. The shovel clanged, smashing his face. He fell back, then rolled, hitting his knees. Again, I swung, this time cracking the base of his skull. The soldier collapsed with a soft groan.

Victor claimed the fallen man's sword, snarling, "It's foolish to charge into a fray without a plan."

I bared my teeth at him. "I already told you my plan. Save Yaga. What are you still doing here, anyway?"

He heaved an exasperated sigh. "I honestly don't know."

Over our heads, a blazing ball whistled. I followed its path, and my heart jolted to a stop.

"No," I moaned before it slammed into the lodge where Yaga was staying. The ground trembled with the impact. Fiery sparks exploded into the sky.

Panic charged through my veins. The flood of fear soaked into my bones. Tunnel vision blinded me to everything but the woman who'd raised me. Eyes locked on the burning lodge, I raced into the street.

"Idris, you bastard," I screamed. "You will not take her from me, too."

"Runa, wait. Your glamour," a voice shouted.

From out of nowhere, a sword slashed. Metal glinted, slicing toward my neck. For some reason, it failed to connect. Grunting and curses rang out behind me. I stalked forward, blind to anything but the burning building.

I ditched my shovel, reaching for my preferred weapon. Power flared in my palms, and a terrifying creature I was far too familiar with flashed through my mind. I launched my duskcat illusion into the world. Around me, half a dozen monster kitties took shape. Screams rang out. Soldiers scrambled for higher ground. One of the braver souls swiped his sword through the chest of one of my illusions.

"They're not real!" he yelled. "The sorceress is here. Find her!"

That I'd been outed so quickly didn't matter since I'd reached the lodge. Heat from fire seared my flesh.

"Dammit, Runa. Don't go in there!" a familiar voice shouted as I threw open the door.

Inside, a hellish scene greeted me. The thought that Yaga was here, suffering, forced me to thrust one foot in front of the other. Smoke clung to the ceiling, flames licking the walls. My lungs burned, and I grabbed the hem of my skirt, pushing it up over my face.

"Yaga!" I shouted, heading for the second floor.

"It's too late. You're going to get yourself killed," that annoying voice bellowed.

Behind me, timbers groaned, then crashed. A pained shout rang out, and I glanced back to find that part of a wall had fallen in, blocking the door. No matter, Yaga and I would find another way out.

Up the steps, I raced. At the top, thick smoke drove me to my hands and knees. Tears streamed from my stinging eyes.

"Yaga!" Fear threatened to overwhelm me, and I choked out a sob. I'd never find her in this. Except I didn't have to see her to find her. Yaga said as much about locating the temple guardian. Yaga herself was a powerful entity.

Forcing the panic aside, I closed my eyes, throwing out my senses. At first, there was nothing. Then, a small glimmer of life sparked in my psyche.

"Yaga?" I coughed, crawling to a closed door, turning the knob.

An iron vice gripped my ankle, dragging me away. My outstretched hand popped off the door.

"Got her!" a gruff male shouted. "Here. I found the sorceress!"

What? No. Not when I was so close. I kicked out with my free leg, and another hand grabbed that one as well. There wasn't time for this.

Terror squeezed me in its sickening grasp. I clawed at the door frame as I was dragged backward.

"Let me go!" I screamed.

My chest expanded, power swelling.

An illusion of fire erupted over my body. My captor screeched, releasing the image of my burning flesh. I lunged for the door, turned the knob, flung it open. A very real inferno exploded from the opening, throwing me back. Hungry flames consumed the oxygen around us. There was no possible way Yaga could have survived.

I pushed my senses out. Nothing answered. Yaga's spirit was a black hole of nothingness.

"No. Not her. Not her!" I shoved my elbows beneath me, crawling. My head swam. Smoke filled my lungs. The acrid scent of burned flesh permeated my nose, scraped down the back of my tongue, and lodged in my throat.

The edges of the burning room drew closer. Black dots spattered my vision, and my will to go further washed away on a thin exhale.

Chapter Thirty-Three

VICTOR

ACHES and pains woke me from an unnatural sleep. The metallic burn of blood and smoke invaded my nostrils. Splintered boards rest on top of me, pinning me beneath their scorched weight.

"Bloody hell." I'd been buried alive.

Memories returned. I'd chased Runa into the burning lodge when part of the wall had fallen on me. Apparently, the chit had left me for dead, consumed with rescuing her precious Yaga. This was the thanks I got for trying to play hero.

Sunlight shone through a crack in the rubble. I struggled to gather my arms beneath me, dragging my weight forward. Pain erupted in my thigh.

"Argh!" I bellowed. Spots swam in my vision. I let my head drop, panting. I trailed my hand down, discovering a piece of debris jutting from my flesh. Just what I needed.

"Hello?" said a squeaky voice. "Is someone there?"

At least it didn't sound like a soldier.

"Here," I grunted. "I'm stuck."

"Hold on." Footsteps crunched, and the board above me vanished.

For a moment, the sudden light seared my eyeballs, and I flinched, drawing the person in front of me into focus.

A child? The boy's unruly stock of bright orange hair glowed red in the sunlight. It was the youth from the celebration last night.

"Great. It's you," I said, failing to convey any sort of joy. "Do you think you can get me out of here?"

The child eyed my situation and bit his lip. "I will try."

"Good chap."

Grunting sounded, and the board resting on my back grew lighter.

"Little more," he said. "Almost there."

Wood cracked, jostling my leg, and I dug my nails into my palms to prevent myself from screaming.

"There. That should do it."

Finally, I managed to crawl out of the wreckage. Once free, I sat on the ground and examined my injured limb. Sticking out of my thigh was a jagged length of timber.

"Outstanding," I groaned.

The child hunkered down beside me, gesturing to the injury. "You want me to—"

"No," I was quick to say. "I'll do it."

The massive splinter taunted me. This was going to hurt. I hesitated.

"I don't mind," the kid offered again.

"I said, I've got it." I gripped the end of the wooden stake. Three short breaths and I yanked. Blood spurted, my flesh tearing.

Agony blazed over my senses. I threw back my head, cursing at the heavens.

Breathing deeply, I opened my eyes to find the boy. Stunned expression on his freckled face, he stared at me.

"What?" I snarled.

"I never heard some of those words."

I glared at him. "Your parents never swear?"

His brows drew tight. "I don't have parents. Some of my children swear, though."

Perhaps it was the blood loss. "Did you say children?"

"Your face looks better now."

"My face?" Strange child. "The woman I was with yesterday. Have you seen her?" Flark, except he wouldn't recognize her without her glamour activated.

"Yes," he said, despite my concerns. "Runa was taken by the dark ones."

Then she lived. Relief flooded me until I replayed his words. "You know her name?"

"Of course. She is Runa Starborn, and you are Victor Custodis."

"How do you know this?"

He frowned, tawny brows tenting with displeasure. "Yaga said you were searching for me and that I should help you, even though sometimes you're not very nice."

"You're…"

"Milton, the temple guardian." His frown deepened. "I attempted to tell you yesterday, but you were not ready."

"Your name is Milton?"

"Yes. Milton the wise. Milton the eternal. Milton the all-knowing. I go by many names."

This was the all-powerful guardian? The goddess Hathor's right-hand man? How…underwhelming.

I scanned the remains of the lodge. Little remained standing but for the stone chimney.

"What of Yaga?" I felt obliged to ask.

"Hathor's priestess fulfilled her duty and journeyed to her next assignment."

Priestess? The scrappy old woman was a divine priestess? Something to process another day. "She's alive then?"

"Why wouldn't she be?" he huffed. "As Hathor's ambassador, like me, she is undying. Before Yaga left, she asked me to give you a message. She said to tell Hot Britches it's past time"—he cleared his throat, cheeks reddening—"you pulled your head out of your fine ass."

I heaved a sigh. She was most definitely alive. "And Runa? What shape was she in when she was captured?"

"Her light was dim."

My chest tightened. I eyed the gash in my flesh, finding it had stopped bleeding. Already, the wound had improved, healing faster than it would have in the mortal realm. One of the benefits of my divine heritage, I supposed.

I took in my surroundings. Half the buildings still smoldered. Bodies lined the sidewalks. Injured civilians, some with bandages on various extremities, wandered the streets, calling out the names of loved ones. Smashed tents and torn banners fluttered in a somber breeze.

Where yesterday, there'd been celebrating and merriment, today there was death and destruction. It was a scene I wasn't unfamiliar with. When a new king rose to power, there were often those who fell in their wake. Still, the sight of this small town troubled me. Made me *feel* instead of leaving me with a cold sense of detachment I'd grown accustomed to. The most prominent feeling was *rage*.

Amberdale had been a beautiful, thriving village filled with many bright souls. For a short time, I was blessed to walk among them. To be "nobody" with them. And dammit, I'd enjoyed myself. Curse Runa and her plan to woo me, for she'd succeeded. What Idris had done to these people was sacrilege.

At my silence, the guardian put a hand on my shoulder. "I will take you to the Empyrean temple now."

"Now? I can't go now! Not with Runa in the hands of—"

"Yaga tried to warn you," Milton's tone snapped with censure. His eyes glowed with an eerie golden fire. "She told you that if power is all you want, then power is all you will have."

I raked my hands through my hair, snarling, "What does that mean? That I must choose? Rescue Runa or reclaim my birthright? Does that mean if I delay saving Runa, she will die?"

The child shrugged. "I am not a seer like Yaga. Only a guide. You must choose your own path."

"Argh!" My frustration emerged as a roar. "Flarking celestial nonsense!"

I staggered to my feet, glaring in the direction of Slyborn Castle. How dare Idris take what was mine? Rage pounded between my temples. If he harmed one hair on Runa's head, I'd find a way to make him pay tenfold. Every moment she was in his hands was a moment too long. Everything within me demanded I storm the castle and tear her from his clutches.

"Hathor will not permit me to appear to you again. This is your only chance. It's a long and difficult journey. We should get started."

For the first time since I could remember, my conscience battled with my goals. The thought of Runa alone with Idris for even one minute threatened to send me charging straight for the castle.

Once more, I gazed at the destruction that surrounded me. These civilians had been powerless. It was a reminder. A male without power was vulnerable. I struggled to temper my fury. This wasn't a time to allow my emotions to get the better of me.

I couldn't very well go up against Idris and his army in my current state. It would be best to face him on equal ground. First, I'd recharge. Then, I'd retrieve Runa. I had faith she could handle herself until I arrived.

Faith.

If only Runa could see me now.

Turned out, I did believe in something other than myself.

I believed in *her*.

"I'll need a horse and supplies," I growled.

"A horse cannot travel where we journey. You must go on foot. Unless you've changed your mind?"

Cursed mystical deities. Cursed prophesies.

I stabbed my hands into the pockets of my tunic to keep them from circling the guardian's scrawny throat. My fingers grazed something, and I extracted the tiny wood carving of a dragon. The trophy Runa had won in the dart game. When she gifted it to me, she claimed it reminded her of my proverbial fall from grace during the trials. If she only knew how far I'd truly fallen that day.

My head swam, and my injured leg throbbed with a pulse, wobbling beneath me.

"Lead on," I ordered, and the mysterious child took my hand.

Chapter Thirty-Four

RUNA

UNFORGIVING METAL CHAFED MY WRIST. My arms ached from being chained to the wall. The damp and cold of my cell permeated my bones. With little but my discomfort to distract me, images of Yaga's blazing room filled my mind.

I shouldn't have left her side. What was I thinking, dancing about like a drunken fool with Custodis? People like me didn't get to pretend they were free. Free of responsibility. Free of my many crimes. Free of guilt.

And I was…

Guilty.

My parents had died trying to protect Raelynn and me. A sacrifice I didn't deserve. I'd failed them. Failed Carcerem. If only I'd dragged my sister through our mother's portal and taken her far from Idris's influence, even if it meant locking her in chains for the journey. Instead, I'd let her slip away.

Much as I had with Yaga.

I never should have let her out of my sight. I knew better. Still, I'd allowed a vulnerable old woman to gallivant around the village unprotected. Then, instead of returning to her side at the first opportunity, I was off rolling in the hay like some light-skirted trollop.

Tears welled in my burning eyes, and I willed them back.

Crying would do nothing to get me out of my current situation. I was Idris's prisoner *again*. Only this time, there was no one around to help me. Not my brothers. Not some undercover allies sent by a queen. Not Victor.

I imagined that after my departure from the stable, he'd grabbed the closest horse and fled. After all, he had little to gain from sticking around. Given his skills with manipulation, I had zero doubts he'd find the guardian and convince them to lead him to the temple. Perhaps he'd even find a way to have the mystic open a portal for him.

I envisioned Victor's perfect body glowing with an ethereal light. *Runa who?* he'd say before the gateway opened and the vampire vanished from my life with the same suddenness in which he'd stormed into it.

Footsteps echoed in the hallway outside my cell door, and I tensed. Torchlight illuminated my prison cell, and Idris emerged.

My stomach clenched. I'd been dreading this moment since I'd awoken in this damned cell.

"Open it," he ordered the guard, and his milky-eyed slave was quick to comply.

Magic pulled at my center. Purple energy glowed in my palms. I conjured a three-headed serpent and sent it lunging at the door.

Idris snapped his fingers, flicking a small ball of energy at my creation, and it vanished in an instant.

I sagged in my chains. I'd figured there was a reason he'd neglected to collar me with a torque.

"Cute." He smirked, striding into the dank space.

Gaze glinting with a disturbing light, he scanned my form.

"Sweet Runa. It's so good to have you back with us. I knew it was only a matter of time."

"Aw, did you miss me?" I pouted.

"Desperately." He sighed in a mocking way. "Tell me. What is my bastard sibling up to these days?"

"Ah. Figured that out, did you?"

Last time I'd seen Idris was in the pit. Custodis had shattered beneath the dragon's fire, turning into a golden god while the false king had cowered beneath his royal chair. Apparently, Idris made the connection.

"I am curious." He narrowed his eyes. "At what point did you become aware of our familial tie?"

"Not soon enough, sadly." It was a shame Yaga hadn't bothered to inform me my captive was, in fact, the lost king.

Yaga. My heart pinched.

"Right." Idris slithered closer, planting his hand on the wall beside my head. "And where exactly is my brother now?"

I pinned my eyes over his shoulder. "Don't know. Don't care."

"Spoken like a jilted lover," he purred.

"Hardly," I scoffed, hoping he couldn't detect the skip in my pulse. "I'm certain Custodis is long gone."

"I wouldn't be so sure about that." He toyed with a lank curl of my lavender hair. "See, there's the pesky issue of the prophecy."

"That old thing." I snorted.

"Yes." His grip on my hair tightened. "That old thing."

I hitched a shoulder as much as my restraints allowed. "Custodis has his own agenda and little interest in your throne." Nor me, it would seem.

"See. I want to trust you, but it's a chance I simply cannot take." Ruthless fingers gripped the top of my head, slamming my skull against the stone. "Tell me where he is."

Stars sparked in my vision, and my scalp screamed. "I don't know," I shouted.

"I don't believe you," he shouted back, saliva spraying my face. "In fact, I'm rather certain he wouldn't travel far from his fated mate."

Laughter spilled from my lips. "You're so stupid. You know nothing."

Idris's palm exploded against my cheek. Pain detonated inside my skull. Bells clanged in my ears.

I tongued the cut in my cheek, snarling, "I am not his fated anything. He couldn't care less about me."

"That isn't how it looked in the final challenge." Golden energy crackled in his palm, and a magical image formed. In it was a picture of the finale. Tiny Runa stood before the fierce dragon, moments away from being burned to death. Then, the image shifted to a view of Victor on his floating platform. His face contorted into an expression of rage, possession gleaming in his glowing gaze. Peering down at me below, he bellowed a war cry and leaped from the relative safety of his platform.

He didn't fall.

Some small part of me had known, but still, doubts had plagued me.

He didn't fall.

When he'd leaped to my defense, he had no idea he was a divine being. In that moment, he'd been prepared to die for me. How was that possible unless...

The mark on my throat. Was it some kind of sacred claim? Was Victor Custodis—the lost king—my mate?

My heart seized, and tears burned my eyes.

Oh, Yaga. Did you know?

The weight of Idris's calculating gaze chewed into my flesh. Too late, I schooled my reaction.

"I know an illusion when I see one." My voice wavered. "That image means nothing to me."

Idris's cruel smirk warned he didn't believe my denial. "Tell me what he's planning."

"He doesn't confide in me." The false king couldn't know about the temple.

Idris heaved a deep sigh of annoyance that had the hairs along my nape prickling. "I suppose you leave me no choice, then." He stepped back. "Guards."

As if they'd been instructed in advance, Idris's milky-eyed guards relieved me of my chains, dragging me behind their false king, up many levels of stairs, and down dozens of hallways until at last we reached the throne room.

Standing beside the sacred arbor was Raelynn, confirming this must have been Idris's plan all along.

Except the brief look of confusion on Raelynn's face indicated she wasn't in the know. As her eyes shifted from Idris to me, her scowl tightened with betrayal.

Ah, were mommy and daddy fighting? Too bad.

Idris settled his royal posterior onto the seat of his throne, and the guards dragged me before him.

Raelynn peered down her nose as if she'd stepped into a pile of bula dung. "What is *she* doing here?"

Apprehension tugged at my insides. The presence of the ailing tree reached for me, and I was helpless not to answer. The kingdom's power twisted around me. Its essence was bitter instead of sweet, tainted with darkness. With pain. Our great tree was sick. That illness spread into everything it touched. Even me.

"Now, now, dear." Idris tsked. "Is that any way to greet your sister?"

Raelynn sneered in return. Once more, I found myself wishing her face would freeze. "That gutter rat is no sister to me."

I forced my lips into the sweetest of smiles. "On this, we agree. I do not consort with traitors."

Rage flashed in Raelynn's milky-violet eyes. She raised her hand, allowing purple energy to crackle in her palm.

"Ah, ah, ah," Idris taunted, clearly enjoying his queen's reaction. "No need to fight, ladies. There is plenty of room for both of you."

Breath seized in my lungs. He couldn't mean...

Raelynn tensed as well, snapping, "You can't be serious."

"Oh, but I am," Idris sang. "Runa has information I need and is proving uncooperative."

Raelynn took an aggressive step forward, raising her clenched fists. "Then beat it out of her."

"Oh, come now." Idris fluttered a bejeweled hand. "We are more civilized than that. Besides, you know how stubborn she can be. She reminds me of you in that way, darling."

Raelynn pursed her lips, tilting her chin. "What do you propose?"

"Only that we bring her into the fold," Idris answered.

Drums took up residence in my skull. My heart pounded a frantic beat.

Raelynn shot me a murderous glare, then leveled a cajoling gaze upon her king. "My love. Don't be silly. Let me spend some time with her in the dungeon. I will get the answers you seek."

Idris slammed his fist into the armrest, sending dozens of burning leaves falling from the sacred tree's limbs. "Do not argue with me. Guards!"

Firm hands clamped down on my arms, dragging my reluctant form up the raised dais to stand before the queen.

"Kneel," the guard commanded, driving my knees into the marble floor.

I peered up into the face of the girl who'd been a fixture in my childhood. The woman who was my last connection to my parents.

"Raelynn, please, don't do this. Think of Mamma. Papa. Remember all they sacrificed for us. We were a family once.

Before *him*. We were happy. Surely, you remember your favorite doll, Princess Poppy. The three of us had so many adventures together."

"We did." Raelynn's glare turned glacial, freezing me in place. "Until you tossed her into the river."

Flark, I'd forgotten that part.

I squared my shoulders, jutting my chin. "I wouldn't have done it if you hadn't pulled the head off of Mopsie."

Despite my deplorable attempt to reach some long-buried part of my sibling, Raelynn grasped my head, digging her nails into my scalp.

Through Idris's milky-eyed influence, her violet gaze gave off an amethyst glow. I realized too late that it hadn't mattered how tightly I'd clung to her hand. She'd been lost to me long before Idris made her queen.

It wasn't my fault.

None of it was my fault.

Nor was it fate.

As Victor said, our choices are our own.

This was Raelynn's.

"Easy now," my sister purred in a way that made my skin crawl. "This will only hurt for a moment."

The assurance uttered in such a devilish manner only managed to increase my fear.

Tears flooded my eyes as helplessness washed over me. I was about to become one of Idris's mindless slaves. My worst nightmare was coming true.

Pain exploded between my temples, and then my world turned white.

Chapter Thirty-Five

VICTOR

DEEP SNOW COVERED my legs up to the middle of my thighs. Frigid winds battered my unprepared frame. My thin tunic and leggings did little to block the cold. My fingertips had long ago turned blue. I feared to check the rest of my extremities.

We'd spent the entire day journeying high into the mountain tops. Such was the way of character-building quests, I supposed. Fates forbid they took place in tropical settings with eager room service.

My companion suffered no such discomfort. The freckle-faced child floated beside me in a climate-controlled bubble. Though I'd asked many times, he'd assured me there was only room for one celestial being within.

I shouted over the fierce howling of the wind. "The conditions of this journey are deplorable. I'd like to speak to the manager."

I imagined Runa's response to my horrible attempt at humor. An image of her saucy smile warmed me from the inside out.

Runa would think I was amusing. Or annoying. Perhaps both. I'd enjoy her reaction either way.

Runa.

Flark, this was taking too long.

"Why do you seek this power?" my celestial guide asked, yet again. And again. And again.

Children and their infernal questions. Though I suspected the temple guardian was an ancient entity and not the youthful boy it pretended to be.

Still, I did not dare to ignore him. Earlier, when I hadn't answered, he'd blasted me to the beginning of the winding mountain trail and made me start over.

"To take back what is mine," I answered for the millionth time, refusing to expound.

"*What is mine. What is mine,*" Milton taunted in a sing-song voice. "Is that all you can say?"

"What do you want from me?"

"Honesty."

"I haven't lied." Not exactly.

"Nor have you told the truth. Is Runa *yours*? Do you do it for her?"

"Yes."

"*Now*, you lie." He folded his thin arms, glaring at the icy terrain.

"When my strength is restored, I *will* free her."

"But you don't set out on this quest for power for her."

"Runa is her own person. She understands what I must do."

He snorted a scoffing inhalation. "Your mate understands that you intend to free and then abandoned her?"

I stiffened. "Runa is not my mate. Not officially. I never claimed her as my Bride."

"Because you didn't need to," he informed me, his manner matter of fact. "There was no need to perform your blood-sucking vampire ceremony because you're a child of the gods and Hathor's chosen one. Instead of a predatory wound, you placed a divine brand upon Runa's throat."

Flark. It was as I feared then.

"Strange place if you ask me." He screwed up his freckled face. "Awfully prominent. Idris placed his mark on his queen's shoulder."

My laboring heart skipped, then raced in my chest, my pulse pounding in my head. "Do you mean to tell me I've claimed Runa for all of eternity?"

"Do you honestly expect me, a child, to explain procreation and claiming to you?"

"Fa-fa-fates no," I snapped, teeth chattering. "What does a freckle-faced kid know about mates anyway?"

"More than you, apparently," Milton scoffed. "You didn't even realize you had one."

Deep down, I knew he was right. I'd claimed Runa. Flark, but that complicated things.

"What about Carcerem's throne? Isn't it yours as well?"

My frozen mind struggled to keep up with the child's endless prattling.

I dared not lie. There was no telling what the brat would do. "I've no interest in Carcerem's diseased throne."

"Why not?"

"I've one of my own to reclaim once I return to my home. One that cost me centuries of blood, sweat, and tears to obtain. One I refuse to give up."

"Seems to me you're rejecting the things that are rightfully yours in favor of something that is not."

"The mortal underworld owes me," I growled, plunging one frostbitten foot before the other. "What is mine, I keep."

"Spoken like an entitled mortal." Milton sighed. "Your world must be incredibly beautiful for you to choose it over this one."

In my mind, I pictured my home. My sprawling mansion, while lovely, paled in comparison to Slyborn Castle. Paved roads, rumbling machinery, and the stench of exhaust fumes drifted on the wind. None of it held up when compared to the natural splendor of this land.

"Did your followers worship you in the mortal world?"

"They did not." I pictured the High Court justices sneering down at me. The bloodthirsty audience, eager to watch me fall.

"Carcerem would worship you," he quipped, his bubble riding an icy breeze. "Many already do. I fear they will lose hope when you abandon them."

I bared my fangs, icy lips splitting with the effort. "Until a new prophecy comes along, declaring the rise of yet another fated king."

"And the mortal world, they are eager for your return, waiting to welcome you?"

"No."

"Then you must have a wife. One you left behind, as you are about to do here. She must be truly special for you to leave your fated mate in Carcerem. Runa will suffer once you're gone. To be separated from one's fated mate is excruciating. It seems cruel to have claimed her, knowing you would throw her away."

Would she? At the thought of Runa suffering, daggers pierced my heart.

"I think maybe you are not deserving of the realm's gifts."

"It doesn't matter what you think."

"Perhaps, but it will matter what the keeper of the Empyrean temple thinks."

"How so?"

"Only those who are worthy shall bathe in Hathor's power. Should she reject you, you will die."

"She won't reject me." I smirked, throwing his own argument back at him. "I am the lost king."

"This, sadly, is the truth, even if you do not believe. You are the lost king. The king who has *lost* his faith in mankind. Who has lost his ability to love. Lost sight of what really matters. Lost his values. His honor."

In the distance, a stone circle took shape in the frosty haze. I rubbed the ice crystals from my weeping eyeballs.

"Is that…"

"The Empyrean temple," my floating guide confirmed.

Thank the gods. I didn't know how much more of the child's clumsy manipulation I could tolerate without punting his magical sphere down the mountain.

At the entrance, he bowed his head to me. "Good luck, Victor Custodis. I hope you find what it is that you truly seek."

The temple door swung open, and a wave of hot air washed over my frozen frame. Warmth beckoned, and I hurried inside, closing the door behind me. Before me was a heated grotto. Steam wafted from a turquoise pool set in its center. Glowing crystals nestled into the walls, filling the space with light. Ferns and tropical flowers poked out from the rocks.

I blew into my chilly hands, rubbing my icy skin. Etched into the stone were ancient runes. It was in a language I didn't recognize. I uttered a curse, trailing my fingers over the carvings, when a golden burst of energy snapped to life. I jerked my hand away, watching as the odd images shifted, the runes changing. Words took shape in a language I understood.

Those who seek redemption shall find enlightenment in the water.

Frozen fabric cracked in my grip, and I drew my frozen tunic over my shoulders. The material was stiff as cardboard. I did the same with my remaining garments, relieved to be free of my bedraggled clothing.

This was it.

At the edge of the pool, I dipped a toe, finding the temperature pleasant enough. Though even ice water would be warmer than what I just trekked through. Once I was submerged up to my shoulders, I moaned in relief, my body thawing. This wasn't so bad. Perhaps the guardian exaggerated when he spoke of death.

I held out my arms and dropped my head back, slushy clumps sliding out of my hair and dropping into the languid waters. I swished my arms. Waiting. Waiting.

Nothing was happening. I cracked an eye open. It was possible I'd misinterpreted the runes. Was there an incantation I'd missed? I exhaled a frustrated sigh and dipped beneath the water to rid the silver strands of the clinging ice crystals. On my way back up, my forehead smacked an invisible ceiling.

My eyes shot open, the surface of the water coming into focus. What the hell? I reached up, and my fingers met an unbreakable force.

I was trapped? Adrenaline spiked my veins. My lungs burned as I pounded the ceiling with my fists. My pulse pounded in my head. My eyes bulged. I might be divine, but I still required oxygen. I needed out. With my pulse racing, I ran my hands over the stones. There had to be a hidden release.

"Why do you seek this power?" a soft, feminine voice asked, the words echoing in my mind instead of my ears.

"What is the meaning of this?" I demanded. "Release me."

My frantic search for an exit revealed nothing. Bubbles parted my lips. My chest ached to expand—to draw in a breath. Spots swam before my tunneling vision. Spasms racked my frame. My body was no longer mine to control.

Against my will, my reflexes took over, and I sucked in a mouthful of water. The thick liquid flowed down my throat. It filled my lungs, and still, I continued to breathe.

I was drowning and breathing all at once. Alive and dead. Everything and nothing.

Serenity filled the hollow space at my center. A void that had been there since my youth. Since I was cut off from Carcerem. It healed me where I was broken. Soothed me where I was hurting. Took away all my pain, making me whole.

"Why do you seek this power?" again, the soothing voice asked.

This time, I was calm enough to hear her.

"Because it's..." I faltered, realizing it wasn't water that flowed through me but obsidian. Through it, I was connected. Connected to something so much bigger than me. The thrust of Carcerem's mountains. The rush of her rivers. Warmth of her sun and tranquility of her twin moons. She was all around me. I was Carcerem, and Carcerem was me.

This feeling. This sense of belonging. It was exquisite.

Voices flooded my mind. Not the deity's. Like me, there were others here. The low murmur grew louder. Only it wasn't overwhelming, each individual speaking in harmony. Hundreds of them. All connected. At the center was the sacred arbor, guiding them, enabling the ebb and flow.

"Why do you seek this power?" the woman asked once more.

"Because it's..." How could I claim this place, this sensation, this magic as mine? It would be like trying to seize the stars. My ignorant words sounded ridiculous now. I was so foolish. So blinded by my own importance.

The presence of the others surrounded me. Comforted me. Grounded me. Our souls were connected. All of us were part of the divine. I was no longer alone. Adrift.

In the darkness, a single flame flickered, calling to me. Instinctively, I sensed it was my mate.

Runa.

She was here as well. The sorceress was a servant of the realm. A keeper of her faith. I reached for my mate, deepening the connection. Only instead of the warmth I expected, cold greeted me. My mate's light was dim.

Runa.

My pulse raced. I had to find her. She was in danger.

The rapture that consumed me seconds ago turned bitter. The comfort I'd found here, connected to Carcerem, filled with obsidian, faded. In its place was something oily and tainted. Someone drained Carcerem's strength, stealing her life force.

The destroyer's presence lingered like stink on a corpse.

Idris. He was killing the kingdom.

"Why do you seek this power?" she asked again.

I needed to fix this. To save the realm from the damage he'd done. A sense of purpose welled inside of me. My mind cleared of all the confusion I'd found in the mortal realm. All the noise, the politics, the posturing. The greed to have more and be more. Nothing was ever enough. The mortal way of life had poisoned me as surely as Idris poisoned this land.

This was what I was meant to do.

"Because it is ours. Because I belong here. I seek this power to return to Carcerem all that was stolen."

Turned out, my goal was true. It was the destination I had wrong.

"Who are you?" she asked.

"Carcerem's guardian," I stated, firm in my belief.

"Who are you?"

From deep in my psyche, I shouted my answer, "Victor Custodis, the lost king of Carcerem. Prophesied heir to the throne."

"Welcome home, child." Her response was warm and inviting.

Water flowed over me, sweeping me up. I rose higher. Higher. Once more, my lungs burned. My temples pounded. I kicked my legs, swimming with all my strength until…

Bubbles erupted. I broke through the surface, flung my head back, and roared at the ceiling. Energy infused every molecule of my being. I glanced down at my body. Every inch of my flesh glowed with vitality, with power, with purpose.

I emerged—reborn.

Chapter Thirty-Six

VICTOR

I STORMED into Queen Elowen's throne room. Unconscious guards littered the path behind me. "Drazen! Kronk!" I bellowed. "Where are they?"

Dirt and grime clung to my tattered clothing. Fatigue dragged at my every step. I'd exhausted three horses on my headlong dash to Copia. Eager to reunite with my allies, I hadn't eaten or slept in two days. The blossoming energy at my center snapped and snarled. Newly awakened, it was an irritated toddler lashing out.

Yet another pair of armored soldiers dared to step into my path, swords raised. I knocked them away with a flick of my fingers. A bolt of golden magic flung their bodies several feet, slamming them into a wall. What I'd intended as a shove manifested as a battering ram. No matter. A battering ram was perfect for what I had planned.

The queen sat on her throne at the base of her sacred arbor. At my unruly entrance, she arched a brow. "Is all this violence truly necessary?"

I offered her the respect of a jerky bow. "Apologies, your highness, but I've no time for pleasantries." And for once, little self-control. "Idris has Runa."

"Yes, I know." She sighed, her calm demeanor out of place for such dire circumstances.

"You know?" I said with a flash of fangs. "Then where are Kronk and Drazen? We need to retrieve her."

"You're too late." She folded her hands in her lap. Her composure resembled my own, back in the mortal world. How annoying I must have been.

"Late?"

"You've been gone for several spans."

"Hardly," I said. "Idris captured Runa just yesterday."

"Time passes differently in the Empyrean temple. When Drazen and Kronk learned of the attack and discovered Runa's capture, they left immediately. Together, they made a plan to sneak into Slyborn Castle to rescue their sister, believing you'd abandoned her and struck out on your own."

An assumption I could hardly blame them for.

"And?" I prompted, perched on a razor's edge.

"They failed, of course," she huffed.

"Those two never did function well without their sister's leadership." Idiots. "And what have you heard about Runa?"

"My spies tell me Idris made her his consort."

Red coated my vision. A high-pitched siren squealed in my ears.

Idris had my mate. Had he touched her? Bent her to his will? Force her into his bed? If he'd laid even a finger on her, I'd cut him apart with a dull knife. Feed his diseased flesh to his duskcats while he watched.

Elowen's voice penetrated the crimson haze in my mind.

"He keeps her brothers chained in his dungeon to use as leverage. We both know she'd do anything to protect them. With Runa's cooperation, Idris is drawing more magic from Carcerem than ever before. By my estimation, the sacred arbor won't survive another turn."

"And Thorne?" I asked through gritted teeth. There had to be someone left to help me rescue her.

Elowen adjusted the delicate folds of her gown. "He and his dragon departed shortly after you did. His beast was weakened by captivity. The two retired into some dark cave where the creature could rest in safety."

Although none of my former teammates were available, I still had options.

"Very well. I'll need to borrow a thousand of your best soldiers. Tell them we ride at dawn."

The queen scoffed, screwing up her ethereal face. "You misunderstand my role in this situation. While I may have assisted you with your escape from the games, that is as much as I can intervene. Under no circumstances will I start a war with Carcerem."

My power swelled with my frustration, expanding inside my chest. Sparks snapped against my fingertips. "You're not serious."

"Quite serious," she said, expression hardening. "I can give you the gift of my wisdom to help you formulate a plan. Along with a place to rest. But that is all. The reason Copia has thrived all these years while others failed is our desire to stay within our own borders and out of others' business."

"Not even if your assistance would grant you untold favor with the new king of Carcerem?"

She smirked. "You've seen Copia. I've no need of your favor."

I gritted my teeth. "Then what do you propose?"

She narrowed her eyes at me. "What I propose is that Carcerem finally stand and clean up their own mess. The current king will expect subterfuge and deception. You are the lost king, rightful ruler of Carcerem. It's past time you acted like it. The power of the gods runs through your veins. You saw what happened when my soldiers attempted to restrain you. Idris's guards won't be able to touch you."

She hammered her small fist onto the arm of her throne. "I say you storm through the front gates, march into the throne room, and challenge Idris directly."

I stared at her in silence, contemplating my options. In the mortal realm, I'd often used manipulation, lies, and deceit to achieve my goals. And look where that had gotten me. "It's a bold plan and, in a kingdom filled with criminals, unexpected. However, once I'm inside, I'll require backup. Some way of keeping Idris's army occupied while I challenge the false king."

The queen grew contemplative. "While fearful, the citizens of Carcerem have been waiting for this moment for ages. Even those who didn't initially join the rebellion may rally behind the lost king. Some of the most prosperous kingdoms are those that have the love and respect of their civilians. Without them, there is no kingdom. Go to your people. Give them hope, give them strength, and they'll support you in return."

I nodded my agreement. "Inspire the people, storm the gates, destroy the king, rescue Runa. Easy." I was most definitely going to die. Hopefully, not until after Runa was free.

The queen held up her hand. "There is one thing you need to know before you go."

Of course there was. There was always a catch.

"You must not, for any reason, damage Carcerem's sacred arbor. Damage the tree, and you'll destroy the kingdom. Idris claimed the throne through unnatural means. Queen Raelynn is deeply embedded in the marrow of the tree. She is like a duskcat who has stabbed her claws in too deep. Rip her away, and she'll take a chunk of flesh with her. You must kill Idris first. Once you've claimed the throne, then you can use your divine gifts and rightful connection to the realm to carefully extract the queen."

Despite Raelynn's many crimes against the kingdom, I'd no desire to be the one to kill Runa's sister. Killing Idris first wouldn't be a problem. The queen, I would leave for her sister to deal with.

I turned to Queen Elowen. "I understand your refusal to lend me an army, but I do have one request."

"What is that?"

"Your fastest ship, finest horse, and clothing suited to a king."

She bowed her head. "That, I can do."

Chapter Thirty-Seven

VICTOR

THE HORSE'S hooves pounded beneath me, driven by divine energy that urged my snow-white steed to an unnatural pace—so fast it felt as if we were soaring. Power thrummed in my veins, Carcerem reaching out to me, prodding me faster. My skin burned with a radiant light. Sunlight glinted off my golden chest plate and gauntlets. The red cape fluttered from my shoulders like a flag, calling all I passed to make ready for battle.

Given my experience in the fallen trials, it was clear the best way to gain Carcerem's attention was to dazzle them with plenty of pomp and circumstance.

Today, I planned to burn brighter than Carcerem's sun.

"To arms!" I bellowed, using a pulse of magic to amplify my voice. "Tonight, the false king dies! Rise up, citizens of Carcerem, and take back your home!" The ground trembled at my command.

I'd managed to rest while sailing along one of Copia's great rivers in the queen's borrowed ship. The moment I hit land and traveled across the border between Copia and Carcerem, I'd unleashed the simmering energy that lurked inside of me.

Lightning cracked overhead, announcing my arrival as I blazed through the villages of Carcerem, a vengeful king on his way to battle.

"To Slyborn!" my command rang out. "Fight for your freedom, for your families. Avenge those who have fallen. Together, we will be victorious."

Villagers emerged from their homes as I passed.

Voices were raised, shouts ringing out.

"It's him, the lost king."

"The prophecy is true."

"He's here to free us."

Tears spilled. Fists shot into the air. Battle cries rang out. Those who were able raced for weapons. Inspired mobs rallied in my wake. My army, with their gaunt bodies, lack of armor, and pitchforks, was nothing compared to the trained soldiers I'd commanded previously. But what they lacked in skills, they made up for in spirit. This army would not abandon their king the moment the coins stopped flowing.

Word spread as I finished the tour of my kingdom. In the last village I entered, people lined the streets, awaiting my arrival, cheering as I flew past.

Chaos erupted behind me.

Chaos and rebellion.

Charging ahead, I left the seething villagers behind me. On the horizon, the castle loomed. My stallion's thundering hooves ate up the distance, exploding against the earth.

As I drew closer, archers scrambled atop the castle walls. With the speed of my attack, I'd caught them unawares. Arrows whistled from the battlements, and I tossed a shield over myself and my steed. Armed foot soldiers raced to greet me. Too late.

I'd barely had any time to practice with my newfound skills, but it didn't seem to matter. With my gods-given ability, my will became reality. With unpredictable results. Regardless, I didn't need precision to destroy the false king, so long as he died.

I extended my glowing hand, launching a sharp punch of energy into the massive gates. They blew off their hinges, exploding into pieces. Shouts and screams rent the air. I galloped into the courtyard, hauling back on my reins.

Beneath me, the stallion quivered, stamping his feet. I dismounted and stormed up the walkway to the keep.

Milky-eyed soldiers rushed to form a barrier between me and the entrance. These miserable bastards would not keep me from my goal. Another blast of energy tore through them like a vengeful tornado, throwing broken bodies out of my path.

Despite the seriousness of the situation, I couldn't help but grin at my success. Where had this power been all my life? It was positively delicious!

Finally, I set my hands on the massive doors. Finding it barred from the inside, I smirked. A small flick of my fingers blasted them inward.

To my surprise, the throne room was packed full of people. So many they spilled into the aisles, cowering against the walls. Unlike Idris's usual audience, those gathered were simple folk. Instead of silks and jewels, they wore the garments of their trade. Aprons and dirt crusted boots. Britches with patches on the knees. They huddled together like sheep in a stockade. Mothers clutched their children to their bosoms. Their expressions were terrified.

Some stared at two fixed points on the wall. I followed the direction of their horrified stares. Suspended against the wall like some kind of macabre pieces of artwork were Drazen and Kronk. I sucked a breath at the sight of them. Several feet above the ground, they rested spread-eagle with their arms and legs bound by golden bands of energy while their heads hung loose upon their shoulders. Various wounds decorated their bodies, some seeping blood as though they'd recently been tortured.

Were they…?

No. Both of their chests rose and fell, their breathing pained and shallow. They were unconscious but alive. Thank the gods.

If Runa's brothers were here, she couldn't be far. I clenched my teeth, struggling to contain my worry. Where the hell was she?

"Greetings, Brother."

Idris's voice claimed my attention. Seated before me on the throne at the base of the sacred arbor was the false king. Raelynn stood at his side, blackened hand on his shoulder. Ready to lend him a burst of power should he require it. I knew all too well what the pair of them were capable of. It was like standing before a loaded gun. Still, I didn't hesitate to stride up the center aisle.

When last I was here, it was as a prisoner. Recently exiled from a world where I never truly belonged. Weakened and manacled. So full of my own importance, I failed to comprehend the danger I faced. Today, I was here, fully aware of who and what I was, as well as my purpose.

The heels of my boots clicked on the cool marble tiles. Once I reached the circle at the foot of Idris's throne, he held up a hand. "That will do."

"I believe you are expecting me."

At my simple greeting, Idris raised a brow. Despite my aggressive entrance, his demeanor remained calm, confident. "You weren't exactly quiet about your intention to charge the gates. I mean, a white steed and cape? Really? They are so last monarchy."

I cast a glance at the cowering villagers. "Hiding behind innocents, are we?"

"I merely summoned a handful of my most devoted supporters to help celebrate this auspicious moment. Allow me to introduce to you the inhabitants of White Bridge, Runa's childhood home. The ones she risked life and limb to protect. Did you know they are the reason she became a thief?"

Flark. If Runa loved these people, I could not risk them.

I masked my concern, saying in a pleasant voice, "And what, pray tell, are we celebrating?"

His lips spread into an approving grin as if he'd been anticipating my question. "Our reunion, of course." Idris scanned my armored form with an appraising gaze. "You look like him. I see it now. Doesn't he look like him?" he said to Raelynn.

The queen peered back at me, eyes darting, posture tense. She was unsettled, and rightly so. To defeat Idris, I'd need to separate her from her mate and the sacred arbor.

"Yes, my king," she agreed, setting her lips into a disapproving line.

I shrugged. "I'm told I take after my mother."

Idris's eyes alighted. "Ah, yes. The whore who bore you, my bastard half-brother."

I furrowed my brow. "Is this the part where we insult each other's mothers? Apologies, as I am yet unfamiliar with the customs here."

He smiled in return. "I have to admit, I admire the misplaced confidence that brought you to my door today. Then again, I wouldn't expect anything less from one of his bastards. Father was quite brash himself. He believed he could flaunt his whores beneath my mother's nose and she wouldn't retaliate. He paid for that miscalculation."

If Idris thought to rile me, he didn't succeed. At the mention of my sire's death, I felt nothing. The former king's failure to keep his affairs in order cost him his life and his throne, leaving his kingdom in disarray. He'd also neglected to protect my mother and me from his vengeful mate. The male meant little to me.

At my lack of response, Idris stood, pacing with sharp, irritated strides, his veneer of control slipping. "You do understand there is nothing special about you. You're not a lost king but a discarded wastrel. You don't actually believe this prophecy nonsense, do you?" He coughed a mocking laugh.

"It doesn't matter what I think. The people of Carcerem believe it. Believe in me." Faith was an influential weapon. One I intended to wield.

Idris shook his head, his expression incredulous. "Aren't you ambitious? Rallying the villagers, pitting them against me. *Me*. The firstborn son and true king of this kingdom. Do you honestly believe you can steal my throne?"

"Actually, I'm here for your head, but the throne will be a nice bonus."

At my threat, Idris turned to face me, making patting motions with his hands. "Now. Now. There's no reason for us to be enemies when we could be allies. In fact, when I heard you were coming, I prepared a gift for you." He snapped his fingers, emitting a small burst of gold sparks.

Motion at the side of the room snared my attention.

To my horror, it was Runa who strolled into view. My breath caught as I took her in.

She was dressed much as her sister in a flowing gown trimmed with delicate jewels. Her dark hair flowed down her back with intricate braids drawing violet tendrils back from her face. Runa resembled the queen down to the white haze that covered her lavender eyes.

My mate was the false king's slave.

Rage smoldered deep within my core, destroying my calm.

While studying my reaction, Idris settled into his throne and held out his hand. As Runa drew beside him, she placed her palm in his. A palm I knew she'd sooner spit in than touch. While smirking at me, Idris kissed her blackened fingertips and placed them on his throne. At the contact, Runa flinched, uttering a pain-filled moan.

The decaying roots that ran beneath the false king's throne

pulsed with a sickening light. Idris's eyes rolled back, and he quivered before straightening. "Oh, that's good. Two sisters. Two powerful gifts. United. The seers can burn. *This* is what fate looks like."

I tensed to attack, stumbling a step before catching myself. No. Not yet. Stick to the plan.

"Look at you, ready to rip out my jugular. While I, being the generous brother that I am, have a proposition for you. In lieu of some messy battle where you will surely die, I propose a trade. Your mortal world for this one. Now that you've regained your strength, you have everything you need to conquer your former kingdom. Runa will open a portal for you, sending you back where you belong. Once you've conquered that pathetic place, we could become allies. Together, we could rule both realms. Think of the possibilities. All you've ever desired is yours for the taking."

I gritted my teeth, reluctant to ask. "And the sacrifice needed?"

Idris glanced at my mate. "I'll admit. Runa was Raelynn's first choice. Sibling rivalry. You understand. However, Runa has already proved to me she can benefit the throne, so I've arranged for another to take her place. Rest assured, the woman's family will reap the benefits."

Rage coursed through my veins, and I exhaled a long breath to slow my racing heart.

It seemed he'd thought of everything. Almost.

Idris drummed his fingers on the arm of the throne. "So, what will it be?" he snapped. "I'm offering you your heart's desire. A chance to return to your world with gods-like power. Runa claimed you're quite mercenary when it comes to achieving your goals. She assured me you'd accept this deal with little qualms."

Regret ground my molars together. I'd given her no cause to believe otherwise.

"Tell him!" he ordered Runa, snapping his fingers.

"It's a generous offer, Victor. There's no place for you here. We both know you've no desire to stay. No *reason* to stay."

Though I realized she was under Idris's control, my mate's words still stung. I had little doubt these were her thoughts.

Idris grimaced in false sympathy. "Runa resisted at first, but once we'd come to an understanding, she shared many things about you. How was that trip to the temple, by the way? I hear it's grueling."

Raelynn shifted restlessly, tapping her thigh. "Enough of this. I'm eager to see this done. Inform the sacrifice that we are ready."

I scanned the mate I didn't deserve and never thought I'd find. As it turned out, it was Runa who was the greatest threat to all that I'd achieved in the last thousand years. Not my nemesis, Magister Steele. Not the mortal Council. Not Idris.

Chapter Thirty-Eight

RUNA

MY HEART HAMMERED against my ribs so hard even the poor villagers of White Bridge could likely hear. Idris, in his cruelty, managed to claim control of my body but not my mind. Apparently, the mating bond I shared with Victor had prevented that. Instead, Idris settled for ordering me about like a puppet while I was completely aware of the atrocities he forced me to commit.

When the false king discovered that Victor had claimed me as his mate, he flew into a rage. His outrage was second only to my own. For Idris to be the one to inform me I was, in fact, mated was no small insult. A slight I'd take up with my mate at a more opportune moment, even though the bond had protected me from the king's nefarious plans.

Idris's rage was such that I suspected he'd planned to assassinate my sister now that she was weakened, claiming me as his queen instead. With Victor's mark branding my neck, that was impossible. Given the intense daggers Raelynn glared at me, I imagined she'd uncovered her husband's thwarted plans as well.

"Dear brother," Idris said with false sympathy, "I understand your reluctance. Truly, I do. Let it not be said that I am an unsympathetic king. Allow me to make things easier for you. Milani!" he shouted, and my heart leaped.

No. Don't do this. Please, no.

The brownie who served us during the trials glided through a door onto the dais.

"Yes, your highness."

"Idris, don't," I managed to groan.

"Silence," he barked, and my lips slammed together.

"Kneel before your sovereign. The true king of Carcerem," Idris ordered Milani.

As Milani sank to her knees, Idris offered her the dagger that rested at his side. "Here, dearest. Thank you for your service to the realm. It's past time you and your family reaped the rewards of your loyalty."

"We are honored, your highness." Milani beamed up at him with hearts in her eyes. "Thank you for this great blessing you bestow upon us."

"Proceed," Idris ordered, dark glint in his smoky gaze.

"Milani, wait!" Victor's bark of objection rang out. Too late.

Without hesitation, the misguided servant held the dagger aloft and stabbed it into her own breast.

Screams rang in my ears, and my head swam. The devoted brownie crumpled at Idris's feet. Crimson bloomed across her simple shift, staining her wheat-colored braids and spilling onto the sacred arbor's blackened roots. The mighty tree trembled, a single leaf tearing from its straining branches, catching fire and turning to ash.

"Excellent," Idris praised, his voice rising over the mummers of panicked villagers. "Runa, take the dagger from her chest."

No. I sawed my teeth into the flesh of my cheek until the metallic tang of blood hit my tongue. I would not. Despite my hard-fought resistance, my limbs moved with a mind of their own, and my legs marched forward. As if it belonged to someone else, I watched my hand reach for the blade and yank it from Milani's still-warm chest.

"Now, you will create the portal you promised my brother. I can't have my consort not living up to her promises. Neighboring kingdoms will believe we are untrustworthy."

Raelynn's punishing grip clamped down on my shoulder, her nails stabbing into my flesh. "Picture the location King Idris's informants gave you earlier and reach out with your senses."

Between Idris's order and my sister's uncompromising guidance, the magic at my core ached to burst free. Uttering a cry of outrage at Milani's loss, I threw out my hand. Wind whirled about the dais, teasing strands of my purple hair. Crimson swirls of Milani's aura wafted from her body, combining with my magic and twisting together, becoming one. At first, the vortex was the size of a dinner plate. Then it grew bigger until it was large enough for a grown man to pass through.

At its center, a blurry image formed, the edges becoming more defined. It was a room filled with dark furniture. Bookcases lined the walls with peculiar objects resting on the shelves. A man with a bald head and neatly groomed beard entered the image and paused, frowning at the portal as if he sensed its invisible presence, then shrugged, moving to sit behind a heavy desk. From a drawer, he extracted a cigar, lighting the end and propping his feet on the desktop.

"Magister Tiberius Steele," Victor snarled.

With my arm locked out in front of me, I managed to twist my head, noticing the vampire's expression. His rage was so chilling that I shivered. I'd never seen him so angry.

"My seers assure me this location has special meaning to you," Idris said, words clipped with satisfaction. "A place called Claymore. They claim it was your home."

"It was," Custodis confirmed.

"And the male seated on your throne?"

"My nemesis."

"Wonderful," Idris cackled. "Come closer, dear brother."

Victor strode up the steps of the dais, stopping before me and the swirling vision of his home. He eyed the image, his brow furrowed in deep concentration, a silent intensity in his gaze.

"All you have to do is step through and reclaim what was taken from you, take your revenge, and kill the male responsible. He is right there, sleeping in your bed, enjoying all you worked for. Step through and claim what is yours. One caveat. Attempt to drag my consort with you, and rest assured, I will slaughter everyone in this room, starting with her brothers."

Drazen. Kronk. My heart ached at the thought of them, so close, and yet I was helpless to save them. I dared not look at their damaged bodies. Flarking Idris had pinned them against the walls turns ago, letting them down only for his men to torture before stringing them back up. He'd claimed they were placed there as a warning to all who considered treason. It was a warning I'd heard all too well.

"Tell him, Runa," Idris ordered, and once more, my words were mine.

I'd not let him end up like my family. "Go home, Victor. This is what you desired all along. I want you to go." As my mother had given me, I would grant him the choice. A chance at freedom.

There was no need for Idris to force the words from my lips. Yaga was gone. My brothers imprisoned. The villagers pawns in the king's twisted games. And I…I currently had zero control of my life, or my body, using my gift to further Idris's agenda— helping him to drain the obsidian from our lands, ravaging our sacred tree. Everything I sought to protect, I ended up destroying.

Despite my soul-deep intentions, I'd become my sister.

"Please," I begged, voice thick. "Use the portal. Go home."

Victor stepped closer and cupped my cheek, his winter-green fragrance flooding my senses. Emotions spilled from his golden gaze as he stared into my eyes, whispering, "Little thief, I am home."

My heart tripped, and I trembled on the verge of tears. Had I misheard him? Surely—

"The portal won't hold much longer," Raelynn's warning interrupted my thoughts. "Time to choose, vampire."

Victor took a step back from me, an odd gleam shining in his eyes. "I choose..."

"Hurry," Raelynn prompted.

"I choose... candied fire zapples."

I coughed on the breath I'd held. "What?" My arm shook, my reserves waning as the portal began to shrink.

Victor grinned back at me. "I choose beauty and laughter. Fierce devotion. Wisdom and courage. Morgue and Fungaria and a dozen younglings. With you, sweet sorceress. I choose you."

I dropped my aching arm, and the portal to the mortal world, to Victor's life, collapsed.

"Flarking idiot," Idris bellowed, "I offer you everything you desire, and yet you decide to stay? For what? Her?" He thrust an accusing finger in my direction, his fury igniting the air. "A common criminal incapable of devotion? Did you not hear her rejection? If words won't convince you, perhaps a demonstration of your mate's affection is in order. Runa, my darling..." Idris purred, his voice a venomous caress.

His oily presence slithered over my nerve endings, a cold, sickening weight curling around my limbs. Whatever he had planned was bound to be devastating.

The king's perfect smile turned blinding as he commanded, "Cut out his heart."

"Idris, you bastard!" I screamed, but the words barely left my lips before my body betrayed me. My grip tightened around Milani's blood-coated dagger, my own hand swinging into motion—an executioner's strike controlled by another's will.

Victor vanished in a blur, the blade cutting through empty space where he once stood. Praise Hathor.

Too bad my relief was short-lived.

Radiant energy detonated like a shooting star, the force of Idris's attack streaking across the dais. A bolt of lethal power struck Victor dead center, the impact a deafening crack that sent him hurtling. He crashed to the ground, landing in a spill of crimson fabric, his golden chest plate scorched and dented —a smoldering crater marking where Idris's magic had struck.

"No," I choked, horror constricting my throat. I'd seen similar blasts annihilate entire villages. Idris had used me as a distraction to mask his assault.

Shockwaves reverberated through my body. Above me, the limbs of the sacred arbor shuddered. Bitter pulses of obsidian slithered up the roots of the tree. My bones ached in sympathy. Carcerem cried, forced to commit the false king's crimes.

Then, a movement—a spark of hope amid the devastation.

Victor groaned, pain-laced but *alive*. His fingers clawed at the scorched tiles as he shed his ruined cape, tossing aside his dented armor with a grunt. He rose, slow but steady, eyes burning with a fury that turned his golden irises molten.

He'd survived! My shoulders sagged, and my muscles became liquid.

"Well, don't just stand there. Kill him. And do not stop until he is dead," Idris barked to someone.

For one heartbeat, I wondered who he'd sent to do his dirty work. Then, my legs started moving.

No. Not me. Not me!

I raced down the steps, launching myself at the dazed vampire. Before he could react, my slashing blade met flesh. Victor reeled back, a bloody gash on his smoking chest.

"Runa, no," he growled.

"Fight back, damn you," I shouted. "He has me in his thrall."

All the times I'd wanted to murder the arrogant man, this wasn't one of them.

I spun and lunged. The blade I yielded sliced under the vampire's raised arm, along his ribs.

Victor recoiled, clutching his side, crimson leaking between his fingers. The sight of his blood fractured something inside of me. Destroying me from the inside out.

"Protect yourself, use your magic," I cried, circling, preparing for another attack.

He shook his head, circling as well, keeping me in his sights. "I do that, and I'll end up killing you. Did you see what I did merely opening the doors?"

"Then kill me!" I screamed, tightening my grip on the knife.

Curse him, but he didn't even raise his arms to block me. He was making it too easy. With a broken roar, I charged, wielding the dagger that had already claimed Milani's life. In slow motion, I watched from a place detached from reality. Watched as the bloody blade descended.

Firm hands grasped my wrist, stopping its descent. Thank the goddess. Ligaments twisted, my bones creaking. The skillful press of his fingers against my nerve endings sent an electric jolt through my arm. My fingers went numb, uncurling from my weapon and dropping the dagger.

Before I could dart away, Victor jerked me closer, clamping his arms around me.

I thrashed in my restraints. *Kill. Kill. Kill!* Idris's command rippled through my muscles, seizing control.

"Fight him, Runa. My mate. My love," Victor said.

Now he claimed me? Curse the bastard and his horrible timing. How was it possible this millennia-old vampire knew nothing about romance?

"Mate?" I spat. "When I confronted you about the brand, you couldn't have told me then?"

"You knew. You just didn't want to admit it."

Flark the bastard. Yes. Part of me knew.

"Fight him. You're stronger than this. The strongest woman I know."

Compliments? Now? "I can't," I spat. "You've seen what he's capable of. He had a flarking dragon in his thrall." What chance did I have?

Victor's expression softened. "Let me help you." Damn him. That slight softening would get him killed.

"Help yourself, *mate*," I snarled, then reared back, slamming my forehead into his nose.

Blood spurted. Victor stumbled. The arms he'd clamped around my torso loosened, and I took advantage. Years of practicing with my brothers, defending myself against other criminals, and Idris's soldiers overrode my desires. My muscles remembered this dance, even if my mind rebelled against my actions. And still, the vampire engaged me. Idiot!

"You should have left when you had a chance." I dove for the dagger, grabbing the hilt and springing back to my feet. "For once, couldn't you do as I asked? Thanks to you, I'll be responsible for destroying yet another life." And this one would finally break me.

At last, Victor seemed to realize the danger he faced, bringing glowing spheres of light into his palms. "But that isn't the full truth, is it love? I think you told me to leave because you're afraid of what would happen if I stayed. Afraid you'd have to let someone in, give up control. To trust."

"I do trust you." I circled, dagger raised, searching for an opening.

"Then prove it."

His elbow dropped, his right foot twisting. There it was. I lunged, aiming for his already damaged ribs.

Golden light exploded. My vision went white. Finally, he'd decided to fight back. I blinked, finding my throat imprisoned in Victor's domineering grip.

"Interesting how our roles have changed. This time, it's you who has a barrier in your mind. Let me in, little thief."

A fiery current jolted my senses. The vampire's presence tested the edges of my conscience. His gleaming eyes peered into my psyche.

Face an inch from my nose, he purred, "Trust me."

Did he attempt to compel me? If so, he'd have to try harder. Idris had a firm hold on my free will. His bitter influence clawed deep into my brain.

Kill. Kill him. The command caused my muscles to twitch, and I tensed my weakened limbs, ready to claw out Victor's eyes.

His thumb stroked a gentle rhythm over the brand he'd left on my throat. "I gave you this mark at a time when I couldn't envision a future for us. When all I could see was my past and what I'd lost. Then Idris captured you, and I started seeing clearly for the first time in decades. Today, I've got both eyes open. The greatest treasure in all the realms is standing before me. I was wrong, letting you slip away. You want Carcerem? I'll give it to you. This kingdom is lost, same as I was. It needs you. Say you will be mine, and together, we'll build a future that will make Carcerem proud."

Praise the fates. He got it. The fallen king had finally seen beyond the end of his aristocratic nose. And I was a captive of Idris's dark magic and unable to respond as I desired.

"Break free of his thrall, little thief," Victor ordered, hammering at my walls. "You've allowed me to claim your body. Open your heart and your mind. Let me in, and I swear I won't disappoint you again."

Those barriers between us began to fracture. Victor was my mate. He was mine. And I was his.

"I trust you," I admitted, letting go, opening my heart and my soul. Starlight sparked along the connection between us. Victor's presence washed over me, filling the empty void within my damaged heart and pushing out Idris's influence. Filling me to the point that all that was left was Victor and me.

I dropped the knife I held, dragging the back of my fingers beneath Victor's jaw. "I love you."

"And I you, sweet sorceress." The hand on my throat disappeared. Victor wrapped me in an embrace, pressing his lips to my forehead.

"He can't do that, can he?" Raelynn's shrill question to her king hit my ears. "The only way he could have broken your thrall is if Custodis's bond with her is more powerful than yours."

I spun to find Idris perched on the edge of his throne, murder in his snarling visage. He glared down at the two of us. I flicked my fingers under my chin and blew him a kiss.

"I'll show you who's stronger," Idris snarled.

Chapter Thirty-Nine

VICTOR

Every hair on my body stood up as though electrified. It was the only warning I received before the rumbling shockwave pulsed through the room. With every bit of speed I possessed, I flung my mate away from me, taking the full brunt of Idris's attack square in the chest.

Pain exploded throughout my nerve endings, and I flew backward, spine bowed, arms and legs jutting out in front of me. The room streaked by in blurry shades of gray and crimson. Ozone's bitter tang filled my senses. Stones exploded behind me as my frame punched the wall. The strength of Idris's blast pinned me there a moment before I plunged to the ground, bones colliding with the unforgiving tiles.

Every inch of me screaming, I blinked up at the domed ceiling, the sudden silence unnerving. Spots danced before my eyes, and a high-pitched, tinny noise filled my ears.

"Victor!" Runa's scream pierced my ringing skull. Cries from the terrified White Bridge villagers accompanied her litany of curse words.

"Are you okay?" Her face swam in my vision.

"Ouch." I exhaled the breath I held, puffing smoke from my parted lips.

"Behold your fabled savior, good people of White Bridge." Idris's laughter rang out. "Is this the sort of king you'd have on Carcerem's throne? This impersonator before you couldn't defend this kingdom from a herd of cottonpelts. It's no wonder his mortal world didn't want him."

"Help me up?" I met Runa's anxious gaze.

"Of course." With trembling hands, she dusted bits of crushed stone from my legs, then slung my arm over her shoulder, lending me her strength as I shoved to my feet.

When last I was brought this low, I faced my adversary alone. This time would be different. I just had to hold out for a bit longer.

I turned my face to Runa's ear. "Focus on getting your people to safety, as many as you can, while I distract him."

"You sure?" She caressed my cheek, sweeping the dust from my skin.

"Go."

Runa nodded, releasing me to slip into the crowd of those gathered while I strode down the aisle.

With a self-assured smirk twisting his mouth, Idris watched my unsteady approach, his eyes narrowed in amusement. Once I stood before him in the circle where he liked to incinerate those he believed to be law breakers, I braced my wobbling legs.

"Is that all you've got?" Thankfully, my voice was strong, failing to reveal the damage he'd done.

His cocky grin spread. "I'm going to enjoy breaking you, Custodis."

"Then give me your best shot," I said, holding out my arms.

Idris drew back his arm and let a glowing sphere fly. I ignited my own magic, coating my palms and knocking the speeding orb skyward, into the ceiling. Stones cracked. Dust rained down on the huddled villagers. Their cries of terror rang out.

Flark. To prevent striking them, I'd need to get closer to my target.

Before Idris could regroup, I rocketed up the steps to the dais and slammed my glowing fist into his unsuspecting jaw. His head snapped back, and he crashed over the arm of his throne, tumbling over the sacred arbor's blackened roots. As Idris tumbled, his queen let out a squeal of distress, abandoning her mate to scurry around the side of the tree and scramble over roots.

The false king glared up at me from where he'd fallen. He swiped the streak of blood from his lip and spat on the ground. Without getting up, he snarled, "So we're to behave as brutes, fighting with our fists? You really are a gutter rat."

I smiled in return. "What's the matter, Brother? Haven't you ever been in a bar fight?"

Idris lurched to his feet and charged. Skin glowing with an eternal light, he leaped root to root. Body tensed, I summoned a wave of magic to shield my flesh and charged as well.

Crash!

Two mighty forces of nature slammed together. Planets on a collision course.

The impact sent a shockwave pulsing through the realm, rippling across the stones and up the limbs of the sacred tree. The castle shuddered beneath us, walls groaning, lamps swinging wildly as dust rained from the ceiling. Cries of the innocents echoed through the throne room. Their fear was a sharp knife against my resolve.

Above us, the great tree trembled. Its glorious leaves ignited from the amount of raw power the king unleashed. They fell like dying stars, fireflies burning up the space between us.

I barely saw the punch before it landed. Idris's fist slammed into my ribs. Cracking. Once. Twice. Bone snapped, fire igniting in my side. Pain shot through me, but I refused to fall.

I twisted into the grapple, using his momentum against him. With a sharp pivot, I flipped him over my shoulder, sending him crashing into the ropy foundation of the tree. The impact rattled the branches, sending another wave of leaves cascading down on us.

The pretender rose from the wreckage, his piercing eyes locking onto mine—not with hatred, but something more dangerous. Coercion.

He coughed a laugh. "You and I both know you cannot win this fight. I've wielded this power for eons while you've toyed with it for a handful of turns. The odds are against you, fallen one."

From the corner of my eye, I spotted Runa. The hands of two children were in her grasp as she guided them to safety with the assistance of her illusions, urging them to slip out the door.

Good girl.

I picked a careful path over twisting roots, careful to keep Idris's back turned to my mate. "You forget. I am Victor Custodis, the lost king who, in his youth, was sent to an unforgiving world filled with mortals. Abandoned by my mother and the land of my birth, I arrived in that place with nothing but the shirt on my back. The odds have always been against me. Yet, I fought. I learned. I plotted and flourished. I will do the same here. On *my* throne."

Idris bared his teeth. His eyes burned. Twin pools of magma as magic swelled his palms. "Foolish, leech," he spat. "Carcerem will never be yours."

Too late, I realized my error.

I'd let too much space form between us—enough for him to wield his full power. I braced my weakened frame, throwing up a shield as he unleashed a storm of raw energy.

Light exploded.

Searing agony tore through my skull as his magic struck like a divine hammer. The world tilted as I hurtled backward. My spine exploded against the trunk of the sacred arbor, splinters of divine bark slicing into my flesh. Pain flared hot and deep, and the taste of blood filled my mouth.

Fates no. The tree! Thank Hathor, the trunk held firm.

That Idris would be so careless was proof of his unworthiness. Unlike the reckless king, the welfare of every living thing in this room remained at the forefront of my mind. I couldn't afford to unleash my volatile power so close to them.

"Who are you fighting for anyway?" Idris asked, voice like rolling thunder. "For them?" He gestured toward the gathered innocents, their terrified faces pale. "Or yourself?"

Another blast slammed into me before I could answer. Magic raked over my already battered body, ripping me away from the trunk and hurling me across the chamber. Gnarled roots scraped my limbs, jagged edges shredding my skin.

"Know that if it's for them, you're an even bigger fool than I thought."

The next strike crashed into me. My ribs caved under the force. I hit the dais steps hard, bones snapping, flesh splitting. My body crumpled onto the shattered tiles, pain roaring through me like wildfire.

"Victor!" Runa's cry pierced the haze of pain.

Gentle hands caressed my cheeks.

I forced my eyes open, blinking against the blood dripping down my face. "Runa, no. Leave me."

"Ah, isn't that sweet," a higher, venom-laced voice purred. "He fears for his whore's safety."

I blinked, dragging into focus the image of Runa's sister where she once again stood beside the throne, having crawled back out of whatever hole she'd hidden in. Idris limped up the steps to stand before her.

"He should since I've been holding back," he spat. "I dared

to hope you would come to your senses and reconsider my offer. I see now it was a foolish dream." His eyes glinted with something colder than malice. "Now you will witness the true strength of this great kingdom—see for yourself exactly why they fear me."

He turned slightly, peering over his shoulder. "Now, my love."

"Raelynn, don't!" Runa's voice was raw with desperation. "He'll kill all of them."

A ripple of terrified voices surged behind us. The people of White Bridge were still trapped within these walls, and their fate now teetered on the whim of a queen who had sold her soul.

Runa's sister raised her trembling hand. Her coal-black fingertips shook, damaged by the level of obsidian Idris insisted she wield.

"Is this why you dreamed of being royalty? To slaughter innocents?" Runa's voice cracked.

The queen's breath hitched. Her milky-violet eyes flickered as if something deep inside her made her hesitate.

"I thought by now you would understand," Realynn snarled. "It doesn't matter what I want. It never has."

Magic coiled around her fingers like a noose tightening.

Runa moved before I could stop her, her arms curling around my shoulders, her body pressing against mine in a desperate, protective embrace.

The air thickened. The magic swelled.

Chapter Forty

RUNA

IDRIS, assured of his victory, grinned down at me and Victor, his eyes glinting with cruel satisfaction. "Do it, my love," he purred to Raelynn. "Open the—"

"Sire!" One of the king's soldiers stumbled through the front door, a crimson stream trickling down his face.

"Not now!" Idris barked, gleaming eyes locked on his sibling.

"But, sire! It's the villagers. They're here."

Idris blinked, finally shifting his focus to the shaken soldier. "What? How many?"

"All of them, sire," the panicked man squawked. "They're attacking the castle. And they've brought reinforcements."

Hope surged within me. The villagers had finally joined the rebellion. Nothing short of a miracle could have accomplished such a task. A miracle or a lost vampire king.

Idris's face darkened. "What kind of reinforcements?"

A shadow stretched across the windows. Shouts rang out from the courtyard. The scent of brimstone thickened the air. My breath caught as the horrifying memory of my final moments in the pit twisted through me.

No. It couldn't be.

Flashing flames and a gust of wind roared in the entryway. The terrified messenger glanced over his shoulder, uttered a shout of fright, and bolted. Smoke swirled in his wake, clearing enough to reveal a familiar fire-breathing figure standing in the doorway.

Cocky grin. Sparkling blue eyes.

Thorne.

"Hey there, beautiful. Miss me?" The shifter winked, standing with his hands on his hips and legs braced like he captained some great ship. His eyes flicked toward Victor. "You started a war without me? I'm hurt."

"You," Idris roared, thrusting out his arm. "You're the one who stole my dragon."

Thorne's grin widened. "And you're the one who dared to enslave him." His voice dropped to a threatening purr. "You should know, he's rather vexed with you."

He cast a quick glance over the room. "Flark. Civilians. That could pose a problem. Nothing we can do about that now, though. Hard to stop him when he has his mind set on something."

His attention swung upward toward my unconscious brothers, and he winced, eyes flicking back to mine. "Shit, wasn't expecting that. Figured they be in the dungeon. If I remember correctly, your brothers are both fireproof, right?"

Not waiting for my answer, he shoved those standing closest to the main isle. "Idiots. Why are you still here? Run! All of you, take cover!

I sank my fingers into Victor's arm. "No. He wouldn't, would he?"

"It's Thorne," Victor said by way of explanation.

"Everyone, clear out!" I shouted as Victor's palms shimmered, casting a protective barrier around me.

Screams echoed. People ran for cover, diving under benches.

Heavy *swoops* pounded the walls, the colossal hammering of wings stirring the air. Emerald scales flashed outside the window. Then, a single reptilian eyeball appeared, followed by a set of bone-crushing teeth. The teeth parted, red embers glowing deep in the beast's gullet.

Not again.

The window exploded, launching shards of glass. Fire roared into the room in a narrow stream.

"Raelynn! Run!" I shouted, some deep-seated instinct overriding my hatred. The fiery blast struck Idris dead center.

My sister's high-pitched scream sliced through the madness.

"Argh!" Idris bellowed, throwing up his glowing palms. Flames detonated against the base of the sacred tree. The explosion tossed me like a ragdoll, ripping me from Victor's embrace.

Pain jolted through my hip and spine, my body colliding with the floor. Smoke scorched my lungs. My arms shook as I shoved myself up, coughing through the haze. "Victor?" I croaked.

A ragged groan answered from across the chamber. "Flarking dragon."

Relief crashed into me. My mate was alive.

Victor pushed himself up, golden energy flickering around his hands. His gaze found mine, sharp and commanding even through the chaos.

"Go, Runa," he rasped. "Help your people." His eyes snapped back to Idris, who was already rising, fire licking at his robes. "Idris is mine."

Before I could voice a protest, two bodies plummeted from the heavens, slamming to the ground with a sickening crack of bone and a string of muttered curses.

I jerked around, my breath hitching as I took in the groaning figures. "Kronk? Drazen?"

If they were free, Idris must truly be injured—giving Victor another chance to end this.

Scrambling to my feet, I rushed to my brothers' sides, my pulse hammering. Both were awake, shifting gingerly but alive. Thank the goddess—because there was no way I could carry them.

Drazen's ruddy face was drawn with exhaustion and streaked with bruises. "How do I look? They didn't damage my best feature, did they?" He glided a blood-crusted hand along one of his horns.

"Like bula dung," I said, bottom lip wavering, attempting to smile.

Kronk groaned, scrubbing a hand over his face and wincing. Across his forehead was a spiderwebbed crack. "Flark, but that hurts. Bastards tried to split my skull open. Almost succeeded." Despite his injuries, he was lucid—and would heal. Relief flooded my chest.

"I could have told them that was impossible." I grazed my fingers along his granite jaw. "Your head is too thick."

A thunderous roar split the air, shaking the walls. Idris's battle cry was a sound I knew too well, one that clawed its way from the darkest corners of my past—the same cry he'd unleashed the night he murdered my parents and stole my sister away.

Dread twisted in my gut as my gaze snapped back to where the false king had fallen. Idris was on his feet once more. His clothing was scorched. Blisters bubbled over his exposed skin, and yet his eyes burned with relentless fury.

Victor stood opposite him, bloodied and bruised but unbroken. Golden eyes blazing, Carcerem's rightful ruler bared his fangs in defiance. A shiver ran down my spine as he threw back his head and roared—a primal, earth-shaking challenge that sent a pulse of power rippling through the air.

Then, with predatory resolve, he charged.

The two collided, locked in a storm of blows, each strike splitting the air and shaking the castle's foundations. Every impact reverberated like a thunderclap, their movements a clash of raw, unrelenting power. Idris, realizing he was losing his advantage, fought with the fury of a raging tempest—wild, relentless, and unyielding. Meanwhile, Victor countered with razor-sharp precision, weaving through attacks and striking fast and true, like wind slicing through steel.

The brothers fought to the death. Only one would emerge from this battle. It was a fight I longed to watch but didn't dare let distract me.

"Let's get out of here before they bring the place down on us," Drazen groaned.

Claws raked at my center, tugging. I glanced at the sacred arbor. Bronze leaves dropped from its trembling limbs in a cascade. Their intricate webbing caught fire, turning into glowing embers and floating away. The craggy roots trembled below the mighty trunk, pulsing, then fading. Pulsing. Fading.

This wasn't Idris's doing. Something was seriously wrong with the tree.

I patted Drazen's chest. "You and Kronk, help the villagers if you're able. There's something I need to do."

Drazen frowned but knew better than to waste his breath arguing with me. "Fine, but keep your head down."

Raelynn. I'd had little time to warn her before the dragon struck. Where was she?

I scrambled up the side of the dais, crawling over the pulsing roots on my stomach lest a stray blast from the battling kings take my head off. On the backside of the arbor, I spotted a ragged scrap of lace.

"Raelynn!"

I scrambled to where she rested, her limbs splayed at odd angles. Smoke wafted from her scorched dress and blistered skin. She'd taken a deadly hit from the dragon's furious blast.

I carefully grasped her hand, and she peered up at me, scanning my visage.

She snorted a derisive huff. "Custodis protected you."

Surprisingly, I was uninjured, other than a few bumps and bruises. The golden light Victor had wrapped me in saved me from the blast. Idris hadn't done the same for his queen.

"It was the same with Momma and Poppa. You were always their favorite. The one they looked after first."

"Is that why you did it?" I couldn't resist asking, despite her obvious pain. "Why you left me and sided with Idris? Out of jealousy?"

"That day at the portal," she said, her voice rasping, "I saw an opportunity and seized it."

I shook my head. "For turns, I blamed myself for letting you go—for not trying harder to stop you. I became a thief, stealing for the people of Carcerem, to atone for the chain of events my failure set off. It took a long time for me to realize that it wasn't my fault." I released the hand I'd clasped so carefully, letting it flop against her chest. "Guilt is a fallacy. It tricks you into believing you had control over something that was completely out of your hands. You're the one who created this mess, Raelynn. You. It was your decision that brought you to this place."

Tears filled my sister's eyes, and she choked on a sob. "You're right. I've made so many mistakes. Because I was a delusional little girl who believed she could have it all."

Whether she was remorseful for her actions or not, I couldn't tell. Regardless, I wouldn't humor her after what she'd done to the kingdom—the lives she'd cost. "What matters now is what you do with that knowledge. Repair the damage you've caused. Relinquish the hold you gave Idris on Carcerem. Help us defeat him."

Tears streamed down Raelynn's blistered cheeks. "I can't. When I realized he intended to replace me with you, I tried to close the gateway between him and the arbor. And failed. It's too late, and there is no turning back. Idris, the tree, and I are intertwined. The floodgates are open, and I am nothing but a conduit. I haven't had control over the connection I created for quite some time."

Explosions crashed at the front of the room. A ball of golden energy whizzed over us, slamming into the wall. I winced, covering my head. The fight between Victor and Idris had escalated. Fates save us, I prayed my mate was unharmed.

"There must be a way to fix this. Maybe if we tried to close it together."

"Do you remember that lake Momma and Poppa used to take us to?" Raelynn asked.

"What? What are you talking about?" This was not the time for reminiscing.

"It was so beautiful there. I'd set my dolls along the bank and pretend I was their queen and they my royal subjects. It was such a pretty fantasy."

Angry shouts filled the air, and another explosion of power prickled my skin. I didn't dare look to see if Victor was wounded. Instead, I focused on my sister.

"Yes. It was pretty. And then I would sneak up and steal one of your subjects, pretending to be an ogre."

"You were such a brat," she choked out. "You threw my favorite into the lake. I waded in to save her, ruining my dress. When I yelled at you, you said, 'A good queen must make sacrifices.'"

Idris's infuriated shot rang out, *"Custodis, you bastard. The throne will never be yours."* Yet another explosion rattled the walls.

In the chaos, my sister whispered, "I'd like my funeral pyre there. Next to that lake."

"Raelynn, what do you mean?" Her burns, while extensive, would heal with the right care.

"I've considered all the options. There is only one way to make him pay for what he's done."

Before I processed her intent, Raelynn raised the knife she'd hidden and plunged it into her chest.

"Raelynn, no!" I grasped her wrist. Too late. The blade pierced deep into her heart. Blood gushed across her pristine gown, and she uttered a mournful groan.

"What have you done?" I cried.

My sister stared up at me. "A good queen"—she sputtered a mouthful of blood—"makes sacrifices. Tell Idris I'll see him in hell."

The light faded from her eyes, and her hand fell limp.

"Raelynn." I clutched her shoulders, shaking her. "Raelynn, no. Not like this." Tears soaked my cheeks, and a sob rattled my frame.

Beneath me, the floor rumbled. The tree's blackened roots throbbed like an oozing wound.

Idris's bellow whipped my head around. Victor lay on the ground before him, forearm braced over his face as though prepared to block a blow that did not land. Instead, Idris flung back his arms, his chest bowing.

"Raelynn, you deceitful bitch!" Spasms shook his body; black veins crawled up his neck.

Victor met my wide-eyed gaze and roared, "Runa, no! Idris first. Raelynn must not die."

I gaped down at my sister. *Now he tells me.* Golden light flashed behind her eyes. The ground cracked below her, traveling across the marble floor and straight up the trunk of the tree. At her center, a sinister, pulsating glow appeared. That blazing light spread, growing larger until it had consumed Raelynn's whole body. I shielded my eyes from the glare.

"Runa, get back," Victor shouted. "Get away from her."

For once, I did as he ordered, scrambling over the writhing

floor to him. He wrapped me in his embrace, and we both turned to Idris.

The false king retreated toward the throne, belting out a laugh born of insanity. "She's ruined everything." He glanced down at his body. From deep within his core, a blinding light glowed, similar to the one Raelynn displayed.

Menacing sparks flared in his palms. "Ah, do you feel it? Hathor's divine essence. Pure and unrestrained. Flark, but it's so good. Too good." He gritted his teeth, clenching his fists at his sides as if to contain the flood. "The dam is broken. Raelynn's cursed us all."

His legs gave out, and he collapsed onto the throne. Above him, the tree rumbled and swayed. Wood cracked like a fractured bone. Gilded energy exploded from the split in the trunk. The leaves above became fiery embers, floating off the tree before raining down.

Idris sat on his stolen throne. His skin charred, and fragments of it flaked off, like the glowing embers of the tree. The unchecked flow of power was tearing him apart.

He sneered at Victor, his tone gravelly. "What do you know? The prophecy was true, except the translation was wrong. You're not the realm's salvation. You're its destruction."

Pieces of his destroyed body floated in the air. He watched them drift away with a bemused expression. "You're too late, lost king. The kingdom bleeds and will never recover."

Thunder cracked. The ground trembled. Idris's body came apart in an explosion of crimson and gold sparks. Victor wrapped his body around me as energy buffeted our frames. Pinpricks of fire pierced my flesh. The sting made me groan. I dared to lift my head and glance at the tree.

Idris was right. The kingdom bled.

I peered into Victor's glowing eyes. "We have to find a way to stop it."

Chapter Forty-One

VICTOR

IDRIS COULDN'T CONTAIN Hathor's divine energy because he wasn't the true king. The unrestrained power that roared out of the tree in a gushing wave called to me, eager for my claim.

I released Runa and struggled to stand. The blast of energy pouring out of the crack threatened to knock me off my feet.

She held up her hand, shielding her vision. "What are you doing?"

"Claiming my throne."

"What?" She scrambled upright, clinging to me. "Victor, you can't. It will tear you apart the same as it did Idris."

I cupped her cheek. "I have to try, for them."

"Them?"

"For the kingdom."

She snorted a broken laugh. "This is a fine time for you to turn noble."

I smirked. "Should my reign as king only last minutes, I'll still expect great ballads to be written about my selflessness. Along with a statue."

Tears filled her watery gaze, and I claimed her mouth in a tender kiss. Showing her the depth of my emotions instead of floundering to find the right words.

Before she tried to talk me out of it, I turned, clawing my way over the throbbing roots. Leaning into the rush of power spilling from the fractured trunk, I finally made it to the base of the throne. Once there, I stood beneath the broken tree and met Runa's eyes.

She peered back at me, palm pressed to her mouth, anguish in her expression. Anguish, and so much more. One final look at my mate, and I heaved a final breath, braced my spine, and sank into my throne.

Energy, bright and brilliant, washed over me in a tidal wave. The sense of rightness, of coming home, filled something long empty. My skull pounded, pressure building between my temples.

"At last. The chosen one," said an ancient voice from deep within my psyche.

"He is late," snapped a different, higher voice.

"Too late," snickered a third, this presence sounding a lot like Idris.

These voices, I instinctively knew, were from the kings who'd come before me. They whispered in my ears.

"What will you do for them? Will you die for them?" Idris snarled. *"Will you control them? Make them submit?"* His poison lingered, slithering down my spine.

The ancient voice chimed in. *"You are king. They should serve you."*

Divine strength sang in my veins. The feeling was euphoric —like bloodlust. The more I consumed, the more I wanted, and Carcerem was giving me everything.

Idris's laughter rang in my head. *"Take more. It's what leeches do, after all. Take all of it. It's yours."*

"Victor," said a sweet voice. "Victor, can you hear me? You

must reel it in. Push back."

But I didn't want to resist. If I could absorb a little more, I'd be the most powerful creature in the realm. With my strength, I could rule them all.

"Victor. It's too much. Your skin is burning!"

I focused on the room before me. My mate peered back, her face contorted in a mask of agony. My mark on her throat blazed with the magnificence of the sun.

"So beautiful. Tell me. Do you love me, little thief?"

"Yes," she wept. "I do love you, you idiot. That's why you have to fight. Don't let it consume you."

"Will you worship your king?"

"Yes!" she shouted. "But I can't do that if you're dead."

"Don't worry, pet. Everything will be all right. I'll protect you."

"But who will protect you?"

I offered her a patient smile. "Gods do not need protecting."

"You're not a god, dammit," she bellowed at me. "Snap out of it."

Soon, she would understand.

"Come to me, my queen." I extended my hand to her. My greatest conquest. My love.

Her bottom lip quivered, and she hesitated, regret apparent in her drawn visage. She would not say no to me.

"You need have no fear." I dulled the raw energy that was vibrating through my fingers, trying not to scare her off. "Come. Rule at my side."

My gorgeous mate heaved a stuttering breath, then took my hand. I drew her closer, bringing my queen between my knees. At last, we would be together as we were meant to be. As destiny foretold.

"I love you," she said, the glow of my divine essence radiating off her perfect face. "I'm sorry, but there must be balance."

Her grip on me tightened, and she smacked her free hand

down on the arm of the throne. Bright amethyst shone in her glowing eyes. What was this?

My skin cooled where she held me, and I glanced down. The magical force resonating in my fingertips began to dim, receding up my forearm. I tried to pull away, but my arm had grown weak.

"Runa?" Her hand inside of mine began to cool, and I drew it up between us. Her flesh had turned black, the darkness spreading up her forearm.

"No," I groaned as a chill enveloped me, the overwhelming flow of divinity ebbing. "What are you doing?"

"Closing the rift. The sacrifice has already been made. Raelynn's life given freely."

The ground trembled, black roots pulsing as they sank deeper into the floor. Runa was shutting down the connection between me and the kingdom, stealing my power.

No. Not her. Not her!

My mate was no better than all the others who'd betrayed me.

Never again would someone take what was mine.

I clamped a hand around her deceptive throat. "Stop this."

"You first," she gasped.

Black veins spread up her arms to her shoulders, then across her chest. Closing the fissure in the tree was taking every bit of strength she possessed. Which of us would last the longest remained a mystery.

I tightened my grip, cutting off her oxygen.

How many games had we played together? Both fighting for dominance.

"You cannot best me," I grated, snarling.

Her pulse slowed under my thumb. Shadowed threads crept up her cheeks. Oily tears slipped from her eyes. "Already. Have."

Thunder rumbled. The throne under me shuddered, and an explosion, so bright it blinded me, detonated.

In the silence that followed, my ears rang.

Confusion clouded my mind. Where was I? My vision revealed nothing but white light. Below my skin, a pleasing energy hummed. I cracked my neck and rolled my shoulders. I'd battled Idris, and then…

Runa!

I gasped, grinding my fists into my eyes to clear them. Across my lap, a gentle weight prevented me from rising. By blurry increments, Runa came into focus. I remained on the throne, my mate resting upon my legs.

"Runa?" I ran my fingers through her hair. "Are you—" Thought returned. She'd healed the gaping wound in the tree, closed the rift between Carcerem, the throne…and me. Something that should have been beyond her capabilities.

"My love," I whispered, gathering her into my arms. Her skin was blackened from fingertip to shoulder, inky veins painted her chest, rising up her neck. Over her mate mark was a new handprint. This one a bruise.

"No! Runa!" I roared. Tears of rage blurred my vision. She couldn't be dead. Not like this. Not ever!

As king, I wouldn't allow it.

I placed my hand over her throat, my touch gentle, aligning my fingers with my mate mark. It was there…a flicker of *something*. Our souls were still connected, though that tie faded with every second that passed.

Due to Runa's heroic efforts, a connection remained between me and the throne. Between me and Carcerem, as it should be. This connection felt natural. Felt right. Balanced.

I drew on that bond, calling on the heart and soul of Carcerem's land, creatures, and people.

Unsure of what I was doing, I sent a simple command. *Heal her. Return her to me.*

The ancient voice I'd initially heard resurfaced. *"King but a minute, and already he's making demands."*

"It's against the laws of the universe. A life lost cannot be given back," the second, higher voice contributed.

"The nerve of this guy." Flarking Idris.

"I do not want it without her," I insisted.

"What did he say?" asked the second.

"The power, the throne, the kingdom. I do not want it without her." It was all meaningless without Runa by my side. In the mortal realm, I'd lived a life of power and wealth but also of isolation and loneliness. I wouldn't do it again.

"What an idiot," Idris scoffed. *"Can he do that?"*

"Well, we certainly can't allow him to abdicate," snapped the second.

"It may be possible," said the first. *"If he gives her a piece of his soul."*

"Yes. Anything," I agreed.

"Anything?" asked the second.

"Demand his firstborn child," Idris said. *"That's what other celestial beings usually demand."*

"Shut up, Idris," barked the second. *"What are you even doing here?"*

"Very well," sighed the ancient voice. *"Place your palm on your mating mark."*

As ordered, I aligned my fingers with the imprint. A warm, radiant light bloomed beneath my palm, like a tiny sun. Runa's delicate flesh glowed at the touch. Heat scorched my flesh, and I gritted my teeth against the burn. The pulsing energy spread, growing brighter, to the point I was forced to look away.

Warmth seared the side of my face. My chest ached. Some unseen force tugged at my innards. Pulling, ripping, tearing. Pain threatened to crack me in half, much as the rift had the sacred tree. That pain broke free of my torso, traveling down my arm to my hand.

Runa's slim frame jolted against me. The eye-watering light pulsed like a solar flare, erupting within my mate. Then, as quickly as it appeared, the fiery heat dissipated, the light growing dim. I cracked my eyelids open, watching as the glow faded from under my palm.

"Runa?" I cupped her face.

Bump. Bump.

Two soft heartbeats reached my ears.

Runa's heartbeats.

At the sound, my own pulse raced.

The sinister tendrils of black vanished from her cheeks, receded down her chest, slid down her arm, and abandoned her fingertips. I held her hand to my mouth, kissing the inside of her wrist.

"Runa, my love. Wake."

She stirred beneath my caressing hands. I rubbed her chilled flesh, and she warmed in response to my touch.

"I love you," I breathed against her lips and she inhaled with a gasp, as if she pulled the words into her pulsing heart.

She blinked, peering up at me. "I love you too."

Overwhelmed, I clutched her to my chest. Runa's arm circled my neck, her grip as tight as mine.

"I saw them."

"Saw who?" I released my mate, absorbing her awe-struck expression.

"My parents. They were with the others in the sacred tree. I was hugging them, awash in peace and harmony. Then suddenly, a void opened behind me. Momma claimed it was you calling me home. That one span, we would all be reunited, but that time wasn't now. The fates still had plans for me, and I needed to get back to work."

My lips curled. "Who are we to argue with the fates? Say you will be Carcerem's queen, and I will rule at your feet."

Violet gaze luminous, she smoothed my hair away from my face. "A generous offer, but I'd rather rule at your side."

"Done. I'd give you anything so long as you swear to never leave me again."

"You're staying then?"

"I may need some convincing. If you're up for the challenge."

"Oh, I'm up for it." Runa grinned a cheeky smile.

Before my queen could make good on her promise, footsteps pounded against the tile. Drazen and Kronk stormed into the throne room, braced for battle. Glancing at the two of us locked in an intimate embrace beneath the swaying branches of the sacred arbor, they relaxed their stance.

"The villagers of White Bridge are safe," Drazen said. "Thorne and his dragon helped the others to capture Idris's men. One look at that snarling beast and they laid down their arms."

"We won," Kronk declared in that deadpan tone of his, stating the obvious.

"We won," Runa declared.

To my utter delight, my mate burst into laughter, and I smiled in return.

Chapter Forty-Two

RUNA

I WORSHIPPED Carcerem's new king with all the heavenly rapture he deserved. Fangs in my branded throat, my fated mate uttered a groan that had me spiraling to the stars. I collapsed against his chest. Both of us were slick with sweat. It had been this way for hours. Turned out, having a divine vampire king as my mate came with many perks.

Victor tucked an arm under his head, pulling me into his side.

"I think we should continue to host the Fallen Trials," he said, as though I hadn't just given him the most earth-shattering orgasm he'd ever received. The scorched sheets I gathered over the top of us proved my point.

Glancing up and noting his lack of smile, I tensed. "You can't be serious."

"I am always serious."

While this was once the truth, my mate had developed a sense of humor during his time here in Carcerem.

"Veto," I declared, making use of my queenly rights.

"Hear me out. We could include the other kingdoms,

366

providing an opportunity to make connections and improve commerce. We could turn the event into a spans-long festival. With dancing, arm wrestling, and vendors who sell candied fire zapples."

Carcerem had a long way to go before we were on the same level as many of the other sacred arbor kingdoms.

"Okay then. We will present your proposal to our advisers."

Kronk and Drazen were quite proud of their elevated status from common criminals to trusted royals. They acted as civilian liaisons, making sure the needs of people were heard by the monarch. Although, much of their work took place in the local pubs.

We'd tried to enlist Thorne, but he'd politely declined, claiming he and his mysterious dragon had personal matters they needed to handle.

"We could use Idris's former soldiers as competitors. Allow them to earn Carcerem's forgiveness."

"It isn't a terrible idea," I admitted. "Since they helped the false king subjugate the villages, it only makes sense that they help rebuild Carcerem's economy."

Once Idris fell, his control over his men vanished. Apparently, only a couple hundred were actually loyal to the crown. The others surrendered the moment Idris's spell was broken.

"And what of your former home? The mortal world," I hesitated to say but didn't want to leave anything unresolved between us. "What about that Magister Tiberius fellow you wanted to destroy?"

"I've a feeling there are others there whom he has wronged, eager to interfere in his plans. Let him rot in his sad little world. I've a kingdom to rule and citizens who worship me."

If I thought my mate was arrogant before, the love of an entire kingdom had completely gone to his head. It was a good thing he had me here to keep him grounded.

"Speaking of your citizens, we are overdue for the coronation ceremony."

"They can wait," Victor growled, rolling me beneath him. "I've more important matters claiming my attention and a bit of worshipping of my own to attend to."

At least he had his priorities straight.

"Yes, you do, my king." I curled my leg over his hip. "Yes, you do."

Hours later, dressed in our royal finery, Victor and I stood before the citizens of Carcerem. Drazen waited beside us with Kronk at the center of the dais, both looking rather noble themselves. In Kronk's beefy hands was the crown he waited to place on Victor's noble head.

Carcerem's sacred tree rose tall and proud at our backs. Gone were the blackened roots. The starved foundation nestled deep within the earth, nurtured by its kingdom. Instead of languishing under the influence of Idris's rot and decay, its bronze leaves shimmered with a celestial light, radiating a healthy glow.

The citizens gathered before us glowed with health and vitality as well.

Along with hope. They had faith that their new monarch would lead them into prosperous times.

The only thing that would have made the moment any better would have been if Yaga had been able to join us. Words couldn't describe the joy I'd experienced when she'd sent a messenger to Slyborn with news that she was alive and healthy. Unfortunately, she'd written saying she was unable to attend the ceremony—though she was loath to miss a good party. She'd claimed the fates had big plans for her and her presence was needed elsewhere. My mate had failed to hide his relief at her absence. Still, I hoped she'd visit us soon.

Victor took a knee before the patiently waiting athos, and Kronk placed his crown on his head. The golden halo of

gleaming branches sparkled against his silver-white hair. The fit
—perfect.

A matching crown already rested on my head. My mate
insisted his queen be presented first.

As Victor regained his feet, Kronk made the official
announcement. "Stand, Victor Custodis. Savior of the Kingdom.
Guardian of the sacred arbor. Divine Child of the Gods.
Unworthy mate of Runa Starborn."

At this last bit, the newly crowned king arched a brow at me,
and I coughed a laugh in return.

Ah, Kronk. Apparently, not even a king was worthy of his
sister.

"Good people of Carcerem." Kronk spread his massive arms.
"I present to you your king. Long may he reign."

Cheers exploded. Drazen raised his hands as well, launching
harmless bursts of fiery sparkles into the air.

In lieu of posturing for his worshippers, King Custodis swept
me into his embrace, forgoing formality.

"It was sweet of you to crown me first." I rested my hand
against his noble cheek.

"It was the least I could do for the little thief who'd stolen
my heart."

I wiggled in his grasp, eager to start the festivities. "Come
and let us live in the moment."

"Together," he readily agreed.

"Together."

Chapter Forty-Three

YAGA

YAGA'S mystical essence floated beside that of the temple guardian. Side by side, they watched as Carcerem's lost king swept his newly crowned queen into his arms. The sacred arbor's new custodians really did make a striking couple.

"Would you look at that? Never thought I'd see the day that our frigid vampire king acted like a fool in love." Yaga cackled.

"Yes. They both appear quite besotted with each other. It's good he's finally focused on the *right* mission," the child with the fiery hair answered.

Yaga snorted. "I thought the dunderhead would never figure it out. Nice ass." She poked a gnarled finger at her temple. "Thick skull."

"He did prove more challenging than most," the ancient child said. "There were several times I believed I'd lose him on the snowy trail to the temple. Once, I almost kicked him off myself."

The old hag's cackle rent the air. "I thought for sure pairing him with his fated mate the moment he returned would have set him on the right path. Some just need a bit more guidance than most."

"You did well, raising the young sorceress and her protectors."

Yaga sighed. "I did, didn't I? I'm going to miss those rapscallions, but my mission in Carcerem is over. It's time I turned my attention to the rest of my flock. Starting with that handsome dragon fellow. I've been mentoring a young lady who will surely knock him on his keester. And none too soon, either. Something big is on the horizon. The realm will need all of Hathor's chosen guardians to play their parts. As well as her sacred trees. There are so few of them left."

"Don't worry. If Runa and Victor are truly committed to fulfilling their duty to Hathor, they will do their part."

"Their path won't be an easy one. Do you think they can do it?" Yaga asked the childlike deity.

"I believe *they* can." The child turned to her, a smile tugging his lips. "I have faith."

Dear Reader,

Thank you for reading Kingdom of Stolen Crowns. Whether you devoured it in one night or savored every twist of fate, your time in Victor and Runa's world means more than I can express.

If their journey moved you, infuriated you, or left you breathless in all the best ways, I hope you'll consider sharing a review—it helps keep this realm alive and thriving.

Thank you for believing in broken heroes, daring thieves, and the kind of love that rises from ruin.

Sincerely,

Stephanie Storm

Up Next

Curse of Ash and Flame

Book 2 - The Sacred Arbor Series

I was born with no past, no power, and one rule—avoid the executioner's fire. Then a glowing sigil appeared on my skin, a dragon tried to eat me… And everything I knew burned to ash.

Sold into servitude in a land that burns magic-wielders alive, Serafina survives by staying small, silent, and far from anything enchanted. But when a forbidden symbol sears her skin, her forgotten past awakens… and something ancient takes notice. As monstrous creatures tear through her village, she flees for her life—only to fall into the claws of a dying dragon and his infuriating caretaker.

Thorne lives with the weight of failure and the relentless countdown of his ailing brother's curse. After all he's endured, he refuses to let the sharp-tongued hellcat his meddling sibling dragged home ruin his last shot at redemption. But the longer Serafina remains in their crumbling mountain stronghold, the harder it becomes to ignore the fire she ignites.

As darkness rises and destiny tightens its fist, Serafina and Thorne are drawn together by forces neither of them can escape. She's reckless, he's ruthless—and the heat between them is a dangerous distraction they can't afford.

With the comet fading and a kingdom on the brink, they'll have to choose what they're willing to sacrifice—duty, desire, or each other. Because if they fail, the throne won't be the only thing that burns.

Will they rise from the ashes stronger than before… or go down in flames?

Also by Stephanie Storm

The Inner Beast Series

<u>Feral Instincts</u>

An innocent mortal—who dies before living. A devoted alpha—who lives for others. Can they overcome centuries of hatred to follow their hearts?

<u>Feral Awakening</u>

A surly drifter who refuses to listen. A feisty outcast who demands to be heard. A simple kidnapping gone wrong.

<u>Feral Longing</u>

She's his best friend's girl. His to protect. And his worst nightmare.

<u>Feral Beauty</u>

A seductive vixen. A grumpy bodyguard. A debt finally paid.

<u>Feral Possession</u>

Can a free-spirited necromancer save a damaged vampire lord from the demons who possess him?

About the Author

Stephanie Storm is a paranormal and fantasy romance novelist who writes stand-alone series connected by ever-expanding worlds. Each of her stories features an exclusive couple with fresh world-building, fast-paced twists and turns, and a heart-melting HEA.

Married to her high-school sweetheart, she lives in rural Missouri where she and her husband have raised two almost-adult boys. Beyond writing, Stephanie adores a good thrift store, spending time with her pet chickens, and watching WWE pro wrestling with her 70-year-old mother.

Learn more about Stephanie and her novels at:

www.authorstephaniestorm.com

Printed in Dunstable, United Kingdom